Martina Murphy has been writing for as long as she can remember. She is the author of twenty-four previous novels under various versions of her name! Her books have been translated into many languages and include the YA award-winning *Dirt Tracks* and the Impac long-listed *Something Borrowed*. She also writes plays and is a qualified drama teacher. She lives in Kildare with her husband, two adult children and two dogs.

Also by Martina Murphy

As Martina Murphy:
The Reckoning
The Night Caller
The Branded
The Bone Fire

YA novels:
Livewire
Fast Car
Free Fall
Dirt Tracks

As Tina Reilly:
Flipside
The Onion Girl
Is This Love?
Something Borrowed
Wedded Blitz

As Martina Reilly:
The Summer of Secrets
Second Chances
Wish Upon a Star
All I Want is You
The Wish List
A Moment Like Forever
Even Better Than the Real Thing?
What If?
Things I Want You to Know
That Day in June
Proof

MARTINA MURPHY

THE WRATH

CONSTABLE

First published in Great Britain in 2026 by Constable

Copyright © Martina Murphy, 2026

1 3 5 7 9 10 8 6 4 2

The moral right of the author has been asserted.

*All characters and events in this publication, other than
those clearly in the public domain, are fictitious
and any resemblance to real persons,
living or dead, is purely coincidental.*

All rights reserved.
No part of this publication may be reproduced, stored in a retrieval system, or transmitted, in any form, or by any means, without the prior permission in writing of the publisher, nor be otherwise circulated in any form of binding or cover other than that in which it is published and without a similar condition including this condition being imposed on the subsequent purchaser.

A CIP catalogue record for this book
is available from the British Library.

ISBN: 978-0-34900-079-4

Typeset in Bembo MT Pro by Initial Typesetting Services, Edinburgh
Printed and bound in Great Britain by Clays Ltd, Elcograf S.p.A.

Papers used by Constable are from well-managed forests
and other responsible sources.

Robinson	The authorised representative
An imprint of	in the EEA is
Little, Brown Book Group	Hachette Ireland
Carmelite House	8 Castlecourt Centre
50 Victoria Embankment	Dublin 15, D15 YF6A, Ireland
London EC4Y 0DZ	(email: info@hbgi.ie)

An Hachette UK Company
www.hachette.co.uk

www.littlebrown.co.uk

For Caroline Hardman – an agent in a million. Thank you so much for championing my books.

Glossary

ASU: armed support unit
Cig: throughout the book, Lucy calls her detective inspector 'Cig'. This is short for *cigre* (the Irish word for 'inspector') and is used a lot among the guards in Ireland.
DDU: district detective unit car
GDPR: General Data Protection Regulations – legislation designed to keep our personal information safe. But quite annoying to access when you're attempting to solve a murder.
IP: injured party, the victim
PULSE: police computer system
SO: suspected offender
SOCO: scenes of crime officer
TE: technical examination (also used as verb: 'TE'd')

Two years ago – Donegal

On the last night of Mary Roche's life, she attended a prayer group run by the new priest, Father David O'Malley. At nine o'clock, after she helped with the clearing up of cups and saucers, she bade a hearty goodbye to everyone.

She'd asked Bridie for a lift home, but Bridie's car was full.

The father offered to drive her but, really, she couldn't put him out. Plus, if Peadar saw the priest driving her home, he'd have a fit. He'd wonder why she didn't ask him, but the days of asking Peadar to do things were long gone.

She didn't know what they were going to do the two of them, but they had agreed to park all the bad feeling until Christmas was over.

In happy tones, she told all her friends that walking home was grand, sure it was only a ten-minute stretch and, patting her belly, she added that a ten-minute walk was better than a zero-minute walk. She could do with a bit of exercise before the Christmas. She and Peadar were heading to their daughter's for the dinner on the day and Mary had to make space for all the food she'd be eating. They'd all had a laugh at that. Mary had that way about her: people liked her. On the way out of the door, she took the time to wish Father David well in Rome.

He thanked her, trying not to beam with delight. But he was going to be talking to the Holy Father, so he had every right to beam, in Mary's opinion. Mary couldn't wait to hear all about it, come January. Then, buttoning up her brown coat, right to the chin on account of the fierce sting in the air, she called out some more goodbyes and set off on the short walk for home.

That December night, it was as dark as pitch, save for the pools of streetlights illuminating the shiny, icy path. Her sensible shoes held fast. She waved at Bridie as Bridie's car drove by, and Bridie and the others waved right back. Then, taking a left, she crossed up a side-street and then a right and she was onto a small dirt track with grass growing up the middle of a rutted road. No streetlights here, only the moon scudding in and out between the clouds, and small copses of trees here and there, but she didn't mind. This was her road, and there, up ahead, in the distance, she could just about make out the light from the living-room window at the side of her bungalow.

She was grand. And safe.

No doubt Peadar was home by now with his feet on the sofa, watching the news.

She wondered what sort of a mood he'd be in tonight. Things between them had really fallen apart and she didn't think they'd ever get back on track. She certainly couldn't tell him now about the letters she'd been getting. She wondered if it was him that was sending them. Trying to drive her mad altogether.

Well, feck him. Mary tucked her chin into her chest and ploughed on.

Tramp, tramp, tramp.

THE WRATH

Then from behind, tramp, tramp, tramp.

She didn't register it at first. But bit by bit, the tramp of feet, echoing her own, caused a slight worm of unease to uncurl inside her.

She slowed her walking without trying to look like she was.

The other footsteps slowed.

Mary speeded up.

The footsteps speeded up.

She stopped and all that could be heard was the call of some night bird.

Maybe, Mary thought, she'd just never noticed the echo before.

Two more steps.

An echo, two steps. And then the echo took one more step.

Mary flinched, couldn't help a yelp escaping.

And from somewhere behind her, an almost identical yelp.

Terror crawled in Mary. Starting in her centre and spreading right out, to the tip of her fingers. She started to walk faster, aiming for home. Mary was no runner and she knew it.

Faster footsteps from behind.

And then a red square envelope on the path in front of her. Held down by a stone. Her name in capitals scrawled across the front. She stopped, horrified. 'What is it you want?' Her voice only shook the tiniest bit. Her face was big and pale in the dark. 'Who are you?'

'Wrath.'

Terror blasted her solar plexus. She tried to scramble backwards. What was this person on about? 'I don't understand. I don't—'

A tall, masked – her mind scrambled for the word – *creature*, holding something heavy, stepped out from behind the trees and came for her.

MARTINA MURPHY

She turned, feet finding purchase on the ice.
Running.
Behind her, running.
Growing closer.
But Mary knew that her life was over.

Present Day

1

The shower isn't as powerful as he likes but it will do. He closes his eyes and glories in the sensation of water splattering over his face and trickling down his torso, washing him clean. Blindly, he reaches for the shampoo and rubs it vigorously through his hair, the smell of fake citrus banishing the odour of iron that seems to cling to his skin. He inhales, exhales. Inhales again and lets out a long, slow breath, opening his eyes, acknowledging that the whole event had gone extremely well. Better than the first time anyway. After that, he'd decided not to do any more, didn't see how he could. But the rage is back. Bigger than before. It's amazing what you can be good at once you have just cause and a basic working knowledge.

Overall, despite the mess, this one had been a job well done. And the death would have been relatively quick. Not like the other time. That had been unfortunate and he'd done his best to learn from it.

He isn't in the business of letting people suffer, he reflects, as he reaches for the conditioner. He even warns them that he's coming, which is nice of him. Or a little cruel of him, maybe. No, he's not a real killer. Not like the ones on TV, dead-eyed and full of murderous intent. Not like the ones he reads about in newspapers, who shoot people for fun or for being unfaithful. He's not scum who breaks into a home and kicks someone to death in front of their children. Nope, he just murders people who deserve it, who hurt others and don't give a shit about it. The ones who swan about living their lives and ruining other people's and just—

The plastic bottle of conditioner explodes in his hand, liquid squirting everywhere.

Later, after he has eaten a jam sandwich – him and his da ate raspberry always – and dried his hair, he finally takes out his notebook. This is his very favourite part, the ticking off of his to-do list.

He turns to the names, written on the first page.

Mary Roche ✓
Jerry Loftus

He puts a tick alongside Jerry's name.
Just one more left.
Then it'll be 'Job done'.

2

'Nothing doing yet,' Dan says, peering through his binoculars at the deserted street below.

We've been ensconced for the last few hours in a small room over a Centra shop in Castlebar. It's used as an office by the manager of the store and he'd been only too happy to allow us to have it for our mini-stakeout, delighted to be part of whatever action might go down.

It's been dark since four-thirty, which was six hours ago. It's barely above freezing inside, while outside the brooding December sky has buried the moon and stars under thick clouds. Rain has begun to spatter on the window and the bustling street of earlier has been enveloped in silence.

Gardaí from three other units are in position up and down the street, but Dan and I have prime view, so we can't afford to get this wrong.

I glance at my phone. 'They left Dublin over three hours ago. They should be arriving soon.'

'Little gougers,' Dan remarks, thrusting a bag in my direction. 'Last doughnut?'

'Half,' I say, though I really want a whole one. Still, I know I'll feel better about myself if I show some self-control. I pull it apart, jam squirting everywhere and pop half into my mouth, licking the sugar from my fingers.

An anonymous tip-off had come in about a planned robbery of a warehouse in Castlebar. It had been deemed credible and Dan and I, along with a number of the regular lads, had been sent out to keep an eye on the premises and to apprehend the suspects. The tip-off had been particularly welcome as we are certain that it's part of a gang of young Dublin criminals who specialise in robbing lock-ups and, on occasion, private houses. How they get their information, we don't know, but they've had a very successful spree until now.

As the old window frames rattle with a strengthening breeze, I think it's the type of evening to be in bed with a massive glass of wine and a good TV movie.

Dan says something.

'What? I was miles away, thinking of wine and TV and bed.'

'I wish I was in your head,' Dan jokes, binoculars still trained on the street. 'I said that Delores has a . . .' He frowns. 'What do you call a woman and a man who are dating when they're over seventy?'

I ignore his ageism and exclaim admiringly, 'Go, Delores!'

'I'm hoping she will.'

'Dan!'

'I'm hoping they'll fall madly in love and he'll whisk her out of our house. What's wrong with that?'

Initially, Dan and his partner, Fran, had been delighted when Delores, Fran's mother, had come to stay. Now, though, with her incessant chatter, her inability to leave the décor alone and her

THE WRATH

propensity for ruining Dan's clothes in the washing-machine, her welcome has grown thin, on Dan's part at least.

'How did she meet him?'

'I don't know. Probably put an ad in the lonely-hearts column for a man willing to put up with irritating women.'

'Stop!' I giggle.

He chortles a little. 'I've met him but Fran doesn't want to. He's annoyed that she's dating when his father is only dead—'

'He's dead ages.'

'Yeah, but you can't say that to Fran. Anyway, I told him that Delores is entitled to live her life.'

'I'll bet you did.' I reach for the second half of the doughnut.

His mouth twitches. 'I just want the best for her and— Hello?'

Just at that moment, a voice crackles over the radio: 'Black Renault Mégane approaching from Market Street, four youths, no lights.'

Dan drops the binoculars, and we move fractionally nearer the window where, under a pool of streetlight, we spot a car, its headlamps off, moving slowly up the road. It coasts to a stop beside the warehouse.

Something catches my eye. 'Feck's sake, who the hell is that?'

Dan follows my gaze.

An old man, in what looks like a green combat jacket, climbs out of a skip, lugging a sleeping bag after him. 'How did we miss him?' I hiss. 'Jesus, if he gets caught up in anything . . .'

The old man starts shuffling towards the car, his hand held out, looking for money.

Long and lithe, a young lad hops from the Mégane, something in his hand, and, without noticing the old man, disappears around the back of the building. Two others, moving like cats, position themselves at the front door.

The old man approaches them.

'We might have a problem,' Dan radios to Control. 'There's a civilian and he's approaching our boys. Stand by.'

The old man says something to one of the lads who says something back and pushes him. The old man stumbles over his sleeping bag and falls. The two laugh as the man scrambles to his feet. He's a little scared now and he attempts to move away but they've got the scent, like dogs on a rabbit, and the second lad aims a kick at his legs and he falls again.

'We have to go in.' I groan. 'We can't let them do that.'

'It'll risk the whole operation and – wait – just wait. Look.'

The fourth member of the gang, smaller than the others, younger, I think, emerges from the driver's side of the car and he helps the old man up and says something to the other two, like he's giving out to them. He hands the old man something and dusts him down before sending him on his way. Then, as the old lad shuffles off as quickly as he can, forgetting his sleeping bag in his fright, this fella berates the other two before getting back into the car. The other two are not happy, but they quickly lose interest in the old man.

'That was close,' Dan remarks. 'Maybe they're not all complete arseholes, then.'

'That lad is just smarter than the others. He doesn't want some homeless guy running off to the guards. He probably made some apology and handed him a twenty.'

Dan nods, turns back to his binoculars. 'Tango alpha one, entry has been gained around the back of the building.'

'Received.'

The two boys bounce back into the shadows at the front. The homeless guy moves up the road and around the corner.

THE WRATH

Dan and I wait, ready to give the order to intercept the car once all the stolen gear is loaded. Already I can feel the adrenaline build. My blood sings.

The tension of the next few minutes is almost better than a glass of fine wine.

And now the front door cracks open and the two boys slide in. 'Tango alpha two, they're all in,' I report.

'Advance to stage-two positions.'

The night grows colder, blanketing the small side-street in a misty fog as we ready ourselves. I know that the other units will be silently approaching the building from all angles. A car will have been positioned at both ends to prevent any escape. Time is running out for this band of criminals.

And then, while the others are inside, the guy behind the wheel exits the car.

'What the hell?' Dan says.

And he moves off down a side-street.

'Jesus, he's . . . he's just leaving.'

Could he have been the one who tipped us off?

'I'll go after him.' It's a no-brainer. I take the key to the front of the shop. 'He'll come out into the street there. You stay here and report back, Dan.'

'You can't, Lucy. Jesus!'

'I can't not. If he's the one tipped us off, he's the best one to put them behind bars.'

'I'll go instead.'

'No, you'll be needed here for the arrests. Tell them I've gone after the driver.'

'Lucy!'

'I don't have time to debate it.'

And I'm out of the office, running down the stairs and into the empty shop. The key turns easily in the door and I'm out onto the street, which is also deserted. The cold breeze makes me gasp, stings my face. Then, through the thin fog, I can make out the shape of a young man about two hundred metres ahead, walking rapidly. I don't call because I know I'll be no match for him if he's to break into a sprint. Instead, trying not to make any noise, I begin to run as hard as I can. I'm twenty metres away when he senses me. He whips his head around and, in the yellow streetlight, I see his face. And I stop. Dead.

I know him.

I don't know who he is, but I've definitely seen him before. And it's not from any intelligence photos.

The déjà vu is disconcerting and I'm not quick enough to react as he takes flight, his runners eating up the ground.

'Stop!' I shout. But even as I do I know I can't pull my gun on him. I try to catch up. He's pulling away. 'Stop! You're under arrest.'

He darts down a side-street and I follow about a hundred metres behind. I can hardly breathe with the effort and my legs will be aching tomorrow. He darts off to the right and I follow. I can barely make him out in the distance now, just a black shirt and jeans.

'Stop!'

He takes another right.

I follow and . . . I've lost him. I stand in the street, listening and waiting. He has to be somewhere. I take out my gun, slide into the shadows myself.

I hear sudden rapid footsteps just up ahead.

I run as fast as I can, feet and lungs burning, until I reach the top.

THE WRATH

Nothing.

He's gone.

Shit. Bending over, hands on knees, I inhale great gulps of air. Damn it anyway!

I radio it in, giving the best description I can, but if he planned this escape, he'd probably scoped out the CCTV and knows exactly what he's doing.

By the time I get back, the car, with everything in it, has been surrounded. Blue lights illuminate the scene, yellow vests crawl the streets, radios crackle and cars rev. The lads who've been apprehended are on the ground, shouting and roaring, hands cuffed behind their backs.

'I'll fucking sue yez for this! You fucking broke my jaw, yez arseholes.'

'Not stopping you shouting all the same, is it?' Dan remarks, to laughter, as the youth promises to 'do' him.

The thrill I'd felt at this operation disappears like soapy water down a plughole. I had failed in my bit.

'We might pick him up on CCTV,' Dan says, trying to make me feel better. 'Like, Luce, you were never going to catch him once he took off.'

'There was a time I would have.' His look of doubt irritates me. 'I used to be a sprinter on my school team.'

'In Achill?'

'Yes.'

He cracks a grin, says, 'In other news, we nabbed those three red-handed. It was beautiful. They didn't even notice their driver was missing, just loaded up the car, and when it came to leave they realised, but we got them right then, before they could even start it. The lad that got away left a jacket behind so we'll have DNA to identify him.'

'I've seen that driver before.' I'm still caught up with the guy I let escape.

'Yeah, in all the fecking alerts.'

'No, he's not been in them.' It was the expression on his face that rang a bell somewhere deep in my brain. Who is he? I shake my head. It'll come to me – it always does.

'We may as well go back.' Dan is limping slightly, and at my look, he grumps, 'Went over on my ankle in a drain at the side of the street.'

An interested crowd has gathered at the end of the road and are being kept back by one of the uniformed members. Someone is taking pictures. Another woman, blonde and busty, seems to be doing a video.

Our three suspects shout obscenities as they're dragged to their feet. Like rabid animals, they shriek and spit and one aims a kick at the guard restraining him.

'That's bloody enough.' Dan's Dublin accent reasserts itself good and loud as, forgetting about his limp, he grabs one of the suspects by the arm and, quite forcefully, thrusts him into the back seat of the car. 'Shut it. You were caught, good and proper.'

A cheer goes up from the onlookers.

3

I've collected my car from the station and by two a.m. I'm on the way back to the cottage in Keem where I live with my mother and my son Luc. Luc returned last night from Spain after his first term as an Erasmus student. I was afraid he might spend the weeks in the run-up to Christmas in Dublin with his glamour-queen/wannabe-actress girlfriend, Cherry. But, give him credit, his first port of call was to visit his cute-as-a-button daughter, Sirocco, who lives down here with her mother, Tani, and her other grandmother, Katherine.

I think of Sirocco as I drive. Her birth, when Luc was just eighteen, was such a shock but now I couldn't imagine life without her. She is the sun around which we all revolve. A cheeky, bossy little madam, with a very quirky way of looking at the world. For a while last year, she had an eerie obsession with death but that passed after my mother enrolled her in dance classes. All she wants to do now is spin on her head the way break-dancers do.

Her other grandmother is not a bit happy about it.

My mother, however, is convinced that Sirocco will be the next Jean Butler. I'm not so sure but I'd never dare say it. And—

My train of thought is disrupted as I spot the car again.

I jam on my brakes, skidding to a halt, bits of grit spraying up as my wheels lock and my little Corsa goes into a bit of a spin.

I'd noticed the car earlier when I'd passed it on the way to work and I'd marked it as odd because it was parked near the edge of the cliffs and I hadn't seen anyone with it or anyone standing on the cliffs admiring the view. But then I'd figured that maybe it was someone who'd pulled in to go for a walk. But the car is still here, hours later.

I peer through my windscreen.

Maybe it's broken down and the driver was forced to leave it. But it's an odd place to pull in, on marshy ground, at the edge of a cliff, just off a narrow road. Little prickles start up my arms. Hair rises on the back of my neck.

I unfasten my seatbelt and, grabbing a torch from the back seat, I get out.

'Hello,' I call.

My voice is whipped away by the wind.

All about is silence. It presses down, like a blanket, broken only by the smash of waves far below. The sky is full of scudding clouds, rain spattering on the breeze. And it's freezing. Every molecule in my body is screaming at me that something is up. I've seen enough suspicious scenes to be able to read what is 'off' and this car, left half-arsed near the edge of the cliffs on a dank night like this, is downright creepy.

I flick on the torch and a cone of light illuminates the way ahead.

Treading carefully, I approach the vehicle. From what I can tell it's a mid-sized Ford, the colour hard to judge in the dark. There's a deep scratch along one side.

THE WRATH

'Hello!' I call again, in case the driver is anywhere nearby. 'Hello?'

Nothing comes back, just the howl of a fox somewhere.

I move towards the driver's side of the car, the bit facing the cliff. The door is slightly open, the window rolled down.

I fish about in the pocket of my jacket because I usually have a pen in there. Finding one, I gingerly coax the door towards me.

I move a step closer.

Something squelches underfoot.

I peer into the vehicle.

It's an abattoir.

4

Of course I have no idea if the blood that covers the front seats, is splattered over the interior of the vehicle and pools just outside the driver's door is animal or human, but I'm not taking any chances. A poorly preserved scene means that evidence will be lost, so I have roused Jordy and Matt from the Achill station and tasked them with securing the perimeter with crime-scene tape.

'Make sure it's the right way up.' I suppress a groan as Matt immediately turns the tape around.

Jordy, wheezing like a poorly inflated pair of bellows, lumbers towards Matt to help him.

Hopefully SOCO will be here bright and early tomorrow: the sooner we get this whole scene examined, the better.

'Luce?' It's Matt.

I turn towards him.

'How far should I go with this tape?'

'As far as you can in all directions,' I tell him. 'We can always bring it in later.' William will decide when he comes anyway.

I'd called William before I'd roused Matt and Jordy.

He'd been sharp on the phone and it had stung. We'd always

got on well but, in the last few months, he's treated me like a stranger he's not particularly fond of. But I suppose no one enjoys being awoken at three in the morning. 'Cig,' I'd valiantly ignored his brusqueness, 'there's a car on the Keem road and its interior is covered in what appears to be blood. There is a pool of blood outside the vehicle too, though it's dark so I can't tell for sure.' I omit the fact that I stood in it. 'The vehicle is unoccupied and has been here for at least seven hours. I don't know if the blood is human or animal but my gut tells me this isn't good.'

'All right,' he says, not even taking a moment. 'Call Achill. Secure the scene. Have you got an ID on the number plate?'

'I've asked Dan to run it through PULSE. I wasn't in the DDU car.'

One of our district detective unit cars has ANPR, an automatic number-plate recognition system, and quite why William would think I'd be driving it home at two thirty in the morning, I don't know.

'All right, what are you thinking?'

'Someone was attacked in that car, maybe dragged to the cliff edge and dropped over. Whoever did it probably left in another car.'

'Okay. I'll put in a few calls and meet you soon.'

Thirty minutes later, he strides towards me wearing a forensic suit. He throws me one and waits until I climb into it. And climb I do, hitching up the trousers and rolling up the sleeves. The only thing that fits properly is the gloves.

Matt, whom I've tasked with scene preservation, records in the logbook that William and I were allowed access at 3.30 a.m.

'SOCO will come at first light but I want to see what we're looking at first, just in case.'

A flare of indignation leaps up in me. In case of what? In case I've got it wrong? I hold my tongue and follow him up a path I've marked as close to the one I walked just under an hour ago. William, always prepared, has brought a heavy-duty torch and the beam illuminates the scene like daylight.

The car is ten years old, a Dublin registration, with that deep scratch running the length of the passenger side. William crosses carefully towards the driver's door and peers in.

'The door was partially closed when I got here. I opened it. I used a pen so there should be no prints.'

His eyes flick dispassionately over the blood-splattered interior. He focuses his torch beam at the ceiling, the light playing on the arc of droplets that seem to have sprayed out in all directions. 'I'm no expert but that looks like arterial bleed to me.' He pauses, the torch hovering over a few circular drops on the door handle. 'We'll need a sample of that too,' he says.

I follow him as he moves towards the back of the car. 'Boot is open,' he says.

I hadn't noticed that.

He reaches out a gloved hand and pushes it up.

It's empty, save for a red envelope, splotches of blood on it.

William picks it up, opens it, pulls out a white A4 page and unfolds it.

Letters, pasted on, taken from magazines and newspapers.

'5/5' is stuck at the top.

Then, one word: 'KaRMa'.

5

The note is shocking in its starkness. More shocking in the icy pitch darkness of a wind-whipped starless night. William and I stare at the ominous word, at the eerie way the letters are arranged on the page, uneven, like they're almost moving.

The sudden sound of my phone with its cheery Wham! ringtone jars. I ignore William's eye-roll at my choice of appropriate crime-scene music. 'Dan, what have you got?'

'The car belongs to a Jerry Loftus. He's living in Ballycroy, so not a million miles away.' Dan calls out the address. 'Give me a shout if you need anything else. I'm awake now anyway.'

'Car belongs to a Jerry Loftus,' I tell the Cig. 'Lives in Ballycroy.' I don't add that Dan is happy to be dragged over because right now there's not a lot we can do and it's better if some of us are bright-eyed come morning.

'Jerry Loftus?' Jordy, who has become almost invisible in the dark, calls from the cliff side of the crime scene, about ten feet away, 'Is that what you said?' His voice ebbs and flows in the breeze.

'D'you know him?'

'If it's the same lad, I think I saw a missing-person report about him.' Jordy walks towards me, taking his newly issued personal device from his pocket. He starts fumbling with it. I suppress my urge to take it from him and key in the information. Jordy is not a technology expert and the new phones we'd all been given courtesy of the Garda Siochana baffle him. Still, while he's all fingers and thumbs, he has a memory for intelligence that is only surpassed by William's. He could have gone far in the force but hard living put paid to it. 'Here we are,' Jordy says triumphantly, gaining access to PULSE. 'Jerry Loftus, from Ballycroy?'

'That's right.' A thump of adrenaline hits my system.

'"Jerry Loftus,"' Jordy reads from his screen, '"missing since yesterday noon. Six foot, slim build, grey hair. Garda are seeking the public's assistance in tracing the whereabouts of sixty-year-old Jerry Loftus of Ballycroy, County Mayo. When last seen, Jerry was wearing jeans, black runners and a red fleece. Mole on his right cheek. He failed to return home after a hiking trip on Achill."' He looks up. 'Must be the same man, eh?'

'Find out who took the report, Jordy, and exactly what work has been done to locate him,' William orders. 'It might save us a bit of legwork. Has this man been found? If so, why is his car here? If not, we need to find him. Lucy, call out to his home in Ballycroy and see if you can get anything for DNA comparison with the blood in this vehicle.' Then I think he realises how late it is. 'Tomorrow,' he says. 'Get on it first thing. Matt!' He strides towards Matt, probably to ask him to man the scene tonight because Matt looks delighted with himself.

'Looks like the Cig is going to include Matt on the investigation,' Jordy remarks. 'He's a good kid, didn't deserve to be left out in the cold the last couple of times.'

THE WRATH

Matt is married to Stacy, a journalist who used to work for the *Island News,* our local newspaper, but who now, thanks to some scoops, writes for the *Irish Herald*. When they were engaged, William had been afraid of leaks on investigations and didn't quite think Matt was strong enough to withstand his fiancée's charms. On the bone-fire case, even though Matt was sidelined, I'd asked him, on the QT, to do some investigating for me. He'd done well but I'd had my knuckles rapped for it. Still, it seems to have had the desired effect. The Cig has obviously decided to trust Matt with some low-level grunt work to see how it works out.

I'm glad for him.

I turn my attention back to the note, photographing it before placing it in a clear plastic evidence bag. Then, to preserve any forensics, I close the boot.

I join William back on the road where he's removing his forensic suit. He's wearing jeans and a bright orange sweatshirt. It's so completely at odds with his natural reserve that I'm not quick enough to hide my reaction.

He catches it and asks, a little defensively, 'What?'

'Nothing.'

Last year he might have made a joke about his clothes but tonight he just gives me a curt dip of his head and leaves.

I stare at his retreating back for a second or two. I so want to ask him why he's treating me like this. We always had a great working relationship, so much so that he came up with a way to save my job on the last case. As I unzip my crime-scene suit, I decide that, like before when I was in the cold, all I can do is my best to prove he made the right decision in including me. If he wants to treat me like he's doing, that's on him.

'I want you here at first light,' William turns and shouts back to me. 'So, get to Jerry Loftus's house early for that DNA sample.'

I don't need him to tell me that, but I grit my teeth and tell him I will.

Jordy comes up behind me. 'What have you done to rattle that cage?'

'He's just under pressure.' I'm reluctant to speak badly of him.

The roar of his car as he U-turns on the road echoes in the night.

6

He wakes with a roar sometime in the early morning, trashing and wrestling with an unseen force. Something is holding him back. He is stuck to the ground. He calls and calls and no one comes and he can't move and—

His eyes pop open with a gasp and, on a huge inhale, he realises with a violent suddenness that he's awake, that he's not stuck to the floor, that he doesn't have to struggle. That he's tangled up in bedclothes. Relief punches through his panic and he flops onto the bed, trying to blink back his stupid tears. 'Get a hold of yourself,' he mutters, scrubbing his eyes and breathing the way he's been told to by the woman he was sent to see years back. In and out, in and out. Little measures of time. He allows the silence to calm him.

Sometime, much later maybe, the quality of the light through the window changes and he thinks that dawn must not be far away. Gathering himself, he swings his legs out of bed and shakily pads towards the kitchen. He needs a drink. Pulling a glass from the press he pours himself a large whiskey. His hand slips on the tumbler as he raises it to his lips, gulping down the amber liquid. The burn reminds him that he is awake.

The dream comes infrequently now, slithering into his slumber like a thief. But when it does, it shakes his head loose for the day. The dream *always begins with the knocking, bam, bam, bam, and as the volume of the knocking rises so does his panic until he's trying to escape but he's stuck and the door is coming in on top of him and he tries to use his whole body to call for help, straining at his chest and balling his hands into fists and then always, inexplicably, he's full of rage and fury and he's red and burning up from the inside and unless he moves he'll shatter into a million pieces and it hurts and—*

He slams down the glass. *Enough. Enough*, he tells himself.

It's a dream. Get a grip.

He yanks his notebook from his coat pocket and pauses, taking comfort in the soft brown leather of the binding. He finds his timetable, marked with a blue sticky tab.

He likes a timetable.

He reads once more all the steps he took to eliminate Jerry Loftus and it soothes him.

He sighs, like a man who has just orgasmed.

Today, he thinks blissfully, as he closes his notebook, *is a day for creating a letter. This will be the second of five.* He gathers his glue, scissors and newspapers and pulls on a fresh pair of gloves. He unwraps a fresh batch of A4 paper and pastes '2/5' on the top.

He's already decided on the message.

You will not know the day or the hour but I am coming for you . . .

7

The following morning, after dodging about a million questions from my mother on why I got back so late last night, I drive to Jerry Loftus's house in Ballycroy.

I take along a flask of strong coffee because the last thing you need on an investigation is a foggy head, and the older I get the harder I find dealing with sleep deprivation. I miss the days when I was bouncing out of the door, eager to deal with the dregs of humanity, thinking I could save the world.

I'm not ten minutes on the road when Jordy calls. 'Jerry's wife, Hazel Loftus, visited Ballycroy garda station yesterday morning,' he says, 'According to her, the last time she'd seen him was at noon the previous day. He'd told her that he was going hiking and he never returned. The guard who filed the report said she seemed upset and kept insisting that something must have happened to him. When he tried to reassure her, she told him she knew her husband and he never would have left her.'

The number of people who say that, I think.

'Hazel also handed over a list of contacts for Jerry, though she said she'd already tried all his friends and relatives. She also gave the guard details of their bank accounts and Jerry's social-media handles.'

That's excellent news. It means we don't have to go wasting our time looking for them and potentially upsetting her again.

'I'll email you all the contacts in case you need them,' Jordy says, and hangs up.

Jerry's house sits on its own in the middle of a vast, undulating brown landscape. At best the location could be described as beautifully savage, at worst depressingly desolate. The tans and golds of the bog stretch on and on to the blue mountains in the distance. Today the sky is grey and heavy with rain. Maybe it's better in summer, but in this bleak midwinter, with the wind howling like a banshee, it's an uninviting place.

I shiver slightly as I park my car in what passes for a driveway, and the sound of my shoes crunching on the gravel seems to fill the whole world. The dormer bungalow is large, newish but unfinished, the plastered walls a grim grey, the windows bare, like a blank gaze. It's as if the owners had lost interest in it. The ring of the bell echoes inside the house. Quick feet on hall tiles and the door is opened by a small, anxious-looking woman, dressed in a drab grey sweatshirt and pyjama bottoms. 'Hello?' Large brown eyes peer up at me.

I show her my ID and the anxious look intensifies. 'Is this about Jerry?'

'May I come in?'

She steps back and I enter an enormous atrium-like hallway. Light pours in through a large Velux window positioned over the stairwell. There's an emptiness in the space. I brace myself and my voice echoes as I say the words I've rehearsed on the way over here. 'Mrs Loftus—'

THE WRATH

'Hazel.'

'Hazel,' I repeat gently, and I'm gratified to see her shoulders relax a little. 'I believe you filed a missing-person report on your husband yesterday morning.'

'Oh . . . yes. Yes, he's missing. He's not here.' Her hands flutter to her chest.

'Well, we located his car but unfortunately he wasn't inside.'

She starts a little.

'We found it in Achill, on the road to Keem beach.'

Her left hand plucks agitatedly at the neck of her sweatshirt. 'I . . . see.'

'I'm here to ask if you could provide me with some of Jerry's DNA.' At her blank look, I'm forced to explain: 'We need it to compare against some DNA we found in the car.' I don't say blood – there's no point in alarming her just yet. Maybe it isn't her husband's, maybe it's not human. Maybe he was carjacked. 'I'd just need a hairbrush or a toothbrush, anything with Jerry's hair or saliva on it. What we do is we test it against anything we uncover in the car.'

Thankfully she doesn't press me for more information. 'He has a hairbrush. You stay here. I'll get it for you.' She turns and moves quickly up the curving staircase. She's barefoot.

I take a moment to survey the hall properly. Large white porcelain floor tiles, stark white walls, a few pictures grouped together on a navy hall table. I peer closer and notice that all of them, bar one, show the same couple. Hazel and a man I suppose must be Jerry. He's tall to her small. My mother would describe him as a long streak of nothing. Lanky, he's all arms and legs with an elongated, though kind face. He has to stoop down to put his arm around his wife's shoulders, which gives him a hunched look. The odd picture out is of a younger man, maybe in his twenties, with dazzling teeth and movie-star looks. He's tall and toned, leaning against a brick wall, one foot planted behind him, wearing a pair of ripped jeans and enormous Docs. It's posed and arty. There's a label under the picture: *Zak 21*, it reads. In fact, there are labels under all the pictures. *Hazel and Jerry at Zak's graduation ball. Jerry and Hazel at Marge and Pete's wedding.* I turn to another photo. *Hazel and Jerry at Jerry's retirement.* Something snags as a familiar face catches my eye. I pick up the picture and peer at it more closely. In the background, just behind a smiling Jerry is Joe Little. He worked alongside me as a sergeant for a while in Dublin. A nice guy. Was Jerry a guard?

'Here you go,' Hazel hands me a hairbrush, which, thankfully, doesn't look as if it's cleaned too often. I place it in an evidence bag. Her eyes flick to the picture. 'Jerry's retirement,' she reads. 'He loved his job in Dún Laoghaire station.'

'He was a guard?'

'Yes. He retired and we came . . .' a gulp '. . . here.'

'I recognise that man.' I point to Joe.

Hazel gives me an over-bright beam. 'Oh. That's nice.' Then, sounding uneasy, 'Can you put the picture back now?'

'Thanks for the hairbrush.' I replace the picture. 'I'll be back if there are any developments.'

'You have to find him. This house . . . this place . . . I can't stay here on my own. I can't be in this house on my own.'

Sudden tears spill down her cheeks, plopping onto the floor and, though I'm in a rush, I can't leave her, not when she's crying. There's something terribly vulnerable about her, in this enormous house in her bare feet. She's childlike, almost. 'How about we have a cup of tea and I ring a friend for you?'

She shakes her head. 'I have no friends here and – oh, God, oh, God, I'm sorry.' She presses the heels of her hands into her eye sockets and her shoulders heave. 'He never would just disappear. Where is he?'

'That's what we're trying to figure out, Hazel. Come, I'll make you some tea.'

I head towards where I think the kitchen should be, knowing she will follow.

I strike it lucky on my first try. The kitchen is another huge personality-free space. More white tiles and walls. Big windows showing an expanse of landscape, dreary and windswept. A red Smeg fridge is the only splash of colour. And the room is freezing.

'What a bright room,' I chatter, as I fill the kettle. 'Have you been here long?'

'I hate it.'

I'm surprised at the venom in her words.

'Windows all over,' she continues, through gritted teeth. 'People seeing in. No houses anywhere. I can't stay here. Moving was Jerry's idea. And now he's gone.'

She paces up and down as the kettle boils, eventually coming to a stop in front of the floor-to-ceiling window that dominates the kitchen. As she peers out, wildness seems to stare back in.

'You don't know for sure that he's gone.' I talk to her back.

'Then where is he?'

'Let me pour you a cuppa and we'll figure out what to do, eh?'

She looks at me over her shoulder. 'I can't stay here.'

I ignore that and pull two cups from a press, locate a bag of sugar and take the milk from the fridge. A few minutes of silence later, I hand her a mug of tea. She hasn't moved from the window.

My eyes are drawn to some photos on the fridge. A younger-looking Jerry with another man who looks strikingly like him. It's a happy snap. *Jerry and Tom at their joint fiftieth.* 'Brothers?' I ask.

Hazel stares blankly at me.

I tap the picture. 'Jerry's brother?'

'I— Yes, yes. Brother.'

My phone buzzes. William.

'Let me just take this.'

Moving into the hall, I keep my eye on her as I press the mobile to my ear. 'Cig.'

'Where the hell are you? Dan is here. We're walking the scene.'

'I'm with Hazel Loftus. She's in a distressed state and—'

'Distressed? Why? What have you told her?'

'Nothing. She's just . . . afraid of being on her own and I—'

There's a tsk of impatience before he says, 'Assign an FLO. I need you here.' And he's gone.

I take a second to gather myself, giving the mobile two fingers before smiling reassuringly at Hazel. 'That's my boss. I have to go but I'm going to give my colleague a ring and she'll wait with you for a while. Is that all right?' Without waiting for her to respond, I dial Phil, a family liaison officer, who promises to be with us within the hour.

William will kill me but I can't walk out on Hazel until Phil arrives. The woman seems to be a ball of anxiety and stress, and there's something else that I can't quite catch. As I sit, watching her clutch her mug of tea like a life raft, I try to analyse what it is that doesn't quite fit about her. Is it what she says? Or her jerky, frantic pacing? Is it how distracted she is?

It's only after, when I leave, on my way to the scene, that it hits me.

It's nothing. Nothing about her fits.

8

I arrive at the scene at half nine and it's a co-ordinated hive of activity. Jordy has replaced Matt and, after he's signed me in, I catch up to William and Dan.

'Nice of you to join us,' William says, without looking at me.

'How is Hazel Loftus?' Dan asks, and I'm grateful because it's his way of standing up for me.

'Anxious, upset, though whether it's over her husband or not, it's hard to tell. I actually don't know what to make of her.'

I have William's interest now.

'It's nothing and everything.' I struggle to explain myself. 'But sure . . . maybe it won't matter. He was a guard in south Dublin. Retired a few months ago. If it turns out he's been assaulted, I'll get one of the lads to check PULSE to look through his cases. In the meantime, I've got a hairbrush from Hazel and it's gone to the lab for comparison against any DNA from the car. What's the news here?'

William waves in the direction of one of the SOCO lads. 'John reckons, like I thought, that there are two sets of blood in that car. One, he says, appears to be a catastrophic arterial bleed while the other looks superficial. He's taken samples. There are also drag marks on the ground at the driver's side as if something or someone was pulled towards the cliff edge. Nothing at the cliff edge, though. There is also, very faint, a trace of what looks like a narrow wheel of some sort. Maybe a bicycle. A number of footprints too. More car-tyre prints. We've got staining on some rocks by the edge of the road, away from the vehicle.'

I study the car, the way it's positioned. 'You'd never see someone being dragged out of the car from either direction of the road if both the driver and the back passenger doors were open. It'd create a bit of a corridor.'

'Might explain the drops of blood on the handle. That's good,' William says, as his phone rings. He steps away, out of earshot to answer, leaving me with Dan.

'It's not just you,' Dan whispers, reading my mind. 'He's in shite form. Poor Jordy got an earful for leaning against the fence post.'

It is about me but I can't say that to him. I can't tell him that William helped save my job by hiding evidence of my dead husband's wrongdoing without putting Dan in an impossible situation.

'Whatever is eating him is big,' Dan muses, his detective instinct kicking in, like a dog after a scent. 'I wonder is it—'

'He's coming back,' I interrupt and, like two kids in front of the headmaster, we put on innocent expressions and try to look like we're discussing the case.

'Human blood,' he says, without any preamble. 'Two types.' A grim smile. 'We won't need the hairbrush. Jerry gave his prints for elimination purposes at a crime scene a couple of years back.

THE WRATH

The blood in the car is his, looks like he was the one on the wrong end of this assault. I'm calling in the divers. Lucy, get Kev to set up the incident room in Achill. I'll ring Jim D'Arcy, see if he's free to do IRC.'

He jabs Jim's number into his phone. I hope the man is free: he's the best incident-room coordinator in the west, meticulous and detail-oriented. No job is left undone. I put a call through to Kev, who says he'd be delighted to set up the incident room. 'Also, Kev,' I say, 'we need to check PULSE to see how far Jerry's missing-person investigation had got in Ballycroy. Can you job it out and get back to us for conference?'

'Sure.' Kev's voice bubbles with excitement. He's one of the smartest young detectives, still starry-eyed with his recent promotion and determined to put the world to rights. He's got a sunny demeanour that will stand to him. He reminds me a lot of myself when I was starting off, and every time I see him a part of me grieves.

'Also get a list of Jerry's cases from PULSE as well. We need people to go through them.'

When William returns, pleased that Jim is free, I tell him about spotting Joe Little in the background of one of Jerry Loftus's pictures.

'It'd do no harm to ask him about Jerry,' William says. 'Get someone to find out if he's still working in that station.' After I say I'll job it out, he says, 'You may as well go with Dan now and call in to Hazel Loftus. Inform her that it's looking likely her husband was assaulted. Ask her the usual questions, see how she reacts. Maybe get a look around if she gives permission.'

'Sure.' I'm glad to leave. His presence bristles with unease.

'Conference tomorrow at ten,' he says. 'Don't be late.'

I tense at the implication that I'm ever late but I let it slide. He's looking to be provoked.

He turns again. 'And good work apprehending those lads in Castlebar, though the lad that escaped is in the wind. I want reports on that as soon as.'

'Feck's sake,' I hiss as, side by side, Dan and I walk away from the site.

It's only when we've made the decision to leave my Corsa behind and travel in Dan's DDU car to Hazel's that he turns to me and says, 'I bet you know what's wrong with him.'

'What's wrong with whom?' I feign ignorance, as I slide on my seatbelt.

'You do know!' Dan sits back and regards me speculatively. 'You do know what's eating the Cig. Spill.'

'I do not.' My lie would work with most people but with a detective as skilled as Dan I haven't a hope.

'You do.' Dan still hasn't started the engine. 'First off, you never, and I mean never, would normally tolerate him telling you not to be late. You would have jumped on him for it.'

'I was keeping my distance from his short fuse.' That isn't a lie.

'And,' he says, 'you're lying to me. What's the story?'

I take a moment, wonder about the best way to deal with this. I don't want Dan digging because I have no doubt he'll find out. And at the same time, I don't want him thinking I'm hiding stuff from him because we're partners and we need to trust each other. I settle for 'Yes, all right, I do know, but it's his personal business.' Which is true.

'He has personal business?' Dan sounds incredulous. 'The Cig? Per-son-al stuff in his life?'

'Hard as that is to believe, yes, Daniel.'

'But why would he tell you?'

Oh, for God's sake. 'I sort of know about it and he doesn't like that I know, all right?'

He chews his lips, ruminating before finally starting the car. 'All right,' he says, but I'm not sure he's convinced.

9

Hazel answers before we get as far as pressing the bell. She takes a step back when she sees us. Then, her expression clearing, she jabs a finger towards me, 'You're the . . . the missing-person person. Sorry I forgot your name.'

'That's all right. I'm Lucy, a detective.'

Another woman appears in the hallway and hovers behind her. Phil must have found a friend to stay with her.

'Can we come in?' I ask.

'Jerry, my husband, is missing.' Hazel is wild-eyed, unravelled. 'I thought you were out looking for him.'

'Hazel, love.' The woman catches her elbow, probably sensing that what we have to say isn't going to be good. 'Let them come in. Maybe they have news for you. This way,' she says, leading us all into the sitting room. 'Now, Hazel, you sit there, on that sofa.'

Hazel does as she is told.

Thankfully, someone has turned on the heat and the house has warmed up.

Telling relatives that their loved ones may have died is hands-down the worst part of the job. No one likes it, though sometimes it's useful. Their reactions can be a good tell. Most people, no matter who they are, respond the same way to terrible news. The guilty ones never quite manage to pull it off convincingly.

Dan remains standing while I perch on the edge of a beige leather chair. Like the rest of the house, the room is bright but soulless.

'Hazel—'

'Just tell me.' She reaches blindly for the other woman's hand.

The best way to do this sort of thing is to be completely straight, leave no room for doubt. 'We believe your husband may have been the victim of an assault. We haven't located him yet but we're working on it.'

'You believe he was?' Her gaze flits between me and Dan. I hate the look of hope.

'A substantial amount of blood was found in your husband's car,' I'm inching out, like a vehicle at a dangerous crossroads, 'and we've matched it up to Jerry. I'm sorry.'

She looks shocked, appears about to say something but her words get jammed.

Carefully, I ask, 'Is there anyone you know who might have wanted to harm him?'

A small, devastated silence as the sentence drops into the room.

Hazel's look of complete bewilderment is worse than any tears.

'Oh, love,' her friend says, sympathy sparking in her eyes.

I can't be here. The last few years seem to have scraped away any armour I used to have. 'I'll make us some tea.' To Dan's dismay, I leave him with the two women.

In the hallway, I take a moment. The worst is over. Now, it's on to the job. Hazel had told me there was no way he would just have gone missing. I have to push through her upset and my unease and get some answers.

The soft murmur of Dan's voice, telling them a little of what we know, fades as I enter the kitchen. After I fill the kettle, I take a walk around the huge space, looking for . . . I'm not quite sure what. The place is so bare, there's nothing here anyway. Some scraps of paper on the windowsill, notes about dinner times and shopping lists and reminders of birthdays. Knowing I shouldn't, I pull open a drawer, rummage through some old birthday cards and receipts. The kettle clicks off just as Hazel's friend pops her head in.

'Can I help at— What are you doing?' She glares at me. 'You can't read people's letters.'

Ouch. 'I was looking for spoons,' I deflect. 'How is she?'

The woman seems unconvinced but is reluctant to accuse me of anything, so she lets it go. 'She's, I don't know, devastated?' It sounds like she's not too sure. She pulls open a drawer in the island. 'Here.' Holding up four spoons and bumping the drawer closed with her hip, she continues, 'Or shocked or something. What exactly has happened?'

'Just what we've told you. Jerry's car was found and it appears that he was assaulted in it. Neither he nor his assailant was at the scene. Are you a member of Hazel's family?'

'No, no, I'm a neighbour from across the way.' She waves vaguely towards the back of the house. 'I'm Roisin. I called over because I needed to talk to Jerry about the Tidy Towns and he wasn't answering his phone and a long thin guard came to the door and explained the situation and sure I said I'd stay with Hazel, the *créatúr*.'

'How well do you know the couple?'

Her voice dips. 'I don't know Hazel that well, really. They only moved here about eight months ago. Jerry is on the Tidy Towns. He likes being involved in things. Nice man, bit of a laugh. I met Hazel once or twice through him. He seems devoted to her. He told us that Hazel likes to keep herself to herself, but I think . . .' She hesitates, as if she's unsure whether to speak or not.

I wait. From experience, I know that most people like to tell you what they think.

'. . . I think it's more than that,' Roisin finally says. 'She reminds me of someone who suffers with anxiety or depression or something.'

A tiny 'plip' like a fish in water as an idea forms, the ripples it makes as I take in all I've learned about Hazel this morning.

I'll use the next few minutes carefully, test what I think.

I do the talking. I wait until the tea has been poured and Hazel has taken a sip before I begin. 'I realise this is upsetting, Hazel, but if you could answer a few questions for us it would help us piece together what might have happened to Jerry. Before that, though, is there anything you want to ask me?'

After thinking for a moment, she says, her voice breaking, 'Where exactly was his car found?'

'On the road between Keel and Keem on Achill Island. The Atlantic drive. A narrow road. Is there any reason you know why he would be there?'

'He – he liked hiking.' It's as if she's fumbling about in the dark for the answer. A hiccup of a sob. 'And how – well, how . . .'

I wait.

'Was there much blood?' A tear plops into her cup.

'Enough for us to assume that the assault was a serious one.

Some of our colleagues would have checked hospitals when you reported him missing but we will be doing that again.' In truth, with the amount of work we're under, it's unlikely the hospitals were checked initially, but it does no harm to soften things up a bit. Gently, I open up the conversation, 'I need to ask again, Hazel, if there was anyone, to your knowledge, who may have wished to harm Jerry?'

There is hesitation. 'No.'

'Now is not the time to protect people. Even if you have a suspicion we can investigate and—'

'There was no one. He would have told me.' A beat. 'I would remember that.'

I leave it a second, see if she'll say any more but her gaze slides to her hands, which are clasped tightly in her lap. I let it go. For now. 'Anyone who would want to harm you?'

She flinches. 'Me? No.'

'You're certain. There were no rows, no bad feelings?'

'No.' She meets my eye.

'Any problems in the family?'

'Jerry has two sisters and a brother. They live in Dublin. I can give you their numbers, if you like.'

I pull out my phone and scan the list of contacts she gave the guards when she reported him missing. 'It looks like you did yesterday, when you visited Ballycroy garda station.'

'Oh . . . yes . . . yes, I did.' Her agreement is a fraction off.

If I'm right about Hazel, this investigation has started badly. I suppress a groan but continue, pressing forwards, hoping I won't have to ask her outright.

'How about your family?'

'My parents are dead. I have no siblings.'

'And your children?'

'Zak would never have done anything to Jerry.' Colour flares in her cheeks. 'Never.'

'Zak is the boy in the picture in your hallway?'

'My boy,' she says, swallowing hard. 'He, well, he had a falling-out with Jerry.'

Now that's interesting.

From the look on Roisin's face, I don't think she's heard about any falling-out.

'But he would never . . .' Hazel gabbles, 'I mean, it was . . . a couple of years ago and, well, he just wouldn't. He's a great lad.'

Everyone is great until they're not.

Across the room, Dan shifts position, pencil poised over his notebook.

'Have you his name and number and we'll try to track him down?' He isn't on the contact list. And that's interesting too.

Hazel hesitates. 'He would never . . .'

'I'm sure he wouldn't but still . . . and I'm sure he needs to know that Jerry is missing.'

I wait expectantly and, after a moment, she stands up and moves into the hall, returning with a notebook. 'Here.' She hands it to me. 'It's there. Under Z. And an address. Not many people have that letter for their first name. Now, he may have changed it, I don't know. He never answers my calls.'

'Thanks.' I pass the address book to Dan who takes a picture of the details. 'Can you tell me what the row with his father was about?'

'I don't know. It caused a lot of upset . . . between us all . . . because why would they not tell me? Jerry said it was nothing and something and it would, you know,' she waves a hand, 'all get blown over. But it didn't. Zak wouldn't come down any more and it upset me and Jerry was devastated. I felt I had to choose a side. It was very hard.'

'Tough,' Dan says, from his corner, and Hazel agrees.

'We'll see if we can contact him,' I say. 'Now, getting back to Jerry. How much did he tell you about his work in the guards?'

'Lots. He wasn't going around dealing with really dangerous people. He was lucky in his postings and, as he said himself, he had it cushy enough.'

Jerry might never have told her the people he was dealing with. And I know from experience that some enemies wait years to wreak revenge. Even if he was just doing regular work, there would have been danger and trauma. Every call is a venture into the unknown. You could be dealing with anything from a suicide to a house break-in.

'Was he always a guard?'

'Yes.' Her mouth curves upwards, transforming her face. 'He loved it.'

I allow her time to enjoy the memory, then say, 'One more thing. I'd like you to visualise the last time you spoke to him.'

The tiniest wince. 'All right.'

Did Dan notice that momentary flinch? 'I need you to close your eyes and relax. We'll start with you getting up that morning.'

'But . . . but I told you. I—'

'It sometimes helps. You might remember something you forgot before.'

'I won't. No. Please. No.'

I wait a moment. 'Please?'

'It might help,' Roisin coaxes.

Hazel looks from me to Roisin, with what appears to be a

THE WRATH

slightly panicked expression, but finally sits back in her chair and closes her eyes. I take her step by step through that morning and she dithers a lot over certain things. What time she got up, what she ate, when she last saw her husband. I let her ramble on, and when she's finished, I flip through the notes I jotted down from the missing-person file. 'When you spoke to our colleagues in Ballycroy, you told them it was noon when he left the house. Now you're saying it was about three?'

'They must have misheard.'

'Okay.' I flip through my notes again. 'And you said this time that he was wearing shorts, but in the last account you said he wore jeans?'

She stares at me, perplexed. 'No. Shorts. That's what I said. He had red shorts on. Sure, it was sunny yesterday.'

Roisin gives a gentle laugh, 'It was raining yesterday, lovey. It's December.'

Hazel straightens herself in the chair. 'It was red shorts,' she reiterates, her tone sharp.

'All right, red shorts.' I close my notebook and, as gently as I can, I ask Hazel to come with me into the kitchen.

I close the kitchen door to give Hazel some privacy.

'Is there anything you'd like to tell me?' I ask.

She moves away from me to the other side of the island, putting a barrier between us. 'I don't think so.'

I wait. Then as her gaze drops, I ask, 'Are you certain about the time Jerry left the house and what he was wearing?'

'Yes.' Her voice is defiant.

'Two o'clock?'

'Yes.'

'I'm a guard, Hazel, and two minutes ago you told me it was three o'clock.'

She stills.

'And yesterday you said twelve o'clock.'

She bows her head.

'Unless there is complete honesty, I will not be able to do my job.'

'I saw him yesterday,' she says, with that intense stare. 'He was here yesterday.' Tears colour her tone.

'You went to Ballycroy yesterday to report him missing.'

'Oh . . . yes . . . yes, I . . .' She holds a hand to her mouth, the other flailing at the air. 'I'm getting mixed up. It's the shock and I want to remember the last time I saw him. I do. I want to remember it.' Soft tears splash onto the countertop.

I tear a strip of kitchen roll and coax her to take it. She thanks me and dabs at her eyes, her shoulders shaking. Finally, she looks straight at me, 'Anxiety makes it worse,' she whispers. 'I'm sorry, I should have . . . but I believed what I said. But I should have . . .'

'It's all right.' It's not but there's nothing to be gained by wishing it was otherwise. 'Tell me why you can't remember the last time you saw him, Hazel.'

'I'm having a few problems.' Her voice is choked up. 'My head,' she gestures with her hands, 'it's stuffy and my memory . . . Things are blurring. It started with, you know, misplacing things, finding my glasses in the . . .' a pause '. . . food-cooler thing. We joked about it at first but words are going now and, anyway, I had tests and I have that thing where you lose your memory, and all the yesterdays are a blur to me. Tomorrow this will be like – like I'm trying to reach it through a fog. And I can't remember when

THE WRATH

I last saw Jerry.' Her voice breaks. 'I can't remember what he said, what he wore. I only know that he's not here.'

The little heartbreaks that make up some people's lives.

'I'm so sorry.'

She says nothing, battling to keep it together, tears bright in her eyes. Finally, 'Jerry minded me, kept me, you know, on the right road. Kept people from knowing. Protected Zak from it. I couldn't have him worrying about me. But now I can't remember when I last saw Jerry. Imagine.'

'We'll do our best to figure it out.' I could cry myself. In cases like this, timings are crucial. CCTV harvesting, though sometimes broad, depends for its success on knowing roughly what time something occurred. 'May I look at your mobile phone? Jerry may have texted you and at least we'd have that.'

'Oh, yes. I never thought . . . I don't use it much.' She pulls her mobile from a little bag concealed under her jumper. 'Jerry made me put it in here and I remembered today.'

The phone is dead.

'Is there a charger anywhere?'

'The charger is beside the fridge on the counter.' She recites it like a mantra.

I locate it and plug in the phone. While it's booting up, I ask Hazel if it's okay for Dan to have a look upstairs. 'A preliminary look only,' I tell her. 'Just to see if we can locate anything to give us a clue as to why he's missing.'

She gives permission and I think she's sound enough of mind to do it. She tells me where the bedroom is and I call to Dan to go and have a look. As he climbs the stairs, I hear the telly going on in the front room. Fair play to Roisin, she's obviously planning on sticking around.

Ten minutes later, Hazel's phone pings back to life.

'The password is on the back,' she says.

That's probably not the best security but I don't complain. Once the digits are entered, her home screen lights up. It's a picture of her and Jerry at the Deserted Village in Achill. Wind has lifted Hazel's hair and she's laughing, her hand up to her head. Jerry looks tenderly down on her. I tear my eyes away from their obvious happiness, banishing the familiar pang of missing out, and busy myself locating the texts.

There are a few that remain unanswered. Scrolling through, I see that they are just general enquiries from a couple of friends. They've come in over the last two days when I suppose her phone had died.

I find the very last text from Jerry. Sent two days ago. At noon: *Stopped in for a bite. Remember I'm back about six. Take two chops from the freezer. I'll cook when I get back. Take it easy, pet. x*

'Did he come home that evening and cook, Hazel? Think hard.'

A blank look followed by an irritated 'I can think hard all I like, it makes no difference.'

'That's fine.' I strive to sound as if it is. 'I'm going to check your fridge, all right?' Pulling it open, I scan the contents. There, on the second shelf from the top, is an unopened packet containing two pork chops. Of course it doesn't prove anything. I turn my attention to the freezer and, aside from a packet of waffles, it's empty. 'Can you remember when you took those chops out, Hazel? And say if you're unsure.'

'Not today I didn't,' she says. 'How would I even think of eating?'

'Okay, so is it possible you took out the chops two days ago and that Jerry never arrived home to cook them?'

Hazel absorbs this before saying slowly, 'Yes . . . yes. That would make sense.'

Jerry had been alive at least until noon two days ago.

It's a start.

I scroll through some more texts but they're much the same. Reminding Hazel to do this and that and the odd time telling her when he'd be back. I can't find a text telling her he was hiking in Achill.

'How did you know Jerry had gone for a hike in Achill?' I ask. 'Can you remember him actually telling you?'

She shrugs, baffled. Then sudden light floods her face, 'He'd write it down for me on a sticky note. Every day he was away. On a sticky note.'

A *whump* of my heart. 'And where would he leave this note?'

'Beside our bed, right on the headboard, so if he was out early, he likes walking, I'd wake up and spot it. And if . . .'

But I don't stay to hear the rest. Pulling on a pair of gloves, I pound upstairs to the landing and into the bedroom where Dan, hunkered down, is methodically searching the bedside lockers. He looks up as I enter. 'Nothing,' he says.

'Did you find a sticky note near the bed at all?'

He doesn't waste time asking what I mean. Instead he shakes his head.

I scan the headboard. Nothing. One set of pillows on the floor, the other propped up against the headboard. I pull the pillows back and . . . nothing. As Dan continues his search, I reach down between the mattress and the headboard and come up empty. Where the hell is it?

Between the duvet and the blue sheets. Nothing. I heft up the mattress. Nothing.

'Would that be it?' Dan points under the bed.

I crouch on all fours to have a look. There's a bright pink square of paper lying just at the head of the bed where it must have fluttered down between the flat timbers of the frame. 'Yes!'

Dan lies on his stomach, ready to crawl into the space, but I'm a better fit, being marginally thinner. 'Let me.' I slide underneath the bed, which is a lot lower than I'd thought, and very gently I peel the note from the floor. Grasping it between my thumb and index finger and digging in my elbows, I start to reverse back out.

It's fecking hard.

I bang my head off a lath and the pain shoots, like an arrow, through my skull.

'D'you want me to pull you out?'

'No.' This is mortifying. 'I'll be fine.'

'Okay.' He suppresses a chortle.

'Don't fecking laugh.' Inch by painful inch, I haul myself backwards. Crawl, bang my head, crawl, smash my head.

'Ouch,' Dan remarks unhelpfully.

Seconds later, covered head to toe with dust, I emerge. I lie there for a moment, my cheek pressed to the floor, feeling as if I've just run a marathon before clambering to my feet. 'Have it.' My voice is too bright.

Dan's mouth twitches.

'Just wait until you hit my age.' I turn my attention to the note. *Gone hiking in Achill. Back 6. Love you.* And it's dated. Good man, Jerry.

After that find, I leave Hazel with Roisin so I can give Dan a hand looking through the rest of the bedroom. It's a massive area – I'd fit the whole downstairs of my house into it and still have space. Cream walls, blue curtains, more neatly labelled photographs. As Dan finishes on the lockers, I begin a search of the walk-in wardrobe.

It's slightly chaotic, Hazel's clothes mixed in with Jerry's. There's a stale smell in it too, as if some of the garments haven't been worn for a long time. I start on the drawers. Underwear, cufflinks, ties, socks. Bright T-shirts that are obviously Jerry's – he must have been a snappy dresser.

'Anything?' Dan pokes his head around the door.

'Nothing. You?'

He shakes his head. 'D'you need help?'

'Take those drawers over there. I'll finish up these ones.'

We continue in silence. Another team will come in and search more thoroughly if it becomes a murder inquiry. For now, we just want anything that might kick start our own investigation.

The last drawer on my side is a mess of papers, biros, books and magazines. A couple of the pens are commemorative ones. A Parker in a fancy box is inscribed with 'On your retirement'. There is a stack of cards wishing Jerry well in his new move. Cards congratulating him on forty years on the force, cards for his sixtieth birthday. Jerry is obviously a bit of a hoarder. I pull out a pile of newspapers and give them a cursory glance. Nothing is highlighted or underlined. It's impossible to see why Jerry might have stored them here. Putting them aside, I make a note to get one of the lads in the station to examine them in more depth, or maybe Hazel could shed some light on why he may have kept them. I pull out another sheaf of newspapers. Something slips from between the leaves and drifts to the floor. It's an A4 page. Picking it up, I turn it over. 'Christ!'

I hold it towards Dan.

Just like the page found in Jerry's car, it's a note using pasted-on letters.

As I shake the newspapers again, three more notes fall out.

Hairs rise on the back of my neck.

Dan breathes, 'Jesus wept.'

10

After we photograph the anonymous letters, we obtain Hazel's written permission to take them and their accompanying red envelopes for forensic testing.

'That's some weird shit,' Dan says, studying the images on his phone. 'Vengeance and hell. Jerry must have been freaking out.'

'And yet he never reported them.' I take the road towards Achill Sound.

'Then he must have had something to hide. Maybe it's to do with the row between him and the son. Maybe he didn't want to get the guards involved. "Vengeance is mine,"' Dan reads. '"The road to Hell is paved . . ."' He looks at me. 'That's a weird one.'

'I think the quote finishes "with good intentions". As in, "The road to Hell is paved with good intentions."'

'Wonder what that means?'

I shrug. 'It means you try to do something good but it all turns to crap.'

'Like being a guard.'

We both have a bit of a snigger.

'Imagine the patience it would take to cut out letters and paste them onto a page. I wouldn't be bothered.' Dan flicks his phone off.

I leave Dan ruminating over the letters as I put a call through to Larry, our CCTV guru. A macho, narcissistic womaniser, he's nevertheless got a serious talent for minute concentration.

'Yo! Lucy.'

I ignore the greeting. He does it to get a rise out of me. I give him Hazel's address and task him with harvesting all the CCTV footage from the area from early on the morning of 1 December.

'I was told noon by Jim D'Arcy,' he says, a little grumpily. 'I'll move the footage up. There's very little to be had, though, just a shop or two along the way. It's only a forty-minute journey. I've put out a call for dash-cam.'

'Good.' I chew my lip, thinking, then say, 'He also stopped for something to eat around noon. That could only have been on the island or on the way there, so make calls to every place that was serving food at that time along that route and see if you can get anything. Also, try for footage from along the road where the car was found. I first noticed it at two yesterday afternoon, though it may have been there from the night before.' I do a mental calculation. I'd driven home from work on 1 December at around five o'clock and the car hadn't been there. 'From five p.m. on the night of the first of December to two p.m. on the afternoon of the second.' I ignore the groan from Larry. 'With house-to-house we may be able to narrow that timeline down. I'd start from five p.m., though, and go until around eight a.m. Chances are whoever it was disposed of the body in the dark.'

He sighs in frustration, a passive-aggressive way of signalling to me that I have no idea what it takes to examine that much footage and hangs up.

THE WRATH

'Arsehole.' I jab the phone off and roll my eyes.

'I think it must be something in the water down here,' Dan remarks cheerfully. 'Everyone is in awful form.'

'Whereas you seem remarkably chirpy.' I give him a sidelong glance. 'Spill.'

'Am I that obvious?' Dan smirks, then says, with a grin, 'Delores didn't come back last night. She spent it with her new man.'

Is it right to be envious of an OAP's love life?

'He's called Fred Keane. Honestly, he's great. We barely see her any more.'

'Fred Keane?'

'Yep. And—'

'So, if they married she'd be Delores Keane.' I giggle a little.

Dan smirks at the joke but huffs out a sigh. 'You'd want to see Fran, though. He was like a priest this morning, saying how immoral it all was.'

We're nearly at the station now. Up ahead dark clouds are building from the Atlantic, like an army on the march. They pile, one onto the other, turning the sky a dark bruised purple and dimming the light.

'Who is that?' Dan's attention has been snagged by a hunched figure shambling along by the side of the road. His brown coat tails are flapping behind him with the breeze from the sea, and his over-large trousers are soaked to the knee. As he trudges along, his boots splash into puddles that he either doesn't see or doesn't care about.

'That's Eddie,' I answer. 'You know, the guy who shouts about religion every so often on the Michael Davitt Bridge?'

'Jesus, he's gone downhill.' Dan shakes his head. 'Poor fecker.'

As we pass, Eddie bends to pick up a bottle from the ground. He examines it before tucking it away in the pocket of his huge brown coat. His beard is longer than I've ever seen it. It comes down to his chest and appears not to have been trimmed in a while. Dark hair spills onto his shoulders from under a battered cap. He stops walking as we drive by, righting himself, his gaze following us as if he's committing us to memory. Eddie had been the cleverest boy in my school. A couple of years older than me, he'd become a professor of something or other before a massive breakdown had led to him leaving his job. He'd never recovered. They said he'd driven himself so hard that his mind broke. People in school had called him a weirdo, which always made me feel a bit sorry for him, but at the same time, I never waded to his defence, just laughed along with everyone else. Teenagers are a cruel species. The memory causes an unexpected flash of shame. Nowadays his older sister looks after him, ringing me now and again when she can't find him, though I get the feeling she's given up on him. He's often to be found wandering the roads of the island, sometimes shoeless, thumbing lifts or shouting about Jesus. He's twirling now, hands outstretched, roaring. In the rear-view, I watch him growing smaller and smaller. He'll probably find a pub in Achill Sound where they'll spot him a coffee and a sandwich.

We're just back at the station when Larry calls. 'Where are ye?'

'Just about to pull into the station.'

'Well, keep going. I was on to McLoughlin's Bar just outside Achill Sound looking for CCTV,' he says, 'and one barman, Tomas, reckons he saw Jerry Loftus that day.'

'Great, on it.'

The bar is a two-minute drive away, across the Michael Davitt Bridge, but just as we pass Centra on Achill Sound, huge slow

THE WRATH

drops of rain spatter the car, hitting the bonnet and windscreen. I turn on the wipers and then, like a switch being flicked, the temperature plummets and what can only be described as a reservoir of water pours down. People outside hurry into doorways, but the more adventurous plough on regardless, heads bent against the breeze. Rain hits the ground so hard, it hops back up again. A disoriented bird swoops in front of us and away. An umbrella tumbles across the road. A gust of wind shakes the car and I'm forced to slow to a crawl.

After what seems the longest time, I pull up opposite the pub, the car stuttering to a halt.

'I'm not getting out in that,' Dan remarks. 'Jesus, my suit will be ruined.'

'Ya big pussy,' I scoff, but I'm kind of glad.

We sit in silence, both of us enjoying the spectacle, I think.

And then, just as quickly as it arrived, it's gone. The rain lessens, light pokes out from behind the clouds and the world calms again.

'Where else would you get it?' I grin. 'The sun and the rain.' I step out of the car into a large puddle. 'Aw, bollox!' My socks are soaking.

Dan meanwhile runs daintily across the road, careful not to ruin the shine on his highly polished shoes. He waits with a smirk at the pub's door as I clump over, feet squelching.

'You should always bring spare socks,' he lectures. 'I can lend you mine when we're done here. I have some at the station.'

'Gee, thanks. Nice to know I'll have dry feet in an hour.'

The barman in McLoughlin's is all eager beaver. He ushers us to a table, pulling out a chair for me – which I quite like – before offering us a beverage. That's the word he uses – beverage – saying it in a fake posh voice that draws a smile from Dan. I probably shouldn't drink any more caffeine, but the coffee is good here and I have no willpower. Dan asks for a sandwich as well so I order one too, and ten minutes later we both have steak sandwiches and a massive portion of chips in front of us.

It's after five and I'm bloody starving.

Tomas pulls up a stool and, just as I've taken a huge bite from my sandwich, without any bidding he launches into his story. I have no choice but to put down my food and wrestle my notebook from my top pocket. I want to kick Dan who is still chomping away.

Tomas is like a dog looking for treats as he recounts his meeting with Jerry Loftus. 'I recognised him because I seen him on the internet just this morning. The appeal to find him came up in my social-media feed. I always have a look at that page because you never know when you'll see someone. There was a documentary on Netflix about a man who was missing for sixty years and wasn't he spotted in a Lidl? The person knew him because he had this wart on his face shaped like a mushroom.'

My stomach turns.

'Tell us about seeing Jerry,' Dan says, through a mouthful of chips.

'Right. A course. Well, when I seen the missing-person post on social, I was going to ring Ballycroy but as a stroke of luck would have it, didn't that guard call me and ask if we had CCTV footage, and I asked if it was about the missing man Jerry and he said it was, and I said, "Well, I seen him, so I did."'

'How sure are you?' Dan wipes a smear of sauce from his face. I risk a chip.

THE WRATH

'Oh, about one hundred per cent. First off, I was only about fifty-two per cent because on social media he was described as wearing jeans and a red fleece but this lad, he was wearing hiking trousers – you know, the sort where you can unzip the bottom half and they become shorts?' Before we can react, he says, 'That's what he was wearing. Black ones. And he wore a blue rain jacket and he had a haversack. But though I'm shocking with faces, shocking, I remembered him because of the mole. Right here.' He points to his cheek. 'I remember thinking it didn't suit him.' He says it like Jerry donned it that morning. 'So anyway, he was the right height too, this man. Tall and tin.' He means 'thin'. 'He ordered a salmon sandwich and a cup of tea and the man with him ordered a plate of pasta. But now, the pasta fella didn't finish his. He came and paid and didn't finish it. Then I went over to clear the plates after the first lad left and I talked to Jerry!' He sounds delighted with himself. 'I asked him how he was getting on, the way you would, like, and he said he'd soon find out as he was going to tackle Croaghaun. I wished him luck and after a bit he left. And that was it.' He dips his head as if to put a full stop at the end, then says, 'Oh, yeah, and the man who didn't finish his pasta called him Jerry, so that's more proof, isn't it?'

'Describe the man Jerry was with.' Dan had stopped shovelling food into his mouth after Tomas mentioned the other fellow. He asks about him now as if it's no big deal.

I wait, pencil poised, food almost forgotten.

Tomas is oblivious to the sudden alertness between us. 'Younger than him, like his son only maybe not. Dark hair, medium.' He looks at me. 'Tinner than you but taller. He wore,' he screws up his face, 'trousers, like hiking ones too, and a grey jumper. They were having a good old chinwag, leaning in and sort of whispering to each other. Then the young lad left.'

'Did you overhear them at any stage?'

'Like I said, he did call Jerry, Jerry. When I was bringing down their food, he said something like "You're just being stupid, Jerry." And they both looked up at me and they stopped talking and after that I was up the other end of the room from them. They were sitting over there.' He points to an alcove, hidden from anyone coming in the door.

'What time was this?'

'Twelve or thereabouts. That was another thing made me think it wasn't him. The social-media post said he disappeared at noon. But he was here then.'

'What time did the other man leave him?'

He scratches his head, screws up his eyes. 'Maybe one? Aw, look, I'm not too sure.'

'And Jerry?'

'Again, I'd be lying if I said I knew.'

'Was there anyone else in the bar at that time?'

'A couple of other people. Two women. They're staying in the hotel down the road and come here every— Ah, speak of the devil, here they are now.' He immediately stands up, straightens himself and pats his hair down.

'Hey, Tomo!' one of the women calls, and he blushes to his fingertips.

'I'm just helping the guards here with their enquiries.'

The women look suitably impressed.

'Do ye remember the couple that were in here last Monday? A long tin man and a smaller tin man. The auld lad was probably as old as her.'

I'm 'her'. I attempt to look nonchalant, but I really want to throttle Dan, who is smirking again.

The girls study me, youth radiating from them like sunbeams.

'Two days ago is a long time in holiday mode,' the taller of the two women eventually says, as the other laughs hysterically.

Tomas titters frantically.

I'd say they've had a few jars.

They sashay up to the bar, drape themselves over the counter.

'Mad, they are,' Tomas says fondly, as he turns back to us. 'There was also two other lads in the pub. One of them is a regular, Paddy Jackson. He lives just up the road.'

I know Paddy. He'll be next to useless but I scribble his name down anyway.

'And another lad, "tank" maybe would be a better way of describing him. Fortyish, strong-looking. Bulging muscles, that sort of a lad, you know.' He eyes Dan up and down. 'Well, maybe you don't but you can imagine.'

Dan remains stoic in the face of the insult but now it's my turn to smirk.

'He had some lunch here but, if I remember well, he sat near the two tin men. He was a tourist, said he was American or something. He might be in again. That's it really.' He leans back in his seat and folds his arms.

Dan recounts everything Tomas has said back to him and he nods.

'Brilliant. Have you got all that, Luce?'

'Yep.' I pop a chip into my mouth and it's freezing. Feck it anyway.

'Good luck on finding him.' Tomas stands up, then sits down again, his voice a confidential whisper. 'Is all that activity up beyond on the Atlantic drive connected to Jerry Loftus?'

'We don't know,' Dan answers. 'Thanks for your help. Just send those two ladies back our way, would you?' He's crossing the *t*s to make sure they really didn't see anything.

As Tomas hops and skips towards the women, I whisper to Dan, 'You can fecking take notes now. I have to eat.'

'I wish I was only starting mine now. It was gorgeous.'

'Not when it's cold it's not.'

The women are approaching warily.

'Ladies.' Dan beams at them and they soften right up, like toffee in the sun. 'If ye'd have a look at this, that'd be great.' He hands them a picture of Jerry. 'Take your time now.'

There's a bit of to-ing and fro-ing, one asking the other if they remember anything, until finally both of them declare that, as he wasn't particularly attractive or young, they would probably never have noticed him.

'Can we go now?' the tall one asks, like we're her parents.

'Sure,' Dan says. Then, in an undertone to me, 'If self-absorption was an Olympic sport, I'd say those two would be in line for gold.'

'And if being a muscle man was, you'd probably come last,' I tease and he fires one of my chips at me. 'Hey, I'm hungry,' I pick it up from the floor. 'Three-second rule.'

He looks mildly disgusted.

'What have we got?' I ask.

'Jerry Loftus leaves his house early on Monday the first, a Post-it note left behind for his wife to find. It says he's going climbing in Achill. At eleven fifty, he texts her to say that he's having a bite to eat, to take some chops from the freezer and that he'll be back in time for tea, which he will cook. We're fairly certain Hazel did take the chops out and they were never used. At noon, ten minutes after the text was sent, we have an ID on him in McLoughlin's bar in Achill. More verification is needed. According to the barman, he was accompanied by a younger man. Son?'

'Tomas said he called Jerry, Jerry. Most people would say Mam or Dad. But it is a possibility.'

'Yeah. Good point. Hang on.' Dan takes out his phone and types 'Zak Loftus' into Instagram. 'There are only four.' Scrolling through them, he frowns. 'All fecking private accounts.' He snaps his phone closed. 'So, back to what we know. Jerry told the barman he was off to climb Croaghaun. How long would that take?'

'With my extensive mountaineering background, I just . . . don't know.'

'Ha-ha.'

'Look it up on Google, you eejit.' I manage to demolish most of my steak sandwich before he finds an answer.

'An experienced climber would take about ninety minutes to two hours, give or take. So, we'll go with ninety minutes. We do not know what time he left the bar, but hopefully CCTV will help there.'

'I do know he would have had to park in Keem or Lough Acorrymore, which is about a twenty-minute journey. So, let's say he began climbing around two thirty, and that's late if he ate here at noon, he should have been finished by four before it got too dark, back well in time for tea. We need to trace his journey from when he left here to the time I spotted his car for the first time.'

'Yeah,' Dan agrees. 'We'll put out a call for the muscle man and the man who was with him in the pub.'

'Also see if we can narrow down exactly when Jerry's car was first spotted abandoned on the Atlantic drive. Someone must have seen it before I did.'

'If it was left there on the night of the first, it may not have been seen until you saw it. I hate to break it to you, Luce, but where you live, that road, at this time of year, only the brave travel along it.'

He has a point. Some days no one uses that road. My house is the last before Keem beach.

My mother had gone shopping that morning, but even if the car was there, she probably didn't notice it. She travels through life scattering fairy dust everywhere. I've always envied her sunny outlook and oblivious nature. I don't know where the darkness in me comes from.

Just before we leave, I corner Tomas at the bar. 'Do you remember how Jerry paid for his meal?'

'No, but if you hold on a second, I can look at the receipts for that morning.' He disappears somewhere into the back and returns holding a box full of paper, which he rummages through. 'There were only six people in at that time of day and it looks like . . .' a big pause as he examines something '. . . four of them paid by card.'

'Can I have the list of cards, please?' With a bit of luck, Jerry might have used one, lending weight to Tomas's ID of him. We might find the mystery man who was with him too.

'Sure.'

Tomas pushes the receipts towards me and I place them in an evidence bag. 'I'll get them back to you when the investigation ends.'

I join Dan at the door. 'We never recovered any of Jerry's credit or debit cards from the car, did we?'

'No, though his wallet could have landed on the floor where we didn't see it. Has the car been taken from the scene yet?'

I put a call through to Matt who says that, yes, it was moved an hour ago.

I ring Forensics. 'Jerry Loftus. I want—'

'Two days' time, at the earliest. Going as fast as we can.'

'Can I actually ask the question, please?'

A resigned sigh from the other end of the line. 'If ye find a credit card in the car, can you let me know ASAP, please. It's Lucy Golden here.'

'I'll take a note of it.'

'Thanks. Two days, yeah?'

He doesn't bother replying, just hangs up.

I glance at my phone. 'It's after six. I think we should call it a day. Conference tomorrow at ten.' I tap my notebook. 'We've got a good bit to go on here.'

On the way home, the roads are slick with recent rain and the dark has settled in. I flick on the radio to hear the news.

'A nineteen-year-old man was today charged with the murder of Peter Fox, a known drug-dealer whose battered body was found in the Westport area of Mayo last year. It is understood —'

I switch station. I have enough crime here without having to listen to more. Over on Mayo FM, an agony aunt is reading a letter from a woman who is wondering if she'll ever find love. I turn up the volume.

11

A teeny-tiny sequined jacket is slung across my hall chair along with a blingy bag. Feck's sake, Cherry wasted no time in coming down from Dublin to see Luc. This woman, whom Luc seems to have chosen over Tani, Sirocco's mother, and I have nothing in common. Gone for ever are my fantasies of having a surrogate daughter who will talk with me about getting fit while we both slosh back cheap wine. Instead, Cherry with her flat stomach and endless chatter of beauty treatments and Botox, might as well be speaking Mandarin Chinese. And the way she looks always makes me feel like some kind of flea-ridden mangy cat. Also, why does Luc never visit her house? Every time he's off college, Cherry's here, floating about the place with *Hello!* magazine and glittery clothes.

'Lucy,' my mother calls from the television room, 'bring your dinner in. I'm dying to hear all about your day.'

I grin. She only ever wants to hear about my day when my job makes the headlines. I can hear the theme tune of *Six One News* through the door. I poke my head in and, to my relief, there is no sign of Cherry. She and Luc have either gone out or ensconced themselves in his room. I hope they stay there. Five minutes later, a big plate of curry balanced on my lap, I'm listening to my mother running through theories about what on earth could have happened in the abandoned car. 'Lorna said bits of fingers were left on the steering wheel.' She waits for my reaction.

'She's wrong.' I fork some food into my mouth and wince. Damn! How many chillies did she put in this?

'They said on the news that the owner of the car was an ex-guard and that he was missing.'

'That'd be right.'

'They said they're going to show footage of the missing guard at the end of the programme.'

'There's no footage.'

'There is. Apparently he was famous.'

'He wasn't. He was just a guard and—'

'And now,' the news anchor says importantly, 'back to the lead story.'

'This is it.' My mother casts me a triumphant look. 'The footage.'

'We have in the studio Leonard Loane. Welcome.'

Leonard isn't one of their normal reporters. He's skinny, looks hyperactive and he wears an unfortunate green shirt that clashes with the emerald set. His shirt claims that he's 'a believer'. He keeps rubbing his nose.

'He's a believer in cocaine all right,' I mutter. Who the hell is this guy? And why is he showing footage on the news and not in a garda station?

'Leonard is blogger, YouTuber and Insta creator. Isn't that right?'

'I am indeed.' Leonard smiles, showing unnaturally white teeth that look like tombstones.

'And you have some insights about the missing man, don't you, Leonard?' the news anchor asks.

Leonard leans forward in his seat. 'Many people won't know this, Colm, but Jerry Loftus, the missing guard, was the guard in my Wowser video. And for those who don't know who Wowser was, he was this chef who insulted anyone who came into his restaurant. He was witty, funny and very popular. Charm the birds offa the trees. Anyway, by chance, a couple of years back, I sat behind Wowser in the cinema and what do I see? Only him assaulting his then partner. So, out with the mobile phone. Now, Jerry was sitting beside me and his is the voice you hear on the video.'

'EEEK.'

My mother jumps.

'Sorry. That was the sound of the bottom of the barrel being scraped. Who put this guy on?'

'Shush.' She's enthralled.

'Did you ever hear of Wowser?'

'No. Now shush.'

Next thing, a poorly lit, shaky video is playing. It zooms in on a woman trying discreetly to get away from a man who holds her upper arm in a hard grip. Next thing a voice says, 'Oy! What's going on there?'

Rumblings of discontent from the cinema-goers. 'You! Leave that girl alone!'

An expletive, bleeped out – from Wowser presumably.

Then, 'I'm a guard, leave her alone.'

'I saw everything.' A woman hops up just as the lights in the cinema go on. 'I'll be a witness, if you like.'

The video camera zooms in on the couple at the centre of the row, focuses on the man's pissed-off face and pans to the woman who has offered herself as a witness. She looks delighted to be involved in all the drama. Next thing, a hand, Jerry's I suppose, drags Wowser from his seat. 'Come on, game's up, come with me.'

And we see the back of Jerry's head – if it is Jerry – leading Wowser away while Wowser's partner, unidentified, follows in his wake. The other woman hesitates, then, looking excited, hurries to catch up. The video goes to black.

'As you can see, a decent man, on his time off, he was still doing his job,' Leonard says sombrely.

'Jesus, Leonard, you're a bottom-feeder.' I snort. Who puts these low-lifes on TV?

'Isn't he saying nice things about the guards?' My mother tuts. 'God knows ye could do with some decent PR.'

'Thank you for that, Leonard,' the news anchor says. 'And now we have someone else Jerry Loftus helped during his long career. Bridie Bird, welcome.'

'Turn this off,' I say. 'That woman is well known in the stations in Dublin. She's always trying to insert herself into cases. I'm going to—'

It's probably good that Luc and Cherry choose that moment to barge in.

'Great,' Luc says, 'you're on RTÉ.'

I hadn't figured either of them as RTÉ fans.

With a 'Hi, Lucy', Cherry settles herself beside me as Luc plonks on her other side. Her perfume gets into my mouth.

'Cherry's ad is on when the news ends,' Luc announces.

'Isn't it exciting?' Cherry nudges me gently.

'That is exciting,' my mother, ever the people-pleaser, agrees. 'I've told everyone about it.'

Cherry had recorded an ad for sausages a few weeks back. It's her big break, she'd said at the time.

'Is that Leonard Loane beside the woman who's talking?' Cherry doesn't wait for an answer. 'I love him. He's only got the most watched videos on YouTube and Insta.' She wriggles to get more comfortable, almost unbalancing my dinner. 'My aim is to be as big on Insta and TikTok as him.'

'You will,' Luc says. 'Just wait until people see you in this ad.'

The news ends and it's followed by the weather forecast. More rain and clouds. Then it's on to the ads. It's like they're aimed at me. There's one for a dating service, followed by some kind of miracle menopause cure and then, to Luc's whoop of delight, Cherry appears in a skirt smaller than the one she is currently wearing, her blonde hair cascading down her shoulders. She's side on, at a gas cooker, a pan of sausages fizzing merrily on the hob as she pokes them. She inhales deeply, cleavage rising under her tight black T-shirt as the camera zooms in to focus on her face, on her satisfied smile, on her pearly white upper teeth as they bite into her lower lip.

'Mmm,' she says huskily.

The camera pans to the sausages. Large and fleshy.

Phallic, I would say.

The camera lingers on the juices spurting out. Pans up Cherry's T-shirt, back to her face and pulls out again. Cherry, fork in hand, faces the camera as she plucks a cooked sausage from a plate and places it between her lips.

'Mmm,' she murmurs, with a suggestive quirk of eyebrows.

'Sullivan's sausages, the only way to satisfy a real woman's appetite,' says the male voiceover.

And on to the next ad.

THE WRATH

What was *that*?

'They told me to channel my inner Nigella,' Cherry says, sounding a little unsure, and I immediately feel sorry for her.

'And you did.' Luc rallies. 'That was, like, I, mean, wow, Cherry.' He hugs her. 'Brilliant. Wasn't she amazing, Mam?' He looks to me. There's a challenge in his question.

'Totally.' I hope my smile is convincing. 'I'd buy those sausages, no bother.'

'Really?' A wobbly smile.

'I would too,' my mother pipes up. 'But, no offence, I probably won't. It's just the Achill ones are the best and we have to support local,' she tacks on.

Cherry's phone bleeps. Flicking it on, her eyes widen. 'Oh, my God.' Now her smile widens. 'People are following me. Oh, wow!'

'Didn't I tell you?' Luc sounds like a proud parent. 'You're going to be huge.' He looks at us. 'She's going to be huge.'

They bounce out of the room, laughing.

There's a silence after they leave.

'That ad was soft porn, wasn't it?' my mother says, after a bit.

'Yup.'

'I never knew what that meant but I do now.'

'You learn something new every day.'

'I quite liked it, though,' she pronounces.

12

Conference the next morning is jammed. For the first couple of weeks, all the might of the guards will be thrown at the case in the hope of solving it quickly. But as the time goes by, resources will dwindle, overtime will be cut – because we don't get as much as the Dublin lads – and guards will be moved to other teams, other cases. Like everything else in this country, we need more money to do a proper job.

I'm fifteen minutes early and it's still hard to find a place in the room. William spots me and beckons me to join him up the front. I'm relieved that he at least wants me at the head of the investigation. A couple of minutes later, Dan joins us. The core team is pretty much the same as usual. Midway down the room, Larry is having the banter with his colleague, Ben. Larry looks as if he's gained a few pounds in the last year but he can carry it, handsome narcissist that he is. Ben, on the other hand, looks leaner and fitter and it suits him. He catches my eye and flashes me a smile. Ben, like Dan, is loyal to me, Dan because we've been through a lot, Ben because of the Sandra Byrne case where I saved his arse. Against the wall to my left, the long, skinny, awkward-in-his-body Mick is chatting away to an equally tall stick-thin guard I don't recognise until I do. It's Susan. And she's had a radical haircut. Gone are the plaits that made her look like Heidi. Instead, she sports a sharp, short pixie style. Jesus, she looks amazing. Like a model. Beside them, Louis, the son of the chief super, is bending Kev's ear. Louis had been shoehorned onto our last case by his highly ambitious dad. We were all wary of him, still are, even though Louis declared to me that he tells his father nothing. He's a Springer spaniel in human form, eager, hyper and a little clueless. Kev, on the other hand, appears clueless but has one of the sharpest minds I've ever come across. I wonder if he's still dating his weight-lifter girlfriend. I search among the crowd for the other usual bodies and spot the three local lads, Ger, Matt and Jordy lounging by the door. Jordy looks as if he's just climbed out of bed and dressed himself blindfolded. Matt is hopping about nervously from foot to foot while Ger wears his usual air of calm.

I wonder who's manning the scene.

I miss Pat, who retired last month. He'd had bad PTSD from years of work-related trauma and, despite William giving him the paperwork side of investigations, he'd finally called it a day. A sad end to a wonderful career.

'All right,' William says easily, and the room immediately quietens. Not for the first time do I wonder how he does it. He flicks on the projector and faces us. 'Thanks for coming, lads. A bit of a rundown on the case so that we're all working from the same page. At two a.m. on the second of December last while driving to Keem DS Lucy Golden there,' he points me out, 'came across a tan-coloured abandoned ten-year-old Ford Focus on cliffs near Dooagh. Upon examination, the scene was sealed off.' A picture of the location followed by an image of the interior of the car is displayed. 'Not pretty as you can see. The area where the car was discovered is boggy. There were drag marks on the ground on the driver's side, suggesting that someone had been pulled, maybe to the edge of the cliff and dropped over.' Images of the drag marks are shown. 'There was also some kind of a narrow tyre print, maybe a bike. We're not sure yet. There were tracks, too, of what appears to be a second car. In the boot of the vehicle, this page was discovered. An A4 piece of photocopy paper, spotted with Jerry's blood, the following message pasted to it.'

The image causes murmuring to start up, the word 'KaRMa' raising the little hairs on my arms.

'There was no blood in the boot, which suggests that the note was not in contact with the body before someone dropped it in. Also discovered in the vicinity of the car, a number of cigarette butts, bottles of water and this.'

'This' appears to be a tiny white pill.

'Again, sent to the lab to ascertain what it might be. From the blood spatter in the car, we believe that one person was violently assaulted, and that the other may have come away with minor injuries. The car will be technically examined as a matter of priority, so hopefully we'll have a clearer picture on that. They'll be dusting for prints so I want someone out to take the wife's prints for elimination purposes.' He turns to me. 'Lucy, what have you got?'

I'm a lot more confident addressing the team than I had been on my first case with them four years ago. William might be treating me a little harshly, but the rest of this team are mine. It's me they come to when they have a problem, way too wary of William to approach him. We've seen a lot, from the night-caller case to the bone-fire murder. I shiver when I think of that one because, despite what everyone has been told, I did not come out of that covered with glory. In order to bond with a hostage-taker, I'd said that I, too, would go out on a limb to protect people I loved. Then I'd confessed which laws I'd broken to do that. I'd sunk my career to help Louis, the chief's son, and to escape from a dangerous situation, and I'd braced myself for the professional fallout such a confession would bring. And then, for some reason, William had stepped in. He'd told me to tell Louis I'd made up a story to get the offender to trust me. William had buried the evidence while Louis and his father had been impressed at my quick thinking and ability to lie convincingly under pressure. The whole thing left me with guilt the size of a boulder.

'Luce,' Dan whispers.

'Are we keeping you from something?' William.

I'm suddenly aware that I've been standing without speaking for a good few seconds. 'Sorry.' I take a breath, launch in. 'As William explained, I found the car, which was identified as belonging to a Jerry Loftus, who had earlier been reported missing by his wife, Hazel.' A picture of Hazel and Jerry appears. I take my time, going through all the information Dan and I had gathered yesterday. I'm pleased to see that William looks impressed. No one else would ever guess it, he's got poker-face down better than a corpse, but I know that when he leans forward and his gaze remains steady, he's engaged. I give them a rundown of the timeline as we know it and then I bring out the juice. 'While we were at the house yesterday, Dan and I did a preliminary search of the master bedroom. We found four anonymous letters on white A4 paper, similar to what was found in the boot of Jerry's

Focus. These letters were hidden in a drawer in the room. His wife alleged she had no knowledge of them but as I've already told you, she's in early-stage dementia.'

The first letter appears onscreen: 'I aM CoMIng foR yOU. RepenT'

'As you can see, letters have been cut from newspapers and magazines and pasted onto the page.'

I flick to the second letter: 'Vengeance is MiNE'

'The third.' 'The ROAd to Hell is PAVed . . .'

'Fourth.' 'The jUDGEmenTs of The lord ArE True'

Then I display all four together and they present an ominous collage. 'As you can see, each letter has what we think are sequencing numbers on the top left corner.' I zoom in on the left corner of each letter.

1/5, 2/5, 3/5, 4/5.

'And the KaRMa letter.' I pull that up and zoom in.

5/5.

No one speaks. It's almost as if the anger in the letters is reaching out and staining the air in the room.

'It's like a countdown,' Mick says, after a moment.

I tap the photos. 'Whoever this is obviously feels that Jerry did something terrible to him or her. Is it family? We know he rowed with his son. Is it someone from Jerry's career as a guard? Is it to do with the mysterious man he met yesterday? Jerry's cases must be examined for possible motives. Take time with them. Of course we have no proof yet that Jerry is dead, but we do know that he's missing and has been the victim of a serious assault. Susan, you had a look at the son for us?'

I'd rung her last night, thinking it might look good for her to get a head start on the case. She's dying to make detective and, besides, like any investigation, the more you learn in the early days, the better.

'I had a look into Zak Loftus yesterday,' Susan says. 'He's thirty. He lives in Dundrum, Dublin, with his partner Abby Devlin. Zak worked as an actor for a while. Abby still does. She's in a panto at the Olympia in Dublin right now. Zak's last gig was in film, though nothing you would ever have heard of. It was called *Big Swinging Mickeys*.'

People laugh, though Susan hadn't meant to be funny.

'Quiet!' William snaps. 'Go on, Susan.'

'I think it was a bit porny,' Susan adds gravely, and beside me, I hear Dan do his best to snort back a chuckle. Around the room, there's a sea of barely suppressed mirth. Beside me, I sense rather than see William tense. You can't afford too much levity on the first day.

Susan continues, oblivious: 'It was X-rated and I think—'

'Enough about the film,' William snaps.

Susan looks startled. 'Sure. Well, Zak gave all that up and now works as an accountant. Self-employed. As far as I can gather, the two of them have been together just over three years. That's it.'

'Thanks, Susan,' I say, before William can respond. 'We also got a list of credit cards from the bar that we need traced. They belong to the people who were in the pub at the same time as Jerry. According to the barman, all the customers bar two paid by card. We may get an ID on whoever was with Jerry through this. That's it, Cig.'

'Thanks. Louis, you'll be on the credit cards. Larry?'

'It'd be better if I had a proper timeline,' Larry says. 'I was told late yesterday, after Lucy and Dan talked to the barman, that the best bet for footage was probably after twelve in Keel. And not before twelve. Or not noon.'

'You knew as soon as we knew,' I snap.

Larry ignores me. 'I know the Credit Union, which is beside the pub, has CCTV so I put in a request and there are some other premises I can harvest footage from too. I'll get that done today. I've also done the usual call out for dash-cam. I'll have more tomorrow, Cig.'

'See you do.' William stands, hands in his pockets, rocking slightly on his heels. 'This, lads, is our fifth case together. As of yet, we do not know that a murder was committed, but someone has been assaulted. Every case is different but investigating it is always the same. The biggest leads we have right now are the fact that he was in McLoughlin's pub at noon three days ago and had been intending to climb Croaghaun. I'll be doing a press conference later asking for people who were in the area to come forward, especially anyone who may have seen him climb the mountain. We will also carry out door-to-door in the area. Thankfully, the houses are sparse. We need to trace the man he was with, find out who he was. CCTV might help with that. Reviewing Jerry's cases will be looking for a needle in a haystack, but it has to be done. We'll start with the more recent ones and work our way back. We may get a pointer or two from his old work colleagues. And finally, we need to interview the son, Zak. He's estranged from his parents so it'd be good to get a read on him.'

Susan's hand shoots up.

'Yes?'

'His partner has an alibi for the last couple of days,' she says. 'She was onstage at the Olympia. I rang to make sure she didn't have a stand-in. So we can rule her out.'

William is pleased at that. 'Excellent.'

Susan looks thrilled with herself.

'That doesn't mean she didn't help Zak plan it, if it was Zak,' Louis pipes up, determined to steal Susan's thunder. And a bit miffed that he's on the credit-card detail. 'They could have hired someone to assault his father.'

'They could have,' William concedes generously, 'but let's not get ahead of ourselves. Larry, CCTV, have something by tomorrow. Jordy, Ger and Matt, divide Jerry's cases up between ye. I know someone has to man the front desk but any free moment, I want ye heads down, looking at those reports. Anything comes up, straight to Lucy with it. Matt?'

'Cig?'

'You are on this case. Don't make me regret it.'

'Never.' Matt amuses us by crossing his heart. Then realises what he's done and tries to rub his neck instead. Then sees we're all grinning and mutters, 'Feck off.'

'Lucy and Dan, hop up to Dublin and visit Zak. Talk to his partner, too, if you can.'

A bloody trip to Dublin, and to Dundrum of all places. That's where I used to live with Rob, my ex-husband, an ex-conman. The last time I was there, the place sang with memories. But I sportingly agree.

'Mick, I want you ringing hospitals. Every hospital in the area and a little beyond. Let's dot the *i*s here, all right. You can also tic-tac with Forensics.'

'Sure.' Mick's got his game face on too. He hates chasing Forensics because he's too nice to kick arse, but the Cig seems hell bent on making him an arse-kicker. He'll keep giving him this job until he toughens up.

'There's the list of friends Hazel gave when she reported Jerry missing, I want bodies out talking to these people. Kev and

Susan, that's yours. If they're too far away to travel, ring the local station.'

That's a step up for Susan. She'll be delighted.

'The appeal for information will be recorded at noon today where the car was found. Larry and Jordy, be there.' He looks at Jordy. 'Be presentable.'

'Do my best,' Jordy says mildly. He gestures to himself. 'But this is what it is, Cig.'

William's mouth tightens at the mild rebuke. 'The rest of ye on door-to-door. Ben, you have the questionnaire ready, don't you?'

'I do.'

'Grand.' William rubs his hands. 'Jim here has the job sheets. Don't forget to hand them back when ye're done. And, as I always say, no assumptions. No pointing fingers. No trying to make the evidence fit. Don't, for God's sake, be swayed by the wonderful news reporting last night when Jerry's alleged hand and back of head arrested some ex-lowlife chef in a cinema.' A smattering of sniggers from those who had seen the news. 'Follow the real evidence. It will fall where it falls and we have to let it.' A moment of silence and I think he's going to say something else but he hesitates. 'It falls where it falls,' he repeats. Then, after another moment, 'Thanks, everyone.' He hurries out of the room, pulling his mobile from his pocket as he does so. I collect the job sheet and meet Dan at the door.

Matt passes us.

'Welcome in from the cold,' I say.

He gives me a delighted thumbs-up.

13

He breathes a sigh of relief as he puts the final touches to Hew Hartt's website with a deep-fake picture of a grave, distinguished man. The site had taken him months to create largely because, to make it work, he'd had to write a few fake pieces on economics and link them to Hew. He hates writing. He also had to give Hew a wife and some work colleagues. Hew has even won an award for journalism that has its own separate fake site. Deep-fake Hew writes very successfully for a number of prestigious publications. He has also published some books that nobody bought but that nevertheless have given him iconic status because no one understood the books either.

Before he makes the phone call, he double-checks that everything looks legit. If the Runt takes it into his head to check up on Hew, he wants him to be more than satisfied.

It all looks good. Great, even.

He readies himself. He can't fuck this up.

Getting the Runt's number had been a walk in the park. An old public Facebook account and a click into contact information and there was his mobile, loud and proud. Getting his address had been a little trickier but hopefully this will work.

As the call connects and the phone starts to ring at the other end, he prays that the Runt isn't the sort of person who ignores unfamiliar phone numbers but, as the Runt is a man whose very job depends on answering unfamiliar phone numbers, he thinks not.

'Hello?'

Yes! A second before he jumps into his Hew Hartt character.

'Hello.' A friendly Brit. 'My name is Hew Hartt. I'm doing a piece for the Business Post and—'

'How did you get this number?'

'I'm a journalist. It's my job, but from Facebook, if you must know.'

'Oh.' He sounds taken aback.

'If it disturbs you, delete your account. But, as I said, I'm doing a bit for the Business Post and—'

'The business paper?'

He can hear the uplift of pitch in the Runt's voice. Excitement or trepidation, he can't tell. 'Yes, the business paper. The name is a giveaway.'

The Runt laughs a bit too much at the joke. He always was a creep.

'We're doing a feature on successful businessmen. We were wondering if you'd like to contribute.'

There's a brief silence from the other end of the line. Has he over-egged the pudding? He'd used the spiel because he himself had been flattered to be included in a two-page spread once upon a time. Two pages all about his uncanny ability to make money and play the stock market. The Runt, however, seems a bit stunned.

'A piece about me?'

'You and others,' he improvises hastily. 'People who run unusual businesses.'

Another pause. Definitely wary. 'Are you sure?' He'd thought the Runt would jump on it. Instead he appears humbled, surprised. It unnerves him.

THE WRATH

'Are you interested in doing the piece or not? It's just I need a quick answer. I've to fill some space and—'

'Yes.' The agreement when it comes is quick. 'Yes. Do you want to interview me now?'

'I'm a face-to-face man,' he says jovially. 'How about a couple of weeks from now? Around eleven a.m.?'

Good to get things over first thing.

'Sure. Yes. Where?'

'In your house.' He doesn't throw it out as a suggestion. 'I like to see my subjects in their own space, I find I can paint a better pen portrait.' He hoped that sounded journalistic and not stupid.

From the other end of the phone he hears keys tapping. He's being checked. After a moment, the Runt rattles off an address and says, 'I'll look forward to meeting you.'

'Me too.'

The line goes dead.

Hew Hartt.

He wonders if the Runt is any good at conundrums.

He gets a celebratory coffee in a run-down, sticky-floored coffee shop just off the main road. A newspaper is tossed carelessly across the table beside him, left behind by the previous occupant of the seat. He pulls it towards him. 'Man's Car Found Abandoned on Atlantic Drive Achill,' the headline screams, and he allows himself a small smile. He scans the piece, then has to reread it, shock causing him to gasp aloud as people look on curiously.

'The guards are at present trying to locate Jerry Loftus and appeal to anyone who may have seen him.'

Trying to locate?

His heart skips, stops, skips.

Trying. To. Locate.

He must have tumbled into the sea. What other explanation is there?

He prays Jerry bloody tumbled but he can't take a chance. He'll have to find some way of fucking up the garda investigation at least until his work is done.

14

On the way to Dublin, we descend into silence, letting the road unspool in front of us. Then, as we hit the early-lunchtime Dublin traffic, Dan remarks, 'I've been thinking about what you said and it makes no sense.'

'I haven't said anything. We've barely talked the whole way up.'

'Exactly.' He pounces like a cat on a mouse. 'Normally you never shut up.' He makes a gesture with his hands. 'You'd be moaning about heading to Dublin, heading to Dundrum, saying the Cig did it deliberately, and instead you've remained schtum so it gave me time to think and it makes no sense.'

'I'm lost.'

'About the Cig. It's not just a personal thing that's bugging him, it's you too.'

I make scoffing noises.

'He said good work to Susan in conference this morning and nothing to us and we were on fire yesterday.' A hint of indignation.

'Detective Dan strikes again.' I keep my voice light, but my knuckles grow white as I clench the steering wheel. How can I tell him? How can I explain? The answer is that I can't, not without dragging him into something I know he'd never want to be a part of. More cars, from the N7 slipway, pour onto the road in front of us. I haven't missed busy lunchtimes in Dublin, that's for sure. 'Why would he be cross with me?' I throw it back at him, staring resolutely out of the window, afraid my expression will give me away.

'Question with a question, that old detective trick.' Dan smirks. 'Look, there was something off with him in conference today, you know it. Plus, not saying "good work" to us is totally arseholey. I mean, you were the chosen one – everyone knows that.'

A shot of grief, like a sliver of glass, pierces me. Not because my career will never recover but because I did let William down and it has changed things. And changed them in ways I'm not even sure of yet.

'I can't tell you, Dan, I really—'

'You can.'

'No. It wouldn't be fair on you, but let's just say the Cig went to bat for me and I think he's regretting it.'

'So, fuck him,' Dan snaps, surprising me. 'Fuck him. How can he regret it? You're the best bloody investigator he has by a bloody country mile and he knows it. If he went to bat for you, he did it for himself. Fuck him.'

Tears prick my eyes but I blink them back. 'Thanks, Dan.'

'You are very welcome.' His jaw is set hard. 'Any-bloody-time.'

'If you weren't gay, I think I'd fall in love with you.'

'If I wasn't gay, I'd be running hard in the other direction.'

'Fecker!' I give him an arm punch.

He laughs.

THE WRATH

*

Zak Loftus lives two roads up from my old address in Dundrum. There was a time I knew everyone who lived here. Work as a guard and people come to you for everything, from dogs barking to alarms going off. And I have a good memory for faces and names. I probably know 80 per cent of the people who reside on this street, but I've never met Zak Loftus.

As we hop out of the DDU car, locking it after us, two women, the younger one pushing a pram, walk towards us. The older of the two is chatting avidly to the younger. And, feck it, I know her. My brain scrambles for her name. Amber. Amber Evertt. Separated. Teacher. One daughter. Came to me begging for advice on her disagreeable neighbours. I dip my head, not wanting her to recognise me. I am persona non grata in this part of south Dublin. Years back, I was the focus of a lot of hate and a lot of gossip when my ex-husband, Rob, stole many of our friends' savings. And then, of course, with him dying trying to save me and Luc, he made the papers again, only this time as a hero of sorts.

'Since when have people stopped putting numbers on their doors,' Dan mutters, oblivious to my growing unease as the women move closer.

Snatches of their conversation reach me, mostly baby chatter.

'Number fifty-five.' Dan blessedly points to a well-maintained house with a blue door. 'Here we go.'

I scurry into the driveway just as the women pass, stealing a glance at them as they go by. Amber, the elder, is still as glamorous as I remember. We never became firm friends as I always felt a little dowdy beside her. And for some reason, I felt she judged me because of it. The second woman, I realise with a jolt, is Amber's daughter, all grown-up. She was thirteen when I left. It unsettles me. Time is passing and I feel I'm just standing still in its flow.

The door of number fifty-five is answered by an incredibly handsome young man. The sort you gawk at with your mouth open, like I'm doing now. He has a bandaged hand and an abrasion on his cheek. He looks tired.

'Zak?' Dan says.

'Yes?'

'I'm Detective Dan Brown and this is Detective Sergeant Lucy Golden. Can we come in? It's about your father.'

'Sure.' Zak leads us to the kitchen and gestures for us to sit down. He clears the table of a number of files and seats himself opposite us. There is no offer of tea, which tells us he doesn't welcome our visit.

'You know why we're here, Zak.' Dan offers him a sympathetic smile which isn't returned. 'Your father appears to be missing. We have reason to believe he was assaulted.'

On the word 'assaulted', Zak winces slightly, just a crinkle of the forehead, but when he speaks, his tone is belligerent. 'I don't talk to my parents, haven't for the last while, so I really can't help you.' He leans back, crossing his long legs at the ankles. He's so young he reminds me of Luc, and through the defiance, I can sense huge hurt.

'Tell us why you haven't talked to your parents.'

The casual pose is abandoned. He leans once more across the table. 'That's nothing to do with anything.' He jabs the air with his finger. 'If my dad is missing, it's got nothing to do with me. My mother is well able to tell you what you need to know.'

'She just said that you and your father had a falling-out. She said neither of you would tell her why.' Sometimes saying it for them opens the floodgates.

'Nothing to do with this. I haven't seen either of them in months.'

'But it has, don't you see?' Dan leans across the table now, his stare flinty. 'You not speaking to your father isn't good for you, Zak. It looks bad. If anything has happened to him, you'll be number one on my list.'

There's a flicker of unease in Zak's eyes and he shifts a little on the seat. 'I don't care. I did nothing.'

'Your father was assaulted. You have abrasions on your face.'

'I fell!' A savagery that takes us by surprise.

'I didn't hear ye come in.' A young woman enters, pretty but with an anxious furrow between her eyebrows. 'Are ye the guards?' Then, before we can answer, she says, 'Aw, Zak, have you not offered them a bloody cup of tea?' Without waiting for Zak to answer, she fills the kettle, then leans against the worktop, eyes darting between us all as she waits for it to boil. 'I'm Abby,' she says. 'Is there any news on Zak's da?'

'Just investigating for now,' Dan says. 'How did you get on with him?'

'Abby has nothing to do with this,' Zak snaps. 'Neither of us has.'

'I've never met either of his parents.' Abby is calm, crossing to place her hand on Zak's shoulder. He reaches back and clasps it. 'I wish Zak would talk to his mother at least but he won't.'

'Don't be so bloody understanding.' He says it with a sort of grief.

The kettle clicks off and an uneasy silence descends as Abby busies herself making four cups of tea, bringing them to the table one by one. Picking up the last cup, she says, 'I'll get out of your way. I've a show later – I need to get a bit of kip.'

'Stay,' Dan says. 'It'd be good to get your take on things.'

Be good to get a read on your relationship, he means.

Abby looks to Zak for permission. 'She doesn't have a take,' Zak says, as Abby slides into the seat beside him. 'Like she said, she never met them.'

'I'm always trying to get him to contact his mother, but he's the unforgiving sort. Aren't you?' She nuzzles him.

He moves away. 'She took his side.'

'What else could she do? Move in with you?' Abby laughs a little. 'You're lucky to have her.' A look at us. 'His mother rings once a month and she rang on his birthday. I feel sorry for her. She sent him a letter once and—'

'Stop, all right! Just stop!' Zak pushes his chair back and stands, turning his back on us, sinking his hands into the pockets of his tracksuit bottoms. His shoulders are hunched about his ears.

Abby puts down her cup and buries her head in her hands.

There follows a silence laden with tension and a sort of hopelessness.

Dan steps in, his tone cool. 'This is not why we're here. We're trying to find your father, Zak, and we need as much information from you as you can give us.' A pause. 'Tell us what the row was about.'

Zak dips his head.

'Zak?' Abby says. Then, lifting her head from her hands, she says, with spirit, 'If you won't, I will.'

He turns, glares at her. She glares back. He heaves a sigh. 'He was . . . that is my dad,' he speaks with difficulty, 'he was cheating on my mother. It was why he moved west. He dragged my mother to the arse end of nowhere so he could get his hole.'

Abby looks at us. 'Zak found texts,' she explains.

'I didn't want my mother to know.' Now Zak turns. 'She's . . . she wouldn't have handled that well. She's . . . well, you met her. She's so dependent on Dad. So, fricking,' he tries to come up with a word, 'helpless, doing whatever he says. But, don't get me wrong. To be fair, he always seemed devoted to her. Anything she wanted, he did, which was why, when I found the texts, I wasn't sure and . . . Anyway, my dad admitted it, begged me not to tell. I told him to stop, to break the relationship off and he said he would. But he didn't—'

'He found more texts,' Abby interrupts. Then to him, 'You should never have looked at his phone.'

'Yeah, well, I did.' He pauses. 'I threatened to tell Mam but he knew I wouldn't. Then, Jesus,' he laughs, 'he leaves a message on my phone a few months back. Was I trying to blackmail him? he asks. I didn't bother replying to that. Bastard.'

'Were you trying to blackmail him?'

'Oh, piss off.'

'Zak!' Abby chides. 'Come on. Sit.' She pats the chair beside her, holds out a hand. 'Come on.' He takes it and lets himself be pulled into the seat. 'He wasn't blackmailing anyone. Were you?' There's a strangeness in the way she asks it, almost looking for reassurance herself.

'No.'

'Did you correspond in any way with him? Threaten him?' Dan asks.

'I cut off all ties. I couldn't be party to that.'

'Is there anyone, Zak, who would have wished your parents harm?'

'No one I can think of. Dad was . . .' he almost chokes on the word '. . . popular and . . .' His voice breaks a little, his anger seeming to dissipate. 'In Dublin, they were very popular and though Dad was a guard, there was never a whiff of trouble from his job. They were both well liked.'

'This was in Dublin?' Dan clarifies.

'Yeah. I don't know much about their time in Mayo. Like I said, I cut ties completely once I found out why he moved. His . . . whatever you want to call her, lover, is down there. My poor mother, stuck in that kip hole.'

'Your dad did receive some strange letters all right.' Dan calls up the photographs of the letters on his phone and hands it to Zak to examine.

'Jesus,' he says, sounding shocked. 'That's . . . Where?' He glances between me and Dan.

'We found them in your dad's wardrobe among his things.'

Zak says nothing for a moment. 'I know nothing about anything like that.' Then, surprising himself, I think, he adds, 'How's my mam handling all this?'

I want to tell him to call her, to make contact, she isn't well, but I can't. 'She's upset obviously,' I say.

Zak dips his head.

'Obviously,' Abby agrees. 'I mean her husband is bloody missing. Your dad is missing, Zak.'

'I know.' Zak closes his eyes and heaves a sigh. 'Jesus.'

'We see a lot of family fall-outs in the job and it's never a bad idea to reconnect.' Dan pockets his phone.

'You've nothing to lose,' I add, standing up. 'You should think about it.'

'And if you remember anything else, no matter how small, give us a shout, yeah?' Dan hands Zak his card and he takes it without a word. 'Oh, by the way, just to check, where were you both on Monday and Tuesday?'

'I was here taking it easy. It was opening night of my panto so . . .' Abby doesn't finish, obviously assuming we have knowledge of what one does on opening nights. 'Both days,' she clarifies. 'I left to go to the theatre around five and wasn't home until after one both nights.'

Dan turns to Zak.

Surprisingly, he flushes, neck reddening. 'I was, eh,' he swallows, his eyes darting a quick look at Abby, 'at work. I work from home but that day, eh, the day he was . . . eh . . . well, I was in town. I was back here after eight that night.'

He's lying.

'You would have come back here after Abby left to go to the theatre.'

'Yes.'

'So neither of you can confirm what the other did, during the day and part of the night?'

They look at each other. 'Nope,' they say together.

'I'll need to check both of those alibis.' Dan throws it out like fish bait, waiting for a reaction.

It's Zak who explodes. 'For God's sake, you hardly think I did anything to my da?'

'It's our job to check facts. Give me the name of the play you're in, Abby, and the name of where you were in Dublin, Zak. Please.' Dan looks expectantly at them.

They both offer up the details and I scribble them down.

'If either of you have got your timings wrong, easy to mix up days, you know, just give us a bell.' Dan pushes the card closer to Zak. It's an invite for him to come clean, to tell us what he was really doing, but he, like Abby, merely assures us that there is nothing more to be said.

'We'll be in touch.'

When we're back in the car, Dan turns to me. 'Zak's lying.'

'He is. I think we'll have to pay his boss a visit.'

A phone call would do it but we both know William would kill us if we didn't do a face-to-face interview while we're up.

It'll be a long day.

15

I call Zak's boss, a gym owner, who agrees to give us five minutes, no more, no less, if we can be at the gym in ten minutes. 'But be on time,' he warns. 'I'm a busy man.'

'And we're not,' I say cheerfully, into the receiver, as he hangs up. 'Idiot.' I throw my mobile into the pocket between the seats and fire the ignition. The gym, which is in Parnell Square, is accessed by a narrow stairway set behind a door flanked by a bookie's and a chipper. On the way up, tatty pictures of Irish sporting heroes are displayed along with inspirational notices advising patrons that without pain there is no gain, and that by coming through the doors of GY gym, they are already champions. Dan and I scoff a bit.

Both of us are a bit winded by the time we reach the top of the stairs. In front of us, pasted to the door is, for some inexplicable reason, an autographed picture of Shirley Bassey.

Dan starts humming 'Climb Ev'ry Mountain' and I get a fit of the giggles.

Then he laughs at me laughing. Finally, after about two minutes, we get it together and Dan pushes open the door.

The brash sounds and strong smells are a punch in the gut. The stench of sweat, rubber matting and frying chips mix with the pumping beat blaring from enormous speakers. Walls of mirrors bounce too-bright light about the place. Huge well-muscled men, who look as if someone took a pump to their arse and forgot to stop, heave massive weights into the air, grunting as if they're birthing a child. The floor vibrates as the weights are dropped with a thump. Near the window, people pedal furiously on bikes or run on machines that are going nowhere. In the far corner, a woman does a series of stretches, togged out in tiny shorts and a barely there top.

I know now why I never go to the gym.

Dan and I make our way through the melee to a door at the far end of the room marked 'business suites'. It turns out to be a grotty corridor with three doors.

'Myles Murphy, manager,' says the sign on the first door.

'Bit of alliteration going on there.' Dan chortles as he knocks.

'Come,' a high voice calls from inside.

A deceptive voice as it turns out. Myles Murphy is a mountain. The only tiny things about him are his hands, which are creepily small. 'Officers,' he intones. 'I only have a few minutes so . . .' He gazes at us expectantly.

Calling a guard an officer is a bit of an insult, but I don't think he means it. Even so Dan, being the meanie he is, will probably hold him up for ages now.

In here, the heaving music from the gym floor makes the wall pound. We have to shout a bit to make ourselves heard. Dan explains loudly that Zak's father has gone missing and that we need to check alibis. 'Just dotting the *is*,' Dan yells over the music. 'Zak works here, is that right?'

'He does. Accounts manager. The only accountant actually but manager sounds better, yeah?' He doesn't wait for us to reply. 'He was here on Monday all right.'

That's odd. We never said it was a Monday we were checking.

'We need exact times.'

'What?' Myles holds a hand to his ear.

'We need exact times!'

'Exact times? I don't have exact times. He comes, he goes. He's the accountant. He flits between all the gyms.'

'How many gyms are there?'

'Six. Started with one and sure our ethos has spread all over the country.' He adopts a lower register again, says, 'GY Gyms, where you go to win.'

'Marvellous.'

Myles beams, failing to pick up on Dan's tone.

'Where are the gyms?'

'Hang on there now.' Myles pulls opens a drawer in his desk, rummages about, producing a sheaf of leaflets. 'There you go now. One for you and one for your colleagues. I'm not being smart but I go out and see the guards on the streets and, no offence, they don't look as if they could run fifty metres after a robber. With our programme now, you can—'

'You've a gym in Westport?'

'Eh, yes. I could offer a special rate to—'

'When did it open?'

'Last February. Very successful. Take that leaflet now and tell everyone.'

'Zak shuttles between all the gyms?'

'That's right and—' He stops as he sees what Dan is getting at before shaking his head. 'Zak is a cool guy. And, yes, I know he had a big bust-up with the auld fella there a few weeks back but he'd never do the likes of, well, making him go missing or that.'

There's a juicy titbit.

Dan keeps his tone even, though I know his pulse would have spiked a little, 'He told us he hasn't seen his father in months.'

Myles colours, and his mouth shuts abruptly. 'Right, well . . .' He swallows hard. 'Maybe I was mistaken. I think I was actually. No, now that I remember it was someone else entirely.'

Dan has zeroed in now. Poor Myles will be like a rabbit with a spaniel in pursuit. 'Someone else had a row with Jerry Loftus?'

'No. No, that's not what I meant. I meant, well, that someone else, not Zak, had a row with . . .' he pauses, clearly wondering how to proceed, 'someone else, not Jerry.'

'Who had a row with whom?'

Myles audibly swallows. 'Me. I had a row with someone.'

'And you thought it was Zak when it was yourself?'

'Yes.' He laughs uncomfortably.

'And Jerry Loftus when it was who?'

Dan's torturing him now. I almost feel sorry for Myles, whose enormous mouth is gaping. 'Just a punter.'

'Funny mistake to make.'

'Yes.' His voice is high and weak.

'If it turns out that you're mistaken about the row and you're lying, well . . .' Dan shakes his head, tosses a look in my direction.

I wince as if it'll be very bad for him.

'Right, let's move on. Is there a clock-in system?'

'It was Zak . . . as well,' Myles blurts out. 'The two of us. I had a row with a punter and he had a row with his dad.' He sounds like he might weep. 'I can't quite remember all the details.'

'Try.' Dan makes it sound like a threat.

THE WRATH

Myles swallows hard. When he speaks, words spurt out like popcorn in a pan. 'He's been acting odd, right, sort of robot-like or something, for a while now but I don't care. He gets the work done. But there now, about say, four weeks back, he came in steaming. He was upset and he shouted at me, which wasn't the best thing for him to be doing. So I told him it wasn't great for him to be shouting at me as I was his boss. He said he was sorry, that he'd just had a gigantic row with his dad. That was it.'

'Can you be more precise? When was this?'

'Oh, God, he'll be annoyed with me,' Myles whines. 'I can't afford to lose him – he's a good accountant. And he's cheap.'

Dan's face is blank. He's scary when he does the whole impassive-guard look.

'About a month ago.'

'Good. Well done. Now, moving on, is there a clock-in system here?'

'Will he know it was me?' Myles asks Dan.

'Yes, probably,' Dan says, 'but he should have told us himself. Now, how does he clock in?'

'He doesn't. He just does the work. Bills me. I don't care how long he's here for.' He moans: 'He'll leave me now for sure. This is terrible.'

'Is there CCTV?'

He twists the top on an energy drink and downs the lot, before registering Dan's question. 'Yeah, but it just covers the door you came in.'

'That's all we need.'

'The door is for the punters. The employees use the back entrance, leads out to the car park.' He gestures out of his window. 'The car park there.' Jumping up, enormous quads in short tight shorts, he crosses to his door and, opening it, points down the corridor. 'The back stairs are through that door.' A moment before he adds, 'Zak won't be on the CCTV unless he decided to press a few weights.' He laughs a bit crazily at that, then glances at his watch. 'I have to go.' He pulls a blue jacket from a coat rack and busies himself zipping it up. Next, he slips his feet into a pair of luminous yellow runners that look way too big for him. His feet are tiny too.

'Is there CCTV in the car park?'

'Maybe.' He finishes tying his laces and looks up. 'I don't have to answer your questions, I know that much, so, sorry, but I have to be going.' He hops up.

'One more thing.' Dan holds up a hand and Myles groans. 'To clarify, you say you saw Zak this week. You don't know what time or how long for?'

'That's exactly what I'm saying. I'm in and out.' He points to the door. 'And now I'm out.'

'Where is his office?'

It's almost comical the way Myles stops suddenly, one runner-shod foot up in the air. 'What?'

'Zak's office. We'd like to have a look at it.'

'I doubt he plotted to disappear his dad from his office.' When we don't respond, he sighs in resignation. 'Right. Come on, this way.'

We follow him out into the corridor to the next door up. Waving a hand, he says, 'Knock yourselves out.'

Zak's office is compact but tidy, cream walls displaying an obligatory accountancy certificate. The floors are wooden and there's a small desk, which takes up most of the space, a heap of neatly ordered files on top. A red chair. On the windowsill, there's a healthy pot plant with red flowers cascading downwards. It's like one I have at home, though mine is the stunted, underdeveloped, unloved version. Alongside the plant, there's a photograph in a red frame of Abby somewhere hot because she's wearing a sunhat.

A filing cabinet with a broken drawer sits in the left-hand corner of the room.

'Does he have a laptop?'

'Yes, but he travels with it. Now are yez done?' Myles makes a production of looking at his oversized watch. 'I have to tell yez, yez are wasting your time. Zak is sound.'

'Thanks for the tip.'

Dan's flippancy elicits a sour look from Myles before he turns away and strides off down the corridor.

We follow him.

'Yez can go out through the front way,' he calls to us, over his shoulder.

'We need to see if there's CCTV in the car park,' Dan explains. We also need to check that he was telling the truth, that there is no CCTV on the back stairs.

Plus, it's good to know the routes suspects have taken because Zak is fast becoming one.

Outside, the biting December breeze catches us. The car park, a tiny tarmacked area, is in an alleyway and the wind is funnelling down through it. I pull my hood up, push my hands into the pockets of my inadequate jacket.

'The lads working in the chipper park here too,' Myles explains, as he walks towards a fairly new electric Renault in a flashy red.

He has the passenger door open just as Dan says, 'Betcha the next phone call you make is going to be to Zak.'

Myles's hand freezes on the door handle. Then, just as he turns to leave, Dan calls idly, 'Actually, just out of curiosity, how did you know we wanted to check Zak's movements for Monday?'

'Because you said so.' He shivers, though I don't think it's from the cold.

'I didn't actually. Did Zak call you by any chance?'

'No.' He laughs a bit too much.

Dan holds out his hand.

'What?'

'I'd like to check your phone.'

'You can't just . . .' His hand flies to his pocket. Then, 'You'll find a call from him all right but it was just, you know, to say he had the accounts ready for me. That's all.'

'Ah, I see. Thanks.'

Myles bolts into his car and roars off.

'You big meanie.' I poke Dan's arm. 'You enjoyed that.'

'If only all witnesses could be so forthcoming with a bit of a glower.'

We laugh and I can hear my mother in my ear giving out to me, telling me that that's no way to treat someone.

Dan glances at his watch. 'Right. Here's the choice. Will we get food and then go back and talk to Zak or talk to Zak now and eat later?'

'I vote we talk to him when Abby's off doing her panto. So . . . eat now?'

'Lead on.'

During dinner, I fill the Cig in on what we've learned so far. I'm half hoping he'll tell us we can stay in Dublin rather than driving home that night but no such luck.

THE WRATH

'Talk to Zak again and call into me in the Achill station when ye get back. What time will it be?'

Dan winces an 'ouch'.

'It's six now. We'll talk to him at seven and probably be back on the road for eight. We should be in Achill around eleven thirty this evening.'

He doesn't tell me it's too late. 'Fine. Talk then.'

I disconnect and think, Fecker, so hard I'm surprised Dan doesn't hear it.

An hour later, Dan and I are standing outside Zak and Abby's house again. There is only one car in the drive so Abby has obviously left for the panto. The curtains in the front upstairs room are drawn. The road is quiet, no cars, no pedestrians, and the only light chasing away the inky darkness is provided by streetlamps.

With a sense of anticipation, Dan presses the doorbell.

Nothing bar the shriek of a child somewhere up the road.

Dan presses the bell again. And then a third time. Finally, from somewhere inside the house, a creaking, shuffling. After a minute, through the frosted pane in the hall door, we see the shadow of movement. The door is opened slowly and Zak stands in front of us, head dipped.

'Did you think we wouldn't find out?' I ask, and Zak's head shoots up. His eyes are puffy with tears and bloodshot.

'You'd better come in.' He pulls the door open.

16

Once more, he doesn't offer us a cuppa. Instead, in silence, we follow him back into the kitchen where he slumps onto a chair. There's a kind of hopelessness in it. It's as if whatever we throw at him will have little impact. A little flutter of uncertainty in my stomach as I try to ask with an authority I'm not quite feeling, 'You actually have met with your dad in the past few weeks, haven't you?'

And there is something in his gaze, surprise and something I can't put my finger on. Relief, maybe. He straightens on the chair, shoulders back. 'Yeah. I would have told you but I didn't want to alarm Abby.' I'm about to ask something else when he continues, 'I was going to tell her so many times but I kept chickening out. She needs all her focus for this panto. It's her big break and I know she'd worry and get distracted.'

There's a ring of truth about that.

'Very noble. When exactly was this big row?'

'About a month ago. After he left that message on my phone, accusing me of blackmail and I didn't reply.'

'Tell us what happened?'

THE WRATH

He gives a one-shouldered shrug. 'What does it have to do with him going missing?'

'Maybe nothing.' I offer an easy smile.

He considers that, long fingers twisting in and out of each other.

'Zak, this is your dad who's missing, you do understand that, yes? You do want to help us find him?'

'It's nothing to do with me. I can't . . .' He shakes his head, then says, 'I was just in from work. Abby was rehearsing or going for a drink with pals, I can't remember. I'd poured myself a beer and the doorbell rang. I was going to ignore it, I was exhausted, but it rang again and again and then maybe a few more times. It sounded urgent and I thought it might be our neighbour. Her mother lives with her and she isn't well, so I answered and he was – me da, that is – standing on the doorstep.' His voice rises, 'He was furious and he was waving a page in the air and yelling about it being the last straw. The anger coming off him was . . .' He shakes his head. 'I said something like "Nice to see you too," and he shoved me in the chest and I stumbled and hit me head. Then I think he was sorry or something and he said he was sorry and I told him to get out. I said that whatever he had in his hand was nothing to do with me. The less I had to do with him the better, I said. Then he just left. Last time I ever saw him.' He says it dispassionately.

'And you didn't tell Abby?'

'No.' He rubs a hand over his face. 'I'm sorry. I feel . . .' He lays his head on the table.

'Are you all right?' Maybe shock's setting in.

'Just about.' He waves a hand. Then, head still planted on the table, he asks, 'Is that all?'

'How did you fall?' Dan asks.

'Tripped over my feet, the way you do.' He speaks without looking up. 'Down onto the ground outside the front door.' He pre-empts Dan's next query. 'No one saw it. Abby will tell you it happened last Saturday.'

'You said you were working in your office on Monday but we can't confirm it.' Dan throws it out to see what his response is like.

'Myles saw me. Did he not tell you?'

'He's hardly credible. You rang him after we left, so we can't really trust that.'

'Then that's your problem, isn't it?' He lifts his head to gaze at Dan. His eyes are flat. 'I don't know what you want me to say. Anything else?'

Ouch.

'If it wasn't you sending those letters, any idea who it was?'

'Nope.'

'If we find out you're not telling the truth about where you were on Monday, it won't look good for you. Do you understand?'

'I couldn't give a fuck,' he says calmly, meaning it and shocking us both, I think. Palms flat, he pushes himself up from the table. 'Now, is that all?' Without waiting for an answer, he leaves the kitchen, throwing back, 'Show yourselves out.'

On the way home, we toss ideas back and forth, both of us reeling a little after our encounter with Zak. 'Did he maybe go down to see Jerry that day?' Dan asks. 'And did something go wrong?'

'You'd think he'd be worried then, wouldn't you?'

'And he's not, is he?'

'No, he lied twice to us and he really doesn't care.'

THE WRATH

We lapse into silence, unable to make sense of it. We're missing something and I don't know what it is. He hadn't seemed all that suspicious until he'd lied about being in work. And it had been such an obvious lie, to us anyway.

And yet, when challenged, he hadn't seemed in the least fazed. Maybe he knows we'll have trouble proving it.

'Did you buy that story about his da pushing him and knocking him over?' Dan asks, after a bit. 'I was just thinking he's a big lad, looks stronger than his dad.'

'That's true.'

'And that hand and those cuts . . . I don't know . . .'

But we'll have trouble proving he didn't fall.

We get back by ten thirty, thanks to empty roads and some breaking of speed limits. Stepping out of the car, a slash of rain hits me square in the face courtesy of the stiff Atlantic breeze. A half-moon is scudding in and out of racing clouds and, below, the ocean grumbles. There's more bad weather on the way. Dan bids me goodbye and, battling the wind, attempts to open his car door without it blowing off while I unlock the door to the station and take the stairs to the first floor. My hair is wet from the squalls and rain drips down my face.

I'm hungry again.

Achill is not a twenty-four-hour station but when a serious case is ongoing, a small skeleton staff remains on duty. The ones working greet me cheerily as I pass the incident room. One of the regular girls from Westport holds out a box and offers me a slice of pizza.

'I'm so hungry I could eat my child.'

Laughter as I lift a slice from the box and bite into it. It's just the right temperature and my stomach growls in appreciation.

'Ye checking Jerry's cases?' I ask, through a mouthful. 'How's it going?'

'Nothing for his last year at work. Mostly routine stuff. We're going back to the year before now.'

'I thought I heard you, Lucy,' William barks, from the door. 'Come into my office, fill me in."

Still holding the pizza, I follow him up the small corridor. His office is in a back room in the station. Sparse as usual with his files neatly arranged into two piles on his desk. His bonsai tree is on the windowsill in its usual position. 'It's grown.' I nod towards it, hoping to break down the barrier that he seems to have erected between us. 'Looks good.'

'Yeah.' He sits behind his desk, steeples his fingers. 'What have you got for me?'

I fill him in, eating the pizza as best I can.

'So, one person of interest who may not be a person of interest, that's it?'

'I beg your pardon?' I swallow the last of the food and manage a bit of a glare. 'What did you say?' It's a challenge to see if he will repeat it. Most people are hesitant to repeat insults.

But William is no such person. 'You heard me.'

'Dan and I were sent to Dublin by *you*. And we made the trip up and back in one day,' I hold up one finger in case there is any doubt, 'and we interviewed everyone of interest and that is what we got. Unless you want us to twist things to fit.'

'Right.' He dismisses that with a sort of mini eye-roll. 'Well, here, Larry found the car that—'

'What is your problem?'

'I beg your pardon?'

'You heard me.'

THE WRATH

'I am your superior and—'

'You know what, William? I don't give a crap about that right now.' He looks shocked. I'm shocked. But I can't pull out now because it's that weird thing when you say something you can't take back and you wish the other person could just unhear it, but you know they can't so you have to keep going. 'What's happened to our working relationship? We had a good one. You even went to bat for me.' I know I probably shouldn't mention it, that it should stay buried, but if this is at the root of his attitude, I need to know. I can't work with someone who resents me at the same time.

He says nothing, but his jaw clenches and he stands up abruptly from the table, sending his seat sliding backwards. Turning his back on me, he stares out of the window into the dark, hands jammed into the pockets of his expensive trousers.

'Do you regret it?'

He bows his head. His shoulders slump. 'You shouldn't have tried to get rid of evidence, Lucy.'

'You should have reported me, then,' I counter.

A long, long moment. 'Yes, but I . . .' he stops '. . . I didn't,' he finishes.

'Then we have to let it go.' I wonder if he can. Will he use it against me another time? I have to nip anything like that in the bud now.

'I am trying but . . .' the words hang in the air as he turns back to me and continues '. . . they want to give you a Scott medal.'

That is so unexpected it takes me a couple of seconds to catch up. 'What?'

'The chief super came to me a few months back. He has recommended you and Louis for a Scott medal.'

The Scott medal is an award for bravery in the course of one's duty. It's not something to be taken lightly. I suck in enough air to vacuum-pack the room. 'He can't.'

'He can and he has. So, you see my dilemma.'

'He's only doing it because Louis is his son.'

'It doesn't matter a damn why he's doing it. The fact is he's doing it and I've learned that what that fella wants he generally gets.'

'Isn't there a selection procedure? Maybe they won't give it to us.'

'We're talking the chief's son here. And if they give it to him, they'll certainly give it to you. You were shot, for God's sake.'

And I don't know why but suddenly it strikes me as funny. The whole mess of it. The whole idea that our cover-up has led to this. And the dour, furrowed expression on his face. 'Oh, shit,' I flap my hand about. 'Sorry.'

'Are you laughing?'

'I don't mean to. I really don't. Sorry.'

'It's not bloody funny. It'll make a mockery of the whole ceremony.'

'I know.' I clamp a hand over my mouth and gulp back the giggles. 'I know and I'm sorry.'

He stands impassively as I struggle to get myself under control.

'Sorry. Sorry. I know it's a big deal and I don't want to besmirch it. And—'

'It'll take a good few months for the whole thing to go through anyway,' he says, interrupting me. 'Be a while at least before we know and, sure, maybe you'll mess up before then.'

I think it's a joke. 'Thanks.'

He offers me the tiniest of smiles before abruptly asking, 'Do you want to know what happened here today?'

'Yes.' It comes out a little high-pitched but at least I'm not giggling. 'Of course. Of course I want to know what happened. But before you tell me,' I adopt a professional tone, just like his, 'I need assurance that we can get on with one another in this investigation. You need to stop picking on me because—'

'I am not picking on you.'

'You are. Everybody's noticed it.'

'Ridiculous. Now, Larry—'

'Dan asked what was up. Dan asked what I'd done to annoy you.'

That stops him short. He respects Dan. 'I wasn't aware,' he mutters.

I don't respond. I'm surprised when he fills the silence. Usually he never would.

'If I have been short with you, I apologise.'

That's a turn-up. 'If you regret not turning me in, then turn me in.' I'm surprised to realise I mean it. I'd rather leave than have him treat me like this. And, to be honest, the guilt I feel at still being in the job lives on my shoulder, whispers to me in the dark. Being awarded a medal that real honest guards and detectives risk their lives for would be like wearing a big crown of thorns.

William looks affronted. 'I made the decision, and I stand by it.' He lets me absorb the words as he crosses back towards his desk and takes his seat. 'Let's just . . .' He waves a hand, dips his gaze from mine and gets back down to business. 'Look, there's a lot going on, it's not just you. It's not just the medal. There's some stuff I need to take care of.' He shakes his head, like he's dislodging his thoughts, refocuses. 'Today, Larry, he did good work. He managed to locate Jerry's car coming onto the island and got

CCTV as far as McLoughlin's bar. He's working on the journey from there. We know now that Jerry left the bar at fifteen ten.'

'That was late. Any footage of the man he was seen talking to in the bar?'

He passes me a photograph. 'A still. We think this is him. It's the person who left the bar about an hour before Jerry did.'

A dark-haired man, royal blue rain jacket and blue trainers with white stripes. His back is to camera but there is an air of youth in the way he holds himself. 'He drove away towards Keem.' Another still of the same bright-blue-jacketed man behind the wheel of a car. This time there's a blur of profile. Another still shows the car from the back. 'The registration is blurred,' I mutter, 'but it's a Corsa.'

'That's right. How did you know?'

His air of surprise is insulting. If things were easy between us, I'd probably tell him so but instead I just say, 'I have one.' I point at the picture. 'I even have those exact wheels.'

'Good catch. I've tasked Larry with tracking all the black Corsas he can find for that day on the island and hopefully we'll strike lucky with a partial reg. We can try getting an ID on PULSE then.'

'Go, Larry.' I don't mean to sound bitter, but he's done better than me today.

'As for everything else, I suppose we'll hear—'

His mobile rings and, with a wince, he answers. It can only mean more work. I study his face for a hint on what is happening.

'They've found a body,' he relays, hanging up. 'Down your way. Coming?' He pulls on his jacket and I jump up, following him out to a DDU car.

17

A young guard, whose name I don't know, has been brought along with us. His job will be to secure the perimeter while William and I check out what the story is. Apparently a couple have reported finding a body in an abandoned cottage a few hundred yards away from where Jerry's car was located. The place had been well outside the search cordon as all signs had pointed to Jerry being dumped in the sea. That's assuming this body is Jerry's, of course.

William, the young guard and I are first on the scene. As we pull up two people hurry towards the car. The girl, Isla, whom I know – she was in the same year as Luc at school – points to the sagging structure of a stone house. 'In there,' she whispers, her eyes huge and distressed. 'The front room. It's awful . . .'

'Stay here, the both of ye.' William's eyes are already on the building. 'Don't leave. We need to take your statements.' He strides away from them.

'I'm sure it was a terrible shock.' I reach into the car and pull out my jacket, handing it to Isla, who is wearing a less than sensible pair of hot-pants. 'Here. Keep warm.'

She wraps it around her shoulders and the young lad cuddles her in.

It's only youth that could tolerate clothes like that in December.

'I know it's a terrible shock,' I begin, 'but –'

'Lucy!' William calls from the entrance of the premises. 'Come on.' He's already donned a dust suit. How the hell has he done it so quickly?

'– the person in there is dead. You two have got to take care of yourselves now, all right?'

'Lucy!'

I roll my eyes, finishing, 'Maybe some counselling to help you deal with what ye saw.' Then, turning, I hurry towards him, pulling on my forensic suit.

A few minutes later we walk through the rotting front door and into the dark building. William flicks on a torch and it illuminates the room. Once loved, now neglected, the remnants of mildewed floral wallpaper hang down in great strips, tipping onto the flagstone floor. The wiring for a light hangs crookedly from a falling-down ceiling. Bits of old rotted furniture, a table and chairs maybe, are black with mould, empty beer cans and beans tins, and old crisps packets, litter the floor; in the huge stone fireplace, there's a mattress. It's not as dirty as the rest of the place but it's not clean either and on it, flat out, lies the body of what I believe to be Jerry Loftus. Jerry's fleece and T-shirt have been pulled up to reveal a wound in his abdomen, which someone has made an attempt to dress using torn-up strips of fabric – bed sheets, I think. A blue regatta jacket is tossed alongside the mattress. Jerry's skin has acquired a greenish pallor and his body has started to bloat. The smell of decomposition permeates the air. Flies are gathering. I think a few rats have visited as well. At the foot of the mattress there is an open haversack, its contents scattered across the foul-smelling room.

For a few moments, William and I stand, observing in respectful silence. This man died here, I think. He was taken from the car and brought to this place. Unlike the car, though, there is no sense of violence, just a calm, unnerving stillness as if he's been laid down almost with reverence. There's even a bunch of wildflowers near his feet, though whether that's deliberate or by chance I don't know.

William spots them too. 'Weird,' he remarks. Then, pointing towards the corner of the room, he says, 'That might just be the thin tyre mark we found at the scene.'

It's a wheelbarrow. I cross to it. It's covered with blood. Someone transported Jerry in it from the car to here.

Jesus.

I walk around the room, stones and glass crunching beneath my feet. The sound of scurrying as creatures run for the dark corners to escape the light is disquieting. To the left of the fireplace, I find a small camping stove, an old kettle and a cracked cup. People come here. Or someone does.

William is poking at the haversack. 'Rain trousers and energy bars,' he says. 'An open first-aid kit on the floor and a red woolly hat. A spare pair of socks.' Then he looks towards the young couple. 'What were those two doing?'

'Looking for somewhere to snog, I reckon.'

William's mouth opens in slight disgust.

'When you're in love, you'll go anywhere.'

I'd done it once in a sand dune with my first love, Johnny Egan, and I blush at the memory. Fecking sand got into everything, making my hair and body itch for days. Though, compared to this stinking hovel, a sand dune is like five-star luxury.

'Oh, this is nice.' With gloved fingers, William pulls from the depths of the bag a mobile phone. He grins up at me. 'Jackpot.'

I grin back and watch as he places it in an evidence bag. 'With a bit of luck we'll have something from it by tomorrow.'

There's a staircase in the room, which looks sturdy enough. 'I'll have a peek upstairs,' I say, testing the first step with my weight.

William turns his attention back to Jerry, taking his phone out and snapping a few pictures.

Upstairs is in better condition, two small bedrooms and a narrow landing. I'd imagine the bathroom was in an outhouse somewhere. The wallpaper has come away in huge strips up here too and a dado rail lies underfoot. The doors into the bedrooms are long gone and I go into the larger one first. An iron bedstead and old dressing-table with a cracked mirror. The windows have fallen in and there's a large hole in the floorboards in the centre of the room. The room looks out onto the mountainside and I'd imagine it's dark even in daytime.

I move into the smaller front bedroom and, as my torch illuminates the chair facing the broken window, I gasp. It's not a chair that belongs here: it's in good condition. Beside it rest two pairs of binoculars. And there's a large mug on the floor too.

'Agatha says she shouldn't be too much longer,' William calls up. 'She was in Castlebar at a conference so she's coming straight over from her hotel. And SOCO will be here soon too.'

'Agatha?' The mug looks fairly clean.

'Yes, anything up there?'

'Who's Agatha?'

He huffs out a sigh. 'Don't you read your emails?'

I don't answer because, really, who has time? Except him, obviously. 'I think you should come up here. It's interesting.'

THE WRATH

I hear his careful tread on the stairs and, as he emerges into the room, he says, 'She's the new pathologist.'

That's right. Palmer has gone.

'A very nice woman,' William surprises me by adding. He isn't a man given to praising people too often. 'Oh, this is interesting. Binoculars.' He frowns. 'Funny how they're still here, though.'

'Yes.'

He bends down, examines them. 'One normal, one night vision.' He peers out of the window. 'What is the view out there?'

'It takes in the road,' I say, knowing why he's asking. 'Whoever was using those binoculars would have been well able to spot Jerry's car driving along that day.'

'And make it to the road before Jerry passed?'

I shrug. 'I doubt it. Maybe if they had a car too, obviously, but still . . .' I frown. 'On foot, I'd have to say no.'

'Unless they had an accomplice on the road?'

'Or unless they saw his car go up towards Keem and just waited patiently, knowing he'd have to come back.'

William nods. 'Come downstairs. I've something to show you.'

I follow him down and he shines his torch onto one of the makeshift bandages. 'Is that a fingerprint?'

There's a mark in blood that certainly looks like a print.

I hear some commotion from outside. Cars and voices and lights. SOCO have arrived.

'Back again.' John, one of the team, comes into the room. He glances down at Jerry. 'How on earth did the poor bugger end up here? Right, just so's ye know, we're getting a safe path marked out and letting Agatha through as she's here. Thought we'd let her go first for a change.'

There would never have been such accommodations for Palmer. This Agatha certainly has them all on their toes.

Ten minutes later, Agatha arrives in, picking her way carefully across the floor, taking care not to slip on the plastic plates. How she's managing it in the booties, which cover sky-high heels, I don't know. She's got a tiny, bird-like frame, enormous brown eyes and huge fake lashes. The forensic suit looks worse on her than it does on me and she has to bunch it about herself as she moves.

'Hello, Agatha,' William says, in a voice he never uses with the rest of us. 'We meet again.' I bristle at his warm, friendly tone.

'How ya, Will.' Her voice is pure Dub with a husky hoarseness, like she smokes sixty fags a day. 'I wish I could say it was good to see you again but it generally just means more work for me.' A laugh that comes from deep in her belly and William actually smiles. Feck's sake. Does he have a little crush? Her gaze turns to me. 'Lucy Golden,' she says, like she knows me well. 'How are you?'

I'm surprised she can recognise me under the garb and I tell her so.

She waves me away. 'Sure you've got great eyes, I always notice a person's eyes, and then there's the scar. Sure it's easy. Don't need to be a detective to spot you.' She turns from me and starts to examine the body.

Great eyes and a scar. Was that a compliment or not? Most people steer away from mentioning the scar. Before I have a chance to process it, she crouches to have a look at the body and starts talking again.

'You died here, didn't you?' she says to the corpse. 'Weren't stabbed here, though, were you? Not enough blood. And someone tried to bandage you up? What was that all about, eh?' She tut-tuts over the wound in the belly. Turns to look at William. 'He's about four days dead, I'd reckon from the decomposition. The colour of him and the foam, lookit, from his lips. You poor fecker.' That's back to the corpse. 'Now, Will, this is probably what kilt him. That there.' She uses a stick to point to the bandaged-up wound. 'I'd put me house on it. Looking like he was stabbed in the stomick, an artery hit, difficult enough to do that kind of thing, so either a fluke or someone who knew what they were doing. I've seen the pictures of the car, so he probably hadn't much blood when he got back here. But sure, lookit, I'll get him back to the mortuary and give you a better report.' She takes a few pictures, wishes us luck, says, 'Goodbye,' to the body and leaves.

'Thanks,' William calls, after her, and I gawp at him. He must sense it because he turns to me. 'Good to keep on her right side. We don't need her turning into another Palmer.' A sudden yawn. 'Christ, I'm wrecked.'

'Me too.'

'Come on.' As I follow, he strides ahead of me into the fresh night air. Across the way, beyond the cordon, the youngsters are having their statements taken by two separate guards, parents standing by. William beckons me towards the DDU car, and from the boot, he pulls out a large flask and two mugs. Unscrewing the top of the flask, he says, 'I keep it with me in case I get caught on a long shift.' Pouring some dark brown beverage into a mug, he thrusts it towards me. 'Here, drink up.'

It's the most disgusting coffee I've ever tasted. 'Jesus, you could build a house on that, it's so strong.'

He looks mildly insulted. 'No one else ever objects.'

They wouldn't dare.

We sip in silence, taking in all the activity that has suddenly sprung up in this quiet place. Lights, generators, forensics vans, garda cars. 'You may as well get off home,' William says eventually. 'Not much else we can do until results start coming in. Hopefully by conference tomorrow we'll have more to go on. See you then, Lucy.'

Normally I'd insist on staying, on seeing the night out, but after the drive to Dublin, after confronting William over his treatment of me, I'm exhausted.

I dump the rest of the coffee out and hand him back my mug. 'Thanks.'

He puts the flask back in the boot and lopes off to tic-tac with John. He'll have a list of instructions on what John should look for and why he should look for it. I peel off the forensic suit and walk down the track, looking for a guard who will give me a lift back to the station to collect my car.

I'm about two hundred metres from a garda car when I sense something. I'm not sure what alerts me – maybe a rustle in the undergrowth? It's enough to stop me in my tracks. I freeze and stare into infinite blackness, dark where the lights can't reach. All is still but my senses prickle. Turning slowly, I flick on my torch, but it merely illuminates the stony road and bogland and, further on, hedgerows. Hairs rise on the back of my neck. I have a sensation of being watched, of all of us being watched. Once more I turn, rapidly this time, the torch juddering, and I hear it. Feet. Running. With a cry, I take off in the direction of the noise, yelling for someone to help me. From behind, someone else joins me.

Up over hillocks and scree and up and up. My breath is coming out in great gulps, but someone is there, ahead. I get glimpses of a coat and hear the sound of laboured breathing. It's hard to run with the torch, but if I discard it—

I fall, tripping over a root, the torch flying from my hands, landing ahead of me, flicking off. My palms slam onto the earth, saving my face but not my knees.

A young guard slides to a stop beside me. 'You okay?' He's breathless too.

'Keep going,' I shout. 'Up there. Someone was there.'

And then a fox runs across the path.

I climb onto my feet. My knees ache. My palms will be sore in a while.

'Could it have been a fox?'

'No, it was definitely footsteps.'

He shines his torch but there's nothing now, no shoeprints on the ground, though it's hard anyway.

'D'you want me to . . .'

It's too late. Whoever it was has vanished. We'd never find them now. And maybe, with the tiredness, I was mistaken. 'Leave it. Maybe it was a fox. Can I get a lift back to the station?'

'Sure.' He jangles his keys.

I take a breath, close my eyes. I wonder uneasily if it was a throwback, a sort of PTSD.

No one is there, not now anyway.

18

My mother has the door open the minute I pull into the drive. She must have been looking out for my car, worried in case something had happened. A well of affection rises in me.

'You work way too hard,' she admonishes, as she goes before me into the kitchen. 'When I heard about the dead man, I said I'd stay up until you got in, make sure you eat. There's stew in the slow cooker. Here.'

She hands me a plate and I fill it with rich, comforting food. 'Thanks, Mam.' Just what I need after a day in the trenches. 'How did you hear about the dead man?' I spoon some meat into my mouth. God, it's delicious.

'Isla's mother called me.'

'How do you know Isla's mother?'

'We're hardly living in New York,' she answers. 'Isla's mother, Louise, she called because she wanted you to know that Isla did not kill that man and was not revisiting the scene of the crime.'

The idea is so preposterous that I splutter half-chewed meat all over the table, causing my mother to rear back from me with a squeal.

THE WRATH

'She didn't want her daughter arrested,' my mother goes on, hopping up to get me some kitchen paper, 'because when poor Denis Long got arrested last time, sure didn't he have all sorts thrown at his house and him an innocent man.'

She'll never let me forget that. Denis and Lorna Long, her best friends, both arrested on my last big case. By me. Though Denis wasn't the saint she thought he was, it has to be said.

'Mop that up now.'

I take the kitchen paper she hands me and clean the table. 'Isla won't be arrested.'

'And I know it looks bad she's hanging around with Graham Lions. But he was only caught shoplifting the once and he got a caution and it's all forgotten now. Put that in the bin.'

'Mam, they'll be fine. Honestly.' I ball up the paper and fire it at the bin. Yes!

'I won't ask you for details on who the person is that you found.'

'I wouldn't tell you anyway.' I speak through a mouthful of stew.

'Is it Jerry Loftus, the hero guard from the cinema?''

'Mam!'

'Sorry. Yes. I shouldn't.'

More silence.

'Anything happen here?' I ask, to distract her, to be distracted by her. Her life is one of simple pleasures, of normality.

'Well,' her voice lightens, 'you missed Sirocco. She came over all dressed up in her school uniform.' A laugh. 'Not that she's actually going this year but Tani couldn't wait and went out and bought one. And Sirocco put it on and she demanded that Tani drive her over here to show it off.'

My heart melts. Sirocco doing anything at all has that effect on me. 'Did Tani come in with her?'

Tani is Luc's ex and the mother of his child. They split up last year and I miss her dreadfully. Cherry, with all her glamour, is a poor substitute as far as I'm concerned.

'She did. Thank God Luc and Cherry weren't here. That would have been very awkward. In fact, Tani was asking after Luc.'

'More fool her.'

'Aw, now, Luc is a good lad. Here.' She pulls her mobile out of her trouser pocket and switches it on, her finger sliding over the screen. 'There now, look.' She passes me the phone and there's a picture of my little grandchild, belly sticking out proudly, hands on her hips, untidy black curls tumbling around her cute-as-a-button face, wearing a white shirt, green pinafore and cardigan and green tights, with shiny black shoes. The uniform is swimming on her.

We both 'Awww' at the picture, though part of me is irritated that I wasn't here, that I missed it. Before I can get too maudlin, she begins to regale me with tales of the rest of her day. My mother is a great storyteller, and though the stuff she talks about is mundane, she has a great sense of humour that elevates it. Hearing her chat about who said what to whom on the Tidy Towns committee or the feud between the two men on the local GAA team helps me come down from the horrors of the day. Finally, she says, 'Oh, and I nearly forgot.' Her voice dips reverently, 'Cherry is going to be an influencer.'

'A what?'

My mother reddens. 'An influencer,' she says defensively.

'You don't know what that is, do you?'

'Someone who influences people.'

'How did that come about? Did she just wake up one morning and say, "I know what I'll do. I'll influence people."'

'Yes,' my mother says. 'Apparently her Insta profile has taken off and she has piles and piles of new followers because of that sausage ad and now she'll be an influencer.'

Load of bullshit, I think uncharitably. 'And what do her parents make of that career choice?'

My mother shrugs. 'She didn't say. But being an influencer is a money spinner, she told me.'

'Let's see if she can influence me to like her,' I say.

'She's not working miracles.'

My mother. She can always make me laugh.

19

He adjusts his binoculars. Focuses. There. He has it.

What a stroke of luck that the Runt lives down in this part of the country too. The house is one of those architect builds, steel and glass tucked into a fold of mountainside. The entrance is flanked by large gates of wrought iron painted bright blue, the colour standing out like a wound in the yellow-brown winter landscape. But, really, you couldn't expect anything more from the tasteless, spineless, grubby little fecker.

A long driveway leads from the gates up to the house and there is a security camera positioned on a pillar to watch people coming and going.

That might be a problem but not insurmountable.

A sudden flash of sunlight on metal and his heart leaps as, through the jam of bare-branched trees that line the driveway, he spots a car winding its way towards the gates, which are opening with agonising slowness to allow the vehicle to glide through. He adjusts his focus again and makes out a figure behind the wheel, and though he hadn't seen him in what feels like another lifetime, he is still recognisable. A bit older, a lot balder but still the ugly little runt he remembers.

The ugly little back-stabbing runt. He breathes deeply to take the edge off the rage that suddenly threatens to consume him. Feelings are best kept

THE WRATH

under control, his daddy always said. It was like having a vicious dog, he told him once: if you couldn't control it, it was no use to you.

As the car crosses the lake and comes towards him, he puts down his binoculars and dons a pair of shades. The Runt sails on by in his fairly new silver Merc without so much as a glance in his direction.

He puts his hire car in gear, takes another breath and tells himself to be mindful, stay in the moment, enjoy the day and relish the moment when he wipes the smirk off the Runt's face.

20

'Luc's girlfriend has decided to be an influencer,' I whisper to Dan, the next morning, just as conference is about to kick off. At his look of curiosity, I add, 'Apparently.'

'I'm not sure you can just decide to be one,' Dan whispers back.

'That's what I thought.'

'Last night we located a body, which this morning has been confirmed to be that of Jerry Loftus.'

William recaps last night for the team, his voice a drone in the background as I hiss, 'But she has loads of followers, so would that make it easier?'

Dan talks out the side of his mouth. 'I guess it would. Are companies going to send her stuff?'

'I don't know. She's the girl in the ad for sausages. Have you seen it? It was on the telly a couple of nights ago and last night too and—'

'That's her? Luc's girlfriend? Jesus. It's some ad.'

'I know.'

'Delores said it should be banned. Said it made sausages into something they are not.'

'Well, she'd know with her new boyfriend.'

Dan starts to shake with suppressed laughter.

'Are we interrupting something down there?'

Too late I realise that the whole room has eyes in our direction. Without waiting for an answer, William barks, 'Preliminary pathologist report, Dan? From Agatha?' Then, 'And for those of you who don't read the emails, Agatha is the new state pathologist. Dan!'

Dan coughs and hastily turns his attention to the paper he's come in with. I feel for him as fumbles with the page. No one likes incurring William's wrath, especially not in front of the rest of the team. '"At twenty-three fifteen hours on Thursday, the fourth of December last,"' Dan reads, neck flushing red, '"I examined, in situ, the body of a male, approximately early sixties. He was lying on his back on a mattress in a derelict house on the Atlantic Drive, Achill, arms by his sides. He was wearing black Columbia hiking boots and black regatta hiking trousers. A blue jacket had been removed and a red fleece and orange T-shirt were hiked up to reveal a makeshift bandage covering a wound on the abdomen. I also observed an injury to the top of the skull."'

The report goes on to say that he'd been dead for at least four days, that he most likely died in the house but that if the wound on the abdomen turned out, as suspected, to be the fatal injury, that injury had been caused elsewhere due to the lack of blood spatter at the scene.

'"A more comprehensive report will follow once I have had a chance to examine the body at the mortuary,"' Dan finishes.

'Lucy, you and . . .' William looks about the room, 'Matt, have you ever gone to a PM?'

'No, and if you don't mind—'

'You and Lucy will attend the PM.'

Matt throws me an anguished look, which I ignore. I can't afford to annoy William now that we've come to a tentative ceasefire, though I get the feeling that it won't take much to set him off again. He really is stressed out about something and it would—

'Lucy?' William barks. Then, 'If people are not going to pay attention, they can just leave.'

'I am paying attention.'

It comes out sharp, and William's mouth opens slightly either to reprimand me or because he's shocked. But probably because he doesn't want anyone to think he's picking on me, he hauls himself back from saying anything. Instead, with a stiff nod, he indicates for me to proceed.

Hastily, I give the room a rundown of Dan's and my conversations with Zak and Abby yesterday. 'In short, Zak stated that his dad is having an affair and that his father was under the impression that Zak was blackmailing him about the affair using these letters. Zak denies this. His movements on the day Jerry was murdered are unaccounted for. During the interview, he lied to us twice. I'd say he's a person we should look into.'

'Okay, we'll get someone on his movements. Larry?'

Larry stands up and, like a showman, waits a moment or two until he has our full attention. 'After Lucy's report yesterday morning that Jerry Loftus left McLoughlin's after midday, I managed to find his car on CCTV.' A toss-away smile in my direction. 'That was a good lead, Lucy.'

If it was anyone but Larry, I'd take the compliment, but he makes it sound like he's throwing me a bone.

'I also managed to get a still of this fella.' On the screen, at the front of the room, I see the picture of the young man William had shown me last night. 'This is the last person to leave the pub before Jerry did. The one the barman said Jerry was with. Unfortunately, we don't have a facial but the bright blue jacket and blue runners are distinctive. This here is another still of a man who left the pub after Jerry. Not as clear.'

That's the large man Tomas the barman described. Even on video he looks enormous. He's wearing a baseball cap and his face is dipped.

'And now here is what I believe is the car the first man was driving. Note the blue jacket behind the wheel.'

The Corsa, with the blue-jacketed man at the wheel, comes into shot and disappears. 'Opel Corsa,' Larry says. 'Like Lucy's, only in better nick.'

'Ha-bloody-ha,' I say, as people titter. My car is only a year old but looks a bit crap mainly because one day Sirocco decided to draw on it using the sharp edge of a stone.

'And then Jerry's car, which we know is his because of that scratch down the side.' He zooms in on the deep scratch on the passenger door. 'Now, was Jerry going after this man? Was he just going in the direction of Keem anyway to climb the mountain?' He lets the questions hang in the air before projecting more footage onscreen, this time of the blue car that had followed Jerry's about ten seconds later. 'After that vehicle, which I can't identify as yet, there are no cars for about ten minutes. I'm trying to get a reg on both the Corsa and this car here because there's some more footage being harvested today.'

'I've also arranged for that still of both men to be released to the media in the hope someone can identify them or that they come forward,' William says. 'That blue jacket is distinctive.

Jordy, anything found in Jerry's case files that bears a closer look?'

'Not yet, Cig. We did a year's worth between us all yesterday but nothing jumping out so far. We specifically looked out for anything that might lead to him being threatened, but nothing. I also had a word with his old sergeant, Joe Little, who was pretty broken up over the news and was full of praise for him. He had nothing to say except that Jerry's nickname was the Good Cop because of that internet video he was in. It was a big thing at the time apparently. Ruined that fella Wowser's career. Jerry got a lot of slagging over it from the lads apparently but the case itself was something and nothing, in the station at least. It didn't even result in a prosecution. Jerry just gave the lad a caution and that was it. Just to be safe, I tracked that Wowser fella down. He's living in Galway now so I got a few lads there to call on him and check his alibi for the day Jerry was murdered. It was solid. He was in work all day. His boss swore to it.'

'Excellent work.' William nods. 'Kevin? You and Susan were talking to their friends from the list Hazel gave us?'

'We've nothing so far, Cig. Most of their friends live in Dublin, so we tasked guards in Dublin to do that. I know you don't like telephone interviews.'

'Good. And?'

'Well, they're snowed under up there. I mean, Dublin is a busy place and—'

'Did they interview anyone?'

'Today, they said.' Kev flushes. 'I'll make sure of it, Cig. Susan and I did talk to a Mr and Mrs Lynch. Alan and Avril. They live down here. They're a young enough couple and Avril said she didn't know Hazel and Jerry that well but Alan did. Alan was a bit . . . What would you say, Susan?'

'Jumpy?' Susan suggests.

Kev nods. 'Anyway, he said he knew Jerry a little from Dublin, he'd met him at fishing competitions once or twice. When Jerry moved down, they fished together now and again, though he said Hazel wasn't too keen on Jerry leaving her. Neither Avril nor Alan admitted to seeing Jerry on the day he went missing, though they do live near Keem, which was the direction the cars drove. Avril alleges that she was meeting friends in Mulranny Park Hotel that day, which we confirmed with the hotel. Alan says he was fishing in Acorrymore on his own, which we haven't managed to confirm as of yet. Avril seemed pretty pissed with him over it too. She'd thought he was in work. And interesting thing,' Kev beams, 'there was a Black Corsa and a Fiesta in their driveway and I saw a bright blue jacket hanging over a kitchen chair in the house.'

'I'd estimate from the video that the fella is about six foot,' Larry says, 'average weight, maybe twelve stone.'

'Alan Lynch would be around that,' Susan says. 'Though his upset when he heard Jerry was missing was genuine, I thought.'

'Me too,' Kev agrees.

'But there was a black Corsa in the driveway?' William asks.

'Yep,' Kev says. 'I didn't take the plates, though. I guess I can look it up on PULSE and if Larry manages to match up a partial, we can go talk to him again.'

'If we get a little more we can haul him in and get a warrant to search the house and get forensics on the jacket. Larry, get on that today.'

'Sure thing.'

'Door-to-door?'

'Just one thing of interest,' Ben says. 'A Linda Hayes?'

I know Linda. She's old Achill. Lives near me.

'Linda believes that she saw Jerry around four thirty in his car, driving back toward Keel from the direction of Croaghaun. I asked her why she thought it was him and she said because he almost ran her over. She caught a glimpse of the scratch on the car.'

That causes a bit of a stir.

'Did this Linda seem reliable?'

'I thought so,' Ben says.

'She wouldn't be one for making things up, Cig. A good head on her.' I'm racking my brains to identify the Lynches. There was a time you'd know everyone in the place but, what with new houses being built and people moving down, it's hard to keep track.'

'That's great work so far. Mick?'

'Well, nothing from any hospitals. Not surprising as he turned up dead last night.'

'Jaysus, the hospitals in this country, you're lucky to come out alive,' Larry jokes.

'That's unfair.' Susan hops on it. 'My dad and all his brothers are doctors. They work hard. I resent – stop doing that!'

Larry has made his hand into a beak.

'Larry!' William cautions.

'I was joking,' Larry says. 'Some people.'

'I wasn't joking,' Susan mutters.

'Forensics, Mick.' William chooses to ignore them both.

'Three things, Cig. Nothing on the anonymous notes as yet.'

'That's hardly a thing then, is it?' William remarks drily.

Mick reddens. 'I suppose not,' he admits. 'Next thing, then. The white tablet we found at the scene is a . . .' he bends to a piece of paper '. . . clozapine.' He looks up. 'Apparently it's a medication to treat people with psychosis. It's given to people who are resistant to other medications.'

William frowns. 'Was Jerry taking any medication for psychosis?'

'Hazel never mentioned it,' I answer.

'Dan, you and Louis find out who the family doctor is and ask him. Don't take all that GDPR crap from him either. Tell him it's a bloody murder investigation, right?'

'Will do, Cig.'

General data protection regulations are the bane of our lives. We all hate them.

'And the third thing?' William turns back to Mick.

'We've managed to get into Jerry's phone and I'll have transcripts from it for later. Also, Jerry's DNA is all over the sheet he was bound up in but also some other DNA that is not in the system.'

'So, two more things?' William is nitpicking.

'The lack of evidence found on the notes wasn't a thing, Cig. You just said that. So, just the DNA, the phone and the tablet. Three things.'

After a moment of tense silence, in which Mick goes redder and redder but keeps his gaze steady, William says, 'I want you to take a preliminary glance at the transcripts on Jerry's phone and see what stands out, then send any interesting texts to Jim to job it out. Louis, you were on tracing those credit cards from the pub. Anything?'

'Well, Jerry's card, of course. He's there. And the two women Lucy talked about yesterday and then, you'll love this, Cig, an Alan Lynch.'

That causes a stir.

'You're sure?'

'Yep. So Alan Lynch, if it's the same one, must have seen Jerry that day.'

'Good work.' William actually beams and I wish it had been Mick or Susan who had found out that nugget of information.

Louis preens.

'This Alan Lynch is looking interesting. As does Zak Loftus. Kev, you take Zak. Try to trace his movements on the day he says he was in work. Susan, you take over on the friends. Let's keep digging. See what more we can find. Lads, by all accounts, Jerry Loftus was a man devoted to his wife, on the Tidy Towns and a good guard. We also have information that he was having an affair, which is at odds with the devoted-husband persona. But he was the victim of a violent assault, and we need to get justice for him. Now, Hazel and Zak were informed last night that we thought we had located Jerry's body. Zak is travelling today to be with his mother. After the PM they'll identify the body. An FLO is with them. Jim has the job sheets. Don't forget to return them. Off ye go.'

Matt meets me at the door and together we walk to the car. 'Any tips for surviving a PM?' he asks dolefully.

'Yep. Don't under any circumstances breathe in.'

He manages a laugh.

21

He sees Phoebe before she sees him. Jesus, he hopes she won't spot him for a while just so he can watch her. He loves the way she's leaning up against the wall outside the coffee shop on a rare break from work, head tipping the stone, feet crossed at the ankles. He enjoys the sight of her raven hair falling across the side of her face as she examines her phone. He loves the teasing glimpse of her profile. People glance curiously at her as they pass but no one bothers her. She's the kind of girl people look at, always has been. He drinks her in, every detail, from her hiking boots to her loose denims and Puffa jacket. She's like a great gulp of cool water on a blisteringly hot day. When she becomes aware of his gaze and recognises him, her welcoming smile is dazzling. He almost wilts under it.

He approaches her, caught in her light.

'You okay, Blu?' A glance at his hand. 'What happened?'

Her nickname for him. No one else ever calls him that and he has no idea where she even got it from, but it is their thing.

Nicknames make them friends.

'I'm okay,' he says. 'And this,' he waves his hand, 'is nothing. I . . . eh . . . fell.'

She reaches up, runs a finger down his cheek, and he would swear that his skin burns at her touch. 'Nightmares again?'

He told her once, long ago, about the nightmares. She never forgot and didn't even make fun of him. He shrugs. 'Nah, just . . . well, yeah, but,' his gaze roves beyond her to the café, 'you said the pasta was good here?'

She hooks her arm through his. 'The pasta is great here.'

He spends the next hour bathing in her glow. Nothing else matters. His whole shitty existence is softened when he's with her. His rage disappears, his smile, a rare thing, reasserts itself and he makes her laugh. He could always make her laugh. If only he could be with her. If she loved him the way he loves her, he wouldn't feel such despair. But he'll never tell her this. He'll never dare jeopardise what they have. He's always been half in love with her, even back in the day, but she wasn't his then and she can never be his now.

Just as the meal comes to an end, she asks, 'You seen him lately?'

That's a first. She's never asked about him before. His heart soars. 'Later today. You can come if you like. He's not . . .' He can't break a confidence. 'Come see him,' he says.

She doesn't reply. Instead she just picks up her phone and tucks it into her jacket. Then she runs her hands through her hair and pulls it from her collar. 'You need to get away, Blu. He's not good for you. He played us all for years.'

He's so stunned, he can't even reply. Shows how much she knows. She bends down and her lips brush his cheek. 'I'll be in touch.'

He leaves her to a taxi and he would have paid for it only for what she said. Who is she to tell him who to mix with? How does she know what's good for him? She doesn't seem to sense his anger because just as she steps

THE WRATH

into the car, she kisses him again and smiles. Then the car drives away and he's left touching his cheek, a bit adrift, a bit unbalanced.

Once she has disappeared from view, he takes a breath, goes in search of a postbox.

Letter number three is on its way.

He has two people he loves in his life. One is Phoebe and the other, arguably his very best friend, is making his slow and unsteady way towards him across the length of the bar. He knows enough not to help him. Finally, he slips into a seat and offers him a smile. Dark hair tumbles over his forehead. 'Good to see you,' he says.

Anger at the injustice of life swells within him. No one, no matter what they've done, deserves this. 'You read the papers?' he asks, with a smile on his face.

A nod and, in a weak voice, his mate says, 'You're a good man.'

Those words always have the power to knock him sideways. 'You are too.'

His mate shakes his head. 'No, I'm not good. You've always been the rock. Only for you, I would've—' He stops. His voice hitches up a notch: 'I thought I had time but they say no.'

'Don't cry, bud.' He fills the awkward moment with chat about how they met as kids and how they clicked.

His friend gives a gentle chuckle, and his heart rises.

'I promise,' he says to his mate, 'that you will outlive them.'

A thin hand reaches over and clasps his own.

He clasps his friend's hand right back.

His heart swells.

Phoebe doesn't know what she's talking about.

22

Matt has turned a funny shade of green as Agatha deep-dives into the body of Jerry Loftus. He's shoving enough vapour up his nose to destroy his nostrils as Agatha, cheerfully oblivious, gives a run-down of Jerry's injuries. Though she's gowned up with a mask and hairnet, her eyes are brimful of joy. And does she love her dead bodies. She chats away to Jerry as she unpeels the layers of his living. Sympathises with him about his broken nose and teeth and the stab wound to his stomach. Hopes it wasn't too traumatic. Apologises as she picks dirt from his fingernails and bags the tiniest of seeds from the sole of his boot. From the corner of my eye, I see Matt looking at her as if she's bonkers but I like the way she's humanising Jerry, normalising the ritual of probing and prodding and cutting. The job is brutal but she's not brutal about it. The previous pathologist Palmer was a dour presence who resented any questions, Agatha positively welcomes them.

No wonder William likes her.

The first of two surprises comes when she carefully peels away the layer of bandages around Jerry's torso. 'Well, well, hello,' she says brightly, prodding with her scalpel. 'What have we here?'

Matt takes a step back. I bend to have a closer look. 'Is that stitches?'

'That's what it looks like,' Agatha gently begins to undo the stitching. 'Not a bad job either, but a little too late, I'd imagine.'

'In *Rambo*, the first film, he stitched up his own arm after it got cut,' Matt says, from six feet behind. 'It was mad.'

'I'm not sure he did this himself,' I say. 'For one thing we didn't see any medical kit lying around in that house. Someone did it for him and left.'

Thread removed, Agatha drops it into an evidence bag and has a good look at the wound. 'This is what killed him all right.' She sounds delighted to have reached a conclusion.

The second surprise comes when she turns him onto his stomach. 'Well, aren't you a man of mystery,' she says, the uplift in her tone making my heart hop a little. 'Look, Lucy. There's going to be a bit of competition as to what killed this fella.'

There is a huge gash right in the middle of Jerry's back, on his spine.

Agatha bends over, prods and pokes. 'Chop wound,' she says. 'It penetrated deep into the body without slicing. That tells me it had a narrow blade but a heavy head. And the direction,' she looks up at me, 'linear.' A moment as she ponders and I feel a chill creep over me. I know what she's going to say before she says it.

'Someone threw an axe at his back, which knocked him down.'

Matt gulps.

Finally, after about four hours, she declares the PM finished. Peeling off her gloves, she says, 'I'll give William another report in the morning and you'll have the full one in about six weeks. Anything important, I'll be in touch. But to summarise, he died about five days ago, that'd be the first of December. My guess is that the axe blow caused him to topple. He fell flat onto his face, which explains the broken nose and teeth and the bits of dirt embedded in them. After wounding him with the axe, it appears that his assailant then pulled it from his back, flipped him over and inflicted the knife wound to the iliac artery. Was it deliberate or just lucky chance? Who knows? Someone, maybe the assailant, attempted to sew it up again. The knife wound is six centimetres in length and three centimetres in width. Vertical with a sharp superior end and a curved inferior end. It went in forwards and then upwards – see the way the skin goes up here,' She invites me to look, so out of some sort of ingrained politeness, I do. 'So that knife, right, cut skin, tissue and the stomick, where it severed the iliac artery. A deep wound. It would have caused extensive and quick blood loss.' She must see a queasy look on Matt's face because she flaps a hand, and says, 'Anyway, to sum up, he was not murdered in that house. It most likely happened in or near the car because I believe that was like a fecking abattoir.'

'Yep.'

'If the assailant knew what he was doing, which, honestly, I suspect he did, he may have dodged the blood spray. There you go. Has it been helpful?' She looks from one to the other of us with her dark brown eyes.

'Very. Thank you.'

'Very,' Matt mumbles, in agreement. 'Thanks, Agatha.'

'You're both very welcome, and as for Jerry,' she turns back to the body, 'I'll keep my fingers crossed for him.'

With that she's back to chatting to Jerry, and Matt and I are free to leave.

*

THE WRATH

Matt's cheese sandwich lies uneaten, curling at the edges in the heat of the coffee shop. 'That was my first PM,' he confesses. 'I hope to Jaysus I never have to do another.'

'Doing it with Agatha is a walk in the park compared to Palmer,' I say. 'The more you hated it, the worse he'd be. You did well, Matt.'

'I may never eat again, though,' he says glumly. 'Why would anyone want to do that job?'

'Some people ask the same about us.' I've had my sandwich and am eating a cake now. Since I've hit my late forties, I crave sugar. 'It's not the best job, is it? You take a lot of abuse from people.'

'I enjoy being a guard on Achill,' Matt says. 'You know yourself the worst we get, aside from cases like this, is Eddie preaching about Jesus outside Supervalu and Malachy moaning about litter.'

Malachy is a serial complainer, though I think he just wants company.

'I'd never want to go as high as the Cig,' Matt continues. 'That fella never just has a laugh, does he? And is it my imagination or is he grumpier than usual, these days?'

'Grumpier than usual,' I admit. 'He has a lot on his mind.'

He sits back in his seat and toys with his coffee cup. 'What is the point in going so far unless it makes you happy? My mammy used to say to me, "Matt, you have to know where your grand is."' He heaves a sigh. 'Like William has obviously worked hard to get where he is and what has he got? A pile of work and no social life. What does he do for kicks?'

'Solves murders.'

Matt laughs softly but I feel sorry for William. He's been good to me and I feel a bit disloyal. But it sets me thinking. When the Cig said he had a lot going on, what did he mean? He even said it wasn't just me that was stressing him out. I can't think it's work – the only other case of note in Mayo was the Peter Fox one and a fella has been got for that. So, is it personal? Does he have a personal—

'My mammy used to say that the people who weren't happy in themselves were the ones who climbed the highest. And when I met the Cig, I flippin' knew she was right.'

If I don't shut this down I may get some more of Matt's mother's sayings and end up listening to him giving out endlessly about our boss, which I don't want to encourage. 'He's a great guard, though, very talented.' I drain my cup and point to Matt's sandwich. 'Bring that with you. You might have the stomach for it later. Let's get back to the station, see if there's anything else going on, all right?'

'Totally.' He shoves the sandwich back into its packet, folds it over and stuffs it into his pocket. 'Lead on.'

23

When we get back, Dan and Louis have just come from talking to Jerry's doctor. I find them both in the kitchen, Dan pouring himself a coffee while Louis talks loudly on the phone to someone he calls 'Babe'.

'It's either a small pig or a woman.' Dan smirks in Louis's direction.

'I'd say it's an AI companion.' I slide into the seat opposite Dan as Matt boils the kettle for us. 'Anything interesting this morning?'

'Nah. Jerry isn't on any meds so it could be from our SO, which would narrow things down nicely. According to the doctor, it's a drug used only when everything else is failing.'

So, our suspected offender is on psychosis medication. Interesting.

'You get anything?' Dan asks.

I give him a rundown of the autopsy findings and he whistles when he hears about the axe, but it's the stitches that steal the show. 'In *Rambo*, he managed to stitch up his arm himself and—'

'That is not what happened.'

'I said that too.' Matt puts a cup of tea in front of me. 'Wasn't it an epic scene?'

Across the way, Louis hangs up on his call and plonks down beside me, totally invading my space. Then he nudges me and, with a wink, asks the lads, 'Did Lucy tell yez?'

The discussion on special effects in eighties movies stops as Dan and Matt look blankly at him.

'Do you want to, Lucy, or will I?' His grin is wide and cheery and my heart plummets.

He's talking about the medal. 'Bit premature, eh?'

He ignores the warning note in my voice. 'We're up for a Scott medal!'

That's met with dumbfounded silence.

'It's for the time Lucy and me stared down the barrel of that nutter's gun. The last case we worked together, Lucy, wasn't it?'

'We're potentially up for a medal,' I clarify hastily. 'And let's not—'

Dan and Matt don't let me finish. Dan whoops and cheers while Matt takes my hand and shakes it hard. I want to find a hole to crawl into. I could kill Louis.

'What's going on here?' Jordy shuffles in with his foil-wrapped sandwiches, which will probably stink the place out the minute he opens them. 'Solve the case, did ye?'

'Lucy is up for a Scott medal.' Dan beams at me like a proud father.

'Potentially.'

'About time,' Jordy says mildly, not sounding at all surprised. But then he calls up the corridor, 'Hey, you lot in the incident room, Lucy's up for a Scott.'

'And me,' Louis pipes up. 'I'm up for one too.'

Ger and Larry pop their heads in. Ger is pink-faced with

delight. Larry slaps me on the back, saying, 'Well done. Now, while you're out saving the world, us CCTVers have a case to solve.' And off he trots, a little pissed-off, I think.

'I'm going to get us all ice-cream to celebrate.' Ger beams at me again and legs it out of the door.

No one bothers to remind him that it's December.

'How'd you find this out?' Dan asks.

'Well, I—'

'My dad told me last week,' Louis barges in. 'It wasn't even his idea. Like I'm not getting it because I'm his son, it's for our bravery. He told me that William is going to write a recommendation too and . . .'

I let Louis's words hop off me. Honestly, that last case has landed me in a whole heap of a mess. It's like I'm trying to put out fires on all fronts.

'Something break?' William looks into the room.

'Just congratulating Lucy on the Scott,' Dan says.

'And me,' Louis whimpers.

My skin prickles with embarrassment.

'*Potential* Scott,' William snaps, eyeing me in annoyance and giving Louis such a glare that he shrinks like a rasher on a pan. 'Now, last I looked, we had a murder on our hands. Our budget is going on extra hours that so far has yielded nothing. We're running out of time and all ye lot can do is yabber on about is medals and giving one another premature congratulations. You,' he shouts at Jordy, 'put away that vile-smelling lunch and do some work. What's the updates here?'

The mood in the room nose-dives.

One by one, under William's furious glare, we relay our morning's work.

I am seething at his treatment of us.

'Our biggest lead at the moment is the cars,' William says, when we're done. 'Aside from Kev, Susan, the house-to-housers and those looking at Jerry's case files, I want all hands on deck helping out with the CCTV. Anything come in on the appeal, Jordy?'

Jordy waits a moment to swallow his sandwich before answering. 'Yes, actually. One of the customers who was in the pub when Jerry and his companion were there rang in. I was coming up to see if we could get someone out to talk to him when I got side-tracked with Lucy's great news.' He says 'great' with a hint of defiance, a little slap on the wrist for William.

William takes a moment, 'Give his contact details to Lucy and Dan. Anything else?'

'Nothing.'

Ger arrives back at that moment with a handful of ice-creams. 'Aw, Cig,' he says, 'I never got one for you. You can have mine, if you like. It's just a Loop the Loop. We're celebrating Lucy's news and—'

'There is no news. There is no medal for anyone yet. Buy ice creams on your own time. Hop over to Larry anyone who has nothing better to do.' A glance at his watch. 'If ye need me, I'll be on the mobile. The Peter Fox case is wrapping up in Westport and I want to be there. Get cracking.' He stalks out.

The room breathes a sigh of traumatised relief at his exit.

'I would have got him one.' Ger hands me a Magnum with a bit of ceremony. 'A special one for you, Lucy. The rest of ye I got Loop the Loops.' The indignant look on Louis's face makes me smile.

That and the Magnum.

THE WRATH

'Hold it for me, Matt, thanks.'
I leg it after William.

He's about to get into his car and I shout, 'It wasn't me. I never told anyone about the medal. But you had no right to talk to us like that.'

He turns to me, gives a shake of his head, steps into his car and roars away.

So much for treating me with a bit of respect.

24

'You found out about the medal the other day and you never said.' Dan is a bit cross with me, I think. He moans about it all the way from the station to McLoughlin's bar where we've arranged to meet Con, our witness.

'I told you, it's not a sure thing. Louis should never have announced it.' I indicate and park up on the kerb just opposite the bar. 'The CCTV we have is from the Credit Union, there.' I point to where the building is, just to the left of the pub. 'It captured Jerry's car driving past. I reckon he parked here.'

'Or there,' Dan points to a small laneway up the side of the pub.

'Handier here,' I say.

We sit for a moment, both running through the last moments of footage we have of Jerry. Or I think we are, until Dan says, 'I thought you'd let me know at least. You don't even seem excited.'

'It's not a sure thing – I said.'

He shrugs and gets out, zipping his jacket against the sea breeze. I've hurt his feelings.

I climb out, lock the car and run around to join him. 'I

THE WRATH

honestly didn't think it was a big deal. It's a long process, a good few months at least until we know. Chances are we won't even be considered.'

He flashes me a sceptical look. 'Whatever you say,' he answers breezily, as he pushes open the door of the pub.

I heave a sigh and follow him inside.

The lounge is empty, save for Tomas, the barman we met the other day, an elderly woman with a violent blue rinse and a red-headed man, in a jacket, cap and gloves, who is squashed onto a sofa nursing a Coke. He stands up when he spots us and waves us over. He's well over six foot, very athletic-looking, arms showing biceps under his tight jacket. A fine specimen of the male species, I think appreciatively. Even his gloved hands, as he splays them on the table to lower himself back into his seat, seem well toned.

Forget Larry, this guy is next level.

'I'm Con.' His voice is a low American drawl, but there's a faint hint of Irish too, I think. 'The barman was saying y'all were lookin' for witnesses for the couple that were in here last Monday.' He points to a seat nearby. 'They was just there. It was lucky Tomas told me because I wasn't watching the news, didn't know anyone was murdered. I thought Achill was a safe haven.' His teeth are so white I bet they attract moths in the dark.

'Things like this don't usually happen.' I rush to defend my home place.

'He told me there was a kid killed in a fire a year or so ago and a woman on a—'

'Can you tell us, from the beginning, what you observed that day?' I interrupt. Jesus, that barman wouldn't want to go looking for a job in Bord Fáilte. 'Tell us everything you remember, no matter how small.'

Con leans back in his seat – well, as much as a man of his bulk can. 'The two were here when I arrived, I remember,' he begins. 'That woulda been about twelve ten. The older guy, he was in black trousers, had a red face, and his companion, I remember he had a blue jacket slung over his chair back. I sat down here, where I am now, and they sort of shot looks over at me. The old guy especially. Maybe they thought I was sitting too close, what with the pub mostly empty an' all. I said, to them, "Not many seats accommodate a man of my proportions," and we laughed and they went back to their conversation. I ordered a beer and a sandwich. It was about, well, I don't know, time passes slow in this place, but I had polished off my sandwich and had another coffee before they started arguing about something. I knew they were arguing because they were whispering and muttering, sort of intense, you know?' He doesn't wait for us to agree, but continues, 'It was a bad fight, what I could see. I wasn't trying to hear anything but I did catch a word or two, here and there.' He screws up his enormous face, eyebrows like twisted caterpillars. 'I think, though I can't be sure, that the older man had annoyed the younger man somehow because at one point I heard the young guy say, "She'd never do that." I heard that clear but the rest was all whispers. Anyway, then the young guy got up and stormed out, and the older guy sort of slumped down and, yeah, I remember there was something on the table and he put it in his pocket and after a bit he left too. That was it. But there was a bad fight of some sort. That I'm certain of.'

I press him on some of the details, encourage him to replay his morning a little more slowly, but he's obviously thought hard about what he's telling us because he doesn't remember anything new. 'Before you came in that day, did you happen to notice any vehicles parked up?'

THE WRATH

'Yep. Two parked on the kerb opposite the pub and another parked up the side. I notice cars – I'm a mechanic. The ones parked opposite, a tiny one. Black. Like a woman's car.' A glance at me. 'Not being sexist.'

Yeah, right. 'And the other?'

'I noticed that more. Scratch on the paintwork. I thought, That's gonna rust right up. Looked like someone got a nail or something and dug right in. That was a Ford. Good American car.'

'And when you left, were those cars there?'

'Nope, both gone.'

'Did you notice any others?'

'One parked up the side of the pub. There was someone in it so I didn't like to look. Blue and it was another Ford, bigger. That's all I got.'

'A Ford, you're certain?'

'Yes.'

'And you're certain there was someone in it?'

'Behind the wheel, yeah. Guy with a red hat. Medium size. But I can't tell you no more.'

Dan scrolls his phone. 'Like this?' He pulls up the CCTV footage of the third car. And, fair enough, there's a man with a red hat inside.

Con peers hard at it, bites the inside of his cheek and chews for a second. A flush appears high on his cheeks, 'Honestly, I only saw the front of it. It was an old car, though.'

'And you're sure this was the same day?'

'Yeah. I came here as I been trying out the local bars. McLoughlin's was my first one on my first full day.'

'When exactly did you leave?'

'A few minutes after your guy. I'm camping down the road there. In a camper.'

'Did you have a cap on your head by any chance?'

'Yup.' He picks one up from the seat and waves it about.

I'll have to tell Larry that we've identified the guy leaving the pub after Jerry. At least we've solved that.

'Thanks, Con.' I hand him my card. 'If you think of anything else, get in contact, will you? There's the email if you can't call, all right?'

'Sure thing.'

'Can I get your details?'

He gives me his email. 'My phone isn't working here,' he says. 'I'm hoping to pick up a SIM but I haven't yet. That's the best way to get me. Good luck.'

We leave him to his pint and head to the bar where we hand Tomas some flyers asking for information with a picture of the man in the blue jacket on it.

'Any idea who he could be?' I ask Tomas, because if the guy is local, chances are he's been into this bar.

'That's a shocking picture,' Tomas says. 'Sure that could be the pope and you wouldn't know it was him. No idea who that is.' He turns from us to hang up the poster.

Dan nudges me and says, in a whisper, 'Now he's what I'd call Scott-medal material.'

I think I've been forgiven.

25

It's early afternoon when Mick bounces in with a ream of paper and a huge grin that splits his face in two. Mick is the jumpy one, anxious, always unsure of himself, so what he has uncovered must be the mother lode.

'It's damning,' he says gaily as, with a flourish, he lays a bunch of pages in front of me. 'And, what's more, that stuff Louis found out about the credit card, with Jerry's phone records and Zak's allegation that his dad was having it off with someone, well, they put this Alan Lynch firmly in the frame for the murder.'

'You're joking!'

'Nope. Here. Have a look. I done like the Cig said.' He sits down beside me, scrunching up close, peering over my shoulder as I read the texts from Jerry and a mysterious 'A'. My space is totally invaded and I shift away, but Mick follows. 'I found the important ones.' He reaches across me and points to highlighted messages. 'Looks like Zak was spot on. Jerry was having an affair but, better than that, it was with someone from down here.'

'Zak said that too,'

'Well, these texts are from just before they moved house,' Mick says.

> 02/04 20:23
> Jerry: **Can't wait to see you.**
>
> 02/04 21:00
> A: **Oh, you'll see me all right.** 😂
>
> 02/04 21:03
> Jerry: **Is that a promise?**
>
> 02/04 21:04
> A: **Oh yeah . . .**

A look at me. 'From reading, I think Jerry forced Hazel to move here because he wanted to keep meeting this A person.'

Bastard, I think.

'Now these.' Mick points to another set of texts. 'Two days after they moved here.'

> 04/04 09:10
> Jerry: **Just waiting until Hazel goes to the shops. She's dithering.**
>
> 04/04 9:11
> A: **Push her out the door. LOL. I'm just around the corner.**
>
> 04.04 9:12
> Jerry: **Wait for me in Keel, outside Beehive. I'll make it worth it.**
>
> 04/04 9:13
> A: **Winner winner chicken dinner!**
>
> 04/04 9:15
> Jerry: **And the sex is on me.**

'It goes on like that,' Mick explains, 'Arranging meet-ups, porny exchanges. I tried calling A's number but there was no answer. Most people don't pick up on unknown callers any more.' He turns a page. 'This was the one makes me think A has to be Avril Lynch.'

> 15/10   11:40
> A: **Last night in Westport . . . amazing. How did you explain it to H?**

> 15/10   11:45
> Jerry: **I said that climbing The Booster was harder than I thought. She didn't bat an eyelid. You?**

> 15/10   12:10
> A: **Is that what you're calling me now? The Booster?** 😂 **I told A that I was working late. It's easy when you've got a job!**

> 15/10   12:13
> Jerry: 😂

'A told A,' Mick says. 'So, a couple with names beginning with A. I'd bet it's Avril and Alan. Turn over some more pages, Luce. Keep going. Right. Those ones.'

More yellow highlighter. As I start to read, he explains, 'Those texts were sent the week before Jerry was murdered. Some are to Hazel, some to the mysterious A, maybe Avril, there's one to Zak too.'

> 23/11   20:00
> Jerry: **Back in an hour, H. Just waylaid at the shops.**

> 23/11   22:00
> Jerry: **Can you call me, Zak?**

> 23/11   22:10
> Jerry: **If you won't talk, I just want to say sorry about the last time we met.**

> 23/11   22:30
> Zak: **Keep your apologies for Mam. If I see you again, I'll kill you.**

23/11 22:35
Jerry: **You've no idea what's going on.**

'Zak doesn't respond after that,' Mick explains. 'But, like, saying he'll kill his da, I thought that was interesting. And now here's these ones from a few days out.' He points down the page.

28/11 22:00
A: **See you soon. Can't wait.**

29/11 8:30
Jerry: **You need to keep your other half under control**

29/11 8:35
A: **????**

29/11 8:50
Jerry: **I think A knows.**

29/11 9:00
A: **Not a chance. Keep cool.**

'And then from the day he died.' Mick reaches across me again so that I get a faint whiff of BO and an eyeful of the back of his head. He turns over the page. 'One to Hazel telling her to take the chops out of the freezer and then these to A, sent around three o'clock.'

'That'd be after the row that we were told happened between Alan and Jerry in the pub.'

01/12 15:00
Jerry: **I am so sorry!**

01/12 15:15
A: **You should be.**

01/12 15:20
Jerry: **I shouldn't have said anything, I realise that. I'm losing it these days.**

THE WRATH

01/12   15:25
Jerry: **I was out of order.**

01/12   15:30
Jerry: **I'll drop by in a bit.**

And that's the very last text of Jerry's life.

The three of us sit for a second, turning the information over. 'These texts prove that Jerry was having an affair ...' I consider my words '... with someone called A – who more than likely lives down here or commutes to here – someone living with a person called A. And we know, almost for certain, that on the last day of his life, Jerry meets with Alan in a pub and they argue. About what?' I don't expect an answer. Instead I flick through my notebook. 'A row which results in Alan saying to Jerry, "She would never do that."'

'Jerry comes clean to Alan about the affair?' Dan throws it out. 'Alan is raging, storms out. Rings his wife, who gets back on to Jerry telling him he's ruined everything.'

That fits. 'When she doesn't reply, does Jerry go to meet her? Is Alan there? Is there a row? But he's not killed then as we have a sighting of him driving erratically at about four thirty.'

Dan and Mick nod.

'Assuming it was him driving,' Dan says.

'Yes.'

'Where did he go after he left the pub?' I turn to Mick. 'Is there a tracker on his phone?'

'Location services were turned off.'

'Crap. That's odd.'

There's silence for a second. Then, blessedly, Mick hops up to get his lunch out of the fridge. 'Fecking starving,' he says.

'Just to play another scenario,' I tease it out, 'what if it's not Avril? What if it's Abby?'

'Jerry having an affair with Zak's partner?' Dan shakes his head. 'I can't see it. And for another thing, it's Zak and Abby. A *Z* and an *A*.'

'*A* and *Z* are close to each other on the keyboard. Maybe she pressed the wrong letter. It happens.' When Dan concedes this, I continue, 'She also has a job she can travel with.'

'But she has a solid alibi for the day of the murder.'

'Yeah, but say Zak found out about the affair. Got hold of her phone. Sent a few texts. Travelled down here?'

'It's too much of a stretch.'

'It also doesn't explain the fact that it was *Alan* Jerry talked to in the pub, and we know it was Alan from the credit-card evidence, and that it was Alan who said, "She wouldn't do that."'

That's Mick.

Dan and I look at him, impressed.

'I'm reading all I can on the case,' he says. 'Susan isn't the only one with a bit of ambition.' He pinks up and peers at his hands.

'Okay, good point,' I concede. 'I was only seeing how it played out. Still doesn't rule Zak out for murder, though.'

'No, but the evidence is stronger for Alan at the moment.'

'Yep.' I gather up everything as neatly as I can and head on into William.

'So, in short, we have an unidentified male in the pub with our injured party on the day he was murdered,' William says. 'We now suspect strongly that it was Alan Lynch, Jerry's friend. We know this because Alan paid by credit card for his lunch in that pub at that time. We have an eyewitness who says that our IP and the suspected Alan Lynch argued and that Alan stormed out of the pub. Alan has denied seeing Jerry that day, but he has a car and a jacket that match our CCTV images of the person caught with Jerry. We also have phone text evidence of an affair between Jerry and a person known as A, who has a partner called A.'

'That's it.'

'And Alan Lynch's wife is called Avril.'

'Yep.'

William sits back in the chair and laces his fingers behind his head. 'There's a lot of people in Mayo whose names begin with A,' he finally says, 'so that's thin enough. But the lie about not seeing Jerry is a bit damning.' Another moment of contemplation. 'What do you think?'

'I don't know the Lynches so I can't offer any insights there, but I agree, lying about seeing him is damning.'

'He'll say his credit card was stolen.'

'He will. We could try for an ID with Con, the American witness?'

'Right, try that, and we'll see tomorrow if Larry manages to match the registration numbers on the CCTV with Alan's car. We'll know almost for sure that it was him then and we can arrest him. Good work and tell Mick well done.'

'Why don't you tell him yourself? You owe the team that much.'

Then before he can react, I leave.

26

It's late afternoon and outside the rain has lifted and the sun is poking fingers through the sheets of grey sky. An icy breeze whistles through the cracks in the old station windows as I wrap a cardigan around my shoulders and try to get up the enthusiasm for another hour of CCTV footage. Ten of us have been tracking, with little success, the route of the three cars of interest. Larry has managed to isolate a number 8 on the Corsa plate, which just so happens to match a number 8 on Alan's reg.

A ping as a text pops into my inbox. It's from Kev: *Met Con in pub again. Talked to him. He wasn't one hundred per cent sure on the ID but picked Alan and another picture out as potentials. Added that the more he thought about it they were having a right go at each other.*

Con isn't totally sure, so I'll have to let that one pass. Damn anyway.

I turn back once more to the endless fuzzy images parading across the screen.

It's a relief when my mobile buzzes some time later. I'm expecting a call about the technical examination of Jerry's car.

THE WRATH

'At last, guys,' I say, holding the phone between shoulder and ear, pen at the ready. 'What have you got for me?'

A moment of silence before: 'Lucy? This is Sylvia, Eddie's sister. He's gone missing again.'

I'm instantly irritated, 'Sylvia, I'm on an—'

'He hasn't been home the last few nights. I was wondering if you could get one of the lads to look for him.'

Sylvia calls me every so often with this. She knows she should ring the front desk but believes it's quicker to do it through me because I grew up here and I'd have pull. Or so she thinks. 'I'm flat out here with the murder investigation,' I answer. 'I'll get one of the lads to ring you later and—'

'No. No. Please, Lucy, I need help. He's — he's not well at all.' She's almost crying and I feel bad for dismissing her. Ever since their parents died, she's done her best to mind Eddie. She'd gone from ignoring the problem to allowing it, in the last few years, to consume her. I think it was when Eddie almost lost a toe to frostbite that she finally got him the help he needed. And he'd been all right for a while, but in the past year or so, he's begun to unravel once more.

'All right, give me the details. I'll see what I can do.'

'Thank you. Thank you.' She swallows hard to get herself under control. 'He normally turns up here when he's hungry, but he hasn't eaten in the house since he came back at some hour three days ago, half dressed, agitated, roaring about the Devil. Telling me to get out. I ended up having to leave the house to keep him quiet. When I came back later that day, he had the place destroyed.'

'Destroyed?'

'Clothes pulled out of the presses, drawers opened, I would have thought I'd been burgled only for I knew it was him.'

'That was the last time you saw him?'

'No. I saw him the next day outside Supervalu. He was filthy. Talking nonsense. On his way somewhere, told me he was purging the Devil. I told him he needed to take his medication, but he said it wasn't working. He threw it away, Lucy.' Her voice catches.

Medication?

'He's convinced that the Devil has poisoned his eyes and his feet. His toes were hurting. I haven't seen him since. I'm really worried, Lucy.'

I grab a pen. 'You're saying that the last time Eddie was in your house was three days ago? That he ransacked it?'

'That's right.'

'Was anything missing?'

'I didn't look. And—'

'Can you check?'

'I tidied up, I didn't miss anything.'

It's a long shot but worth a try. 'Can I ask if you have stripy blue and yellow sheets?'

'Yes.' She sounds surprised. 'How would you know that?'

I click my fingers, motion for the lads in the room to quieten. I put Sylvia on hold as I explain to the team who Sylvia is and what she has just told me. 'I'm putting you on speaker now, Sylvia,' I say, then ask, 'Can you check if those sheets are there now?'

'Sure. But what has this to do with Eddie?' We hear her moving from one room to the next and the sound breaks up as she begins rummaging about, muttering to herself. Finally, after about five minutes, she comes back on the line. 'Both sheets are missing.' This is followed by a soft cry. 'Have you found him? Is he wrapped in them? Is he all right?'

THE WRATH

The atmosphere in the room tenses at what we've just uncovered.

'Sylvia, as far as we know he's still alive, all right. Now, I'm going to need you to calm down,' I click my pen. 'Tell me about Eddie's medication.'

'He's not taking it, I told you.'

'What does he take?'

'Oh, sorry.' More footsteps, more rummaging. 'Clozapine.'

And there it is. The tablet we found at the scene. Eddie. The sad little lad in school. The boy who'd lost both his parents.

Feck it anyway.

How does he fit into all this?

'Thanks, Sylvia. We'll send someone out to get DNA samples from Eddie's things, if that's all right.'

'Why?'

'It's procedure, and we'll look for him as a priority, okay?' She keeps quiet: she knows something's up. Any other time, we'd just ask the lads to keep an eye out for him. 'If he arrives back in the meantime, do let us know and, Sylvia, based on what you've said, he may be a danger to you so don't let him in.'

'He'd never harm me.' She backtracks rapidly. 'What are you saying?'

As she's growing ever more panicked, I scribble out a Post-it for Dan to ring William with an update. See what he wants us to do. Maybe he'll initiate a full-scale search. Maybe he'll want something more concrete before he does. As Dan gets on the phone, I cut back to Sylvia, halting her anxious questions. 'Where would Eddie go? Would you know his favourite haunts?'

'What are you going to do to him?' Raw fear for her brother.

'Find him. Bring him back.'

She hesitates but she knows we're her best bet. 'He likes the bogs, knows them well. He sometimes just sits there, staring. He has a couple of pairs of binoculars, I bought him a pair and the other pair he has are our father's. He uses them a lot. I think he likes Dooagh and around there. From when he was a little lad, he loved it there.' Her voice catches in a sob. 'I do be always afraid he'll jump into the sea one day. And he likes the abandoned houses too. Minding them, he says, for the people who'll never come back. I just leave him at it. It keeps him happy and out of my hair.'

I steel myself against her pain. 'Grand. We may need you later, so stay by the phone.'

'He'll be all right, won't he?'

'I'll do my best to make sure he is.' I know it's not enough. If Eddie proves difficult, if he becomes a danger, I can't help him. 'Thanks, Sylvia.'

She hangs up.

'Right,' I say, to the lads, who are all looking at me like dogs after treats, 'Dan is talking to William. Larry, take a skeleton crew and keep up with the CCTV. Let's see now if we can spot Eddie on anything as well.' I yank my jacket from my chair and pull it on. 'I'll let ye know what's happening.'

Dan is in the kitchen, giving William an update over the phone. There's a lot of 'uh-huh' and 'right, right' being said. Finally, he turns to me. 'He wants to talk to you.'

I take the phone, press it to my ear. 'Cig?'

'This lad took sheets matching the description of the ones we found around the wound, is that right?'

'Yes, and he's also taking the same medication that we found on the ground near the car. He owns a pair of binoculars and hangs around the old houses, his sister says. The timing fits with the taking of the sheets too, three days ago.'

'Did the sister notice any blood on his clothes?'

'She didn't say.' Damn, I should have asked. 'He's filthy, though, so she might not have noticed.'

'All right, let's keep any search low key for now. You know the area. Get a map, make a list of vacant houses and their locations up that way and put a team together to check them out. I'll sort a couple of drones. Task Jordy and Matt to take a car to do registration checks on vehicles entering the Atlantic drive. That way we can keep a discreet eye on who is going in and out. And send someone to get DNA from the sister. We can run that against the scene.'

'Grand. And if we find him at one of the houses?'

'Call me.'

I turn to Dan. 'Let's get cracking.'

27

Drone footage seems to confirm some activity near an abandoned house up by Lough Acorrymore. Pictures sent to my mobile show the unmistakable image of a figure peering out of a broken window. There's another shot of a person sitting outside in the rain, head in hands.

Dan and I have positioned ourselves about ten metres from the tumbledown stone building. We need to establish without doubt that it's Eddie inside and not a tourist. You'd be surprised at how many people think dilapidated buildings are something to be explored.

Rain is bouncing off our hooded jackets, and in the rapidly darkening day the bungalow ahead is a fuzzy blur, shape-shifting through the deluge. Dan and I are taking turns at looking through binoculars at the cottage. It's Dan's turn now. He has a remarkable ability to remain perfectly still while I find that I have to move every so often or my legs stiffen up.

Bloody age.

'Looks like something's stirring,' Dan says, and I pull out my own binoculars. They're wet and slippery. As I adjust the lens, the cottage solidifies. It takes a moment of scanning across the building before I locate the doorway. A chaotic figure, dressed in over-large clothes, stands framed in it. He's rocking to and fro and shaking his head.

We wait, still not sure. Let's see your face, I urge silently. Come on, look up.

And the figure does.

'That's him.'

Within the hour, a tactical team has assembled, the road has been closed down in both directions and Sylvia is on standby in case we need her. A negotiator is on her way. The lifeboat crew is on alert and two ambulances wait further down the road. Plans are being drawn up as to how we should approach this. Eddie, meanwhile, has retreated inside, oblivious.

He will see nothing until we want him to.

I'm on the edge of things now, waiting for the signal to go in. Dan is conversing with one of the lads from the armed support unit, and I'm waiting on William to show up. My phone rings. 'Hello, DS Lucy Golden.'

'This is Graham. We did the technical examination on the Jerry Loftus car? You were asking about a credit card?'

What timing. I roll my eyes. 'That's right.'

'We haven't found one.'

'Marvellous.' I hang up, thinking how like the Cig I sound.

As I watch the final preparations for Eddie's arrest fall into place, there's a buzz in my veins and my head zings. This is why I do this job, I think.

This is the reason.

28

William arrives five minutes later. I watch his approach, phone to ear as usual. I can't make out what he's saying but he isn't happy. He gesticulates wildly, shaking his head, then standing still and closing his eyes. What's up? I wonder. Surely this is a great breakthrough.

He jabs his phone off, looks at it for a second and pockets it. I feel a sudden dart of concern for him. There is hopelessness in his demeanour, but before I can analyse it, he gets himself back under control and crosses towards me. Indicating the lads on the ASU, he asks, 'Almost ready?'

'Twenty minutes or so,' I answer. 'Dan is bringing the negotiator.'

'Good.'

'Did something happen? I saw you on the phone.'

'That was about the Westport case that's finishing up, nothing to do with this.'

'The one you rushed off to earlier?'

'The Peter Fox case, that's the one.' He says it grimly, like it's a bad memory.

'I heard on the radio that they were charging someone.'

'They did.'

'You don't seem that pleased?'

He shoots me a look before laughing slightly. He doesn't reply, though.

So, he was telling the truth when he said it's not just me being nominated for the Scott medal that has him in such foul humour.

'What happened?' I brace myself. 'You can't keep taking it out on my team.'

He flinches. 'I'm not.'

I don't dignify that with a response. Instead I turn away and focus my attention on the cottage that is rapidly disappearing into the gloom of late evening. Silence is my best bet, I reckon. I almost smile as I hear him sigh. Then he says, 'The young lad they're charging, he's barely eighteen. He had nothing to do with it.'

I turn around. 'What?'

'He pleaded guilty. His DNA was all over the scene but he didn't do it. I know it, the lads know it, but this kid, he knew all the details, even ones that weren't released to the media. He says he was off his head on drugs, that he just killed Peter Fox, that he didn't know what he was doing.'

'Maybe it's true.'

'Nah. Way too much forensics at the scene, it led us straight to him. It was cut and dried, Lucy.'

And I know what he's saying so I say it for him. 'Too easy.'

'Yeah. One would almost think he'd agreed to be set up for it before it happened. A convenient hair of his found on the body. It reminded me of the murder of Daniel Coyle in 2011, Jude Manly in 2013 and Adam Lewis in 2019. And do you know what they all have in common?'

'Nick Flannery.'

'Yep.'

Nick Flannery was a man we'd encountered last year. A gangland criminal from Limerick. We'd helped him solve the murder of his daughter and grandchild. He is one of those people who wear violence like a suit.

'I say this to the team, to the super, but no one wants to know. A solve is a solve. It looks good for the stats. The young fella is going down.' A second later he adds, 'Flannery is laughing at us. At me. I wouldn't mind but I bloody went out on a limb for him when his daughter was killed. On a bloody limb.'

Why would he go on a limb for that thug?

'I've done background on the young lad who confessed,' William tells me. 'He's got a habit all right, got beaten up a few years back because he owed some fella a few bob. There's never been a whiff of violence from him, and we're supposed to believe that he went out and killed a man.'

'Was money missing at the scene?'

'Of course. Sure they were setting him up for it, weren't they? There was DNA from two other lads on the body but, hey presto, they turned up, said they'd been asking after a car the guy was selling. CCTV shows them in the area, shows them outside his house. They're Flannery's men. Bloody laughing at me.' His tone is one of quiet fury.

'So, what happens?'

'Nothing.' He massages his eyes with the heel of his hands. 'Whatever way I look at it, it's all stitched up tight. I'd love to know what Flannery's promised him.'

'If you find that out, you can promise him more.'

'He won't go against that fella.'

He's right. It'd take someone far stronger than an eighteen-year-old kid to go up against that head case.

'What can you do?' I ask. 'There's no point beating yourself up over it.'

He dips his head. There's something more. Something in his demeanour reminds me of myself. And slowly it dawns on me. He's going to act.

'Cig?' I take the liberty of touching his sleeve. He meets my gaze with his ice-blue one and for some weird reason my heart flips. What the hell? I want to tell him to be careful, to let it go, but my words are stuck. How can I tell him not to take action when I'd once done it myself?

'I got into this job to get justice for the right people,' William says. 'And—'

'The negotiator is here.' Jude, the tactical leader, joins us, and I whip my hand away, flushing. 'We've the sister primed. We're going to go hail him. Stand by.' He marches away, back to assume command.

The moment, whatever it was, is gone.

'This is it, then.' William, his eyes not meeting mine, peels himself off the wall where he's been leaning and prepares to follow Jude. He hesitates slightly. 'What I told you, it's just between you and me, eh?' He taps his nose.

'Peter Fox probably deserved what was coming to him.'

'Yeah, but that kid doesn't.' And he's gone, head dipped against the breeze.

Across the grass, a dishevelled Sylvia paces nervously, her arms wrapped about herself. Darkness has come, the sun making its way to the other side of the world, but up here, lights will be switched on, illuminating everything for metres around. And then, just as I think it, the lights come up, dazzling in their intensity, showing every blade of grass, every loose rock and pebble between us and the ramshackle cottage, which has now been surrounded by armed detectives. The boggy brown landscape beyond the house lies in a cloak of darkness.

'Eddie, it's Sylvia. Are you in there?' Her voice blasts through the evening. She sounds strong, composed. 'Can you come out, please? There are people here who want to talk to you.'

For a moment, there is nothing but the whip of wind, and then a keening sound, eerie in the night, rises from the cottage. The hairs on my arms stand to attention.

'Eddie. It's Sylvia. Your sister. Please come out.'

The keening grows. 'The Devil is here.' His voice carries in the silence. It sounds strange. Strangled. A long, low moan. I suck in my breath.

'Then come out and leave him there,' Sylvia says. 'We can fight him together. These people are here to help you.'

His shadow flits by the window. 'I saw him. Fiery red. He did things. "Blessed are they who hunger and thirst for justice for they shall have their fill. Blessed are the clean of heart and –" oh, oh . . .' He starts to wail. 'He made me forget. He made me forget. He made me forget.' And more howling.

'Eddie, do you remember what Mam used to sing to you when you'd get scared of the man under the bed? Remember?' Her voice wobbles, hiccups with tears, then wavers as she croons, '"Who's that man scaring my man, don't give in, we can fight him, so we can. A biff and a boff, knock his head off. He'll soon give in 'cause we shall win!"'

There's something heartbreaking about the bravery in that song. Something painful in Sylvia's singing of it here, in this

THE WRATH

godforsaken place, with Eddie's reedy voice joining in. I swallow hard, shake my head and try to gain a bit of distance. Eddie's mother died of an overdose when he was quite young yet she made up that song for him to comfort him.

Sylvia starts the tune again, then stops abruptly. Bending over, her arms about her stomach, she sobs like she's vomiting. I have to look away.

From the house, Eddie continues to sing.

'Don't hurt him.' I hear Sylvia's choked plea. 'He's a good man, he's just . . . he's just lost.'

An image assails me, brutal in its suddenness. Eddie in the schoolyard. My father has turned up, out of the blue, to collect me: he's bringing me out on the boat and I'm so excited. Eddie is excited for me. He's waving and waving and I'm embarrassed, even though I'm only eight. I don't want Eddie to be excited for me. I don't want people to think I know this weird boy. 'He's a good lad,' my dad whispers to me. 'He's just lost for a bit of affection.'

I'm brought back to the present when Eddie stops singing and begins that eerie keening again.

'We can help you,' Sylvia shouts, stronger now. 'Keep singing, Eddie, let the people in to help.'

A moment later, Eddie shouts back, sounding terrified, 'It's different this time.'

'Every time is different. I know that. We can do it together.'

'He's here. He's here. I saw him.'

'Ask him what he wants, Eddie.'

Shadowy figures move silently across the roof of the building.

'Evil. Death,' Eddie howls. 'The Devil is coming. He wants to consume our souls, slash our stomachs, he wants to make us bleed and the force is here and I can't see for red and the man is begging and he's a sacrifice.' His voice drops and it's hard to make out what he's saying. The armed men on the roof ready themselves.

The negotiator whispers in Sylvia's ear, and she says, 'Can me and my friends come in and talk to him, Eddie?'

'"Wrath does not come without warrant. It is deserved. Vengeance is mine, says the Lord. I will take vengeance and I will—"'

The men on the roof drop down into the building.

As Eddie's voice pitches even higher, more men run towards the front door, which yields easily.

Across the bog, we watch as lights move around inside the house. There's more of that eerie howling, some shrieks but no shots. Finally, after what seems a long time, we get the call that it's clear to enter.

William, Dan and I run across the bog as Sylvia struggles to accompany us.

We hear roaring and shouting from inside the house. Eddie, eyes blazing wildly, is rolling about on the floor, legs kicking, hands cuffed. His left wrist drips blood. 'Satan disguises himself as an angel of light,' he roars, eyes wild. 'You shall not kill me for I shall be reborn.'

It's distressing to see him like that.

'We need you to relax,' one of the men instructs calmly. 'We will help you.'

'No. Nooooo.' His legs flail.

'You can't go arresting him.' The man turns to me as William leaves my side and moves carefully behind the group. His tread is soft. 'That lad needs serious medication.'

'I give no opportunity to the Devil, begone. Begone. I am the Lord your God. If you believe in me you will live for ever.'

THE WRATH

Eddie is tasered from behind.

His body jerks and stills. His final kick sends a knife spinning across the room. A medic is called in.

I toe the knife. 'I think we may have found our murder weapon.'

29

Eddie is sedated before being treated for non-life-threatening injuries at the scene. He's loaded onto an ambulance and Sylvia, who is in tears and shivering violently, hops up into the vehicle to join him.

'He'll be taken care of,' I say, but she fixes me with a blank stare and turns away.

I think she feels I betrayed her.

I bag and tag the knife.

As the cottage is being sealed off, William tells Dan and me that we can leave. 'I'll see ye in the morning. We should have an update on Eddie's mental state by then.'

We bid him goodbye and, as we head towards the DDU car that'll bring us back to the station, I suddenly realise how cold I am, the rain jacket I'd been wearing no match for the wild weather. My fingers are numb, my face frozen.

'I find it hard to believe he did it.' Dan voices what has been nagging me. 'For one thing, he's so far gone, he'd never have been organised enough.'

'He may have just got lucky.' I play Devil's advocate as I slide in behind the wheel and fire the engine. My frozen hands fumble with the gearstick. 'And don't forget the medication he takes, and sheets identical to those missing from his house were found at locations associated with the crime.' I put the heater on full blast and pull off.

'Maybe he came across the incident?'

'Or, as Sylvia said, he threw his pills away and had a psychotic breakdown, thought Jerry was the Devil.'

'Yep, that might fly,' Dan agrees. 'We won't get any answers until he comes around, though.'

My phone pings with a text and I pick it up.

'I'd give you a fine for using your phone while driving,' Dan warns mock-sternly.

I pay him no heed, using one hand to steer the car and the other to flick through my contacts to dial Larry to see what he wants.

'Jesus Christ,' Dan mutters.

'Easy mistake to make,' Larry chortles, as he answers at the other end. 'Did you get my text, Luce?'

'I did but I didn't bother reading it. What's the story?'

'Two digits identified on the car now.'

'Great work. Keep going.' I hang up. 'Eddie and Alan are neck and neck as suspects.'

'With Zak a close second.'

And we groan. Dan's phone pings.

'D'you fancy dinner in my place?' Dan asks, reading it. 'Fran says he's made a curry.'

'Do you even have to ask?' I swerve and take the road to his place.

*

'Damn, Delores is here,' Dan moans, as I pull into his driveway, tyres crunching on gravel as I coast to a stop. 'She was meant to be out.'

I love Delores. Well, at a distance. I wouldn't fancy living with her because she's exhausting. Non-stop talk, even in her sleep, Dan informed me once.

She greets us with a delighted clap of hands as we enter the house. 'There he is, my son-in-law,' she chirrups, before turning to me. 'Hello, Lucy. How are you? How's your mother? I was only saying to Fran that I haven't seen Lucy's mother in a while. Wasn't I only saying that, Fran?'

'Only saying what, Mam?' Fran shouts from the kitchen where presumably he is elbow deep in curry-making.

'Only saying that I haven't seen Mags in a while?'

'Yes,' Fran shouts back.

Dan shoots me a look of comical despair. He's a man who likes solitude and quiet and time to think. Delores is someone who blows all that apart.

'Where is Fred tonight?' Dan asks, as we divest ourselves of our jackets. Taking mine, he hangs it on a coat-stand just inside the door.

'With his daughter. She doesn't like me, so I didn't go.'

'Their loss is our gain,' I say, and ignore a dig in the ribs from my work partner. 'How could she not like you?'

Dan's house is a quirky mix of old cottage and designer furniture. It smells of food and warmth and soap.

'I suppose she's a bit put out about our relationship.' Delores's voice dips: 'Like some other people.' She gives a not-so-subtle gesture in Fran's direction and misses the glower he gives in return. 'But, as I said, I have my life to live and, as I don't interfere in anyone else's, I don't expect interference in mine. Isn't that right, Lucy?'

'Something smells good.' I sidestep the question. 'What kind of a curry is that, Fran?'

'Aubergine and chickpea,' he says. 'I thought we'd have a vegetarian night.'

'Far from aubergines and chickpeas you were reared,' Delores mutters fondly. Patting the seat beside her for me to sit down, she asks, 'How are you, Lucy? Tell me now, how's your mother?' Then before I can answer, another thought strikes her: 'Did you ever do speed-dating?'

'Eh – no, I never did.' I'm wrong-footed by her ability to change gears and subjects. 'Thanks, Fran,' I say, as he hands me a bowl of curry. It smells good. I pick up my fork, about to dig in.

'It's great fun. That's how I met Fred. A charity thing. What you do is you have a few minutes to impress the men. They all take their turns coming to talk to you. I impressed loads of them but only one of them impressed me and that was Fred. He's nice, isn't he, Daniel?'

'Uh-huh,' Dan says, which could mean anything. 'Naan bread, anyone?'

'He's a try-hard.' That's Fran.

'Would you do it, Lucy?' Delores valiantly ignores her son. 'Your mother was saying the last time we met that she'd love to see you settled.'

Dan starts to cough on the bread.

'Mam, stop!' Fran pleads. 'Jesus. Sorry, Lucy.'

I could kill my mother. 'I'm very happy as I am.' Even as I say it, I know it's not quite true. But what's the alternative? To go out with someone and never fully trust them? 'And even if I was going to date, I wouldn't do speed-dating.'

Her face drops and she pulls ever so slightly away from me. 'It's better than Tinder.' She's insulted.

'You've used Tinder?' Fran is appalled. 'Please tell me you haven't used Tinder.'

'I tried but they're a young bunch on it.' She looks at me. 'There are dating apps for older women I was thinking of exploring but sure I've Fred now. Your mother—'

'Honestly, Delores, no offence but I don't want to speed-date. I'm very glad you found Fred.'

'So am I!' Her sunny mood restored, she regales us with tales of how Fred is very useful. 'He can turn his hand to anything. He made a lovely rocking chair for his daughter there about three months ago. It was to help her accept us but it didn't work.' She spreads her arms as if to say she wouldn't be here if it had. 'Still, she loved the chair anyway.'

I let her talk pass over me, eating the curry without really tasting it and trying valiantly to ignore all her hints about the different ways to find love. A mild depression settles about me like dust.

On the drive home, I banish Delores's words from my head by concentrating on the case. I think about our three suspects as I pull into my driveway, and as I raid the fridge for cheese to go with the acidic gone-off wine left open on the kitchen table. Zak, angry at his dad with no alibi; Alan Lynch, who allegedly had an argument with Jerry in the hours before his death; and now Eddie, mentally ill, disorganised, whose DNA has been found all over the scene and whose medication was found near the car.

I hope it's not Eddie.

Yet Zak doesn't convince me as a suspect.

THE WRATH

Alan, maybe, if we can find out what the row was about.

A ping from my personal mobile jerks me out of my reverie.

On that case we discussed earlier, I hope I don't need to remind you that it's just between us.

I long to reply that he is reminding me but, in the end, I chicken out and send back a thumbs-up.

Knowing I won't sleep, I open my laptop and access the Peter Fox file, just to see how damning the evidence is against that young man.

30

I'm glad I'm early to conference the following morning because twenty minutes after I arrive, the room has filled with the whole team and it's stuffy and overheated. Someone has put tinsel around the windows. I wonder how they found the time. The walls are weeping condensation. Outside the sky and the ocean merge into a glowering grey.

There is a hum of celebratory anticipation, though, a sense that maybe the case has broken open a little.

'As ye're aware, we arrested a Mr Eddie O'Shea last night under section twelve of the Mental Health Act in a derelict house not far from the cottage where the body of Jerry Loftus was discovered.' William indicates the areas on a magnified map that has been tacked to the wall. A red circle shows where the car was found. 'Eddie O'Shea, whom most of you will know, has been taken to hospital for a psych evaluation. We won't be getting anywhere near him for the next couple of days at least.'

One or two detectives groan but we need to tread carefully. It is imperative that Eddie is of sound enough mind when we speak to him so that whatever he tells us will stand up in court. Because he has suffered a psychotic episode, whatever he tells us will have to be checked and double-checked anyway.

'Until we can talk to him, we'll focus on the areas of the investigation we have control over. If these lead us towards Eddie as our main SO, happy days, but I will not tolerate any bias. Let the information take you where it takes you.' A picture of the knife retrieved last night is projected onto a screen. 'This was taken from Eddie last night. It's been sent for testing. On a preliminary examination, it matches the description Agatha gave of the murder weapon. No axe located, though. The DNA retrieved on the sheets is being run against Eddie's DNA as a matter of urgency today. Our IP's car was TE'd yesterday. What have we got on that?'

Mick hops up. 'I've got the technical-examination report here. In plain language, the car was a 2015 Ford Focus. On the exterior bodywork, a deep scratch was observed in the passenger side of the car, most likely caused by a sharp-pointed object, a nail or a key being dragged along the surface.' He looks up. 'I know that mark was there prior to the incident but I'm including it anyway, especially if it was deliberate.'

'Good call,' William remarks. 'We'll ask Hazel or her son if they can remember when it happened. Kev and Susan you're on that.' He gestures for Mick to continue.

'Now, Cig, I have exciting stuff to tell you but I'll do the boring bits first.'

'There are boring bits?' William is genuinely baffled.

Beside me Dan stifles a chuckle.

'Well, maybe some bits are more *exciting* than others,' Mick offers, and hurries on before William can respond. 'The car was in working order. Besides the scratch, no external damage to the bodywork. Blood, Jerry's, was located on the exterior driver's door, on the front wheelbase, on the tyres, suggesting that he bled out both inside and outside the car. A number of red fibres were found inside the vehicle. They're being tested today. There were four sets of prints found. Comparison tests were run and Jerry's and Hazel's have been identified. Two others are as yet unidentified.' Then he pauses, taking his moment, and I hope to God it's worth it because William has a short fuse where Mick is concerned. 'As we know, the location identifier on Jerry's phone was switched off but when his car's onboard computer was examined the satnav from the car records that after Jerry left McLoughlin's he didn't go straight to Croaghaun. What we know now is that he drove his car towards Keel and stopped in for two hours, right here.' He points to an area on the map just outside Keel. 'And it's interesting for two reasons, first that Kev and Susan confirmed it's in the area where Alan and Avril Lynch live. Now maybe his car broke down. Maybe he drove over and waited in to see if he could talk to one of them alone.'

William smiles. 'Excellent,' he says.

Someone claps and Mick's chest puffs up. I'm delighted for him.

William is pleased, I can tell by the satisfied way he rocks from the balls of his feet to the heels. 'I believe we were trying to get an ID on Alan yesterday from an American tourist who'd been in McLoughlin's. Any joy?'

'No,' Kev pipes up. 'He was torn between two, one of them being Alan Lynch. But the other auld fella picked him out. A Paddy Jackson?' He looks across at me and Dan. 'Ye said he was there in the pub on that day too?'

Jesus, I'd forgotten about Paddy. He's a rampant alcoholic, though.

THE WRATH

'I know Paddy from coming into the station,' Kev continues, 'always a bit drunk, but I caught him on his way into the pub yesterday. Sober he was. Showed him a few pictures and he picked Alan out as quick as you'd pick the nut caramel in the box of Roses.'

There's a bit of a dumbfounded silence at the analogy.

'I hate the nut one,' Susan breaks it. 'Coffee all the way.'

'Orange one for me.'

'He picked it out like his favourite chocolate,' Kev amends, to mocking applause. 'Excuse me for trying to inject some flair into my investigative reports.'

More laughter.

'That was a good bit of initiative, Kev,' I say. 'Well done.'

'Ta. I just did it on me lunch break there yesterday.'

'Okay, so that all looks pretty nasty for Alan Lynch,' William remarks. 'How's the ID on the black Corsa going, Larry? Is it Alan's car, do we think?'

'This was the clearest image of the plate I could get.'

A fuzzy still is projected onto the screen. Larry zooms in on the reg. 'If you look you can just make out a three and an eight.' He zooms in some more.

'I think the eight is a stretch,' William remarks.

'I can see them,' Kev pipes up, and then, of course, the whole room breaks up into a discussion of what they can and can't make out. Someone says they can see an R, which Larry loudly declaims as the eight.

'Anyway,' Larry talks over the hubbub, 'Alan's reg has both those numbers in it, in those exact places, so I guess what we do regarding him is your call now, Cig.'

'We have a blue jacket, a partial registration on a black Corsa, the fact that Jerry was almost two hours parked in the vicinity of their house on the day he was murdered. We know he wasn't murdered at that point as he was spotted driving erratically at four thirty later that day. Though was it him in the car? We have Alan's credit card used in the bar when he told Kev and Susan that he was fishing all day. That's suspicious. And we have eye-witness accounts of a row between Jerry and Alan in the pub. All right, here is what we'll do. Louis, do you have a list of the transactions for that card?'

'Yes, Cig. The bank sent that on, along with the card's ID.'

'Good. Were there any transactions in the days prior to the day of the murder?'

'Yes. A few.'

'Good. That'll dilute the I-got-my-card-stolen defence they all use. I think we've enough. Let's arrest Alan and his wife. And draw up a warrant to search the house. Larry and Ben, you head out and bring them in. Lucy and Dan, prepare for the interview of Alan Lynch here later. Bring Avril Lynch to Westport and we'll arrange for her to be interviewed there. Anything else?'

'There's a bit more on forensics,' Mick says. 'That KaRMa note found in Jerry's car. The paper used is a generic A4 80 gsm. Nothing special about it or anything that stood out. One thing they did note was this.' He projects an image of the KaRMa letter onto the screen and enlarges it. 'That K,' Mick says, 'if you look carefully, you can see, just under the letter, what appears to be a year?'

Once more the whole room leans forward, squinting.

'I need glasses.' William is annoyed.

'I can see it,' Kev announces. '2023.'

'You've some eyesight,' Louis remarks, sounding miffed.

THE WRATH

'No one in our family ever wore glasses,' Kev tells us. 'Except for my mother's brother but he was like the black sheep anyway.'

'What's wrong with glasses?' Jordy asks. 'How did that make him the black sheep?'

'That wasn't what made him the—'

'Can we concentrate for a second,' William says sharply, and Kev's mouth snaps closed. 'Mick? You were saying?'

'Yeah, right, well, Forensics think this K was taken from a 2023 magazine. So, like, well, that's it.'

I pull out my phone. Call up a few images. Zoom in. 'It's *OK!* magazine,' I say. 'If you look, the date of publication runs underneath the *OK!* part with the year just underneath the *K*.' I pass my phone up the room and William stares at it, looks at the screen.

'The typeface looks the same,' he allows. Then, to me, 'So what are we saying? This letter is two years old or that the sender is a hoarder of newspapers?'

'Either one,' Mick says. 'Other than that, there was nothing to identify where the rest of the letters used in KaRMa came from. There was a partial fingerprint and it's being run against the ones we have already.'

'Larry, any more for me? What about that second car? The blue one that was parked up the side-street.'

'Nothing yet. Though that tourist, Con, said he saw it too and that it may have been an old Ford.'

'Good. Lucy?'

I give the room a run-down on what the PM uncovered yesterday and on the rest of the developments.

And Kev adds that he has contacted all the GY Gyms and none of them saw Zak on the day of his father's murder. 'Wherever he was, he wasn't in work,' he states.

And there is no news from door-to-door.

'We found nothing from Jerry's files in the last three years,' Jordy says.

'And I had a quick glance through the old newspapers that were recovered from Jerry's house. Nothing was highlighted, but flicking through them, some of the papers have court reports on Jerry's cases. Others are local papers with pictures of Zak starting school, that kind of thing. There was one paper with a big feature on Jerry's retirement and an interview with him but I don't think we can read much into them.'

The meeting finishes up quickly.

'Alan Lynch, here we come.' Dan rubs his hands in delight. 'I love a good auld interrogation.'

31

Alan Lynch is a tall, gangly, geeky man. His face is narrow with a long nose on which a pair of glasses perches. He has a habit of pushing them up with his index finger and leaning forward earnestly to talk to us. Forty minutes into his interview he has relaxed sufficiently to be holding a mug of tea and eating a couple of digestives. He'd been petrified at first, tears welling in deep-set dark eyes as he swore he'd do anything to help solve who had killed Jerry. Ask him anything, he'd said, his palms spread wide. 'I don't understand why I'm here, though, under arrest. And my wife . . .' He let the words trail off in a sniff of upset.

But the tears have cleared, and now that we've built rapport, it's game on.

'Just to clarify, Alan,' I say, 'what was it you did on the first of December?'

The biscuit breaks in half, crumbs coating his trousers. 'Damn.' He busies himself brushing down his clothes as Dan and I look on in silence. Finally, he holds the bits of biscuit towards us. 'Eh, what do I . . . will I?'

'Just dump them on the table there,' Dan says helpfully. 'We'll worry about it later.'

He obliges, face flushed.

'Last Monday.' I get back on track. 'Can you tell us again what you did? All the details matter, so tell us everything.'

'I'm not sure that would help. I just went fishing.'

We let the words drop into the silence.

'Eh ... my wife, Avril, whom you arrested too, she was meeting some friends in Mulranny so I took a day off work as well and got my fishing gear together and I drove out to Lough Acorrymore. D'you know it? It's a great place to catch a few trout.'

'Yeah, I've heard. So, you fished and ...?'

'I just fished.' He's hesitant, making a lot of weird gestures. 'There was another fellow or two down at the lake but I kept myself to myself. I like the peace and quiet. About maybe five, I packed up my gear and came home and made myself a cup of tea. When Avril got in, we had dinner together. And we watched a bit of TV. That was it.'

I run through what he has said again, just to make sure I've got it right. After he confirms that I've understood him, I ask, 'Did you spend all your time on the lake that day?'

'Yes.'

'Did you need to come back into Keel for any reason during the day?'

'Once I'm at the lake, nothing will rout me.' He laughs a little.

'The day before that, can you tell me what you did?'

'I went to work. I'm a carpenter, and I'm working on some new builds in Westport. Triple time on a Sunday, they needed to get them finished.'

'Keep going.' I smile, like I'm pleased with him.

'Em, I had lunch in a coffee shop there with a couple of the lads – Coughlin's. Then I went back to work and came home about six. I went for a run on Keel beach after tea.'

'Good stuff. And, say, the day after Jerry was found? What did you do that day?'

'How will all this help Jerry?'

'We're not sure but all details matter. Try your best to be as specific as you can.'

He shrugs, not seeing the harm in the question. 'Much the same. I didn't know Jerry was dead or I never would have gone to work. I'd have been . . .' he swallows hard, rubs his face '. . . Jesus, broke up. I went to work that day. Took lunch on my own around one. Came home and about eight Avril and I went for a pint in Gielty's. That was it.'

'Great. Tell us about your friendship with Jerry.'

He jerks a little at the question. 'Mainly I meet him to fish. I met him through the angling club in Dublin. Then, last year, Avril got promotion down here and we moved. When we heard Jerry and Hazel were coming, we were delighted. Well, I was. Avril doesn't know them, really. It's hard to get to know people here – it's all a bit clannish.'

That's not very nice, I think. My mother wouldn't like to hear that. 'Go on.'

'That's it. Jerry and I, you know, fished and maybe we had dinner together and that. Lately he said that Hazel isn't herself so we just . . . well . . . Avril will probably tell ye this, but Hazel didn't like us. I don't know why. Maybe it's the dementia making her sort of hostile. Dementia can do that apparently. Avril wouldn't visit after a while.'

'How does Avril get on with Jerry?'

He shrugs, though he seems easy with the question, 'Quite well, I guess.'

'All right, let's go back to the day of the murder. You say you spent all day fishing and you didn't go anywhere?'

'Yep.' His jaw tenses and his shoulders hunch slightly.

'What did you do for lunch?'

'Just . . . brought it with me.'

'And yet you paid for food in McLoughlin's at noon that day.'

A look of terror creeps into his eyes. My senses pop.

'My . . . eh . . . credit card was . . . stolen a few days before.'

'You said . . .' I make a big deal of looking at Dan's note-taking '. . . aw, yes, that you went into Coughlin's in Westport for a sandwich the day before the murder. Your credit card was used there.'

His mouth opens in an O.

'And the day after the murder you stated that you and Avril went for a pint in Gielty's and the card was used in the bar there too?'

'I . . . well . . . maybe someone was following me around.'

That lands with all the uneasiness of an off-colour joke.

We leave the silence to build, and he reddens so much, I think he'll start to cry again. He looks like a man on the edge, one tiny push and over he'll go, babbling his truth everywhere, so I leave it. Stretch the moment out. Hope that the dam of what he's holding back will burst right open. But instead he says, 'I need a solicitor.'

Fuckedy-fuck. That was badly played.

'Of course. No bother.'

We end the interview and flick off the DVD.

THE WRATH

William, who had been in the observation room, joins us in the corridor and I brace myself for a bollocking. To my surprise, though, he says, 'You did well.' At my look of incredulity, he adds, 'We know for sure there is something he isn't telling us so let's dig.'

We already know that there isn't a lot to learn about Alan Lynch. He has never even had a parking ticket. From his social media, I glean that he grew up on Dublin's southside, the only child of a rugby-playing father and a socialite mother. Various cute pictures of him as a kid with his handsome father litter his Instagram page. He attended a private secondary school, played on their rugby team but his ability didn't match his dad's. When he left school, he qualified as a carpenter. He married Avril four years ago after meeting her on Tinder. She's ten years younger than he is. They have no children. His Instagram profile picture is of his wedding day. A trawl of his Instagram feed throws up pictures of Avril smiling artfully at the camera, while other photos show pieces of wooden furniture and bowls that he's crafted. He's quite the artist. And, finally, we hit on a picture of Alan with Jerry. Both men are in waders and fishing gear and they hold, between them, a ginormous fish. Whoever took the snap managed to capture something that radiated happiness. The post reads, 'Two fishy blokes'. In the background, a sign says *Dodder Angling Club*.

It was taken five years ago. I move back further and there are more snaps of the two men, usually with a fish. There's one with Hazel squeezed between them and she looks a little bewildered. Maybe that was the start of the dementia. I scroll forward again, then back. 'There are no pictures of him and Jerry on this feed in the last four years. Isn't that weird?'

'And what about Jerry's social media?' Dan asks.

'He didn't have any, I guess with him being a guard.'

'It's odd, all right. Maybe they fell out back then. I mean, Hazel doesn't look too happy in that pic.'

'I'll get Matt to talk to whoever knew them in the angling club. But if they fell out, it's hard to believe Jerry would move down here, isn't it?'

'If his lover was down here, it'd be reason enough. And sure, maybe, I dunno, Alan heard Jerry was here and met with him the other day to warn him away?'

So many bloody maybes.

Thirty minutes later, we hear from Westport that Avril's interview has ended. 'There was nothing that they could find,' Ben reports back. 'Either she's the best fecking actress I've ever come across or she's genuinely puzzled about why they were arrested. Her alibi checks out. She was in Mulranny. She was back by six, she had dinner with Alan, whom she did say was a little off. Said he was like a briar the next day too, but she just assumed it was because something he was working on wouldn't fit into a house right and he had to adjust it. She maintained that she barely knew Jerry, that—'

Bang!

Some of the pieces that were puzzling me rearrange themselves. I leave Dan talking to Ben as I make a phone call to the guys on digital forensics. I've just scribbled down a number when Dan arrives back. 'Showtime again,' he says. Then, 'You look buzzing.'

I grin. 'Just let me readjust our questioning a little.'

He knows me well enough to say, with a wink back, 'Go for it.'

32

Alan has decided to double down and is giving us a no-comment interview. A deeply frustrating thing when the cautioned suspect chooses to remain silent. Calmly, I fire off the questions that he has already answered so he can sit there, saying, 'No comment,' and feel in control. That way he'll be cocky when the axe falls, and even if he says nothing, we'll know by his reaction that we're on the right path. His solicitor, provided by the state, sits alongside him, tapping his pen irritatingly on a notebook. Money for jam, he's thinking.

Question after question earns a one-shouldered shrug and a mutinous 'No comment.'

'Tell me again what you did on the day of the murder.'

'Describe the other men you say were fishing at Lough Acorrymore.'

'Did you pay for lunch using your credit card in McLoughlin's?'

'What do you say to the fact that we have a witness who can place you in McLoughlin's bar on the first of December?'

'If you were in McLoughlin's bar, why would you not tell us?'

'Another witness says there was a bad row between you and Jerry.'

That earns an upset-sounding 'No comment.'

'Can you tell us about that row?'

'Tell me when you first began a sexual relationship with Jerry Loftus?'

He rears back from the table, his head jerking, like he's been hooked by a rod. 'Stop!' he yelps, then claps a hand over his mouth.

'When did the relationship begin?'

And slowly, like a building falling, he starts to disintegrate. His eyes fill, silent tears spill out, he palms them away. Then his shoulders shake and he cries some more. Soon after that, as his solicitor gawps, Alan, head on his arms is weeping onto the table. It's not the nicest table and I wouldn't put my face anywhere near it but now is not the time to tell him that. I pass across the box of tissues and ignore the way Dan is kicking me under the table, wondering how I'd figured that out.

'It's all right,' I say eventually. 'We're just after the truth of what happened that day, Alan. You know some of it and we need to hear it or we'll never find out what happened to Jerry.'

The mention of Jerry's name starts a fresh wave of what can only be described as grief. His solicitor sighs loudly, his easy money well and truly shat on, and looks in irritation at his client.

'Are you going to tell Avril?' he hiccups out. 'I couldn't bear . . .'

'We won't be telling Avril anything but it may come out somehow.'

'I didn't kill him. I never would . . . I . . . I loved him.' He brings his gaze to mine. 'I really, really loved him.'

Many people kill for what they think is love. 'So, help us.'

Alan dabs his eyes with a tissue, before blowing his nose and rubbing it vigorously. 'I saw him that day.' The admission costs him: he starts to shiver. 'I'll never forgive myself . . .' He swallows before busying himself pushing the tissue into his sleeve. 'I . . . I couldn't admit it when ye called because Avril thought I'd gone to work. But I couldn't tell you that I'd gone to work because you would have checked and that would have looked worse, so I opted for fishing because it was handy. Even with the fishing Avril was pretty annoyed.'

We wait.

The solicitor's pen taps into the tension. I have the urge to take it from him and shove it down his throat.

'She'll go mad altogether if she thinks I was with Jerry. I normally don't lie to her but, honestly, I hadn't seen Jerry in a couple of weeks and I just wanted to see him and the only day he could get away was that Monday.' Another second. 'We hadn't met up as much as I thought we would – Hazel gets frantic if he leaves her, goes to pieces. I think she . . . suspected somehow. And Jerry is soft . . . he was soft,' he amends. 'He just couldn't bear her to be upset. Maybe he feels guilty, I don't know, but he never upsets her. That day, though, he was all for the meeting and I probably should have wondered why.' His expression darkens. 'I could tell, right from the off, that something was bothering him. He was weird with me. He was asking all sorts about Avril – did she know we were meeting, did she know about us. He was obsessed about people finding out, and I guess I can't blame him because he was a guard.'

Dan will get that: it had taken him years and a lot of courage to come out to the lads in the station.

'I actually think he was losing his mind with the secret of it all,' Adam goes on. 'He had fallen out with his son because his son had accused him of cheating and he wanted him to end it.' He gives me a sharp look, 'Apparently there was bad feeling there. You should chat with him.'

'We are investigating everything,' I answer. 'Go on, you were saying you met Jerry on Monday the first?'

'Yes. In McLoughlin's, but you know that. I think it was about noon. And I knew from the minute I saw him that he wasn't in good form but we ordered some food and we talked a bit. It started off with me asking him about what he had told Hazel and he said he'd told her he was climbing Croaghaun. But he was sort of distant, not paying attention, so I asked him what was the matter. And he pulls this page out of his pocket, a photocopy of this cartoon note, and he lays it in front of me and he says, "Well?" I just looked at him. Then he says that that was the latest one. In his trolley, he said. And he gave me this look, sort of challenging, and I didn't know what he was on about. The letter said something like "The road to Hell is paved" and I laughed at it and he says, "Did Avril send that?" I thought he was joking. I said, "Some building firm probably left them everywhere." And then he said, "No, I have the original letter at home. It's not the first. It's someone who knows about us. I think it's Avril. You'll have to stop her." Now Avril is a lot of things but if she thought I was cheating on her, I wouldn't be standing here, you know what I mean? And anyway, like I said to Jerry, if I challenged her on it, the whole relationship between me and Jerry would come out so I said, a bit pissed off, that Avril would never do that and he leans across the table at me and he hisses in my face, "Then it's you, and I will never leave Hazel so you're wasting your time."' The memory affects him. He has to blink furiously to halt the tears and I think, quite uncharitably, what an irritating weepy man he is. 'I was hurt by that, really hurt, so I said, "How do you know this letter is about us? How do you know it's not about something else?"'

'What else?' I ask.

'I dunno. It could even have been his son trying to spook him. But, like he was a guard, it could have been from one of his cases. Like anything. Why would he think it was about me?'

'What happened then?'

'Nothing. I just got up, paid for my food and left.'

'You got up, how?'

'Just up.'

We were told he was angry. I wait to see if he will add anything, but he doesn't. I'm forced to ask, 'And after that?'

He looks from me to Dan and back. 'That was it.'

'Alan, come on.' I hold up my mobile. 'We're checking your phone right now.'

'We exchanged texts, yeah, and I went home, cried my eyes out because I knew it was over, and I texted him that he'd ruined everything. I don't think we could have come back from it. He said he was coming over.' He visibly shivers and more tears start up. 'And he did. He – he parked away from the house and like, when he came I just, you know, told him that was it. I told him I knew what he thought of me now and what he thought of Avril, and that there was never going to be any future for us and that there was no way we could be, you know, friendly any more. And then he left. Oh, God . . . when I think of it now, I should have . . .' The rest of his words are lost in blubbering.

His solicitor rolls his eyes.

'You did what you thought was best at the time,' I say.

'I did but—'

'Let's just go over this story again.' I ask Dan to read his statement back to him and Alan agrees that, yes, that's exactly what happened.

'Just for clarity, what time did you arrive at the pub?'

'About noon, I said.'

'And we know from your credit-card receipt that you left around one thirty. Where did you drive after you left Jerry?'

'Straight home. I was back about two as far as I remember.'

'And Jerry called over at what time?'

'Well, he parked a little away from the house so no one would see and walked about five minutes, but around four maybe?'

'When did he leave your house?'

He shrugs. 'I was so upset, I don't know.'

'Roughly?' My voice is a little harsher than I had intended, and Alan looks like a dog I'd just kicked. From the corner of my eye I see Dan wince.

I must reel in my distaste for this guy.

'About half an hour.'

'Thirty minutes.'

'Yes, he came inside, I couldn't have him on the doorstep, and then he wouldn't go. But he did after I told him there was no way back.' More sniffing.

'Thanks, I know this isn't easy and—'

'It's hard. He was the love of my life.'

'What exactly happened when he was in your house?'

'He just begged and pleaded and said he was sorry but I said I was done. That was it.'

I wait but he doesn't bite.

'Why didn't you want to tell Avril that you were meeting Jerry?'

'It would have annoyed her.'

'Why?'

THE WRATH

'She'd asked me to go with her to Mulranny to meet her friends. All their husbands were going. I said I had to work.'

'Had you already arranged to meet Jerry at that stage?'

'No. I just ... I just ... well, I didn't want to go with Avril.' He grimaces. 'Look, the pretence is killing me. It's bad enough living with her but having to go and put a show on for the world, well ...' The sentence drains off.

'Are you saying you wouldn't mind if Jerry left Hazel and set up home with you?'

'It's all I ever wanted.'

'So why haven't you told Avril?'

'Jerry would go ballistic. It was his idea, you know.'

'What was?'

'That I get married.' He makes a face. 'I know. It's horrible what I did but Jerry said unless I got a wife we couldn't be seen meeting up. Said people would gossip otherwise. He was paranoid. So I married Avril and what happened? She got promotion to Castlebar and we ended up here in the arsehole of nowhere.'

Larry is probably laughing in the observation room. He knows how I feel about people disrespecting my home place.

'Jerry Loftus told you to marry Avril so you did?'

'Yes. I know it was—'

'And now you're stuck in a marriage you never wanted?'

'I feel guilty as hell. I know I should tell Avril the truth but what would I do then? She'd throw me out – she's the one with the big job. I'd be in a mess.' He sniffs and dabs his eyes. 'When Jerry retired and moved here I thought it'd be great. I thought, Finally, we're going to come clean but no. It was the same shit secrecy. Sometimes I thought he must have other men but he always denied it.'

I wait a moment to get my tone just right. 'That must make you angry, though.'

'Yeah. It was all totally unnecessary. He's a selfish bastard but, God,' he groans, 'I just . . . I couldn't help myself.'

'Did you ever tell Jerry you were angry at him?'

'No . . .' he bites his lip, his eyes shiny '. . . because I was afraid of him dumping me if I did. In the beginning, he kept dangling this carrot in front of me and I just kept on following. He told me that when he retired he'd leave Hazel but he didn't. Instead he said she'd dementia and he couldn't leave. That suited him, so it did. I was done with him after Monday. I'm devastated he's dead but I was done.'

'Jerry led you on for years, entreated you to marry to keep up the pretence, didn't leave his wife when he said he would, and then you believe he used his wife's diagnosis of dementia so he could stall coming out. Is that right?'

He starts to sob hard again. 'I was so stupid.'

'That is a lot to be angry about.'

'Yep.'

He doesn't seem to realise he's putting himself slap-bang in the frame as someone with plenty of motivation to assault Jerry.

'I could understand if you lost it with him on Monday,' Dan pipes up. 'It's a crappy way to treat someone.'

'It is,' Alan says, as his solicitor starts to cough in quite an alarming way.

I know exactly what he's at. He can't intervene to save Alan so he's distracting him.

I shove a glass of water towards him and keep my gaze on Alan. 'It's a lot to be dealing with.'

Alan suddenly realises he's talked himself into a corner. 'Jesus, no. No, I didn't. Christ. No.' He folds his arms, looks towards his solicitor who is gazing at his client as if he's the stupidest man ever. 'No comment.'

Two hours later, Forensics come back with a match for Alan's fingerprints in Jerry's car, but William isn't convinced we could swing another six hours' detention for him. 'Those prints could be from any time. I mean, if they were lovers chances are he was in his car. Have we anything else?'

'No,' I admit glumly. 'Anything new from the wife?'

'She hasn't a clue what's going on,' William says. 'She spent most of the time venting on him for not telling her he was meeting Jerry. They did lean on her, tried to see how she felt about Jerry and, honestly, she just kept referring to him and Hazel as the weird old couple that Alan seems to like.'

'Any chance she was spoofing? Maybe she did send those letters.'

'Even if she was and even if she did, it's unlikely she could have killed him herself given the extent of his injuries.' William rubs the bridge of his nose. 'While I'm not ruling out Eddie, I think that Weeping Willow is our best bet for a suspect at the moment.'

I snort with laughter. 'Weeping Willow is right. He grates, doesn't he?'

'So hard my skin is raw.' William cracks a rare joke and the accompanying smile transforms his face. 'That was good work figuring out the messages were for Alan, not Avril.'

'It was so obvious I was kicking myself I didn't figure it out sooner. Like, it didn't make sense that Jerry would tell Alan he was having an affair with Avril. What man would do that? Plus, in Jerry's house, it looked like he was really minding Hazel, labelling the pictures and all that. Not the home of a man about to leave his wife. Maybe he would have if she was a stronger person, but she's vulnerable. And that photograph of the two men on Instagram, holding the fish? Alan looked happier there than he did on his wedding day. And then I remembered that both the barman and our witness Con had referred to them as a couple. So, when we got Alan's phone, I recognised the number. The same number that Jerry's texts had been sent to. I got them to check for the messages and, bingo, there they were. Honestly, if Jerry was straight and was having an affair with Avril, he'd probably have left his wife before now because men do that.'

'Hey!' He looks insulted.

'A lot of men would do that,' I amend, 'especially when it's a younger, more attractive model.'

'You insult my sex.' He huffs out a sigh. 'Big question, do you believe him?'

'I think he's a self-absorbed narcissist with leaky eyes and a lot of anger buried under those tears but his grief did seem credible.'

'He's lied to his wife for years, though, and thought nothing of lying to her about where he was going last Monday.'

'Yes, a credible liar obviously.'

'Keep an eye on him.'

'Anything found at the house?'

'No axe, if that's what you mean.'

Damn. 'Is there any update on Eddie?'

'Nothing yet.'

'Okay.' I'm pulling open the office door when I turn. He looks at me questioningly. Taking a breath, I say, 'I had a read of that Westport file. There's not a lot you can do to help that kid, Cig.'

He stiffens.

THE WRATH

'You obviously tried your best. It's not your fault Nick Flannery blackmailed a young lad to confess to a murder. That's on him.'

He shakes his head. 'No, Luce, it's on me. It's my bloody job to get the right people.' Regret colours his tone, like dye in water. He rallies. 'And yours. Hop it, go on.'

'I just think—'

'Hop it.'

Sterner. I wonder what he'll do.

33

Luc is wearing a white suit. At first I think, in my addled puddle of a brain, that I've let myself into the wrong house. But no. There he is, with Cherry, standing in the hallway. He's wearing a white floppy jacket and a flowing pair of trousers. Underneath the jacket, he sports a wide-collared white shirt.

'Has someone gone and put you sitting on the right hand of the Lord?' I ask.

He glowers at me.

Cherry raises her eyebrows in open disapproval at my remark before linking her arm through his in what I suppose is a gesture of support. I like that. She's also dressed in white, though it suits her a lot better than it does my son. Her dress is long, made of sheer satin, and clings to her curves, like a river following its bank. Her streaked blonde hair is piled on top of her head in what appears to be a haphazard bun. Over the past few days, her lips have grown bigger and she's acquired a beauty spot on her left cheek. 'Hi there, Lucy.' She eyes me up and down and finds me wanting. 'I think Luc looks awesome. Here.' She hands me her sparkly mobile phone after first pressing some buttons. 'We're

THE WRATH

Instagramming Achill, mainly the beaches. That's Luc, in the picture.'

I glance down at it. Luc is attractive in a sort of scattered, unkempt way, but here, to my amazement, he is all sculpted perfection. In the photograph, he's barefoot and ankle deep in the sea, his slightly long hair whipped sideways by the breeze, strands falling across his face. The white suit billows about him. The sky is a moody mix of grey, black and blue with a long slender ray of sun streaming out through the clouds and hitting the sea behind him. 'Good photograph.' Jesus, his feet must have been freezing.

'Sixty thousand likes so far.' Cherry takes the phone back. 'Oops, sixty-one thousand.' She beams up at Luc, who, in front of me, tries not to look too pleased with himself. 'I tagged the beach and the location,' she continues, talking to me, 'and all my followers are promising to come and visit here in the summer.'

'That's marvellous. Fingers crossed they won't all arrive at the same time. How much did that suit cost, Luc?' All I can think of is that the idiot better not have spent his fecking rent money for college on it because it's the sort of thing he would do.

Both of them snigger a little. 'Cherry's profile has soared, Ma,' Luc says, as if that should explain everything. 'I have to change.'

'Me too.' Cherry makes to follow him down to the room and then, at my look, adds, 'I'll change in the bathroom.'

Satisfied, I leave them to it and go in search of my mother. She's in the kitchen, reading a book about serial killers. 'I made a pasta bake. It's over there on the counter. Just heat it up.' Then, lowering her voice and closing the book, she hisses, 'She's got Luc done up like a pimp.'

I giggle. 'She took a nice picture of him, though.' I dish up some pasta and flick on the microwave.

'Haven't I seen it? Haven't I spent the last hour looking at pictures of the two of them in their white. There's this ridiculous one where they're both glancing back at the camera with their hands in the air.' In a whisper she adds, 'Luc'll be a laughing stock around here if people catch a look at him and—'

She stops abruptly as Cherry, wearing a pair of wide-legged ripped jeans and a blue sweatshirt, sashays in. Unpinning her hair, she shakes it out and it tumbles around her shoulders. 'Sixty-one thousand and one hundred,' she announces. Then, for our benefit, 'Likes.'

'Marvellous.' The microwave pings and I take my dinner to the table. It's a little cold but I'm starving.

'I was just saying to Lucy how lovely you and Luc looked in the pictures,' my mother gushes. 'I suppose you're finished with it all now?'

'I got sent yellow suits for the photoshoot tomorrow,' Cherry says, crossing to the kettle and flicking it on.

My mother makes an anguished face behind her back.

'Have you any oat milk left?' Cherry pulls open the fridge. 'Oh, no, just dairy. Shit.' She closes the fridge and pulls some dry-looking crackers from the press to nibble on. 'Ye could do with a vegan shop down here,' she says.

This is the girl who has a massive profile for selling sausages.

My mother makes no comment and it's my turn now to roll my eyes. 'Our biggest claim to fame down here is our Achill lamb,' I tell her, and she looks like she might vomit.

'So why the yellow?' my mother asks her.

'It'll match the heather on the bogs.'

I try not to laugh at my mother's attempt to seem cool with that. In truth, I'm a bit horrified myself. Achill Island is not a yellow-suit place.

THE WRATH

'If you'd like to join us tomorrow, Mags, you can.' Cherry frowns as she studies my mother. 'I might have something you could wear. We could use an elderly person in a picture.'

'That sounds marvellous. I'll think about it, let you know in the morning.'

Cherry turns her gaze on me. 'If you're doing nothing you could—'

'I'm trying to solve a murder so . . .'

'Oh, yeah, bummer.' She takes another three crackers. 'For Luc.' And off she goes.

My mother waits until the door closes after her. 'Yellow suits, holy Jesus.'

'I thought you liked the pictures. Isn't that what you told her?' Then I add piously, 'You can't play both sides.'

She pulls a face at me and huffs her way out of the room. She'll be in a bad mood now but she always does this, gives out about something, then totally denies it, especially where Luc is concerned. I'm not doing her dirty work for her this time. If Luc wants to wear a yellow suit and get his picture taken on the bog in this wet weather, then off with him.

My phone vibrates with a reminder to call the Tracys. I ring them once a year, more out of duty than expectation at this stage. My very first case as a Dublin detective was one in which two children were abducted in broad daylight and never found. One boy, who alleges he was also snatched, managed to escape but was so traumatised that he couldn't remember much about it. I call his parents just to check in. The boy, David, is eighteen this year, so I can ring him directly now. I glance at my watch. Nine-thirty. Not too late. I dial his number.

'Yeah?' He's got a thick Dublin accent.

'David Tracy? It's Lucy Golden, I was the detective on your case when you were—'

'I remember nothing. Never will.' He hangs up.

I'm not entirely surprised by his abruptness. He's put it behind him, probably doesn't want any reminders. His mother was never that helpful either. She was sympathetic for the two missing children but I suppose she didn't want to upset her own child. Maybe, a voice whispers, I have to let it go.

But I just can't.

No bodies means there's still hope.

It's two o'clock in the morning when I wake up. At first I can't grasp what jerked me from sleep and then, like a light popping on in a dark room, I have a moment of recall, which I instantly dismiss. No, I think. It couldn't be. And yet . . .

It's worth checking out even if they will all think I'm crazy. I make a call – there will be no one in the lab so I leave a message. 'I want the results as soon as possible, Edgar. The file is the Stephen Larkin case. Thanks.'

I lie awake the rest of the night.

34

Three days later nothing much has broken on the case and the sense of frustration is spreading. We're counting down the minutes until we can talk to Eddie. I've just decided to have another chat with Zak – we still haven't found out where he was on the day of the murder and I'm sick of feeling so powerless – when I get a call from reception to say that Zak has just arrived at the station and has asked to talk to me.

For one mad moment, I think maybe he's here to confess, that the case will be over and we can all go and pat ourselves on the back, then spend the rest of the week catching up on all the admin crap that comes with the job. I still haven't filed anything on the arrest of the Dublin gang over a week ago despite irate emails from the powers-that-be.

In Reception, Matt is doing his best to talk to a woman about driving licences while fielding questions from her young lad. 'Where are all the robbers kept?' he asks Matt, with big round eyes. 'Did you ever kill anyone? Have you got a gun? If I karate-kicked a boy in my class would I be in trouble?'

I'm smiling at the young lad's question as I approach Zak. He's smiling too until he spots me. He stands, unsteadily, holding onto the chair for support. Has he been drinking? 'I believe you asked to speak to me? As it happens, we wanted to talk to you too. Come on through.'

'Where is that man going? Is she a baddie? Is he a cleaner?'

Zak laughs. 'Aren't kids great?' There is a definite slur in his voice.

I wait until we're in the corridor behind the front desk before I turn to him. 'I have to warn you that if you've been drinking I can't talk to you. What you tell me will be completely compromised and—'

'I have motor neurone disease,' he says.

I hadn't expected that.

'Shit,' is my well-considered response. Then, flushing from my toes up, I add, 'I'm sorry. Sorry for saying shit and then for thinking that you were . . . drunk. I'm—'

He holds up a hand. "S why I wasn't in work the day Dad . . . Well . . . I've been having all sorts of tests without Abby knowing. I'd been having falls and getting tangled up in my feet and I knew that, well, something was wrong. And I had an appointment the day before my dad . . . and they told me and . . . I couldn't find a way to tell Abby and then Dad went missing and you and that other guard came with all your questions and I could hardly tell ye when she didn't know, and that day, I was . . . look, I know I was . . . it's the disease. I get . . . angry, you know. Anyway, the day my dad was . . . you know . . . assaulted, I was at home. My mate came over, Myles from the gym . . . He covered for me, which was stupid, I know, and anyway . . . I told Abby yesterday, like there was no right time. My mother hasn't a clue what's going on, keeps asking about Dad. Things are . . . well, they're terrible.' His honesty scrapes me raw.

THE WRATH

It's a moment before I gather myself and say, 'Come on into the kitchen. I'll get you a coffee.' Grinning a little, I add, 'We've this great coffee machine. Come on, see the one and only perk of this job.'

He smiles back, and a few seconds later we land in on top of Larry, who is explaining rugby to a young guard, who has volunteered to help check Jerry's cases. She's gaping at him like he's a god as he expounds on some rule or other, his chest puffed out. I'd bet my house she has no interest in the sport. 'Can we have the room?'

Larry is about to object but then he spots Zak, who looks visibly upset and beats a hasty exit.

The young guard remains. 'Can I get you anything?' Fair play to her.

'We're grand. Thanks, though.'

'I'll leave ye to it, then,' she says, picking up her lunchbox and taking it with her.

'Best way to get a male detective off your back is to cry.' I'm being totally sexist in an attempt to relax him.

'I get that,' he says lightly.

I ask him what kind of coffee he likes and make a flat white for both of us. When he's sitting, sipping from Dan's mug – it's the cleanest in the place by far – I say, 'Thanks for coming in to explain. I'll have to verify that with your doctor and Myles, you understand.'

With great care, he places the mug on the table and unzips his jacket pocket. His hands are clumsy. Maybe they were before and I didn't notice or maybe in the past week he's deteriorated. After a bit of digging around, he hands me some pages. 'Names and contact numbers. And a photocopy of my appointments.'

I feel like a monster taking them from him but I can't just accept his word for it . . . though I believe him one hundred per cent. 'I'm really sorry again,' I say. 'That's hard news.' Ever the detective, though, I glance quickly through them and note that, yes, on 30 November he had a neurology appointment at one o'clock in James's Hospital. But the next day, he could still have . . . I let it go. It's unlikely he'd have been able to kill anyone.

'I think it's going to be harder on Abby.' He sips his coffee. 'I'm not a great bet. Me ill, my mother with dementia and my father murdered. She didn't sign up for that.' A moment and his voice bleak, he says, 'I offered to leave her.'

I don't know what to say to that. Where is Susan when I need her?

'She said no, but Abby is a fun-time girl. I'm not . . . I'm not letting her throw her life away on me.'

'She's a grown woman. She knows her own mind.'

He says nothing to that but I get the impression that his mind is made up.

'Can I ask, Zak, the day your dad came to your house, shouting and roaring and accusing you of sending the letters, did he say anything else?'

He looks a little startled at the change in subject and I feel awful. He's just told me he's terminally ill and I'm still on the job, pumping him for information.

'Like what?'

'I don't know. Anything you may have thought of as odd, or that jarred. I don't know, really. Just fishing.'

'The only thing I remember is that I think he would have liked it to be me. I got that impression. I can't back it up but, yeah, I think he wanted it to be me.'

'Explain that?'

'I dunno . . .' He shifts a little in the seat. 'I think, like, when you don't know who is sending you stuff, you want it to be someone you know.'

'Okay.'

Zak shrugs. 'That's all I got.'

'Would you have any idea who might have sent the letters?'

'Jesus.' He splutters out a disbelieving laugh. 'I don't know. Maybe the husband of his mystery woman? That'd make more sense, yeah?' And then, just as quickly, his anger vanishes. 'He was a good man too, you know.' He gulps. 'A good dad.' He waits a moment, before hauling himself upright. 'Funny how life works out, yeah? If that's all?'

'Yes.' I tap the paperwork he's handed me. 'And good luck with everything.'

'Think I'm past that now,' he says, with a wryness that makes me smile.

'Luce!' Dan virtually skids into the room, almost colliding with Zak. 'Oh, hey, hello?' He gawps at him 'I didn't know . . .?'

'I'll fill you in. Thanks, Zak.'

Dan waits until Zak has left, then says, 'You'd better fill me in on the way to Mayo General because Eddie is interview-ready.'

35

Eddie's doctor, Conrad Johnson, tells us that Eddie is stable, that in his opinion the man had a psychotic break with reality because he hadn't been taking his meds. 'He's lucid enough now but his memory is shaky. What he tells you, take it with a pinch of salt.'

I'm gutted. I'd half suspected this could be the case. How could a man in the depth of psychosis remember anything? It's deeply frustrating, especially if he has vital information for us. Even though I know his DNA will be found on the body, the knife and the sheets, I have trouble believing that, even under extreme mental illness, Eddie would have been capable of murdering Jerry. But, God, he must have seen who did.

The doctor leads us to a room that has been provided especially for the interview. Just as we are about to go in, he says, 'I don't know how many other psychiatric patients you've interviewed but it's best just to treat him like you would any other person. You may find his face is a little expressionless, but that doesn't mean he's not engaging with you. I've treated Eddie before. He's an intelligent man and he'll be taking it all in.'

'Thanks.'

He pushes the door open, lets us go ahead, then follows. It has been agreed that he can sit in to monitor his patient. It's not normally allowed.

Eddie is at a table, his solicitor alongside him. His beard and hair have been trimmed and he looks twenty years younger than when we last saw him. He's uneasy, though, his runner-shod foot tapping a rhythm on the floor.

'Hi, Eddie,' Conor says, getting his attention. 'I've brought some detectives to talk to you, like we discussed.'

'Uh-huh.' Eddie waves a hand at two chairs and Dan and I take seats opposite him.

The doctor positions himself near the door. 'I'll be here, Eddie, just in case you need a break.'

Eddie brings his focus to me and Dan. His eyes widen and crinkle up in what I think is a smile as he says softly, 'Lucy Golden. You give me lifts.'

'Yeah, whenever I see you walking about with no shoes on.'

'I'm all cured now. It won't happen again.' A shy joke. 'So your loss.'

I laugh slightly and am suddenly blasted back to the day my dad picked me up from school, Eddie hopping about, foot to foot, restless, following us across the yard as the other children screamed and played, oblivious. 'I want to come too,' he'd said. 'Please can I come, Lucy?'

'No!' I snapped.

His face filled with disappointment and—

Dan stands on my foot. Jesus, what just happened there? Sounds of the schoolyard recede and I refocus on Eddie who is staring at me curiously. 'You look good, Eddie,' I say.

'Aye.' He sounds calm but there's a glassiness to his gaze. Then, surprisingly, he heaves a great sigh and says, 'I'm not sure I can be of much help. That, all that stuff,' he shakes his head, 'it's all jumbled and foggy and buried, like, d'you understand me?'

'All we want you to do,' Dan says, 'is to tell us as best as you can what you do remember.'

I'm grateful that Dan has taken over. Something about Eddie unsettles me. Something not to do with this crime.

'It might not be right.' I come back once more as Eddie rubs his shorn face. 'I mean, I don't know if I killed him.' He looks at the doctor. 'Maybe I did. Maybe I just can't remember. Oh, nooo.' He starts to hyperventilate.

'If we thought you did,' Dan jumps in, 'we'd be charging you now. All we want is for you to tell us what you remember. Let us do the rest. Deal?'

Eddie settles his gaze on Dan, who is at his most charming and trustworthy. He nods. 'Sure.'

'And no matter how outlandish it sounds, that's what you remember and that's what we need,' Dan says. 'So don't censor yourself.'

Lovely, Dan, I think.

Eddie licks his lips and glances at me. 'I always wanted that one there to admire me. This will put the nail in that coffin.'

Dan chuckles, building a rapport at my expense as my face flames. Red-hot shame pours lava through my veins as I think about how casually cruel I was to this poor man in my youth.

'Tell us what you remember.' Dan speaks softly, like you would to a nervous animal.

Eddie shifts a little in his seat. 'I do remember seeing the cars,' his voice flattens out, 'a brown and a blue. And like, then, right, something happened. I got this feeling, a voice telling me this isn't right, and I just went over and I don't know but I saw the red Devil. I was invisible and he drove off in his chariot. And the man was Jesus, with the blood coming out of him. I brought him to the house and fixed him up and tried to keep the Devil from getting his soul. Tried to get him to rise up.'

Jesus's sake, I think, as I jot it down.

'Anything else?' Dan asks, as if what we've just heard makes perfect sense.

'There was a thunderous voice, outside, telling me to surrender him but I wouldn't. I thought it was the Devil. Then I'm here.'

Dan takes time to absorb the story. The doctor shifts position on his chair. Eddie's solicitor looks uneasy. 'You say you remember seeing the cars?' Dan eventually says.

'Aye.'

'Where were you when you saw them?'

Eddie blinks as if he hadn't thought about that. 'It was obviously the house,' he says. 'Not the one you found me in but the other one. Where I put Jes – Jerry. Where I have the binoculars. I go there when I need . . . when things are . . .' he glances at me '. . . when I'm bad and I just sit and let the voices come and . . . well . . . I have these night vision binoculars. My sister bought them for me.' He fires a look in my direction. 'I don't like the dark ever since . . . and, well, I use them. I was using them that night.' He stops.

'If I give you a map, can you show me the house you mean?' Dan asks, after a moment. He pulls an enlarged area map from his pocket. 'This shows all the vacant properties, Eddie,' he explains. Unfolding it, he lays it on the table.

Eddie studies it, his long fingers, nails scrubbed clean, tracing the wavy lines. Counting the houses. 'This one,' he says, and Dan hands him a pen to mark and initial it.

'So, you're in the house, where exactly?'

'The room that faces the road, upstairs. I have a chair that I took from a skip and the binoculars, and I sit, watching, keeping guard.'

We wait.

Eddie raps a finger on the table. He reddens. 'I just, I want the sun to know that it's safe to sleep and safe to come up in the morning.'

'So, you're sitting upstairs in that house, looking through the binoculars, telling the sun that it's safe to come up and—'

'I don't talk to the sun. It's more a mental thing.'

'Fine. And you're doing that and what happens?'

'The sun was just gone. The sky was red but the first star had come out. When I see the stars I know the sun is safe. I know the sun will come up the next day. My mother always said that once the sun is shining on your face it's a good day.'

'That's very true,' Dan agrees.

He's being kinder to Eddie than I ever was.

'So, you're sitting there, happy that the sun is safe, and what happens?'

Eddie stills, like a dog twitching on a scent. 'I see the first car,' he says. 'I didn't know 'twas the first car, it was just a car, but it stopped, sideways, like this.' He makes a sideways motion with his hand. 'And I'm thinking maybe it's broke down, you understand. Maybe he has a flat tyre or his engine is gone or he has to make a phone call and I'm thinking it's most unfortunate, that the sun going down has taken the energy from his car, and then I see a red person.' He stalls. 'I didn't know it was the Devil. He runs from the car, carrying something, and then I see another car.' His speech is getting faster, the words tumbling, his hands twisting one into the other. 'I see the lights anyway and I'm thinking the first car will crash into the second one and I'm there looking but I can't do nothing because I'm too far away and then doesn't the second car stop, screech. Goes off the road. I hear it. And then, I don't know. The Devil is there.' He's blinking rapidly and pulling his sleeves down over his hands, rocking.

From the corner of my eye, I can see the doctor about to interject.

'Don't think about the Devil just yet.' Dan is calm and his voice soothes Eddie. 'You're doing great. Isn't he, Lucy?'

'Brilliantly.' I hate myself for saying that. What do we care once we get the information? 'But stop us if you want to.'

Dan darts me a look, not happy with that. He's a true predator. I was like that and I don't know what's happened. 'You said that the first car stopped. Now think hard, Eddie. Earlier you said you heard a voice. Is that right?'

'I know now there was no voice. I mean, how could there have been?' Eddie asks. 'But I did. And the next thing I know I was invisible and watching. And,' he judders, 'I saw the Devil. He was red. That night, it's like,' he shakes his head, 'like a yawn that turns into a scream. It's muddy and soft and loud and I took the man. I know I done that.'

'What man did you take?'

'Jesus. The cut-up man.'

We wait but Eddie stays silent.

'Can you tell us where was the Devil was when you took the man?'

'He must have been gone.'

'Did you see him leave?'

A long moment. 'I saw a chariot but,' he winces, 'it was probably a car.'

'But you saw the Devil.'

He blesses himself.

'Describe him for us if you can.'

He dips his head in one fluid gesture, focusing his eyes on the table. He rocks slightly. 'Red. Top to toe, red. And teeth shining out from his face. His face was red.'

'How tall was he?'

'Fathoms tall. Fathoms wide. And . . . No, no, that's not right. He wasn't fathoms wide. He was normal wide and taller than the car, but not fathoms because I didn't have to look up and up.'

'That's great,' Dan says, though I know he's thinking this is a waste of time. 'Did he wear clothes?'

'Maybe. I don't . . .' he shakes his head again '. . . Just red.'

'Hair?'

'Red, all red.'

'Thanks.' I know Dan is frustrated, but he hides it. 'After the Devil left, what happened? Close your eyes if you want, describe as much as you can remember. What sounds were there?'

'I don't want to close my eyes, I don't do that. I never close my eyes.' He pushes back from the table, suddenly panicked.

'That's fine.' Dan is unruffled. 'Some people just find it useful. Sure, if you can, describe what happened afterwards.'

'You're doing really well.' I'm trying to make up for my faux-pas earlier.

He takes a moment to compose himself, mopping his brow with a handkerchief he pulls from his jeans. The action twists my heart. 'I can't remember.' He swallows hard. 'I think I must have been in shock. It's not every day you see the Devil. But I remember thinking, The Devil must have done that, when I saw the man. He was trying to crawl back into his car and he was . . .

blood, blood everywhere.' His breathing gets shallow. 'Blood and a knife in him. And I told him to wait. Yes, yes, I did.' With mounting excitement, his eyes catch fire as the memory tumbles in. 'And I took the wheelbarrow and I brought him to the house. I got sheets and I fixed him up. And then I left him. He was to rise in three days, the voice said, and—' He stops and his jaw drops as horror crawls across his face. 'Did I kill him? Did I kill him by leaving him? Is this—' His breathing becomes panicked. 'Did I—'

'Enough now.' The doctor stands and crosses towards us. 'That's enough for now.'

'But did I do—'

'The man was seriously injured,' I interrupt him. 'He was bleeding out. He wouldn't have survived.' It's the greatest kindness I can do him. Pushing my card across the table, I add, 'If you think of anything else, give me a call.'

Without a word, his face blank again, Eddie takes it and examines it. He's still twisting it up and down and sideways as Dan and I leave.

It's only when we're outside in the bracing December air that Dan groans, 'That was a bit of a waste. The only thing we learned was that he had the hots for you. Still has, by the look of it.'

I unlock our car. 'We also learned that there was a blue car and a brown car at the scene. We know, too, that that was how he got the knife. He must have pulled it out of Jerry.'

'I think it was weird that the Devil,' Dan makes quote signs with his fingers, talking to me across the roof of the car, 'left it behind in the first place when he managed to take the axe.'

'You think it was Eddie's?'

Dan shrugs. 'If Eddie was as deranged as he's having us believe, maybe he thought Jerry was the Devil and tried to kill him or he could just be stringing us along. Trying to mess up the evidence. I wouldn't go being all nice to him just yet.' The last part of the sentence is loaded. He pulls open his door and sits into the car.

I join him. 'I wasn't being all nice.' I switch on the engine, put the car into gear and pull out of the parking space. 'He's not faking his illness. That's ridiculous. He's been ill for years.'

'And what was all that at the beginning?' Dan changes tack, turning to face me in his seat, 'You were sort of blank or something.'

'You tell me,' I joke lightly. 'You're blank most of the time.'

He knows a stall when he sees it but he doesn't push it.

I say, 'If it was sunset, whoever it was might have looked red from top to toe.'

Dan nods. 'That's true. Good call.'

We drive for a bit in silence, until Dan says, with a grin in his voice, 'Delores and Fred have booked a holiday abroad for the new year. Would you think it'd be okay to change the locks while she's away?'

I break out in giggles and soon he's off, treating me to stories of his partner's irritating mother, and the mood lightens until my phone rings and it's Jordy.

'Eh, Lucy, it's Jordy, I'm off today but I've someone here, at my house, I'd like you to meet. I'm not sure how you'll explain it to the Cig, but it might help the investigation and, well, are you on the road?'

'I'm with Dan.'

'Bring him along but I don't need a lecture, right. I'll meet ye in my house.' He gives us an Eircode and we say we'll be there in thirty minutes.

36

The young man wearing the black hoodie is standing way too close to the middle-aged woman in the bus queue. It's subtle, but he, who had been brought up on city-centre streets, can spot it like measles. He positions himself in their vicinity and waits until the bus pulls up. That's when the kid does it. Just as the woman climbs the step to get on the bus, the kid dips his hand into her back trouser pocket and pulls out her mobile phone.

'Give it back,' he whispers, in the young man's ear as he places a hand on his shoulder. He knows just how to make it land like a sledgehammer. 'Give it back,' once more, all silky soft, 'or vengeance is mine.'

The young man is about to turn around to tell him to piss off but something in him has an ounce of self-preservation because he calls to the woman, 'Hey, you with the red coat, is this your phone?'

The woman turns. Is it me that youngster's talking to? she's wondering. Then she spots her phone, smiles and takes it from him. Thinks, You should never judge a book by its cover. She thanks the youngster before hurrying down the aisle into a seat.

The young man is shaking because fingers on shoulders can do horrible things if they press down hard enough.

He guides the young man away from the bus. Still in his ear, he says, 'One thoughtless action can ruin someone's life. You think about that now, you arsehole, as you go about your day.'

Then he leaves the young man standing there, rooted to the spot, shell-shocked, not quite sure what has just happened.

He celebrates his good deed with a jam roll in a coffee shop. Raspberry always. It's good to have saved someone's day from potential ruin, he thinks, as he examines his accounts on his laptop. He conducts his investments like an orchestra as money grows before his eyes.

A child's voice and his attention twangs.

A father and son have sat opposite. The man, so like his own dad, tall and big and fun and smiley. The boy not so much like he was as a kid, except that he, too, laughs hard at whatever his father says. This little boy laughs with his whole body, the giggles pouring out of his mouth right from the centre of his belly. It fills the immediate area and makes people smile.

The two of them have chips and tall glasses of fizzy orange in front of them. They wear the same tops with the name of a football team on it. They pretend to steal food from each other's plates. The father reaches out and tosses the son's hair. The son—

'Sorry, have you got a problem?' The father looks straight at him.

Has he been staring?

He must have been.

He flushes right up. This dad, so like his own, glaring at him. His heart hammers. He shakes his head. 'I have no problem. None.'

The dad takes a moment. Then he stands up, holds out his hand for his son and they carry their chips and their drinks to another table. He sees the dad having a word with the waitress, then she turns and he has to go.

He was only looking.

THE WRATH

*

As he walks through the town, his good mood slightly dampened but he's still managing to enjoy the cold bright sunshine, he catches sight of the headlines. Despite Promising Leads, No Charges Yet in Garda Murder Case.

Promising leads.

My arse they have promising leads, he thinks. The only decent lead they had, he's managed to fuck up for them.

Plus, they'll never catch him if they think he's just done it the once.

37

Jordy's house is exactly what I imagined it would be. Part of a terrace of eight, with tiny front gardens, his place looks like it's been unoccupied for decades. Overgrown, peeling paint and windows with a thick layer of dirt so it's impossible to see in. We ring the bell, which doesn't work, so I rap on the letterbox and after about five minutes, Jordy answers the door. I've only ever seen him wearing his garda uniform and on the odd occasion, at get-togethers, a pair of jeans and a jumper, neither of which ever fit him properly. Today, he's in tight blue track bottoms and a blue sweatshirt, with the words 'They said, "Just do it," and I failed.'

'Nice threads,' Dan remarks, with a grin, striding ahead of me into the house. 'Now, big question, how the fuck did you wangle a day off?'

'I applied ages ago.' Jordy adds no more to his explanation, merely waves for me to go by and then, closing the front door, he shuffles behind us, coughing and wheezing, into his kitchen.

The room is tiny and as run-down as its occupier. If it were a bit cleaner, it'd look quite retro, but instead the red presses are dirty, their doors hanging crookedly. A spindly table and chairs take up most of the space. A man, sitting on one of the chairs, is the spit of Jordy, but cleaner.

'Maurice, my brother.' Jordy waves in the direction of the man as he introduces us. We all shake hands. I know by Maurice's firm grip and his 'How are ye?' that he's a guard as well. There is just something about the job that moulds people into a 'type'. 'I've heard a lot about ye from this fella here.' He thumbs to his brother.

'Tea?' Jordy asks, and both Dan and I utter a hasty 'No, thanks.'

Jordy looks mildly surprised, shrugging. He pops the tab on a can of lager and slides into a seat. 'Maurice is a guard too,' he says, 'and we got chatting about the case.' And before we can say anything, he adds defensively, holding up a hand, 'I don't want to hear it. I remember, Lucy, you told your mother details one time and it got in the paper, and as for you,' he smirks at Dan, 'we only solved that last case because you told your girlfriend, sorry, boyfriend . . . eh, partner,' he settles on, 'you told your partner about it. So, I don't want to hear it.'

'No one will hear anything from me anyway,' Maurice placates. To us, 'I have certain information you might find useful. At least, I think you will.'

He even sounds like Jordy: the wheeze and the chestiness.

'It might throw all the stuff we've found out so far up in the air.' Jordy takes up the baton. 'And I don't know how it fits together, but what Maurice told me, it's too much of a coincidence. I think so, anyhow.'

They have our attention now. 'Go on,' I say.

Maurice begins, 'I was a DS like you, Lucy, working mainly in Donegal. It was a grand place, a bit of a robbery here and there, some border trouble but not much. But about two years back, there was this case—'

'Wait until you hear this,' Jordy interrupts.

'Mary Roche, a woman in her sixties, was found with a severe stab wound in her back and three others on her stomach on a dirt track two hundred metres from her house. She hadn't come home so her husband went out looking for her. He alleges that he saw someone fleeing the scene and that he found her, on the ground, bleeding out, a knife in her abdomen and that he tried to help her. He managed to trample all over the scene. His DNA was everywhere, on her clothes, body, everything. There was other evidence found on Mary, fibres, that sort of thing, that didn't match anything the husband had, but apparently Mary had been out and about that day, shopping, buying clothes, meeting friends, mixing with a lot of people. In the evening she'd attended a local prayer group. We took DNA from that group and asked other people she'd interacted with to come forward. We did rule out some evidence, but we couldn't trace everyone and there were a couple of fibres found on her that we never traced. During the investigation, we learned that Mary and her husband had been going through a rough patch. One of her friends confirmed to us that they had barely been on speaking terms. We asked him why and he denied everything but we found out he'd been having an affair, that he'd wanted to leave her, that she was refusing to entertain it, the usual. He admitted to being angry with her, and in the heel of the hunt, he was charged with her murder, a conviction I couldn't stand over – it was almost too easy. He pleaded not guilty but the circumstantial evidence was damning. Anyway,' he looks at us keenly, 'you're probably both wondering why I'm telling ye this.'

'Yes,' we answer together. If it were any other guard, I'd think this was a gigantic waste of time, but Jordy, though he has never bothered trying to advance through the ranks, is razor sharp in a deceptively sloppy way. I trust his instincts.

'Not only was Mary murdered with a stab wound to the torso,' Maurice leans towards me, 'not only was her iliac artery severed after a couple of botched attempts but, and this is the big thing, the wound to her back was strongly suspected to be an axe wound.'

'There you go,' Jordy pronounces. 'Identical to Jerry.'

'You can go on PULSE and check the description of the wounds, but the whole MO sounds very similar to Jerry's. A bit messier, maybe – it took her a while to bleed out. And also during the investigation, I was told, by a priest, that Mary had said to him she was receiving anonymous letters.'

'Are there any copies of the letters on the file?' A *whump* of pure adrenaline pours through me.

'According to the priest, Mary destroyed the ones she had. He said she'd been afraid of whoever was sending them. She also mentioned that they were biblical in nature, telling her that vengeance was coming, that they came in red envelopes, always on a Monday, and consisted of pasted-on words.'

'Identical to our case,' Jordy says.

'They *sound* identical,' I clarify. 'Did you believe this priest?' I ask Maurice.

'I did. Why would he lie? There was a blood-soaked red envelope with a page inside underneath Mary Roche's body when she was found but it was beyond saving. Anyway, they said at the time that the envelope may have had nothing to do with her, it could have been there for weeks.' He pauses, lowers his voice: 'I believed at the time that whoever wrote those letters killed her but we had no letters. They were gone. I couldn't prove a thing and, without the letters, it all pointed to the husband.'

'He could have written them,' Dan says.

'He could have but there was nothing in the house to say he did. No red envelopes, no photocopy paper, not even a pot of glue. There was an axe, but no traces of Mary's blood were found on it. And, like I said, the husband alleged that when he arrived on the scene, he caught a glimpse of someone else fleeing. They were in red and there were red fibres found on Mary. '

Red, I think. Like the Devil. Like Eddie said. And there were red fibres in Jerry's car.

'Anyway, when Jordy said that Jerry Loftus was getting letters too, in red envelopes, I just thought it was odd, that maybe I was right and that Mary's husband is innocent. To this day, he still says he had nothing to do with it. He'll miss out on parole if he keeps it up.'

'You say Mary was murdered two years ago. That's a long time if the cases are connected.' Dan doesn't seem to be buying it.

He dips his head, acknowledging the truth of that.

'Is there any connection at all between Mary and Jerry?' Dan turns to Jordy. 'Does that name feature in any of the cases you've gone through?'

'No,' Jordy says. 'And we've gone back five years now.'

'Then I don't see how . . .'

'I think we should at least look at the possibility that Jerry and Mary could be connected,' I say. 'There are interesting parallels between their murders, don't you think?'

'I do,' Jordy says.

'Can I get a look at Mary Roche's full paperwork, Maurice?' I ask.

'You can.' He winks. 'I took it with me when I retired.'

'Send me a jpeg of Mary too, maybe an old picture and one

around the time she died. We could show it to Hazel and Zak, see if they recognise her at all. Let's track down that priest and also talk to Mary's husband. Be good to suss him out.' See if I believe he's innocent, I really mean.

'And, eh, how are we going to square all that with the Cig?' Jordy shifts in his seat, looking wary.

'You just leave it to me,' I say, with a lot more confidence than I feel.

38

William looks from me to Jordy, his left eyebrow raised and sceptical. 'Let me just get this straight,' he says, and I know by his tone that he's going to tear us apart. 'You and your brother were chatting about the job –'

'He's a guard too. We shoot the breeze like that,' Jordy says calmly, and I admire his ability to smooth over the truth.

'– and he just happened to mention that he was tortured over a case he handled two years ago.'

'Mithered,' Jordy says. 'Losing sleep over it, the lot. It was his last case before he retired.'

William leaves a pause.

Don't fill it, I mentally beg Jordy.

And he doesn't. Interlocking his hands over his bulging stomach, he smiles amicably at the Cig.

'And this case your brother mentioned just so happens to be a copy of the case we are handling now.' Another arch of eyebrow. 'What a coincidence.'

'I could hardly believe it,' Jordy says.

'I can hardly believe it,' William says drily.

THE WRATH

Jordy flushes. I beam brightly. 'So, Cig,' I say, 'I think it's worth having a look at. I've booked a slot to talk to Peadar Roche, Mary's husband, for later today. He's in Castlerae so only about two hours up the road. I know you don't want a potentially innocent man in prison.'

He flashes an incredulous look at me. Yep, I'm using what he told me against him.

'And I traced the priest Mary confided in. We can talk to him too,' I hasten on.

'You've been hard at work sorting it all out, seeing as Jordy only told you this morning.'

He wants the truth. I bat it away. 'I believe it could be a good lead. None of our current suspects are convincing me. If we could find a connection, it might open things up. Jordy is going to talk to Hazel, see if she can remember a Mary Roche. It's worth a try, Cig. Just let me and Jordy have a go at it.'

He ponders, thinking about how thinly the resources will be spread, no doubt. 'All right,' he eventually says. 'You've got two days to find a link between them. If you don't, we're concentrating on the information we have. I can't afford detectives haring off on wild-goose chases. Go on, hop it. Forty-eight hours. That's it.'

He bends his head to the paperwork as Jordy and I leg it from the room.

'He didn't believe the story we spun him for a second, did he?' Jordy whispers.

'Nope, but do we care? Get a picture of Mary and let's get cracking. It's down to you and me, Jordy.'

The priest, Father David, who is now living in Galway, welcomes me into his house and, after cutting me a slice of apple tart, which he says he made himself, tells me everything he remembers about Mary Roche and what she told him about the letters she was receiving.

'She definitely said a red envelope?' The apple tart is stale, or maybe it's just not a nice recipe, but I gamely swallow it, trying not to gag.

Father David nods. 'She was terrified, I remember, and I . . .' he pauses '. . . I was so bloody young. I know it's only a couple of years ago, but I've aged a lot since then.' His sigh is filled with remorse. 'I told her to either go to the guards or try to talk to her husband about it all.' He closes his eyes. 'But he was a killer.'

His words give me a jolt. 'You believe he killed her?'

'Isn't that what you lot said? Sure, they even found the knife sticking out of her with his prints all over it.'

'And the letters, Father?' I wince at calling this youngster 'Father' but it's force of Catholic habit.

'He probably wrote them, sure, it doesn't matter now.' It seems only to occur to him then: 'Why are ye asking, anyway?'

'Something has come up about the case. Thanks.' I pull on my jacket.

'I was only trying to help her. If she had told me about the husband's affair and the state of the marriage, I might have advised her differently.'

'We can only do our best at the time. It was good advice.'

He looks at me in irritation. 'If you'd been responsible for a person getting killed, it'd haunt you.'

I think of Rob. 'It does,' I answer.

A couple of hours later I'm outside Castlerae prison. I've only ever been inside it once before when I was a guard in my early twenties. I'd accompanied one of the senior detectives and sat silently as he'd talked to some guy who'd agreed to offer up information in exchange for a reduced sentence. I'd been scared, my palms slick with sweat, although I'd done my best to appear cool with the whole thing, but the sound of our echoing footsteps, the ring of voices, the clang of metal and the air soaked in suppressed violence had freaked me out a little.

Almost thirty years later, I enter the place as a detective sergeant and it's still intimidating. This time, though, it's with the hard knowledge of the few hundred men who are locked away from society, deemed too dangerous to be trusted in the outside world. They and I are now hemmed in by the large wall and the locked doors that are the signature of any prison. I have always felt there is something unnatural in the separation of one set of people from another, yet what else is there to do? I know Larry would argue that people who have committed these crimes are unnatural but, having dealt with some of them, I believe that sometimes it's just unfortunate chance that lands people in here. A wrong road taken and the way to a normal life lost. Maybe lost in a bruising childhood or a fierce moment of fury, in a longing for a drug-induced oblivion or in a strong right hook.

But lost.

I wonder if Peadar Roche is one of that sort. Or is he innocent?

He's waiting for me in the small dull room, handcuffed, round-shouldered, his head bent, showing a cap of close-cropped grey hair.

'You can take the cuffs off,' I say to the guard with him. He does as instructed and the cuffs open with a small clink.

Peadar rubs his hands but doesn't raise his gaze to me.

'Hi, Peadar, I'm DS Lucy Golden. I'm here to ask you about your wife's murder.'

No reaction.

Sometimes getting someone in this situation to talk to you is like hunting a rabbit. You have to sneak up on it and startle it out of the long grass.

I let the silence build until he begins to squirm. Then, 'Did you murder her?'

His head shoots up. 'No.' And there it is, writ large across his face. He is telling the truth. How could anyone think otherwise? It's in the simplicity of the admission startled out of him. There is no bluster, no justifying, just a simple 'No.'

'I believe you.'

He eyes me warily. 'No one else did.'

'I'm not no one else.'

His face floods with emotion and he seems incapable of doing much but staring at me, almost as if he thinks I'm messing with his head.

'Would you have any idea who might have done it? Think hard.'

'Do your poxy job yourself.' A burst of anger, like an over-full kettle. 'Why should I help you shower of incompetents?'

The guard makes a move but I shake my head for him to stay put. Peadar Roche needs to vent.

'I'm doing a life sentence for something I haven't done. I'm stuck in this awful hell of a place, day in day out, and you lot put me here. Now you want my help? Get lost.' He holds up his hands. 'Guard.'

'Honestly, you're right,' I say, as the guard clinks the cuffs back on. 'I don't deserve your help. But you deserve mine for what has happened. If you know anything at all, it will help you. I'm on your side, Peadar.'

His gaze is cold but he hasn't interrupted, which is a good sign.

'Cards on the table? We're investigating another case with a very similar MO to Mary's murder. We're wondering if there's a link. We heard Mary was getting letters?'

'I never saw any . . .'

I have him. I do a mental fist bump.

'. . . but she got them, I know that.'

'How?'

'Because she said to me once that she knew I was trying to mess with her head to get a divorce. That no matter what I did or how many letters I sent it wouldn't happen.' He eyeballs me, 'That's how I know.'

It's a bit thin.

'But you didn't send these letters?'

'Why would I bother? I could have just walked out.'

'Why didn't you?

'I wish I bloody had, but it was Christmas and I didn't want to rock the boat until afterwards.' He shakes his head.

'And was there anyone who might have wished Mary harm?'

He shrugs.

'Your new partner?'

'Unlike Mary, my new partner, who is waiting for me to get out, is a lady. It would never cross her mind to do that.'

'On the night it happened, you said you saw a figure. Can you describe it?'

'It was dark but I'm certain the figure had a red jacket. Maybe all in red. And they were running. Fast.'

Though I'm somewhat hardened to investigations, that detail

sends a chill right through me, the hairs rising on the back of my neck.

'In what direction were they running?'

'Away from Mary. Carrying something. She was on the ground, gasping and that.'

'When you say "all in red", what does that mean?'

'Red top to toe.'

'Did it remind you of anything?'

I'm pressing him for 'Devil' but he just looks blankly at me before barking out a laugh. 'Santa? Giving me a Christmas present of a dead wife.'

I remain poker-faced as he continues to laugh a little hysterically. Finally, he sobers up and I push a picture of Jerry Loftus across the table. 'Do you know this man?'

'Isn't he the lad that was killed on Achill there?'

'Yes.'

'I never saw him in my life.'

'You sure?'

He takes another look. 'Aye.'

I feel like banging my head off a wall. I'm missing something here. We all are. 'Thanks, Peadar.' I tuck the picture back in my bag and pull on my black jacket, preparing to leave.

'You won't forget about me, will you?' The hard-man act is gone now.

'No. You can count on it.' I might not be able to do anything about the lad in Westport, who is confessing to a crime he never committed, but maybe with Peadar I have a chance to balance the scales for the Cig.

He holds my gaze, nods briefly.

It'll take me days to banish the sounds of this place from my head.

39

It's late when I get to talk to William, who seems never to sleep. No matter the day or the hour, William is sure to be found in his office, either on Achill or elsewhere, depending on what is the most pressing case. It dawns on me as I sit down in front of his desk that I have no idea where he even lives. I can't imagine him in a rural setting, he's always bemused by the goings-on in Achill, by the way people know one another. He probably buries himself in the city.

He gazes at me expectantly, 'Anything?'

'Not yet but—'

'Jordy said neither Hazel nor Zak recognised Mary Roche. He went and showed them a picture of Peadar Roche, too, but they didn't know him either.'

Damn. Damn. Damn.

'Jordy's brother, what's his name, Maurice, is handing over all his information on the murder tomorrow. I cannot believe he took files with him when he retired.'

I ignore that. We'd all probably do it if we thought a case had been badly handled. 'The husband is telling the truth, I'd bet my house on it.'

'It's not the husband's case we're working on. It's Jerry Loftus, an ex-guard. The chief is pressing for updates, had the bloody nerve to tell me to hurry up with it, like we're all here scratching our arses. Shoot me if I ever get like that.'

I resist the quip to tell him I could save him worrying and just shoot him now. William doesn't always get my jokes and there's a bit of history between him and the chief, plus Louis, the chief's son, who was shoehorned into our last investigation, looks like being a fixture on the team now. And he's such a brown-noser that none of us quite trust him not to go running to Daddy when he's aggrieved. 'Anything turn up here?'

'While you were out gallivanting, we—'

'I wasn't gallivanting, I was pursuing a potential lead and—'

'While you were out pursuing a potential lead, we had some more results back from Forensics.' Then, grudgingly, 'Mick is playing a blinder. The toe of his shoe is worn out from kicking people up the hole.'

'Mick was always dedicated.' I'd championed him and Susan from the start. Mick had just been a little slow to get going, mainly because he's terrified of William.

He ignores that as he flicks through some paperwork on his desk. 'Here we are. The knife had Eddie's prints all over it. And I mean all over it. No other prints. And the sheets, DNA from both Jerry and Eddie. The red fibres . . .' He bends his head to read off the page, looks up at me. 'Basically, I'm told by Mick that the dye and the composition of the fibres were analysed and that if we managed to obtain more of them we should be able to compare them.'

'There were fibres found on Mary Roche that were never identified. Can we ask the lab to run a comparison?'

William groans. 'If they were red fibres, yes. Otherwise just leave it until we have a link.' He pauses. 'Plus that woman's fibres were deposited twenty-four months back. It's a little unlikely—'

'Anything else?' I interject quickly, before he can talk himself out of it.

'We've a couple of regulars going through Eddie and Alan's belongings to see if any more red items can be tested. We're trying to identify that third car now, the blue one that followed Jerry after he left the pub. We ran a PULSE check on every blue Ford car registered on the island. Of that list, ten were identified as potential and a few of the lads went out to talk to the owners. We were lucky, got to speak to all ten and we're satisfied, for now, that none of them were around that day. Larry then went and examined other footage harvested from the Achill Sound area and, hey presto, we found another car that matches the one seen soon after Jerry left the pub that day. We can't pinpoint when it arrived but it was captured leaving on the sixth of December. We've isolated three numbers on the plate. We're running the numbers against all the blue Fords registered but nothing yet.'

'The sixth? That's like five or six days after the murder.' I'm sceptical. 'Why would someone leave it that long to get away? That's the potential lead Larry's pursuing?'

'*Touché*, but this lead isn't costing me two missing members of my team.' He taps his desk with a pen. 'All right, have a gander over Mary's murder file tomorrow, see what you can uncover. I'll talk to you at some stage. I mightn't be around most of the day.'

'Dossing, are you?'

'Chance'd be a fine thing.'

But he doesn't elaborate.

40

As I pull into the driveway, my mother hauls open the front door, looking uncharacteristically alarmed and a little at sea. She has obviously been on the lookout for me. Something has happened.

My hopes of a chilled-out evening disappear, like an Irish summer. My hands tighten and grow slippery on the steering wheel. A couple of years back, my house was broken into by an ex-offender, with a grudge, who'd held my mother and Luc at knifepoint. I don't think I've ever fully recovered.

After a few seconds, which seem endless, I realise that if something truly awful had occurred she would have rushed down to meet me, or she would have phoned work. Whatever it is, it can't be too bad. Whatever it is, it's fixable.

Oh, God, maybe Luc has gone and got Cherry pregnant? That would finish me. I love Sirocco but one cute grandchild is enough.

Deep breath, Lucy.

I unclench the steering wheel and hop out of the car. 'What is it?'

'Luc is very, very upset.' My mother scurries to meet me,

THE WRATH

follows me as I walk towards the house. 'He's down in his room and he won't come out.'

'Why?' The last time Luc took to his room he was about to become a father. 'Cherry's not . . .? She's not . . .?'

'She's gone.' My mother follows me into the kitchen, whispering now.

Aw, feck, there's no dinner.

As if reading my mind, she says, 'How could I cook when there was all this upset?'

'How is it upsetting if Cherry has gone? Thank God, I say.'

'Lucy!'

I pull a packet of biscuits from the press and wrestle a couple out. 'What happened?'

'They went out this morning, happy as Larry, Luc carrying all her gear and she ordering him about, the usual. Then about three o'clock, he comes back on his own and when I asked where Cherry was he said that in the middle of the photoshoot she'd told him she wanted to go home.'

That's a bit odd. 'Why?'

'That's the thing, he says he doesn't know, but I think he does. He's very upset.'

'Maybe she had an emergency at home.'

'Well, you'd think Luc would be with her then, wouldn't you? I mean, he's besotted with her.'

And he is. I'd never had a man treat me the way my son treats Cherry, but then again, I've never shone as brightly as her either. 'I'll have a word.'

My mother makes a face.

'What?'

'Be nice.'

'I am nice.'

Her over-bright smile isn't encouraging but it makes me determined to prove her wrong.

I have negotiated with all sorts of people, I tell myself, as I make my way to my son's bedroom. I've got the truth out of suspects who were full sure that they wouldn't talk to me. How hard can it be with my own son?

I tap on his bedroom door. 'Luc, are you all right?'

'Go away.'

'Well, I live here so technically . . .'

'That's just a lame joke.'

'Sorry. Can I come in?'

'No.'

Feck it. I dither for a bit, then ask, 'What happened? Mam said Cherry has gone home.'

'She has. She's finished with me.'

Why would she do that? Was it because he was too needy, too helpful? Girls like a bit of a challenge, just like lads do. Luc wasn't much of a challenge as far as I could make out. 'Was it because you were too much of a pushover?'

'What?' Then, 'No!' I detect a sob in his voice. 'I did . . . Ma, I did everything. I was really good to her, like I tried to . . .' He stops, hauls his emotions back. 'She just . . . Well, she's gone.'

'She's not . . .' I close my eyes, fling a prayer heavenwards. 'She's not pregnant, is she?'

'You're obsessed with my girlfriends getting pregnant!' he shouts, half tearfully. 'You made Cherry feel uncomfortable every time she came to my room. She used to sit on the floor in case you came bursting in. Did you know that?'

THE WRATH

'No, and I wish you'd told me because I might have relaxed a bit more then.'

'You're . . . that's . . . It's your fault she's gone. You're so judgy. I saw your face when her ad was on the TV!'

'Oh, for fuck's sake,' I snap. 'She wasn't so uncomfortable that she didn't spend all her time here. I mean, where were her parents?'

He doesn't answer.

I lean against the door and groan inwardly. From up the corridor, my mother tuts in disapproval. Yes, I've probably made it all worse. 'Look, Luc, if she's broken it off, she owes you an explanation. But if she doesn't give you one, there's nothing much you can do. I am sorry, truly, for what has happened. I am. I know you loved her.'

And I hear it, the unmistakable sound of a sob being stifled and, fuck it, I don't care. I open his door and, though he initially resists my arms, he eventually lets me hug him. Then my mother comes in and hugs us both.

Cherry has lost the contract for her sausage ad because her ex-boyfriend posted a picture of her wearing a 'Meat Is Murder' T-shirt. 'Then there was this big pile-on,' Luc says, 'like of everyone, the meat-eaters saying she should lose her job and the vegans saying she sold out. And there were threats against her and like it's gone viral.'

For fuck's sake. 'Let's have a look.'

He finds the post and hands me his phone. My mother peers over my shoulder.

'Nan, please, don't.' Luc looks anguished.

My mother pats his hand and sits down.

The picture is of a younger, more natural-looking Cherry, her hair a dark brown and her face make-up free. She's sipping a juice drink and pushing her chest out to showcase the 'Meat Is Murder' message.

'She looks nice.'

'It doesn't matter what she looks like. Look.' Luc jabs the comment section. The text under the picture reads *Just thought the world needed to know that @CherryBomb is not such a #sausagegirl She's a #liar. #misleader #truthtelling #anotherlyingbitch.*

And the comments. Whoever invented the word 'pile-on' had it accurate. Vile, gleeful and celebrating the downfall of a young woman.

> @Roxyrox;
> You sold out for a sausage, you vile bitch
>
> @Luciann
> Delighted to see you go down. Your ad is disgusting.
>
> @Mik69
> Giz a blowjob, why not.
>
> @LucG
> You fucker. I will bury you.

I tap the phone. 'Luc, don't engage with these people.'

'If I see him, I'll kill him. How dare he do that to her?'

'Unfortunately she's a vegan and all he can be accused of is being a total prick.'

Luc glowers.

'And how would you having a go at him help Cherry?'

More glowering.

'It still doesn't explain why Cherry broke up with you, pet,' my mother says. 'Why would she do that? It's not as if you did anything wrong.'

There is a moment of silence and, because I know my son so well, I know that he has messed up somehow. 'What did you do?' I ask, trying not to sound accusatory.

He glances up at me from under his tangle of hair. 'I just . . .' He shrugs. 'Well, I said I'd told her so. Like I knew she'd get found out.'

'You said that to her while all this shit was pouring into her phone?' On his nod, I snort. 'For God's sake!'

'I know. It was . . . Look, I know I shouldn't have,' he sounds defensive, 'but the way I said it, I didn't mean it the way you'd mean it.'

'Pardon?' I'm offended.

'Let's just calm down.' My mother is evidently sensing a row.

'Calm down, my arse. What do you mean, Luc?'

'Lucy!' My mother barks. 'Stop it.' She turns to Luc. 'Tell us what way you meant it, pet.'

She's right. I'm supposed to be the parent.

Luc flicks a look at me. 'I didn't mean it in a judgy way. I just meant it in an informative way. Like, you know, I told you that would happen.'

My mother tilts her head sideways. 'It does sound a bit judgy, though, Luc. I can see why she may have been upset.'

'Yeah, well, I apologised to her but she was just crying and all and she just said I was a prick. And I got cross and said I wasn't a prick. All I was doing was pointing it out to her and she said she didn't need anything pointed out to her and that I was just like all the other arseholes and for me to piss off.' His voice catches a little.

'Don't upset yourself,' my mother can't bear to see him sad, 'Cherry knows you're not a . . .' She hesitates, reluctant to say the word.

'Prick?' Luc mutters.

'Yes,' she says. 'She knows you go out of your way to help her.'

'I do,' Luc agrees. 'I'm not like Dad. '

And there it is. The reason he's such a pushover, determined to be thought of as a nice, dependable guy. I swallow a lump.

'Oh, pet, your dad wasn't all bad.' My mother sounds like I feel as she hops up to embrace him. 'Didn't he jump through a window to save your life?'

'I know,' Luc says, his voice muffled from my mother's hug. 'But he really upset Mam, and I just never wanted to do that to Cherry and—'

'All you have to do to be a good partner, Luc, is to have Cherry's back.'

I have his attention. If he needs anything from me now, it's honesty and that's hard for me in relation to Rob and relationships in general. As my mother releases him, I continue, trying to keep a lid on my emotions, 'Thick and thin, Luc. And that doesn't include threatening violence on people who hurt her. It means being whatever she needs you to be. All I ever wanted from your dad – all anyone wants – was a wingman. Cherry needs to feel that she's never alone dealing with crap. If you think you can handle that, call her. If not, you're better off out of it now.'

As the words fall into the room, I dip my head. I'd laid my own heart and longing out there too.

Luc takes a moment. 'I don't want to lose her. I . . . I really like her.'

I bring my gaze to his. 'Then you know what to do.'

A long silence. Finally, he offers me a small smile. He knows how much the admission has cost me but he's not quite sure how to acknowledge it. 'Thanks, Mam.'

'No bother.' I offer him one back.

As he leaves the room, he touches my shoulder briefly and I rub his hand, and then he's gone. It's like a goodbye. I have the strange sensation that I've lost him. He's someone's else's boy now.

When I turn back to my mother, her expression makes me uncomfortable. It's like she can see right through me into the lonely woman I fear I'm becoming.

'Oh, Luce,' she says, and she looks as if she might cry.

I deliberately ignore the emotion. 'Yeah, I can't believe I'm trying to get him back with Cherry.'

And she manages a laugh.

41

I fear Dan is going to get sick, he's laughing so much when I tell him of Luc's latest problems.

'She's a vegan.' He cracks up. 'Jesus Christ, that's hilarious.'

'Shut up.' I thump him. 'This is serious. He's bloody heartbroken. If Cherry doesn't get back with him, he'll be devastated.'

'Who'll be devastated?' Larry enters, all slick suit and shiny shoes. I don't know why he dresses like that: he barely sets foot outside the office, glued as he is to the CCTV. When we ignore him, he says, 'Wild guess. Something to do with Lucy's young fella.'

'How the—'

'Oh!' He raises his fist in triumph. 'We all know the look you get when your son – what's his name?'

I don't answer.

'– Liam or something has fecked things up.'

'For your information, my son rarely fecks things up.' This lands like a hammer on a metal floor, the clang of the lie reverberating around the room. 'Plus, what do you mean you all know the look I get?'

Jordy shuffles into the room. 'Eh, Luce . . .'

'Oy, Jord,' Larry settles himself in front of his computer and switches it on, 'what look does Lucy get on her face when her young lad has done something?'

'Aw, now.' Jordy puts up his hands. 'I'm not getting involved here, none of my business. I have that file for you, Lucy.'

'Good.' I turn my back on Larry and follow Jordy from the office. I hear Dan and Larry chortling away, the feckers.

'Do I get a look on my face?' I whisper to Jordy, as we make our way to the incident room where a box containing all the paperwork of the Mary Roche investigation is laid on the table. Not waiting for an answer, I pull open the lid and peer inside at the copious amount of filing we've to wade through. 'Shit.'

'I'm thinking,' Jordy sounds a bit defeated, 'that there is no way we'll manage to get through all that stuff today.'

'Then we'd better sort out what we think is important.' I pick up a sheaf of pages and a photograph slides out and flutters to the floor.

Jordy bends down to retrieve it. I wince as his knees crack. Handing it to me, he says, 'Mary Roche. Neither of the Loftuses recognised her. Hazel, the poor woman, you couldn't be asking her anything. She's all over the place. Anyway, no one recognised her.'

I do.

I've seen her before.

'I said—'

I hold up my hand to stop Jordy distracting me. I fecking know this woman. Or I've seen her in the course of the investigation.

And then with the suddenness of a firework exploding, I know the link she had with Jerry.

But do I know why they were both killed?

After the drama in my house last night, I can take a good guess at it.

'We have it, Jordy,' I tell him, with a delighted laugh. 'We fecking have it!'

42

At eleven o'clock he pulls up to the garish blue gates of Leonard's palatial mansion. Far from that the little prick was reared, he'd bet. He remembers Leonard from back in the day. He had been a likeable gobshite but just not cool enough for the three of them. They were tight, and back then they were like a family. No one else mattered.

None of them realised that the little fecker was watching them so closely. And even if they had noticed, they never would have suspected that he could sink so low as to pull their world asunder. And, what's more, continue to do it ever since.

He smiles grimly as he presses the buzzer on the gate.

'Hello?'

'Hew Hartt.'

'Aw, great. Can you look at the camera? It's just above the gatepost on the right.'

The image he'd put on the website looks nothing like him. He glances upwards, smiles, hoping the shades and his growth of beard will fudge things a little.

'Hew Hartt, the journalist?' Leonard sounds cagey.

'You've been on my website.' He manages a light laugh. 'That picture is years old and I'd looked my best that day.'

Leonard laughs back. 'Aw, yeah, sure.'
The gates slide open and he's in.

Leonard is waiting for him at the top of the driveway and, from his attire, he appears to be going for a hipster vibe. Loose jeans, sandals — in fecking December — and a stripy top that looks as if it's woven from wheat. The whole outfit only serves to make him appear in need of a good feed.

He pulls his car to a stop and Leonard runs lightly towards him, his hand held out in welcome.

Oh, good.

So far, all his scores have been settled outside. He makes a point of it. Murders are harder to solve, apparently, what with tricky weather and the insects and animals that like to feast on bodies.

Leonard is caught in a sticky web now and he doesn't even realise it. He enjoys the man's look of surprise as he steps out of the car. People are always surprised when they see him. Especially when he wears the red sweatshirt, jeans and shoes. They think he looks a little odd, and he does. But red hides the colour of blood quite well. Before the man has a chance to pull away or think how different he is from his website picture, he grasps his hand in his gloved one. Pumps it. 'Hello,' he says. 'We meet again.' He drops his accent.

Leonard seems not to have noticed. 'Again?'

'Yes.' He squeezes Leonard's hand ever so slightly, not enough to raise alarm, not yet. 'Don't you remember?'

Leonard frowns.

'I guess I made the same impression on you that you made on us.'

The penny drops. Len gasps, realises something is off and tries desperately to wrestle his hand free.

Ever so slowly, enjoying the look of naked terror on Leonard's face, he begins to crush Leonard's hand in his own. Leonard's eyes pop.

THE WRATH

'*You ruined our lives with what you did, do you know that?*'

'*I never meant—*'

'*Was it revenge because we laughed at you? Was it—*'

'*No, no.*' *Beads of sweat pop out all over Leonard's forehead.* '*Like I told the guards, I was just trying to illegally record the film and I—*'

'*I have no respect for liars.*'

'*It's the truth. I swear I—*'

'*That footage shows no film.*'

'*Yes, because a woman was being assaulted in front of me.*'

Oh, a little bit of spunk. Nice.

His grip loosens and Leonard takes advantage, slipping and sliding away.

He reaches into his car and pulls the axe from the front seat.

Leonard, barefooted, has made it to the back of the house.

Holding the axe, he raises it above his head, keeping it steady and straight and hurls it through the air.

It clatters to the ground a foot from the little bastard.

No!

He runs full tilt as Leonard disappears behind his back wall. Bare feet do not travel well on gravel and Leonard is not fast. He catches up, grabs his shirt and knocks him to the ground, face first. Standing astride him, pulling out the knife, he says, with composed fury, '*It was only a little pinch. Far worse is done on women every day and Phoebe got over it.*' *A flash of Phoebe with her smiles and her kindness.*

Leonard turns his head. Says, as he spits gravel from his mouth, '*Of course she did. Didn't she make money from it? Set herself up nicely, so she did.*'

'*She had talent. And she was gracious enough not to press charges. People respected that.*' *He bends down, knife held aloft.*

Unexpectedly Leonard laughs. '*You don't know, do you?*'

He freezes. 'Don't know what?'

'You deluded fuck.'

It's like a slap in the face. He rears back. One time his mother had called his daddy that. Then she'd left.

'Let me tell you something,' Leonard says, blood and teeth falling now from his mouth. 'Phoebe was the one set it up. She was the one told me to be there. "Sit behind us," she said. "Record what you see." She wanted to use the video for blackmail.'

He won't believe that. Phoebe wouldn't. The knife goes in hard and fast.

Leonard shrieks in pain, clutches his side. Screams, 'It was all her. It was never meant to be public but then that stupid guard and the woman got involved.'

'No!' Jab.

'That's why we sold it to the papers,' Leonard gasps. 'Phoebe needed money. I needed money. She's the one— Stop!'

Jab. Jab. Jab. He barely hears the rest of Leonard's incoherent rambles: his head is roaring, a volcanic eruption of fury and wrath.

After, when Leonard has shut up and is still, he collapses beside his car. He is soaked in blood.

Calm again.

That was not the clean murder he'd hoped for. Somehow, he knows what Leonard said is true. There was always something too unlucky about the recording of the video.

He thinks if he could cry, he would. He feels the way he felt when his mammy left him and his daddy for another family.

His therapist said once that some things are too deep for tears and maybe this is one of them. The betrayal.

He struggles to his feet.

The fucking betrayal.

43

It takes a few goes to locate the video of the assault, the one I'd seen on the TV a few days ago. I try various combinations before searching *video cinema guard assault* and *Leonard Loane*. And there it is.

I pass my phone to Jordy. 'See what you think.'

'Jesus, me eyesight isn't that good.' He shuffles off, unhurried, looking for his glasses. I gaze after him in mild frustration.

He returns a few minutes later with an enormous pair perched on the end of his nose. Taking my phone, he holds it close to his face.

I resist the urge to tell him that maybe he needs a new pair and wait as the video plays out. He says nothing the first time. Instead, he plays it again until finally, handing my phone back, he says, 'That's Mary all right. And that's the Wowser video, is it? The one we all dismissed?"

'Yes. There's your connection.'

'Okay.' He makes a face. 'So they're both in that video. Why would they be killed? What have they done?'

I jab the screen. 'This guy, Wowser, he was a big chef at the time. This video ruined his career, didn't it?'

'So you're thinking . . . revenge?'

'Yeah. Look, the guard and the woman, both drawing attention to him here. Both gone.'

Jordy nods. 'Both killed with the same sort of knife, outdoors, unidentified red fibres found at both scenes.'

A sudden cold fear catches me. 'If that was you, who would you take out next, Jordy?'

'I would have taken him out first, but the guy that filmed the video.'

'We need to find him. And fast. See if he's getting any letters.'

I try to reach William but his phone is off, which is unusual. I'm reluctant to text or mail him, so in the end I leave a voice message telling him to call me urgently, that we may have a breakthrough.

'What now?' Jordy asks.

'I think we should just try to run with this ourselves until William tells us what he wants. We've another,' I glance at my phone, 'eight hours at least before the forty-eight are up, so let's have something decent to give him when he eventually calls. For now, you see what you can find out about Wowser, about the whole case back then. I'll get on to RTÉ, see if I can get Leonard's contact details from them.'

44

There has been no answer on the mobile number that RTÉ provided so I've decided to take Jordy and drive towards Bangor Erris where Leonard lives. On the way to the car, Jordy fills me in on the video and reads aloud bits from the newspapers he's printed out.

'The woman with Wowser in the video is Phoebe Shine,' he huffs out, trying to keep pace with me. 'I have to say, Luce, I'm her biggest fan. She's changed quite a bit since that video, let me tell you.'

That's so unexpected, I stop, turn and he bangs into me.

'Sorry,' he grins, 'but she's a super actress. If she's part of this case, I have to be there.'

'If that happens, I'll do my best to have you there.'

He beams delightedly, which is so unlike him.

'Come on, fan boy,' I tease, as we head towards the car park. 'What else?'

'She's a great girl, survived a lot in her childhood and then she—'

'I was talking about the news reports, Jordy.'

'Of course. Yes, right.' He waits until we're in the car before shuffling some pages and reading them by holding them up close to his face.

'Well, I rang Joe Little again, the sergeant in Dún Laoghaire and he said again that that Wowser video started off as something and nothing. Wowser, a.k.a. Brian Walsh, was hauled in by Jerry, but the whole case came to zero. His girlfriend, that'd be Phoebe, declined to press charges. It turned out that the woman who said she'd seen it all, Mary Roche, had actually seen nothing so Jerry let Wowser off with a caution. The whole thing would have blown over but the video was released to the media. Joe Public got in on the act and crucified Wowser. Jerry became a minor celebrity. There was a lot of auld righteous outrage. I mean, don't get me wrong,' he clarifies hastily, ''tisn't right what he did but the stuff that was done on him was over the top. Someone wrote,' Jordy scans a page, '"Cut off his cock and shove it down his throat." Then someone else offers to do it and then someone else tells them to join the queue.' A glance at me. 'Wouldn't it make you weep for humanity?'

'He did hurt the girl.' I pull out onto the road.

'He did that but, by God, he paid a high price. According to Google, his restaurant was firebombed, he was assaulted in the streets, he lost everything, and Phoebe left him.'

Most of me thinks he deserved it but I know of murderers who haven't lost everything. In fact, some have even gained by their act, getting their share on any jointly owned property, profiting off the savings accounts. 'What Wowser did was wrong.' I'm not willing to defend him, too reminded of Eamon Delaney on our last case to empathise with men who abuse women. I nod towards the articles. 'I'm thinking it makes for a good motive, though, eh?'

THE WRATH

'Man who loses everything takes it out on those who caused his downfall?'

'Something like that.'

Jordy makes a face. 'Devil's advocate. Murder is a big step. Lots of people go through the cancel mill and don't murder people.'

'Lots of people get dumped by their spouses and don't murder people, but there are some who do.'

'Aye.' Jordy chews his lower lip. 'He does have an alibi for the Jerry Loftus murder, though. I checked it out myself. '

'I know, but two people associated with the video are dead, one of them a bare six months after it was filmed. Let's see if Leonard can shed any light on things for us.'

45

Forty minutes later, with only a few hours of William's deadline left, Jordy and I are nearing Bangor Erris. The last time I was here was when I was doing a stake-out for the night-caller case. Bangor is a small village with one road, great swathes of Mayo bog spreading out on either side. The Oweniny river winds its way in, out and on, and Leonard Loane, as far as I can figure, lives on the far side of the river, about a kilometre from the Bangor walking trail, which is a thirty-nine kilometre walk from Newport. It's been described as the loneliest place on earth, and as we drive the undulating bog road, with not a soul in sight and all the world a misty grey, the eternal sky blending into the landscape, I can well believe it.

The gates to Leonard's house are open, almost as if he's expecting us, but of course he can't be because we had no way of contacting him. The long tarmacked driveway, slippery with rotting leaves from the bare trees on either side, curves, after a few hundred metres, in a large sweep about the front of an extravagant house. Property is not expensive in this part of the world, but Leonard still must be earning a packet to afford this place. I'm in the wrong job, I think.

THE WRATH

As I step from the car, I have an eerie feel that something is off. I follow Jordy to the door and he rings the bell.

The sound echoes inside the house.

No answer.

The silence is thick out here.

Jordy presses the bell again.

Nothing.

'Hello!' I call. 'Leonard Loane? This is Detective Sergeant Lucy Golden and Garda Jordy . . .' I look at Jordy, suddenly aware that I have no idea what his second name is.

'Donal Jordan,' he offers bashfully.

'Garda Donal Jordan. We have a few questions for you if you could just open up.'

Not even the twitch of a curtain.

'I did look at his social media before we left,' Jordy says. 'His last post was a week ago identifying Jerry as the guard in the Wowser video.'

I rap on the door again. 'Maybe he's away.'

Jordy raises his eyebrows, asks, 'Why was the gate open?'

I was thinking the same myself. There is a prickling under my skin and my heart rate has soared. I point left. 'You take that side of the house, Jordy, I'll take this. Shout if you see anything.'

Maybe it's the isolation of the place, or the oppressive weather, or the way the wind keens across the lake, but it's a bit freaky. The dark is creeping in too; whatever light there is bleeding away behind the clouds.

And the way the house stands over it all, casting a shadow.

Just as Jordy disappears left, I round the corner of the house towards the back.

I hear and smell it before I see it.

The lazy hum of flies.

The stench of a recently dead body.

Oh, Jesus.

'Jordy!' I shout. 'We've got someone here. We need to preserve the scene. Get on it now.'

William arrives two hours later, as dishevelled as I've ever seen him. Agatha Grimes has been and gone, making some crack about me being a cadaver dog in a previous life. SOCO are examining the grounds and the interior of the house for anything that might help. I fill William in on what Jordy and I uncovered as he stands over the body of what was once Leonard Loane. He stares impassively down on him.

I know that's for show. I know he'll be going bloody mad with another murder on his patch. A murder of someone relatively well known, too. The papers will be all over it.

'You're getting great at finding trouble, aren't you?' he remarks wryly. 'And you think this relates to Jerry Loftus how?'

'Jerry Loftus and Mary Roche,' I correct him, and he shoots me an impatient look, not fully convinced. I go through the whole Wowser-video theory.

'So you're saying none of our other suspects fit? We've wasted the last week chasing the wrong guys?'

I don't go there. What's the point? Instead I talk about Leonard. 'Agatha thinks he was assaulted before he was killed but, obviously, she won't know until she examines him.' I point towards Leonard's face. 'But the jaw does look to be broken, as are the fingers.'

His hand is completely misshapen.

'It looks like he was killed just hours before ye arrived. Any sign of notes? Axe wound? Anything more concrete to link it?'

THE WRATH

'The video links all three,' I say, 'and—'

'William, Lucy?' It's John, one of the SOCOs. 'We found this on the bed.'

A note, in a red envelope. One word. 'Karma'.

And I think, thank God.

46

The investigation spins off in another direction, like one of those tops kids used to get that whirled all over the place. Everything we have is examined once more. The CCTV from Leonard's house unsurprisingly stopped working but at least the date and time it was stopped help to pinpoint exactly when he was murdered.

'Yesterday morning,' Larry tells the room. 'The last footage we have is this.' He presses play and images from nine cameras appear on the board at the top of the room. He zooms in on one. 'Here is Leonard and I've watched this over and over. All he does is watch TV or pop into the kitchen to grab some food.'

'Bit like yourself then, eh?' Ben quips.

Laughter before Larry adds, 'But he's jumpy. He doesn't seem to settle for too long.'

William turns to Ben. 'You were tracing Wowser, weren't you? Any luck?'

'Yep, Cig. He's actually going by his real name nowadays, Brian Walsh. He really took a bit of a nosedive after that video was published. He's currently working in Express Pizza and a bit of a recluse by all accounts. Now, if anyone should have been

THE WRATH

aggrieved over that video, it was him. He lost everything. We've the lads in Galway primed to arrest him and bring him here later today.'

'Good. You and Larry can take it.'

I'm annoyed at that. Me and Jordy got this lead: the least he could have done was let me and Dan question him. I'd bet my house that Wowser is behind it all.

'Susan, you were asking Hazel about the scratch on Jerry's car. Any luck?'

'No. She can't remember. Just said it was there one day when they woke up. She thinks it was a long time ago. '

'Any pictures of the car? Anything we can try to date it to?'

She looks incredulous. 'Who would take pictures of a car?'

'It may be in the background of something. Look.' He turns impatiently from her. 'Jordy, anything from Phoebe Shine's people?'

We'd contacted Phoebe's agent last night after Leonard had turned up dead in an effort to speak to her.

'Nothing, Cig,' Jordy says. 'They said they'd call last night. I'll call again.'

'Cig.' A hand shoots up from the back of the room. It's one of the regular lads, Mark or something.

When William indicates for him to continue, he says, 'Phoebe Shine rang on the confidential line. She gave me her number. She wants to talk to us urgently.'

'Jesus Christ, when did this happen?'

'Last night.'

'Last night – and you only come with this now?' William doesn't wait for the poor lad to answer. 'Do you know how many times people promise to speak to us, then think about it and pull out, Mark? Did you not learn in Templemore about striking while the iron is hot?'

The poor fellow looks hot himself. 'I didn't want to disturb anyone. I just thought—'

'Don't think, just do. Lucy,' William turns to me, 'for the love of God, get the number from that idiot there and ring Phoebe right now.'

'Sure.' I push my way through the crowd, all of whom are trying not to look at Mark, everyone knowing what it feels like to be on the receiving end of William's tongue. 'Come on,' I say to Mark, 'let's get that number.'

He follows me out of the room. 'I just thought—'

'Look, if anything like that ever comes in, you call someone. Play it safe.'

'I've really messed up, haven't I?'

'Everyone makes mistakes at some point,' I say, feeling sorry for him. 'Sure, I messed up years back and it's all forgotten about now.'

He frowns. 'I'm not sure it is because—'

'Let's just . . . Just give me the number.' I hold out my hand.

He digs through a file and hands it to me.

'Go on back in.'

'Can't I just stay here with you, see what happens?'

He's scared, I think in amusement. 'All right.'

The number rings out. Shit. He'll be in big trouble if we can't get hold of Phoebe.

On the third attempt, thankfully, someone picks up with a husky purr. 'Hello.'

I introduce myself and, after a pause, 'I rang last night,' Phoebe says. 'My agent contacted me, told me about . . . about Leonard.

THE WRATH

Said ye wanted to talk to me. Can I ask a question?' Her voice breaks a little.

'Sure.'

'Was it anything to do with the letters he was getting?'

A bright jewel of a question. 'How do you know he was getting letters?'

'Because he asked me if I was getting them. He was scared. And I got two yesterday.'

47

Phoebe is sobbing as she answers our questions. It's odd because she's also smoking heavily, not an easy feat. Jordy and I are in her trailer, which is where she spends the time when she's not needed on set. It's nicer than my house, except for the fug of smoke hanging heavy in the air and the overflowing dustbin. Jordy is puffing contentedly beside her, which isn't exactly allowed but she seemed to calm down when he agreed to join her in a cigarette.

'You said you heard about Leonard and that you think you may be next,' I say. 'Why?'

She scrubs a hand across her eyes. 'Len rang me, maybe a month ago – we keep in touch, you know. He's not, like, a friend or anything but he's good to keep onside. You can't trust him, you know. Anyway, looking back, he sounded a bit spooked. He said he was getting these weird letters and he wondered if I was getting them too. In red envelopes, he said. Now, Leonard has done some shit in his time, you know, bringing people down, so I wasn't surprised if some freak was targeting him. I told him I'd had no letters but then last night . . .' she swallows hard '. . . two arrived.'

'Two?'

'Yes.'

'Have you got them there?'

She places her cigarette on the side of the ashtray and, in one fluid motion, stands up from the table and reaches into a press, giving us a view of her pert backside. As she pulls out the envelopes, a load of other papers tumble onto the floor.

'I hoard.' She winces at the mess, then steps over it to hand me two envelopes.

With gloved hands, I take them from her. Opening them, I extract the A4 pages. The pasted-on letters are in capitals.

LYING BITCH

The second one reads, LAST FILM YOU WILL MAKE

They look identical to the others but something is off. I can't figure out what it is.

'No Bible references.' Jordy gets there before me.

'Yeah. Good catch.' I take a look at the envelopes. They weren't posted either. This is a bit different. 'How did you get these?'

'One of the runners handed me them yesterday. I thought it was fan mail until I opened them.'

'Would you get many crank letters at all?'

'No.' She shrugs. 'I'm not, like, mega-famous.'

'Not yet,' Jordy says, and she offers him a shy smile.

As I place the letters in evidence bags, I ask, 'Would you recognise this runner again?'

'Probably not.'

'That's all right, I'll track him down. Now, just a few more questions. What do you know about this video?'

I hand her my mobile and, as the video starts playing, she visibly pales. 'Damn.' With shaking fingers she picks up her cigarette and inhales as deeply as a dementor sucking out the soul of Harry Potter. A tear tracks down her cheek.

'Now, now.' Jordy pats her arm. He's entranced by her. She's his dream woman, beautiful and a kindred smoking spirit to boot.

'That video was . . .' A pause. 'Is Wowser out to get us?'

'It's a line of enquiry we're investigating. We're arresting Wowser today. Anything you tell us may be helpful.' I don't tell her that, apart from Wowser, she's the only one alive from that video.

'The video was my fault,' she says softly. 'I always felt bad about it.'

'Explain that to me.'

'He used to hit me. And when I challenged him, he'd brush it off as a joke. Like it was slaps on the bum or whacks on the head, nothing too hard, just unexpected. I doubted myself and he made me so many promises. He was going to kick start my career, set me up. I think he did it just to keep me dangling. In the beginning, I loved him. He had a great personality when he wasn't being a dickhead.' She sighs shakily, flicks ash onto the floor. 'We met in drama school. He was a great actor, the best in the year, he could do anything, but he was just passing time. His heart was always in cooking and flavours. We were the best-fed drama students ever.' She looks a little wistful at the memory. 'And then, sure, the restaurant came about and he swore he'd use the profits to make me a star. To make us all stars. I believed him. He was funny and charming and, yes, his profile was helping mine. But,' another drag on her cigarette, 'after a while, I realised he was just playing me. He's good at that. Knows what to say to keep you reeled in so you'll do just about anything for him. He puts you down and brings you back up. Took me years to see it and when I did, and I only did because my mother said it to me, I got really mad.'

She looks at Jordy, at me. 'I did a terrible thing. I always felt mean about it. I befriended Len – he wasn't always the horrible pap he became. In those days, he was a bit pathetic, hanging around us, looking for Wowser's autograph, selfies with him, whatever. And I guess, well, I started to show him a bit of attention and he lapped it up, like I knew he would. I mean, what I did was as bad as what Wowser was doing to me.' She takes a moment to get herself under control. 'And when Len was, you know, half in love with me, I let a few bruises show, only they weren't real, I used stage make-up and,' she swipes a hand over her face, 'made out Wowser was worse than he was. I confided to Len that I'd love to get a video of Wowser hurting me so I could blackmail him into paying me off. Len jumped on it. He wasn't even looking for money. And then it all went wrong and I couldn't use it and Len decided to go public with it. He knew gold when he saw it. And he got paid a shitload of money and he was generous enough to offer me half. And I took it.'

More tears spill down her cheeks. 'Our relationship was over by then. I mean, I had to leave Wowser after it all came out, and when I did, I had nothing. I needed the money. I didn't press charges, though, because I felt so bad about what I'd done, and if I did press charges, it might have come out in the wash and . . . It was so shameful to me.' She looks at us. 'I've never told anyone that before, you know.'

'You think Wowser is behind the letters?'

'Who else could it be?' She stubs out her cigarette and lights another. 'I just wanted to blackmail Wowser. I figured he owed me. I never meant to get anyone killed.'

'Of course you didn't,' Jordy says, as if blackmail is nothing to worry about.

'Ten minutes, Phoebe.' Some young lad pokes his head into the trailer, bounces out and slams the door after him.

'I tried calling Leonard after I got the letter but there was no answer. I . . . Maybe he was . . . he was dead by then, wasn't he?' More tears, more ash onto the floor. 'And it's all my fault.'

'It's not your fault,' Jordy says. 'We all do things we regret. And Wowser was hitting you.'

'He was and it made me angry, you know?'

'I do.' Jordy nods. A man who wouldn't know a ruffled feather if he saw one.

'Did you ever tell anyone you and Leonard had set the whole thing up between you?'

'No. Like I said, I was ashamed.' Her shoulders start to shake as her sobbing escalates.

'Now, now,' Jordy says kindly. 'We're here, we'll mind you.'

'Five minutes, Phoebe!' The boy pops his head in again. Then, horrified, he splutters, 'You're ruining your make-up.'

She ignores him as she turns big pleading eyes on Jordy, who visibly swells with importance. 'What can I do?'

'We have Wowser in custody as of this minute,' he tells her gravely, in a very un-Jordy-like way. 'He's going to be cooling his heels for a while and then we'll grill him. Don't you worry, we'll keep you updated.'

'Eh . . . just saying,' the young lad interjects, 'Make-up will need to see you, Phoebe.'

'I'm in the middle of a crisis.'

'Yeah, but . . .'

'Out!' She points her cigarette at him. 'Out!'

THE WRATH

He glances at his watch. 'Four and a half minutes,' he says, with spirit, before legging it.

'You have another cigarette there,' Jordy tells her. 'I always like a cigarette when I'm under stress.'

He must be constantly under stress then.

She nods. 'Me too.'

'Jordy will stay with you,' I say, because they seem to have bonded, 'and you know what, we'll get a couple of local lads to come down here as well.' They'll jump at it. The food here looks amazing. 'I'm going to see if I can track down this runner fellow.'

Before I go in search of him, I walk the set. I even walk down to the main road and back up again. The journey from there to the set is via a long single lane. Temporary traffic lights are installed at each end but there is no CCTV, just security guards monitoring the cars going in and out of the main set. But after observing them for a while, I know that all you have to say is that you're an extra and they'll let you by. They don't even have a list of names to check off. It takes me a while to get a list of the runners, a lot of disgruntled muttering, and it's only after I threaten to close down the filming that ten young lads are sent to me.

'Which one of you delivered two red envelopes to Phoebe Shine yesterday evening?'

Two young lads redden up like tomatoes. Odd.

'You two,' I zoom in on them. 'Go on, the rest of you.'

Lad One looks at Lad Two.

'I never did,' Lad One says. 'Cross my heart. I never did.'

Lad Two stares down at his tatty Nike runners. 'It was me,' he admits. 'What's the big deal?'

'Can I go?' Lad One asks. 'The director wants a cup of soup and—'

'Go on.'

He sprints off and I turn my attention to Lad Two. 'What age are you?'

'Twenty.'

Thank God. Any younger and I wouldn't be able to talk to him. 'Right, tell me all about the person who asked you to deliver the letters.'

He looks relieved. 'Just some guy. He was in the extras' car park and he called me over as I was walking to set and asked me to deliver them.'

'What did he look like?'

'I dunno. It was raining and cold and dark, and I wasn't exactly looking. He had shades on. I think he was tall enough – his head was almost at the ceiling of the car. And he gave me four letters. Two for her that evening and two today.'

'Have you got the other letters there?'

He pulls two envelopes, folded up, totally battered, from his back pocket. 'Hard to keep them looking good.'

'Indeed.' I place them in an evidence bag and he looks on, bug-eyed.

'Did I do something wrong?'

'Anything could have been in those letters. Aren't you warned about doing things like that?'

He reddens. 'Yeah, but people do it.'

He got a few bob for it he means.

'How much did he pay you?'

'One hundred.'

More like two, I reckon.

THE WRATH

I ask him again about the man. I go through it in detail but there's nothing else he can say. He didn't even get the colour of the car.

'If you see this man again,' I hand him my card, 'I need to know. It's very important.'

'Can I go now?'

'Yeah.'

He pockets the card and hurries off.

By the time I get back, Jordy is seated in a fancy chair at the side of the film set. He's wrapped up in a sheepskin blanket and smoking contentedly. His gaze is paternal as he nods to Phoebe, who is now dressed in evening wear for a shoot of a dinner dance. 'They say never meet your heroes,' he wheezes, 'but they're wrong. She's amazing. The Fiona to my Shrek.'

I laugh as he chuckles. 'I'm just going to call the Cig with an update.'

'Phoebe's got four letters so far,' I tell William, some minutes later. 'I think she's in imminent danger. The person responsible was here, in the extras' car park, yesterday evening. He bribed one of the crew to deliver the letters to her. The set is easy to access, no security on it.'

There's a long silence from the other end.

'Cig?'

'Well, whoever is doing this, it's not Wowser. It can't be. Stay there, keep an eye. They're giving him another going over in Interview Room Two now but I think we're flogging a dead horse. Are we sure these are all connected to the video?'

My heart plummets in disappointment. 'But it has to be. Jerry was the guard, Mary was a potential witness, Phoebe and Leonard were setting him up. Now, unless all four have another connection that we don't know of, it has to be the video.'

'I'll get Larry to give you a bell in a while after the interview concludes. Should only be another ten minutes. Hang tight.'

'Is he tall?'

'Tall, good-looking and very personable.'

And he's gone. And before I can think about what all that means for our investigation, another call comes in. 'DS Lucy Golden.'

'Hiya, Lucy, it's, eh . . . Eddie here.'

'Oh, hey, Eddie. How's things?'

'Better, eh. You said I could call if I remembered, eh . . . anything else.'

'Of course. Go ahead.' He sounds good.

'The Devil, he didn't get into a chariot. Surprise. Eh, it was a Renault, I'm pretty certain. My sister has one. Blue.'

That doesn't fit. 'You sure?'

'Yeah. As I can be.'

'Great. Thanks, Eddie. Bye now. Take care.' I put the phone down. We're looking for a Ford. Con, the witness from the pub, said he saw a Ford parked against the side of the pub. A blue one. Could he have got it wrong? He got the other makes right so it seems unlikely. And Eddie? His information will be laughed out of court.

I'm on my way back to Jordy when Larry calls.

I brace myself.

48

'Wowser has nothing to do with anything,' Larry says, sounding a bit pissed off, probably because he didn't nail his man. 'He was a decent enough guy, actually, said back in the day he was a cocky arsehole, deserved everything he got. But more importantly, all his alibis check out. He was in work both days the murders were committed. You played a blinder there, Luce.'

I ignore his snarky tone. 'Did you confront him about the video? Did you tell him that everyone was now dead bar him and Phoebe?'

'No, no, I didn't.' A beat, a snort. 'Jesus, course I did. You know what he said? He was upset. Wondered if he could be next. I mean, he was genuinely upset. Plus, the Cig told us that the guy you're looking for was at the film set last night. D'you know where this fella Wowser was?'

He doesn't expect me to answer.

'Helping in a homeless shelter. Trust me, this is not our guy.'

He is totally annoyed and I don't blame him.

'Is William there?'

'He won't tell you any different.'

'Someone connected to the video is doing this. We're missing something.'

Larry gives an exasperated sigh and there follows a muttered conversation, no doubt Larry bitching about my refusal to face the facts.

Then next thing I know, William says, 'I've the lads combing through all the witness statements again, Lucy. But that fella, the video guy, Leonard, he had a lot of enemies. Wowser was the first guy he exposed but he was a fast learner, made a pretty good living digging the dirt on others after that. And, apparently, he rang a lot of people asking them if they were getting those letters. It wasn't just Phoebe.'

'But we know for a fact that three of our victims got letters.'

'That's not proof of murder. The actress, I'll bet she gets creepy letters all the time, as do the guards.'

He has a point.

'Plus, Mary was murdered two years ago. And the evidence against her husband was damning.'

I know he's playing Devil's advocate, but it's frustrating. 'The husband's conviction was too easy, and you know what you always say about too easy.' Before he can reply, I plough on: 'Also the letters our IPs got appear to be identical. Red envelopes, pasted on.' I tell him about Phoebe's letters being slightly different, that I think it's way more personal with her than it was with the others. 'Look, Wowser must have found out and—'

'If you don't believe Larry, believe me. The man was nowhere near those scenes yesterday. His alibi for Jerry's murder is solid. Now, I did think he was a bit too sweet to be wholesome but you know me, a cynic.' Then he adds, 'And, honestly, this fella couldn't throw a party never mind an axe. He's tall but puny.'

THE WRATH

'If Wowser isn't a possibility, the question Ben and Larry should be asking is if he knows who's doing it. It's connected to that video. I know it is.' I pause for breath.

William takes a moment to let me cool down.

'If you get back in time you can have a crack at Wowser yourself,' he says. 'Otherwise, we're releasing him at the end of the six-hour detention period. Is there a garda presence with Phoebe Shine?'

'There will be. Two detectives. Jordy is with her now.'

'Leave Jordy with her as well. It's good if she likes him.'

That's decent of him: I know we're short on resources. I wish it was someone other than Jordy, though. I'm not sure he'd be much good in a fight.

I disconnect the call and make my way back to Jordy. He's still tucked under his blanket, Phoebe by his side, lighting a cigarette for him. 'I'll send you some of my more expensive ones when I get the chance,' she says, placing the cigarette between his lips.

I give Jordy the news that he's staying put for now.

'It'd be my honour,' Jordy says, grinning up at Phoebe. 'Sure, we'll have a grand time.'

'We will.' Phoebe beams. 'Jordy is great.'

'You'll have two other lads with you, and they'll be armed.' I feel odd leaving him here, like abandoning my kid in a supermarket, but Jordy seems happy enough. 'Take care, right,' I say to him, and he flaps a hand at me to get going.

By the time I pull into the station car park, it's pelting rain. Through the windscreen of my car, I spot a man matching Wowser's description at the front desk.

Aw, no, they must be letting him go.

I leg it out of the car, across the tarmac, rain lashing my face, and push open the door.

Wowser is signing for his things. Dan and William look on as he pockets his phone and zips up his jacket.

'Who is doing this, Wowser?' I'm breathless with the fifty-metre dash and have to hold onto the door frame.

Wowser turns towards me. His fingers are long and slender. In no universe would they be described as fat. 'Who are you?' He looks mildly surprised. He's tall and, yes, very good-looking. No wonder Phoebe fell for him.

'DS Lucy Golden, I just want to know who is—'

'We asked him, Lucy,' William says wearily, 'in the interview.'

'Asked me what?' Wowser says.

'If you know who's doing this.'

William glares at me.

Wowser pockets his phone and his wallet. 'Jesus, I don't.' He looks upset. 'How would I? Jesus.'

'You're free to go,' William says.

'I hear you're a good actor.'

'Lucy,' William says softly, 'he's free to go now.'

'I'm a good chef, or I was.' He sounds despondent. 'I was never an actor. Anyway, I've done nothing.' Now his voice hardens. 'Nothing.'

With a bit of a glare, he walks past me.

And with another glare, William does an about-turn and leaves me on my own in Reception.

Damn anyway.

49

My mother can always tell when I'm not listening to her. I'd asked about Luc and she'd told me there was no word from him as yet, that Cherry was not at her apartment but that Luc was tracking her down. Then she had mentioned she had other news for me that might be described as 'some news of the night'. So, I fix a smile on my face, to make it look like I'm listening. Instead, I think about the case. I've spent the last few hours going over witness statements, wondering how Wowser fits into all this. Because he does. He has to. I read back the transcripts of the interviews we've held and something in Alan Lynch's jars. I just can't put my finger on it. I've missed something and my brain is too tired to figure it out, and yet, I can't let it go.

I become aware suddenly, as I chew a slice of lukewarm pizza, that silence has descended on the kitchen. My mother's chatter has faded away and she's looking at me with a mix of disappointment and challenge. 'What do you think?' she asks.

'Mmm,' I pretend my mouth is too full, 'great.'

A moment. Her eyes narrow, 'That's all you can say? Did you know already?'

'I had an inkling.'

'The last time you saw the woman she wasn't engaged.'

Best to say nothing, I reckon.

She folds her arms, nods, as if satisfied with her conclusion. 'You weren't listening.'

'I was. You were saying about an engagement, and I said I'd had an inkling.'

'What engagement?'

'Your friend.' Part of me relishes the challenge of convincing her, of seeing how much I can get away with.

'Delores,' she says.

'Delores is engaged?'

'Ha! I knew you weren't listening.'

That's impressive. That was worthy of a level-four detective. 'All right, sorry. Go on, you have my full attention.' I put the pizza down. 'How did you find this—'

'You need to let work go when you come home, Luce,' she says, with some concern. 'I know you still don't sleep and you get bad dreams. I hear you rattling about in the early hours and then you're gone for the day, seeing God knows what, and I worry. I mean, this place—'

'Tell me about Delores.' I thought she hadn't noticed the way I wander around the house at night, trying to shake off nightmares. They've changed from blood-soaked to ones in which I'm drowning. I've always had a terror of water.

'– has gone to the dogs. Are you any nearer to getting someone for that –'

'Delores?'

'– poor man? And him an ex-guard. And now this other fella out in Bangor. That video fella we were only laughing at last week. I mean, who'll be next? And I saw you on the news today, walking with your boss. And I'm telling you, the camera did you no favours.'

'Are you or are you not going to tell me about Delores?'

Her mouth snaps closed. Then, 'Will you listen this time?'

'Yes.'

She takes a second to compose herself before bursting out brightly, 'She got engaged today! I was there! Well, it was me and Lorna. Having coffee! In a hotel! For Lorna's birthday! And across the room from us, this man got down on one knee to ask this woman to marry him and it was Delores! Imagine! And when she'd helped him back up, because apparently he was not supposed to be kneeling down at his age, she said yes and Lorna and I cheered and she spotted us and we all had a drink of champagne. His name is Fred and he seems like a very nice man.' She lowers her voice: 'No oil painting, mind you, but looks don't matter at our age.' A moment, then, 'Delores was thrilled.'

Not as thrilled as Dan will be, I reckon.

'Now, she was a bit worried about how Fran would take it but I said if he loves you he'll be delighted.'

Dan must love Delores a lot, I think.

'Now, I'd never go again,' my mother says, with a shudder, 'Men are all very well but would you want more than one?'

And yet she keeps trying to match-make me. 'You certainly would not.'

Her face falls as she realises what she's said. 'At my age, I mean. Up until sixty is a nice time to remarry but after that men just become a problem. Now this Fred has bad knees, and that's going to be a problem, but a man of fifty, he wouldn't . . .'

As she rattles on about Fred Keane, my mind wanders once more, flipping over the facts we have.

'Are you listening?'

My phone rings and it's Dan. It saves me from another ear-bashing. 'Sorry, Mam, I've got to take this.'

'It'd better not be work!'

'Hiya, what's happening?'

'She got engaged!' He says it in a whisper but even that can't disguise the delight in his tone. I think he's outdoors because, in the background, I hear a car go by and, further off, raised voices. 'Isn't it flipping great? And guess what, old Freddie boy has a few bob. He didn't tell her because he was afraid of gold-diggers.'

'So, this call isn't about the case?' I tease.

'Once I'm out of the station, I let it all go,' he says. 'Just wait and let the mind do its thing.' Then back to the engagement: 'Fran is going ape. Yelling at her that she's betrayed her first husband and she's in there bawling her eyes out.'

I feel a stab of pity for poor Delores. 'That's terrible. Is Fred there?'

'No, she wanted to break the news to us herself. And— Oh, hang on, she's coming over. Wait a sec.' He covers the receiver but I hear footsteps crunch on gravel.

Delores's voice is muffled. 'Can you give me a lift, Dan? I will not stay in that house a moment longer. Fran is being completely unreasonable. Honestly, so much for gay sons being close to their mothers.'

'Sure, no bother, just let me finish this call. Lucy,' he says into the receiver. 'I—'

'Is that Lucy? Give it here.' Delores comes on. 'Hello, Lucy, I suppose you heard?'

'Congratulations. I'm delighted for you.'

'Thank you. And Daniel here is such a support. I always thought he didn't like me but he's a rock.'

THE WRATH

'I'll bet,' I say.

'He'll make Fran see sense, won't you, pet?' That's directed at Dan. Then, 'Bye-bye, love.'

Fumbling sounds as she hands the phone back.

'Luce, I'll see you at conference tomorrow. Jaysus, you missed the most boring interview we've ever had at the station. Wowser was grand, cooperative, a bit annoyed because he was missing a day's pay in work but there wasn't a shred of evidence to link him to anything. Larry was really pissed with you. I was laughing my hole off delighted we hadn't been given it.'

'Yeah, serve Larry right.' I snigger. 'Talk tomorrow and try not to be too gleeful in front of Fran.'

'Cross my heart.'

The line goes dead.

50

'As of now,' William says at conference the following day, 'we have two murders on our patch. Because of certain links, we're investigating them together. I know it's a pain in the arse, lads, and I know it eats into any spare time ye wanted off, but I appreciate all your efforts. The first murder, as we found it, was Jerry Loftus and we do have a number of suspects. His lover Alan, who said the last time he saw Jerry was when he came to his house the afternoon he was murdered. They argued. Alan had opportunity and a possible motive in that he was in a secret gay relationship with Jerry. We also have damning forensic evidence against Eddie O'Shea. His DNA is all over the scene, on the knife and on sheets used to wrap the body. And, finally, we have Zak, Jerry's son, who was not in work on the day of the murder, but as we subsequently found out, he was at home with his friend, who has already lied for him once. But the man has motor neurone disease so is unlikely to have been able to kill anyone. Kev, you're checking all that?'

'Zak checks out, Cig. I think we can rule him out.'

'Okay.' He addresses the room again: 'And then we come to Leonard Loane. He was, it has been established, murdered soon before we arrived on the scene, severely beaten, a blow to the head, possibly a kick from a steel-toed boot rendering him unconscious and cracking his skull. He was stabbed a number of times with a knife similar to the one used in Jerry's murder and he had broken fingers. The link between the two men is that both Jerry and Leonard were receiving letters.' He displays them onscreen. 'We found all five in Jerry's case and two in Leonard's. He may have thrown others out. A video, taken over two years ago, which resulted in the loss of Brian Walsh's business, links the two men. Brian Walsh, a.k.a. Wowser. Yesterday we interviewed Brian Walsh and there is no evidence to link him to any of the scenes, though we know that he lost the most when that video was released to the media. He was cancelled for a short while and his business set on fire. He has spent the last few years trying to atone, he told us. Now, we also have this lady here.' He puts up a picture of Mary Roche. 'Murdered barely six months after the video was taken. She, too, was getting letters according to her local priest, though we have no evidence of them. She, too, was in the video, but at the time of her murder, there was damning evidence against her husband and he was subsequently charged and sentenced after a trial. Here, for anyone who hasn't seen it, is the video in question.'

He plays the by now familiar video.

After the screen goes to black, he says, 'Ben, just to cover ourselves, can you see if Alan Lynch or Eddie O'Shea has any links to Leonard Loane? Is there a connection there? If not, are we looking at someone who hasn't come into the picture yet and maybe will once we link the murders? And if there is no link between the cases, well, we have a mountain to climb.'

Silence descends as we imagine just how bloody hard that mountain will be. Two murders in our patch and limited resources. 'We can't assume anything,' William reminds us. 'So, I propose we have a thorough review of all the evidence we have so far.'

My phone pings and William glares at me impatiently. I take a surreptitious glance at it.

An email from Forensics.

'Any more CCTV, Larry?'

As Larry drones on about finding a sticker on the blue car, the one that followed Jerry's from the pub, which identifies it as a hired vehicle, I take a sneaky read of the email.

> Luce – I thought I'd send you the jargon-free version. We ran a comparison test on the red fibres from the Jerry Loftus scene and from the Mary Roche scene. They are identical. Their chemical composition is the same, as is the dye chemistry. Man made, one hundred per cent polyester. I've enclosed an image to give you an idea.

'Cig,' I say, then realise that Larry is still talking. 'Sorry.'

'As I was saying,' Larry sounds miffed, as well he might, seeing as I handed him a dud interview yesterday, 'I'll call the car-hire company today, Cig, see if they can give me a name of whoever hired that car. They might be able to identify it on a partial plate, a colour and the make.'

'Good. Lucy, hope what you have is as good as what Larry gave me.'

'I think it is.' I hold up my phone. 'I requested a comparison between red fibres found at the Mary Roche scene and the fibres found in Jerry Loftus's car and they are identical.'

A ripple of unease goes through the room, because now we may be looking at three connected murders, which is serial-killer territory.

'It goes some way to proving that her husband may not have killed her.'

'Any fibres found at Leonard Loane's scene?'

'Well, no, but they haven't finished there yet.'

'Grand. Mick, chase that up, yeah?'

'Yes, Cig.'

'Anything else come in from them?'

'The note found in Leonard Loane's house was identical to that found at the other scene. There was a partial print on the Karma note, but not enough for court or anything like that. Eh, some other things . . .' Mick flushes bright red. 'Important things. Hang on.' He pulls out his notebook from his back pocket.

'You're meant to keep that in your breast pocket,' William snaps.

Mick wisely says nothing, just flips some pages, his face growing ever more puce. 'Oh, yeah, here we are.' He looks up nervously and William's face is not encouraging. He really does pick on poor old Mick. 'There was a boot mark on the tiles in Leonard's kitchen.' Mick's voice shakes the tiniest bit. 'It was compared to shoes and boots in Leonard's wardrobe but there was nothing that matched up with it. We believe it may have come from the SO as Leonard only had one visitor before the video was wiped and it was his sister. It's been sent out to the main shoe distributors to see if it can be identified. Also, there was some soil deposited by these boots and that's being analysed too. And it appears that our SO took a shower in Leonard's room after the murder. Traces of blood were found on the stair carpet and in the grouting on the tiles. More as I get it.' He closes his notebook and is about to shove it into his back pocket, then remembers. William waits until Mick has put away his notebook correctly, ignoring the fact that poor Mick is all fingers and thumbs.

Finally, after a few excruciating moments, William turns to Ben. 'You were working the Leonard Loane scene, Ben. What have you got?'

'Door-to-door is a whole heap of nothing. There are no neighbours nearby. There was no forced entry, so we think Leonard knew this person and was possibly not threatened by him. CCTV is non-existent. No phone was found at the scene, so we've asked the phone company to send down records and, eh, his computer, I believe, was sent for technical examination.'

'That's right,' Mick pipes up. 'Nothing yet, though.'

'Kev, you were talking to people Leonard exposed. Any suspects there?'

'Yeah. I worked with Susan and Louis on it, Cig. We traced a number of people he exposed over the last eighteen months. We've managed to talk to ten of them so far. Of those, five have been out of the country for over a year, though we're obviously double-checking that. We're nailing down alibis for the rest of them, and it'll be easy enough with the timeline we have for the murder. Most of them have agreed to have their prints taken, with a couple admitting they won't be shedding any tears over him. We'll keep at it.'

'All right. If the murders are connected, whoever killed one killed them all. Lucy, Dan and Kev, go back over all the witness statements in the Jerry Loftus case. That's your priority. Let's make sure we've done as much as we can there. Mick, stick with Forensics on both cases. Ben, Susan, Louis and Ger, carry on with the Leonard Loane case. I'm keeping Jordy with Phoebe Shine for today anyway. Jim has the work sheets. Get cracking.'

*

THE WRATH

It's early afternoon and outside the sky is a winter blue, the ocean almost green. If it wasn't mid-December you could be forgiven for thinking it was a spring day. The temperature is dropping, though, and they're predicting heavy rain for the west coast. A status orange apparently. Nothing new there. Kev has left to buy us all a box of Jaffa Cakes. His weight-lifting girlfriend swears by them for energy. Across the way, Dan rubs his eyes, yawning.

I'm getting started on Alan's statement for the second time. I've left it a while to read, just to let my mind settle.

'It's a bloody emotional nightmare,' Dan says, apropos of nothing. 'I have Fran whingeing in one ear, Delores bawling in the other, and they both want me to sort it out.'

'No one ever tell you to be careful what you wish for?'

'Feck off.' He fires a pencil at me. 'Gloating doesn't suit you, Luce.'

'What are you going to do?'

'Nothing,' he declares. 'Fran'll come around. Either that or I'll hire whoever is doing this shit,' he taps the Jerry Loftus file, 'to pay them both a visit.'

'Stop!' I giggle. 'You're so full of compassion. It's hard for Fran to see his mother moving on so soon. I mean, if you died, imagine if he found someone else that quickly.'

'Life goes on.'

'I love you, Dan, but you really are emotionally stunted.'

He shrugs. 'An advantage in this job.'

He may have a point. Dan finds it easier to detach than I do, that's for sure. Images haunt me for a while after I put cases to bed, especially when young people or children are involved. It's probably why I keep trying to solve the long-ago case of the missing kids in Dublin. I pick up Alan's interview statement again and start to read.

> *I think it was about noon. And I knew from the minute I saw him that he wasn't in good form but we ordered some food and we talked a bit. It started off with me asking him about what he had told Hazel and he said that he told her he was climbing Croaghaun. But he was sort of distant, not paying attention and so I asked him what was the matter. And he pulls this letter out of his pocket, like a photocopy of this cartoon note, and he lays it in front of me and he says, 'Well?' I just looked at him. Then he says that that was the latest one. In his trolley, he said. And he gave me this look, sort of challenging, and I didn't know what he was on about. The letter said something like 'The road to Hell is paved' and I laughed at it and he says, 'Did Avril send that?' I thought he was joking. I said, 'Some building firm probably left them everywhere.' And then he said, 'No, it's someone who knows about us. It's not the first letter. I think it's Avril, you'll have to stop her.'*

I reread. Slower.

And there it is. Plain as day. Winking at me brightly from the text. We bloody missed an opportunity. I must have been off my game. It's some consolation that the Cig didn't pick up on it either.

I look up the date of Alan's interview and then I tell Dan to grab his coat: we've somewhere to be.

He asks no questions, just looks delighted to be getting away from paperwork.

THE WRATH

We're leaving just as Kev is coming back in with three packets of Jaffa Cakes. 'Where are ye—'

'Thanks, Kev.' I grab a packet, and Dan and I leg it.

51

The weather is bitter, a sharp breeze cuts through my thin rain jacket and I hastily wrap a scarf around my neck. Battling the wind, I open the DDU car and slide inside, turning on the engine and firing up the heat.

'Where are we off to?' Dan asks.

'No idea yet.' I dial Hazel.

She answers, sounding distracted, barely registering my question.

'Hazel,' I repeat, 'what day do you do your shopping?'

'Hello? Who is this? Jerry?'

'It's—'

'Hello?' Thankfully someone takes the phone from her.

'Hello? This is Abby.'

Abby must still be down here, her big break in theatre sailing away from her.

'Hi, Abby, this is DS Lucy Golden. Can you find out what day Hazel and Jerry did their shopping and where?'

I hear her ask, and a voice replies.

'Thursdays in Tesco, Westport. She's seems very firm about that one.'

THE WRATH

'Thanks.' I wait a beat. 'Listen, I'm sorry to hear about Zak.'

The longest pause before she gulps out, 'It's unfair, isn't it? He went to Dublin last night, and he's going to the doctor today for more tests, wouldn't let me go with him – he won't let me do anything – so I said I'd mind Hazel. Sometimes you just . . . well, you just have to stand by until someone realises you're not going anywhere, isn't that it?'

Her words cause a lump in my throat. 'Take care,' I stumble out.

Abby hangs up.

I turn to Dan. 'Tesco. Westport.' At his puzzled look, I explain. 'Alan said that Jerry found one of the anonymous notes in his trolley. It has to be a shopping trolley, like when else would he have one? There must be some CCTV we can examine from that Thursday, see if anyone put it there.'

'But what Thursday?' Dan asks.

'I'm banking on it being the Thursday before he met Alan.' Even though I know it was probably three weeks ago and maybe the CCTV has been wiped, it's worth a try. William will go mad if he finds out we missed a potential lead.

We're in mega-luck. The manager of Tesco seems to have been expecting us. 'That lunatic finally contacted you, did he?' he says.

Dan and I exchange puzzled looks as the manager bids us sit. He's a neat little man with perfectly parted hair. He reminds me of *Mr Ben*, a children's show I used to watch as a kid. 'I hope he wasn't too aggressive with you but, then again, you're both guards, you'd be used to that. We're not equipped to deal with it here. He was some boyo. Came up here, demanding footage. It was the Thursday of November the twenty-seventh. I told him

I'd need authorisation, we can't be giving away our CCTV willy-nilly. Then he tried to pretend he was a guard himself. As if anyone would let that lunatic into the force.'

Dan hides a smirk. I know what he's thinking. If we're not lunatic when we start, we sure are by the time we retire.

'I had to get security to escort him off the premises. I told him that if he brought a guard with him I'd let him have it. I've held it for him ever since. I had been going to dump it this week if he didn't show. Wait one minute now while I locate it, I have it in a drawer somewhere.'

'Wonder why he didn't contact us?' Dan asks me, in an undertone, as Terry, the manager, starts poking about in his filing cabinet.

'He was afraid the letters were about his affair,' I answer. 'I guess he wouldn't have wanted that known.'

'Here we go.' Terry holds up a brown envelope. 'Now, he wanted a particular section of footage, but I just downloaded everything. He seemed like the sort of man who'd come back looking for more or complain that what I'd given him wasn't right, so I just wanted to give him all we had. Get rid of him.'

'What section did he want?'

Terry looks at us. 'Has he not told you?'

'Terry,' Dan says, 'Jerry Loftus was the man who was murdered in Achill two weeks ago. We've only become aware of this footage now.'

Terry pales, staggers slightly and has to grab his desk for support. 'Oh, dearie me. Oh, dearie, dearie me.' He pulls a white handkerchief from his sleeve and starts to mop his face. 'How dreadful.'

'Sorry now for giving you a shock but we need to know what part of the footage he wanted to see.'

'The bread aisle. Apparently he'd left his trolley unattended and, well, someone had interfered with it and he wanted to see who it was. I thought he was going a bit overboard about it but maybe not.'

'Do you remember what time this was?'

'Afternoon. Maybe two. We were busy.'

'Thanks.' I pocket the envelope. Larry will hate me for landing more CCTV footage on him when he has such a lot to be going on with but if someone put a note in Jerry's shopping basket, we may get ID on whoever is sending them. And if we can match up fibres or boot prints from the crime scenes to this note-dropper, we'll have our man.

The manager sits down unsteadily as we leave. We really have given him a shock. But he rallies: 'Don't forget you can get thirty per cent off your Christmas shopping if you spend over three hundred euro before the twenty-second.'

'Hey, Luce.' Kev glances up from some paperwork as we arrive back. 'I have—'

'Hold that thought,' I say, heading for Larry.

He's on the phone. 'I don't know what branch of yours the car came from.' He sounds annoyed. 'Just that it's one of your cars. I'd be obliged if you could check it. Yes, I bloody know you have thousands of cars but we have a person murdered, which I think trumps your complaint.' He holds up a finger to stop me talking and I bristle a little. I don't normally think of rank, but I am his senior and he constantly talks to me as if we're on the same level. Or as if he's above me.

'Funking shower of morons,' he says, as he covers his receiver. 'They can't even check— Yes, hello.' He's back talking to them.

'I'll need the information as soon as. Look, I can't see how you'd be busy in December. I can't see how— Yes. Yes.'

'Larry—'

He shushes me. 'Thank you.' He reads out the partial reg of the car. 'Yes, that is all I have. And it's a blue Ford . . . Yes. Blue . . . Yes, Ford . . . Yes, I know that's your most common one . . . No, I don't know the year but I can send you an image of the wheels if that'll help narrow it down . . . Thank you. If you could do it ASAP and— Unbelievable.' He glares at the phone. 'She flipping hung up on me. Yes,' he swings around in his chair, 'what can I do you for?'

I lay the flash drive in front of him. 'CCTV of Tesco shopping centre in Westport for Thursday, the twenty-seventh of November. Isolate the bread aisle around two o'clock and look for Jerry Loftus. Someone put a note in his trolley, we think.'

And the bulb goes off in Larry's head. 'Oh, fuck me. That's what Alan said in his interview, wasn't it? Jaysus, you missed that, Luce.'

'Thanks, but I'll get it back. Can you make that ASAP?'

'I can but you'll bloody owe me. That interview yesterday—'

'William gave you that, not me.'

'It was your idea to haul him in.'

'You would have done the same.' I tap the flash drive. 'ASAP, yeah?'

I know he's giving me the two fingers as I leave. Larry is a sexist arsehole but he's got the focus needed for CCTV. He's probably the best around and he bloody knows it. I turn back, just at the last minute. 'By the way, maybe widen that search. Someone told me that that Ford might actually have been a Renault.'

'What? When?'

'Yesterday.' I make to leave.

'Are you sure?' Larry calls after me. 'I'm not making a fool of myself over—'

'A Renault?' Kev says. 'Was that the car you originally said was a Ford? The blue car that followed Jerry Loftus's from the pub?'

'Yep. But I got a call yesterday to say it may have been a Renault.' I don't say it was Eddie who called me.

'Paddy Jackson said it was a Renault too, but I thought he'd got it wrong.'

'Paddy Jackson said it was a Renault? Why didn't you say?'

'Because that Con fella you interviewed knew his cars. He got the other makes right and you said—'

'But Paddy ID'd that Alan Lewis was in the pub with Jerry when you asked him. Con couldn't.'

'Yeah, well,' Kev shrugs, 'you use the bits of information that work, don't you?'

I'm not entirely sure of his ethics there but I say to Larry, 'Two witnesses out of three say a Renault followed Jerry's car from the pub, Larry, so get on it, all right?'

After Larry has muttered something unsavoury under his breath and made a big deal of calling the car-hire crowd again, I ask Kev, 'Did Paddy say if he saw anyone in the Renault?'

'No. He said when he saw it that it was empty.'

Con had seen someone. Odd.

'OK. Right, keep at those statements.'

The investigation is hotting up, I can feel it like champagne in my veins. And the excited look on Dan's face tells me he feels it too.

52

Phoebe calls him. His head rolls when her name appears on his screen.

'Hey, Blu, you still on to meet me at the end of the week?'

'Yes. Yes.'

'You all right?'

She knows him too well. Can sense his despair, his anger. He lightens his tone, makes it warmer. 'I will be when I see you.' It's not a lie.

'Yeah, me too. Things aren't too good here. I'll fill you in when I see you.' She sounds shaky.

He knows she has a garda escort. Two young lads and a fat fella. He knows what time she leaves the set each day: he doesn't need her filling him in.

His plan is hasty this time, but he thinks it will work. The elimination of these people is meant to be: he prays and suddenly he has the little bit of luck. Mary Roche on Twitter or X or whatever that toxic platform is called boasting about seeing a celeb being naughty. Turned out she'd seen nothing, the stupid bitch. And Jerry Loftus, he'd almost given up there. But then that piece online, taken from a local paper, 'Garda Retires After Sterling Service' and an interview with Jerry in which he'd talked excitedly about his new house. His new location. A bit of legwork and there *he was. That had been a good day, rain sleeting down as he drove past the house, Jerry and his wife hopping into their car. All it had taken was a bit of stalking. Deciding that on Jerry's next hike, he would strike and the whole—*

'Blu? You all right?'

'Sorry, I'm just . . . I'll see you, Phoebe,' he says. He can't resist adding, 'Take care now.'

53

Thirty minutes later Dan and I have bunked off to grab some food in a cool little pub in Newport, two massive coffees in front of us and plates of fish and chips. It's the kind of food I crave in wintertime. A young couple, who should probably be in school and not drinking pints, are wrapped about each other on the sofa opposite. A turf fire burns merrily, its sweet aroma filling the small space. Christmas lights twinkle from the shelves and a real tree, fragrant with pine, stands proudly at the top of the room. I'd forgotten that Christmas is only a couple of weeks away.

Dan and I barely talk as we eat. I haven't had breakfast and I'm starving. Finally, popping the last chip into his mouth, Dan says, 'Any news from Luc yet? How's the reconciliation going?'

I glance sideways at him, glad he's not talking about the case but not particularly wanting to talk about Luc. 'Something tells me you just want to be entertained.'

'Of course I do. And your Luc is just the man to do it.'

'He's said she doesn't want to talk to him but he's going to keep asking her until she will.'

'So he's a stalker?'

THE WRATH

'He is not a stalker.'

He chuckles.

A ping, as a message pops into my email. It's from Larry. Three videos and a text message: *Isolated these videos. I'm running a reverse image search on what looks like the note-dropper but it's not the clearest picture of him. Do ye recognise him?*

I click into the first video as Dan peers over my shoulder. As I asked, it's the bread aisle in Tesco. 'Jesus, that's a lot of different breads,' Dan remarks.

A few customers mooch up and down, dragging children, pushing trolleys. We even spot a shoplifter, who shoves a few rolls up her jumper and zips up her coat.

'There's our man.' Dan points to the lanky figure of Jerry, pushing a small trolley in front of him coming up the aisle. He holds what appears to be a shopping list, glancing from it to the shelves and back. Finally, after some fruitless searching, he abandons his trolley and walks along the shelves until he finds the loaf he wants.

I freeze the video and there, clear as anything, is a person in sportswear and a hooded jacket, head covered and bent, moving towards Jerry's trolley. Running the video again, the man reaches it, bends over and moves on. I pinch the screen to magnify the image but it pixellates. Jerry returns to his trolley, spots the envelope and looks quickly about. Shoving it into his pocket, he moves at speed down the aisle, out of shot.

'Not much there,' Dan mutters, frustrated.

I turn to the second video. This shows Jerry entering the shop thirty minutes prior. Ten seconds later, our suspect enters. He sets off in the same direction as Jerry.

The third video is taken from the shop's exit, facing the car park. Jerry is ejected from the store by two beefy security men. He stands up and dusts himself off, yelling something as he does so. Five minutes later, our SO leaves. He stands still for a moment, legs just visible in shot, before turning sideways and moving in another direction. It's at that second we catch a glimpse of profile. I freeze it. Make it slightly bigger.

Dan and I peer closely.

Then closer still.

What we are seeing makes no sense and then all of a sudden it does make sense.

'The cheeky bastard,' Dan whispers. 'We should have copped.'

Our dropper of notes is our American witness, Con.

54

'I'm going to ignore the fact that ye could have got this information a week ago,' William says, sounding a little pissed off as he pores over the picture. 'Tell me it all again.'

'This was the tourist we met in McLoughlin's, who told us that Jerry and Alan were arguing in the pub,' I say. 'His information sent us after Alan. It was credible. He was also the man who correctly identified the two cars opposite the pub so we tended to believe him when he said the car parked up the side of the pub was a Ford. Larry has been on a wild-goose chase for ages with that intel. Con was also one of the people who paid in cash in McLoughlin's on that day, so we have no proof of his name. And we've checked now with the camping crowd in Keel where he said he was holidaying and they'd never heard of him.'

'Marvellous.'

'Look, we can't check everyone out who offers us information and, anyway, he mixed fact with fiction and that's always the hardest to spot.'

'Have ye heard back from Jordy yet?' He ignores my outburst.

'No.' I'd sent the picture of Con to Jordy, wondering if Phoebe could help us with an ID. 'He said Phoebe's on set and he'll talk to her when she gets a free moment.' I don't add that Jordy was telling me that this surveillance was the best gig of his life. He'd been put up in a spare bed in Phoebe's hotel room while the two detectives had had to remain in the corridor. She'd treated him to a high-end steak-and-chips dinner. 'I'll be able to tell everyone I spent the night with Phoebe Shine,' he'd chortled into the phone.

When he'd finally stopped crowing, I'd told him to get to Phoebe as soon as he could and he'd promised he would.

'Say it's someone connected to that video, could we ask Wowser if he knows him?' Dan asks.

'No,' William says. 'It might backfire on us if this guy is a friend of his. Cross-reference all Wowser's associates with pals and associates of Leonard Loane too.' Hopefully Jordy will ring back soon and save us all this work, I think.

'Hop it,' William says. 'That's a hell of a job to catch up on.'

So much for forgetting we're a week behind.

I'm deep into Wowser's Instagram page when all of a sudden Luc pops into my head. His rage at what had been done to Cherry. The way he'd threatened the guy on Instagram. 'Who was Wowser's best mate back in the day?'

'Why?'

'Because if it's connected to the video, whoever is doing it is doing it for Wowser. It's got to be someone who loves him deeply. Or thinks he loves him.'

'I'm sure Lord Google will provide.'

Half an hour later, we've discovered that Wowser has lots of best friends. Most of them look like hangers-on, though.

'It has to be someone who goes way back, someone who really

cared about him.' Someone, I think, with an axe to grind against people who hurt his friend.

We start using different search criteria now. It's easier when you've got something to look for. At the time of the assault video, there had been masses of coverage, most of it sensational stuff from the rags. I don't recall any of it, but then again, I'm not really into pop culture. A lot of ex-girlfriends climbing out of the woodwork claiming they, too, had been abused. Friends saying they'd always known he had a dark side. Well, yeah, I think, he made his best living from insulting people.

There are at least a hundred search pages. I go into page ten, hoping it'll be earlier career stuff. Nope. All still about Wowser's fall from grace.

'Lucy, here,' Dan calls from his station. 'Look, I added in a year to the search results, one when Wowser was just making a name for himself. Fifteen years ago. Come see.'

It's a newspaper snippet. A filler. The headline reads 'Chef Insults and Customers Result!'

Pretty clever piece of rhyme, I think. The article is from seven years ago.

> Chef Brian Walsh is wowing customers with his unique menu combining great food with the acid sting of insults. This journalist, having been led to a table by Brian himself, was told to sit down to take the weight off the floor. The nearby diners laughed appreciatively. It is true that I am not a slim man but I was taken aback by the casual cruelty of the jibe. But in this establishment anything goes, it seems. It must be said that the food was astonishing. Mouth-watering goat's cheese and beetroot salad to start followed by pan-seared cod. Insulting your punters is a risky premise for a business but one that seems to be working. At the end of the evening I asked Harvey Adams, Brian's friend and business partner, why they felt the

need to insult people. He responded: 'We're both sick of the arse-licking that goes on in restaurants and in everyday life. People networking, making friends and alliances and using it to shut other people out. Me and Brian, we were shut out for years. Now is our time and you either get with our programme or piss off. We serve great food, we make no effort to lick your arse. Our staff won't take crap from you. We are bad ass. Come here if you want to be fed well. Come here if you want to grow a pair. The world is hard and crap, get used to it, stand up for yourself. Maybe, you know, get some real fucking problems, you idiots. And in the meantime, amid the chaos, eat Brian's good food.' Some people might say he has a point. Will I be returning? Probably.

Accompanying the article, there's a picture of a younger, undeniably handsome Wowser with his arm slung around the shoulder of a beefy young lad with ginger hair and a face full of freckles. *Brian Walsh with his best pal and finance manager Harvey Adams.*

'Finance manager and best pal Harvey Adams,' Dan says. 'What do you think, Luce?'

I try to recall Con and overlay his features onto this youthful Harvey of fifteen years ago. 'I think it's the same guy. That nose, still squashed, and see the freckle, right up the nostril, that's the same.'

'We think our SO is called Harvey Adams,' Dan shouts. 'Get on it, lads.' He prints out the article and picture and hands one to us all. I task Kev with digging up what he can about Harvey's past.

I key in 'Harvey Adams, finance manager, Wowser'. There isn't much, it's as if Harvey deliberately kept a low profile and let Wowser take centre stage, but about forty minutes later, I hit the mother lode. It's in the *Sunday Business Post*, a two-page spread profiling successful people.

"'Harvey Adams is the powerhouse and silent partner behind celebrity chef The Wowser,'" I read aloud. "'Many will be surprised to learn that he doesn't have a background in food but he does have an aptitude for making money. Before he invested in Wowser's restaurants, Harvey was the star trader in Seeker and Seeker, making the company and himself millions before throwing it all in to support his friend Brian Walsh. 'Brian and I go back a long way,' he said at the time. 'We've both battled hard to get where we are. He's been there for me and you can't ever underestimate that.' Fiercely loyal, he didn't have the greatest start in life but discovered an aptitude for maths when in foster care. He subsequently acquired, with a lot of support, a business and maths degree and joined Seeker and Seeker as a stockbroker. With an impressive ability to do mental maths and a nose for a profit, Harvey soon made more money than he knew what to do with. 'I needed an investment and what better than my best mate's restaurant.' The pair have since invested in a string of successful eateries across the country as well as in Wowser's food videos.'"

'What was his bad start?' Dan asks.

'This.' With a flourish Kev plonks a printout in front of me. 'It's a piece from one of the nationals from twenty-eight years ago. A Harvey Adams, who looks very like that boyo there,' he points to the picture of Wowser and Harvey with their arms about each other, 'failed to attend school for over a week, and when there was no word from the boy's father, a guard was dispatched to the address. When she knocked, the door was open and she stepped into a slaughterhouse. Harvey was lying asleep on top of the rotting corpse of Daddy, who had been murdered.'

'Feck me,' Larry has just entered the room, 'and I thought the woman I was with last night was bad.'

'Feck off, Larry,' Susan says, from across the room. 'The poor little boy.'

'Aw, yeah,' Larry scoffs, 'the poor little boy who went on to butcher people.'

'Allegedly,' Susan snaps. 'And imagine getting over something like that. It takes guts.'

'You haven't heard the best bit,' Kev says. 'Dad was an enforcer for a well-known drug cartel and apparently was renowned for bringing his young son along to experience what happened when you cheated people. His speciality was axe-throwing.'

There's a 'Jaysus' from Ben.

'Anyway, a rival faction beat Daddy to death in his home as the boy looked on. When they left, Harvey apparently tried to get help. He called into a neighbour and she ignored him. Then he tried to flag down a garda car, but they said they thought he was going to throw something at it. He was a bit of a wild young lad apparently. When he was found, his words were that no one came.' Kev shrugs. 'Poor young fella, but, anyway, after that he was in and out of foster homes, in and out of trouble, issues with anger but he eventually settled down, and in school, they discovered he had an uncanny ability for maths. With help, he went on to college and joined Seeker and Seeker and we know the rest.'

'When did he meet Wowser?'

'As a kid, in school. They were very tight.'

'And it's definitely the same guy?'

'Same name, same job at Seeker and Seeker. Looks alike.'

I sit back in my chair and stare up at Kev. 'That is seriously impressive research.'

He beams brightly. 'I know, right?'

'Anyone interested in what I have to say?' Larry waves a page about.

'If it's not misogynistic crap,' Susan snaps.

Larry laughs. 'Me? A misogynist? Sure I love women. And when they can cook, I love them even more.'

Some of the lads laugh as Susan calls him an 'arsehole'.

'Larry, what do you have to offer?' I try for the weariness of William but I only sound feeble.

'Charisma, charm.'

I raise my eyebrows.

'Well,' he begins, with a smirk, 'thanks to the bad leads of various witnesses taken by serious detectives, I had to reassess this car and—'

'Just get to the point.' God, I could strangle him.

'The lads in the rental company confirmed that the image I sent of the wheels showed they were from a Renault. Not a Ford. And with the three digits I provided, they narrowed it down to two Renaults. But only one was blue. And guess who it was rented to?'

'Harvey Adams?'

'Bingo. He's set to return it in two days and I've requested that it be brought in for a technical examination. That's if we don't manage to nab him first.'

And that sets the chatter going.

'If he's set to return the car in two days,' I say loudly, 'it means that either today or tomorrow, he'll go after Phoebe. I'll just give the Cig a heads-up, see what we'll do.'

I barge into William's office without knocking. He's talking to someone on the laptop and he stiffens when he sees me.

'I'm on a call, Detective,' he snaps.

His face has gone red. That's weird. He looks guilty. I wonder if it's a woman.

'Sorry, but something big has broken and we—'

'Is that Lucy?' A voice from the laptop. My heart jack-knifes. I glance in horror at William, who glares at me.

'Nick, I have to go.'

'Let your little star say hello at least.'

Nick Flannery. Gangland crook. I'm not going to engage with that monster. What the hell is William up to?

'Hello, Lucy,' Nick Flannery calls. 'I hear you're solving more murders up that way. Aren't you delighted that the Peter Fox one in Westport got wrapped up so nicely?'

'She's not on that. That's enough.' William snaps the lid of his laptop down. He glares at me. 'You're not meant to barge in.'

'And you're not meant to be liaising with known criminals.'

'Be careful there, Lucy.' His voice holds a singsong of warning. 'Don't talk about things you don't fully understand.' His eyes are ice and, in that moment, I feel I don't know him at all. He's always been a bit of an enigma, but I'd always thought he was one of us. Now I'm not so sure. He lets the silence fall before suddenly switching back to the William I'm familiar with. 'What's the story, then?'

'What are you doing?'

'Asking you for an update.'

We stare at each other. I take in his white shirt, grey tie, jacket slung over his desk. Ice-blue eyes, tired. Mouth in a firm line. He looks the same but my perception of him has done a huge one-eighty. What is he?

'Lucy!' he barks. 'Update. Now.'

I have to cop on, put this moment behind me for now. I'll

worry about its implications when the case is over. I give a succinct rundown, through gritted teeth, of where we are. 'I still haven't heard from Jordy, but I do believe we need to beef up security on Phoebe. If Harvey is returning the car in two days that leaves tonight and tomorrow if he plans to strike.'

'And our other suspects?'

'Eddie is still in hospital so not a chance. And he was there when Leonard Loane got killed. Alan, it transpires, may actually have been telling the truth. Zak is ill. Harvey is the only person who connects all three murders. He must have lost everything when Wowser went down.'

Though these killings smack of more than money. The letters and the stabbing. They're personal.

'What do you propose?'

At that moment Dan charges in.

'You're meant to knock,' William thunders, stopping him in his tracks, like a cartoon character.

'Sorry. Just, well . . . It's Jordy.' He holds my phone out. 'You left it on the desk.'

'Jordy?' I press it to my ear. 'What's up?'

'Phoebe recognised the picture. She says it's Wowser's friend Harvey. The three were tight back in the day. She said Harvey was broken-hearted when she split with Wowser and they went their separate ways. He kept in touch with her over the past couple of years, kept on at her to visit Wowser, kept trying to recreate what they all used to have. She says he's a great guy, really kind. She never told him she set that video up. But they're meeting tonight.'

I look to William.

'Should we let the meeting go ahead?' he asks.

'No! Jesus.'

He holds up his hands. 'Hear me out. If she cries off, he'll smell a rat and we may lose our chance. It's very tight to try to get a tactical team together, to find a decoy. It could be a disaster. This girl is an actress, right?'

'Actor,' I correct automatically. Then, 'You cannot use a civilian.'

'If she's a half-decent *actor*, and she agrees, we might just nail this bastard.'

'She'll have to agree one hundred per cent,' I say.

'She'll agree.' Jordy's voice from the speaker. 'When I told her we might have to bring her to a safe-house, she went ballistic. She said there was no way she was letting the crew down, that she needed to be here to finish the film. She said she wasn't going to cancel the meeting and that if we wanted to arrest him, this was our chance.' With a swell of admiration, he adds, 'She's some woman.'

'There you go.' William is satisfied. 'And you think she'll be all right for it, Jordy?'

'I do.'

'If it went wrong and the papers got hold of it, we'd be dead meat,' I say.

'Any other suggestions?' William looks at me curiously.

'Yeah, she cancels on him and rearranges for tomorrow and we put a plan in place for then.'

'She can't rearrange for tomorrow,' Jordy says. 'She's flying out to Spain in the morning to begin work on another movie. Tonight is the only window.'

'All right. If Jordy says she's good for it, I'll take his word,' William says. 'If it goes wrong, I'll take whatever's coming. Where has she agreed to meet him, Jordy?'

'At the Palace Hotel in Enniscrone where she's staying, Cig. Fabulous place.'

'How many entrances and exits?'

'One main one, one through the car park, another from the leisure centre and another through the kitchens, so four. Phoebe is on the fifth floor, room five oh nine.'

'Okay. We'll get a small team together and cover all the entrances. We'll place people in room five oh nine and arrest him on sight.' A glance at me. 'He'd better be our man because this will bloody blow our budget.'

I don't dignify that with a response. Who is he to talk and him conferring with criminals?

'You two, make your way up to the film set, I'll make ye responsible for bringing Phoebe in. I'll be in contact with the plan later.'

55

At eight o'clock, after filming has wrapped amid much cheering and drinking, Phoebe steps into the car that will take her to the hotel. It's not your ordinary run-of-the-mill vehicle: it's bulletproof, which eases my mind somewhat, though as Dan said, Harvey tends not to use bullets. Jordy hops into the back alongside her. 'Can't leave my best girl just yet.' He grins.

'Some girls have all the luck, eh?' Dan laughs, closing the door after them and hopping into the front alongside me.

On set, the party is still going but Phoebe declares she's relieved to be getting away from it. 'Too many drugs and not enough cigarettes.' She lights two in the back and hands one to Jordy.

As they puff contentedly, I drive slowly away from the trailer and onto the kilometre-long narrow dirt track, which will take us to the main road. In case Harvey is keeping tabs on her arrival, the plan is to bring Phoebe to the hotel but place her, under our protection, in an alternative bedroom. Harvey has arranged to collect her from room 509, but he will be arrested the second he sets foot in the foyer.

'FS is on the move,' Dan informs control.

THE WRATH

FS is the code name we've given the operation. Short for 'Film Star'.

From the corner of my eye, I catch a glimpse of a young lad, head bent over a mobile phone, glancing in our direction. It strikes me as odd that he's down here by the trailers and not at the party. I'm about to shake it off when I realise it's Lad Two, one of those I'd initially suspected of handing the letters to Phoebe.

'Something up?' Dan asks.

In an undertone I explain what I've just seen.

'You want to check it out?'

'Yeah. Give me a minute.'

Rolling the car to a stop, I get out, running as best I can across the uneven ground towards Lad Two. Oblivious, he's pocketed his mobile and is moving back towards the party. I grab hold of his jacket and yank him towards me.

'Hey.' He jumps in fright. 'Get lost.'

'DS Lucy Golden. Take your mobile from your pocket and hand it to me.'

He struggles against me, but I've caught a fistful of jumper along with the jacket. I grab his arm, wrestle him to the ground and attempt to cuff him.

'This is illegal. You can't look into my private stuff.'

'I can when I think you're doing something suspicious.' I grab an arm.

He keeps struggling.

I grab the other and finally manage to get the cuffs on. Then, with another bit of a struggle, I pull the phone from his pocket.

'Did you just send a video to someone?'

He glowers at me. 'Just a weird fan, that's all. He paid me.'

Feck's sake.

'Were me and my colleagues in this video?'

'Might have been.'

I close my eyes. Shit. Shit. Shit.

He'd caught a taxi to the extras' car park, then made his way down the lane and into the trees. He'd taken all he needed from his haversack. His lucky red clothes, a small sharpened axe.

He's ready.

He feels it now.

A ping on his phone.

William tells us to keep with the plan. 'What will the video tell him other than that she's leaving the film site with security?' he says. 'That's if it's Harvey who requested the video.'

'It was Harvey all right.' I glare at the young lad in front of me who has just identified Harvey. 'Okay, Cig. And the young lad, Alex Henderson?'

'Keep his phone and tell him we'll be in contact.'

I pocket Alex's mobile and he groans.

'You're lucky it's not more serious,' I snap, turning on my heel. 'Did no one ever tell you not to take money from strangers?'

I ignore the two fingers he gives us.

The video is on his WhatsApp. So she knows, he thinks. He hopes she's scared. Split-second timing and luck. That's what he needs now.

I've made the executive decision to put the boot down and am doing eighty kilometres per hour on the narrow road. The temporary traffic lights are fixed in our favour so I have no fear of meeting anyone else. Besides, I can take hairpin bends with the best of them so this driving is easy. My aim is to get to the main road as quickly as I can because from there it's only a short trip to the hotel, and once in the hotel, Phoebe will be completely safe.

The roar of a car grows louder. It's moving faster than he anticipated. It will be upon him in seconds. He throws out the spikes.

Something explodes.

There's a bang and a crash and the car is suddenly out of my control and spinning on the tight road, bouncing on two wheels, Dan's head hits the passenger window and blood blooms onto the airbag, which bursts into our faces. A scream comes from somewhere and I realise it's me, a primal roar of fear, smashing head first . . .

And up he goes, up and over the stony ground.

56

I don't know how long it is before I come to. Not long, I think. My neck hurts as I turn to look at Dan. He's unconscious. And from the back there is only silence.

'Dan.' I give him a gentle shake, panic spiralling. 'Dan, please. Wake up.' This cannot be happening. 'Please, Dan.'

Slowly his eyes flicker open, he emits a small groan. 'Jesus, Lucy, I always said you were a terrible driver.'

Relief makes me want to weep.

He tries to move and groans. Blood is dripping onto the floor under his foot.

I can't think what it means or I'll lose it.

As I turn to check the rear seats, my arm roars in protest. I've hurt it somehow. Jesus, Phoebe isn't there. My heart hops in fear. Jordy is missing too. Maybe he escaped with her. Maybe he's brought her to safety.

'Tango alpha. Tango alpha.' The radio crackles. I pick it up, left-handed.

'Tango alpha. We've crashed. Something has happened to the car. Request ambulance and assistance. One guard is down, one missing. FS is missing.'

'Received.'

Dan lifts his head, blood drips from somewhere and I can't bring myself to look. 'I'll be back.' My voice is surprisingly firm. 'I need to locate Jordy and Phoebe.' Jordy doesn't even have a weapon.

The door screeches in protest as I push it open. Gingerly, my head spinning and my legs wobbling, I pull myself from the vehicle and stand, staring out into the forest that surrounds both sides of the road. Our front tyres have been torn to shreds by a set of spikes.

Jesus.

A glimpse of blue amid the brown trees catches my eye.

No.

No. No. No, no, no, no.

Splayed just off the road, face down in the dirt, an axe in his back, blood pooling all around him is Jordy. I hunker down, touch a finger to his neck. My hand is slippery with blood but I think I detect a faint pulse. 'Jordy, stay with me, please. Stay with me. I'm going to get Phoebe, you keep breathing, all right.'

My instinct is to stay here and protect him, but that won't help us. I take off my jacket and lay it over him, and then I do what I've always done: I push everything away, bury it deep and zero in on the here and now. I need to find Phoebe.

Where do I start? It's so black up here, just a green tinge in the distance from the traffic light.

There's a torch in the boot of the car and, after a bit of fumbling with the twisted metal, I pull it out. When I flick it on, the light offers some comfort.

In the car, Dan's breathing has become laboured.

Forget about it, Lucy, I tell myself.

A sudden noise has me reaching for my gun but before I get to it, Phoebe, covered with blood, zigzags into the space and collapses at my feet, shaking and sobbing.

The relief at seeing her makes me weak.

I drop to my knees, cradle her, tell her it's all right. She doesn't seem to be injured and I realise that the blood must be Jordy's. She's incoherent, blubbering, panicked.

'It's okay, it's okay,' I repeat over and over. 'I'm here. It's okay.'

I have to get her away, and if it means leaving Dan and Jordy temporarily, that's what I have to do. I pull out my gun, saying, 'Phoebe, we have to go. Come on, up you come.' My arm about her, I raise her. With gentle encouragement, I manage to get her to take a few steps.

Rapid footsteps behind.

I spin around as an enormous man in red plunges headlong into us. 'You bitch,' he roars, 'you setting-up bitch!'

I know now why Eddie said he was the devil. Harvey's face is twisted in red-hot anger. Hate. Fury. Wrath. Wrath, that's the word.

Phoebe screams.

I try to get a shot off but the man tosses me away like a rag doll, grabs Phoebe by the hair and holds his knife to her throat.

My gun spins across the road.

57

'Harvey, you don't need to do this.' I'm on the ground, the back of my head throbbing. 'Let's . . . let's calm down, all right?' I have to engage him. Keep him talking until back-up arrives. I slowly get to my feet. The world sways like a merry-go-round. I half wonder if I'm dreaming.

In the distance I think I hear sirens, but they sound way off yet. I hope he hasn't registered them. It'll only spook him.

'Ah, you know my name.' He smiles a little. 'Well, well, you finally caught up.'

'You were clever.'

'Not bloody clever enough,' he snarls, and his grip on Phoebe tightens. He pulls her to him, pressing his face to hers as she tries to twist away, 'Why did you do it, Phoeb, huh? Why did you ruin us? Why did you do that to Wowser and me, hey?'

'He hit me, that's why!' Phoebe says it with sudden spirit. 'I don't let someone hit me.'

Harvey wallops her with a savage ferocity then drags her up again, barely conscious. 'That's a hit,' he says. 'Wowser didn't hit you like that.'

I swallow the bile in my throat and take a small step towards him, trying hard not to let the panic show. 'Listen to me, Harvey,' I say softly. 'You need to let Phoebe go. She was a victim too.'

His head swivels in my direction, 'Do you know what a victim is, Miss Scar Face Policewoman? "He hit me, he hit me,"' he mimics Phoebe, as he shakes her. 'She doesn't know what a hit is. I've seen what a hit is. She's just a whinger. Me and Wowser, we never whinged, just done our best with what we had, both of us, together, every step of the way. We had each other's back and you, you bitch, you fucking ruined him!' He yells the words into Phoebe's face. 'You fucking bitch, you ruined him. Ruined me. "He hit me,"' he mimics again, shaking her. Then, on a sob, 'I thought you were my friend, Phoebs.'

'I was, I am.' She speaks through a mouthful of blood, spitting out a tooth. 'I loved you, Harve. It was never meant to go that way. I was just trying to teach Wowser a lesson. It got out of hand. We were the three *amigos*, remember.'

'I do remember.' He's crying. 'Wowser said we were family.'

'Yeah. We were. You're a good man.'

He sniffs hard. 'I am. I am a good man.'

'Yeah.'

'Leonard said it was all your idea.'

'No.'

For a second, he looks uncertain. 'He said you told him to go to the papers.'

'That was all him. You've got to believe me. I like you, Harve. I never would have hurt you.'

'Yeah?'

For a second all is silence. I try not to think of Dan bleeding out in the car. Or Jordy dying on the road. I keep silent. Phoebe is getting to him. Already his grip is loosening on her.

'Harve, please, I know Wowser's your best friend and I know—'

'He's my family, my only family, and I won't have him for much longer. He needs help and . . . I'll save him.'

'And I'll help you do that,' she says.

She's said the wrong thing. I can read it in the slight narrowing of his eyes, in his sharp inhalation. Phoebe continues to talk even as the air grows still, even as Harvey cocks his head sideways and begins to hyperventilate. 'No one ever fucking helps,' he says slowly. 'No one ever comes.'

And he lifts Phoebe by the throat and the high, piercing scream of a terrified woman rings out.

And bam!

Harvey stumbles, rights himself, his grip still on Phoebe.

And bam, again.

Harvey teeters like a great oak on the verge of collapse, the knife drops from his grip and, as Phoebe twists away, he smashes to the ground, his leg shattered.

I grab my gun and stand over him. 'Don't think about moving.' I turn to my partner, who, despite being trapped in the car, has got a shot off. 'Thanks, Dan.'

He manages a smile as his gun falls from his hand and his eyes flicker closed.

58

'I'll help you do that.'

The words had spiralled him back to the day they came for his daddy.

They had gone to mass. His daddy loved mass. He especially loved quoting from the Bible. He taught Harvey loads of passages. There was poetry in them, his daddy said. And truth. Always truth.

But even better than mass that day was the BIG surprise.

When they got home, there was a birthday cake on the table and his daddy had bought him a balloon with a big 8 on it and a pocket-knife, all for his very own.

He thought his daddy had forgotten, but no.

Then bam! Bam! Bam!

The door shook in its frame.

His daddy grabbed his hand and told him they had to run. He pulled him across the kitchen, and just as he had the back door opened, the front door fell away and three men in black with masks over their heads and hammers and pipes in their hands burst in.

They pushed him away and surrounded his daddy and he did nothing.

He stood there and listened to his daddy cry out and, like a big baby, he did nothing.

THE WRATH

He didn't even try to pull them off his daddy or run and get help or tell them to stop.

He did nothing. He was a BIG coward.

After, when his daddy lay on the floor and didn't move, when bits of his head wouldn't go back in his head and his leg was in a funny position, he tried to help him then.

But he had left it too late.

He had lived with the shame of it until now.

59

I can barely recall what happens after that. I'm suddenly aching all over and have to be helped to the ambulance because I wouldn't move, wouldn't get out of the way so they could attend to Harvey. There is a lot of noise from sirens and helicopters and radios and somewhere in the distance media lights and chatter.

I refuse to go to hospital, instead watching as Dan is cut from the wreckage of our car. He's stretchered off, a medic holding a bag of blood aloft as he's loaded into the back of an ambulance.

'Do you want to go with Dan?' William crouches beside me as I sit in the back of another ambulance, a silver wrap around my shoulders.

I can barely look at him.

'No,' I whisper. Dan will be OK. I need to be with Jordy when they take him away. I was the one who left Jordy with Phoebe. It was my doing and I need to be here for him.

'Jordy's dead.' William's voice snags. 'There isn't anything you can do for him now.'

'I want to be here.'

THE WRATH

He pats my hand and stands up. Walking across to the other detectives on scene, he starts issuing orders.

I wonder how he can carry on, how he can keep going when Jordy is dead?

I'd always liked Jordy, a good guard with great instincts. He was first and foremost a local guard, knowing the ins and outs of business on the small Island of Achill, but he was also fierce in an investigation. And you never felt that your career was threatened by him. He brought you information in good faith, never wanting praise or recognition. He just saw it as doing his job. And only for him and his brother, the monster that Harvey is might have escaped us.

His instincts led us here, to this place of slaughter.

William offers to drop me home and I don't have the energy to resist. He wisely says nothing on the way, just turns the heat up in the car and plays the dulcet tones of Lyric FM in the background.

'Can you stop the car, please?' I ask, just as we enter Keel. 'Now.'

He pulls quickly into the side of a road and I stumble out and puke all over the path, heaving and retching. And then I start to shiver so violently that I can barely stand.

William joins me and wraps me in his jacket, rubbing my shoulders, telling me it's just shock setting in. 'We see crap that's not normal,' he says.

'But Jordy!' And the tears I hadn't been able to shed tumble out and I weep all over his coat and he pulls me to him and rubs my back and tells me it won't get any easier, that this job is shit, that all we can do is our level best and that I've done a great job and I'm one of his best detectives.

'I'm not five.' I sniff. 'You don't need to say all that.'

'I know.'

His calmness calms me and soon the two of us are just standing there, in the dark, looking out at the ocean, listening to its eternal heartbeat. A big fat moon is on the horizon and the night is clear. It's beautiful.

'Bit better?' he asks, after a while.

How can I be better? Jordy is gone, and this man, whom I'd always admired, even though he'd been hard on me, has a hidden side that's bloody dangerous. 'I just want to go home.'

He jangles his keys. 'Come on so.'

60

The next couple of days pass in a haze of shock and pain. I lie in bed and think that I can't do this job any more, that there is too much sadness in the work. My partner is in hospital, my colleague is dead and my boss is a crook.

During this investigation, I interviewed witnesses and tore their lives apart, asking personal questions that in the end had no bearing on the case. Zak had to submit personal medical information to satisfy me that he didn't kill his father. Alan and Avril had their marriage paraded in front of me in an interview room; Alan cried when he admitted his sexuality and I was so cold that I found it mildly irritating. Eddie O'Shea, whom I'd been asked to find as a favour to his sister, had been surrounded and tasered like a wild dog, and instead of being horrified, I was delighted because I'd located the murder weapon.

What has the job turned me into? Have I become a monster too?

And the lingering worries that I can't let go. What will happen to Hazel? How will she cope in the years to come? How will Zak be? Will Abby stay with him? In no other job would I witness so much personal pain and be expected to keep going. What is the point of it all?

Have we actually helped anyone? Four people are dead.

On the third day, Luc slides into the room. He brings tea and toast every morning at eleven for me, and so far I've tried my best to chat and be upbeat and listen to how he and Cherry are getting along because, apparently, after a lot of grovelling, she forgave him and all is rosy once more.

'There's someone to see you, Ma,' Luc says. 'Is it OK if she comes in?'

'No, I'd rath—'

'Hi, Lucy!' Like a rainbow into my drab world, Cherry pokes her head around the door. Why do I always look my worst in front of this girl?

Luc beats a retreat.

Great. I never know how to talk to her.

'How are you?' Cherry sounds way too happy for this bedroom as she plonks herself down on the bed beside me and I yelp at the sudden pain.

'Sorry! Oh, oh, sorry!' She jumps up and that hurts me too. I watch as she hurriedly pulls up a chair. 'I always seem to do something stupid around you, don't I?' she says, not sounding that bothered.

'I hadn't—'

'Anyway, you're probably wondering why I'm here. I just . . . well . . . I want to say thank you.'

Surprise gives me the impetus to haul myself up in the bed. 'For what?'

'I know it was you told Luc to make that nice speech about him being my wingman and having my back and only doing what I needed him to do.'

So Luc had listened to me. Verbatim. Something loosens in my chest.

'And I thought his speech was lovely,' Cherry goes on. 'No one was ever completely in my corner before.'

'No?'

'No,' she says, without explanation. Without self-pity. 'And, like, then I thought, who cared about the stupid ad or all those stupid horrible people? If Luc is there, it doesn't matter. I bet you don't care about horrible people. You meet them all the time and you put them away and, like, that's so cool. And you had all that hate the time your husband robbed everyone and nearly ruined the whole country, didn't you, and here you are, still going strong. So, I said, Cherry, be like Lucy, pick yourself up and dust yourself off and keep doing what you do.'

'Well, I—'

'I didn't even like the ad anyway. It was sort of porny. But, like, my other job taking pictures of beautiful places and people and clothes is worthwhile, isn't it?'

'Eh, yeah.'

'Maybe not as worthwhile as yours,' she admits, after a bit of consideration, 'like what you did, saving Phoebe Shine from that nutter.' She taps her heart. 'That was epic.'

I never in any universe thought Cherry would be the one to bring me back from the brink. 'Thanks.'

'Luc says you're a legend, and I didn't really believe it but she's like a real celebrity and everything. So well done.'

It's slightly patronising but I'll take it. 'Thanks.'

She sits for a couple of minutes more, then says, 'Right. I don't know what to talk to you about right now. But I got you a present.' She digs down into a carrier bag and pulls out a sheaf of fashion magazines.

'They always cheer me up when I'm sick.' And she dumps them on top of me and I wince with pain. And off she waltzes, and a few minutes later I hear her and Luc chattering away in the kitchen.

Thank you, Cherry, I think.

61

A few days afterwards, Jordy is buried and his funeral is on TV. He would have loved that. He's given a guard of honour and a military band and all sorts of plaudits. No one says he smoked so hard that his lungs must have been black or that he was a raging alcoholic in his day or that he always looked like he'd just crawled out of bed. No one says that.

And I hate it because it's like they're talking about a stranger.

'And now his brother Maurice would like to say a few words,' the priest says, after the communion has been given out and everyone has sat down again.

I managed to drive myself to the hospital so I could be with Dan when I watched the funeral. I couldn't face seeing all the lads from the station, absorbing their grief as well as my own, or the curious ones, wanting the full story of what had transpired on the road that evening. I just needed to be with my friend. We've been given a room where we can watch it in private.

Dan is still recovering. He's had pins put in his leg, and his arm is in a sling and he had some internal bleeding, but he's on the mend now. It'll be slow but he'll get there. And because we're guards, no one mentions the mental trauma, though we'll get counselling, which will help.

We watch Maurice ascend the altar steps and take his place at the lectern. A hush descends on the mourners. As Maurice begins to talk, the microphone screams with feedback. Unfazed, he spends a few moments adjusting it, ignoring the media. He has the same slow and easy way about him as Jordy had, and it's comforting and sad all in one go.

'I don't have notes,' he says, when he starts to speak again, 'because Donal, eh, Jordy was my little brother and I knew him like myself. To listen to all his colleagues and to read the papers, no offence, but you'd think the man was a saint. Well, I'm here to tell you that he wasn't.'

A shuffling of unease and Dan cheers.

'Go, Maurice,' I say.

'He was just an ordinary bloke who wanted to be a guard,' Maurice continues. 'Maybe hours of watching *Starsky and Hutch* had a hand in it, who knows?' There's a ripple of laughter at that and Maurice smiles, so like Jordy that I have to gulp back a sob. 'Jordy gave his all to the job. His marriage fell apart because of the hours he worked keeping people safe. He was unfit, he drank, and he could have made smoking an Olympic sport. Jordy was singlehandedly responsible for keeping the brewers and the cigarette companies in business over the years.' A laugh of recognition from some of the lads in the station who are sitting up near the front. 'Being a guard is not an easy job and I know Jordy saw things that most normal people don't. And yet he stayed himself. He saw evil, he encountered abuse, and he stayed even. He never took his fears out on anyone. He always tried to do right by people. And let me tell you, that's easy for a saint. It's so much harder when you're an ordinary bloke, like my little brother.'

Maurice swallows hard, inhales and says softly, 'Love you, Jord.' He takes a second, then moves away and, in the silence, as he returns to his seat, someone starts to clap and then the whole church is on its feet and cheering, and Jordy would have enjoyed it.

The camera pans the congregation, and I spot Matt and Ger and Larry and Ben and William. Then the chief super, Louis's dad, and he's clapping too and surprisingly mopping his eyes with a hankie. And right at the back, Phoebe Shine, her cheeks wet with tears.

I turn to Dan, and we hug each other. Even his eyes are moist.

As the final hymn starts, I ask him when he's getting out.

'It'll be another while. Not sure I want to, though.' There's a cheeky grin playing around the corners of his mouth. And I think that Dan, too, doesn't let the bad stuff hurt him.

'Why?'

'Delores has insisted that she must take care of me as Fran won't be there during the day. So, she won't be leaving any time soon. And my own bloody mother, who I don't talk to, wants to come down and visit. I almost lost the will to live when I heard that.'

It's the first time I laugh in days.

Dan catches my hand and says, 'It'll be fine. We'll keep at it, you and me, right?'

And I know we will. Because we can't do anything else.

I leave Dan around four and meet William in the hospital foyer. He's still wearing the suit he wore to the funeral. 'Hey,' he says.

'Saw you on the telly,' I say shortly, then add, 'Dan's awake if that's where you're heading.'

'I wanted to see you first,' he says. 'Join me for a coffee in the canteen?'

I don't want to. I can barely look at this man any more. Plus, the coffee in the canteen is rank but William never seems to notice such things. For years, he's been the only customer of one of the dingiest bars in Achill. The canteen here is actually a step up.

'Please,' he adds, sensing my reluctance.

I nod. I'll walk out if he tries to justify being in contact with a known gangland leader. He may have gone to bat for me but what he's doing is way off the scale. I find a seat while he heads up to the counter and returns with a couple of very flat-looking cappuccinos.

The place is quiet, and I've chosen a table far away from the rest of the customers.

'When are you due to come back?' he asks, pushing my coffee towards me.

'Tomorrow.' I have to gear myself up, move on, tackle new cases.

'Take it easy when you do.'

I take a sip of coffee and try not to gag.

William, as always when he has something to say, starts first to talk about work.

'Larry and Ben did a great interview with Harvey last week. Forensics matched those red fibres up to his red clothes. There were also traces of blood from all our crime scenes on the jumper and shoes. When he said it was the Devil, Eddie wasn't that far off the mark.'

THE WRATH

I think I owe Eddie a visit. I'll keep in touch with him to make up in some way for how I treated him in school.

'It was quite beautiful, actually. Larry managed to tie Harvey up nicely despite his denials and the mainly no-comment interview. We matched his boot marks to Leonard's house, his blood to blood found in Jerry's car and red fibres to both Leonard and Mary.' He dips his finger into the froth of his coffee and stirs before licking it off. After a moment, he adds, 'Look, I need to tell you about Nick.'

'I don't want to know.'

'You might not want to know but you need to know. I can't have you thinking I'm, Jaysus, liaising with criminals. How will we work together?'

I shrug. I don't know what he can say to justify it.

'Nick and me, we grew up together, all right?'

I look at him in surprise.

'He was my best mate for years. We were gougers, there's no doubt about it. When my family . . . Well, after they died, Nick's ma took me in.' He pauses. 'She brought me up, Lucy, and that makes it complicated with us. Nick went his way, and I went mine, and I requested a transfer from Limerick because I was afraid I'd be compromised. Then when his daughter got murdered last year, sure, there he was in my back yard again. I did my best for him but,' his face grows grim, 'then he tries to fuck me over with the young lad confessing to that crime him and his bloody henchmen did. So I contacted him and we came to an agreement. He'd offer up someone who deserved it.' He pauses. 'And that's it.'

'The young lad was charged, he's going to trial.'

'Another fella saying he did it will cast doubt on the prosecution case, you know that.'

'Clever.'

'Yeah.' He smiles. 'A career-ending move, though, if it ever got out. I just want you to know. I can't have you thinking what you were thinking.'

I wait a beat. 'Is Nick's mother still alive?'

'No. She died many years ago, begging me to help him, and I tried, but I think we both knew it wouldn't happen.'

'Sorry.'

'I did what I did in the last case for her.'

'I get that.'

He smiles at me across the table and I smile at him, and somewhere in the space between us, the horror of this case lessens. William has my back. I know it without him having to say it. Yes, he treated me like shit but he is a man who believes in justice and that young lad in Westport wasn't getting it. And it was killing him.

'In some good news, they're releasing Mary Roche's husband next week. And he'll sue us for a packet.'

I join in his laughter.

We've achieved that at least.

62

He doesn't recognise Wowser at first. It's only when the guard points him out, sitting at a table right beside the door, that he sees, yes, it is him. Wowser sits up straight, head high, he's shaved and had his hair trimmed and even got new clothes. Harvey feels ridiculously touched.

'You look good.' Harvey smiles at his best mate as he slides into the seat opposite. 'The new treatment working?'

'Why'd you do it, Harve?'

The question knocks him off balance, Wowser looking at him like he's some sort of a weird specimen in a jar.

Harvey opens his mouth to reply.

'Why'd you do it?' Wowser asks again, before Harvey can frame the words. 'You killed people, Harve.'

'You know why,' Harvey answers. 'The video.'

'That video is old news, Harve.'

His world is off kilter, tipped sideways. 'You were dying. Aggressive MS.'

That was why he killed Mary Roche two years back.

'I'm not dying.'

'Yeah. You said the stress of Leonard's video was a contributing factor and caused—'

'No.' Wowser shakes his head, looks shocked. 'Nothing wrong with me. I hope you didn't do anything on account of me.'

Harvey can't think of what to say. Wowser was diagnosed shortly after the video and had blamed the video and told Harvey that only a coward would stand by and let them get away with it and—

'I never asked you to hurt anyone,' Wowser says, after a moment. 'You know that, right?'

Hadn't he? Harvey's mind scrambles backwards. All those days where Wowser cried in his arms with the misery of it, those days when Wowser could barely walk, the days when Wowser moaned that action should be taken against people who ruin other people's lives.

'Harve,' Wowser says again, softly, 'I was really angry at the time, but I never actually asked you to do anything. I've rebuilt my life.'

Harvey blinks. 'But you—'

'Did nothing.' Wowser speaks calmly, like you would to a hysterical child. 'Now, I can't say I'm sad they're gone, but none of it was my doing.' He heaves a sigh. 'I hope you understand that I can't be your friend any more.'

In shock, Harvey watches as Wowser stands up, smiling a little sadly, before leaning towards him, winking and whispering, 'Thanks, though.'

Harvey gasps aloud as people look across.

Wowser, without a stagger or a stumble, walks swiftly from the room. He even looks like he's wiping away a tear.

A class actor, a manipulator. Phoebe's words float into Harvey's head. For the first time in years, Harvey starts to cry.

63

It's my first day back at work and I'm being spoiled. My colleagues insist on offering me unsolicited cups of coffee or, in Kev's case, presenting me with Jaffa Cakes. It won't last, though. Some awful thing will happen and all attention will be diverted away from me.

I'm at my desk, filing all the shite paperwork. Still, it's probably better for me right now than heading off to a crime scene.

I've just logged in a report on a pair of brothers who were caught selling counterfeit cigarettes outside the church when my phone rings. It's the forensics lab and I wonder if they've called me by mistake.

'DS Lucy Golden,' I say.

'Hey, Lucy, it's Edgar.' His voice drops. 'How's things? I heard about Jordy. That was rough.'

'It was. What's the story? Why are you calling?'

'You left a message for me some time ago, to run DNA on the cuff of that jacket that was left behind at the scene of the warehouse robbery in Castlebar?'

My heart quickens as the detective part of me wakes up. It seems like another lifetime. I'd forgotten about it.

'We compared the DNA against the DNA in that other case . . . What was it?'

'The Stephen Larkin case.' One of the children who'd been abducted in Dublin fourteen years ago. I've been searching for them for years.

'That's right. The DNA on the jacket matches Stephen Larkin's DNA.'

'Jesus,' I whisper. 'Are you sure?'

'Yes.'

Stephen Larkin is alive.

Jesus.

Edgar hangs up and I'm pressing a number into my phone. Smiling. Heart banging hard. This will be huge.

William answers my call.

'Cig,' I say. 'I've got a case I need to work on and you won't believe it.'

ACKNOWLEDGEMENTS

Thanks as always to my family, friends and readers. Without you all, I wouldn't have the confidence to keep going in this rollercoaster business. Your love for the books (and for me) is the gift that keeps on giving.

Thanks to all who came to my *Bone Fire* book launch. It was great to meet so many people, especially ones I had only met via the internet – including the carers group. It was an honour.

Thanks to the Maynooth Bookshop for the great book launch and for their support over the years.

To Aideen and Vincent of the *Liffey Champion* – ye are the BEST!

Thanks to my agent, Caroline, and all at Hardman Swainson for their dedication to my books – champions all.

Thanks to everyone who helped research this latest Lucy Golden outing – from the detective who reads them to make sure the plots hang together, to retired detective Brian Willoughby, who answers all my email queries, no matter how ridiculous, with great insight and knowledge.

Thanks to all at Achill Tourism for getting behind Lucy – she is for ever in your debt!

Thanks to everyone who gave the book publicity the last time around. I appreciated the wonderful reviews in print and it was great to meet the *Six o'Clock Show* team again, be interviewed by Declan Meehan and a thrill to be on *The Pat Kenny Show*.

Memories made!

Thanks to my publishers, to my new editor, Jen Shannon, and massive thanks to Hazel Orme: without her keen eye for a smooth sentence, and for spotting that every second character was named 'Mick', this book would be a very confused reading experience indeed!